THE SPIRIT CHASER

Kat. Mayor

Cover by Bespoke Book Covers

ISBN: 1535246588
ISBN 13: 9781535246583

Special thanks to my friend and Beta reader, Brandy. You rock, girl! To Laura, for helping with my wayward commas and giving me great editing advice.
To Scott Mike Stanley, who created a wonderful inspirational sketch of Enchanted Hill Manor.
And to Jennifer, Pam, Judy, and Candace. I am blessed to have the best coworkers in the world!

TABLE OF CONTENTS

1	1
2	21
3	29
4	39
5	49
6	58
7	69
8	83
9	91
10	105
11	113
12	119
13	129
14	136
15	148
16	157
17	172
18	190
19	201
20	215
21	222
22	236

23	259
24	265
25	272
26	282
27	288
28	295
29	299
30	311
31	320
32	327
33	336
34	341
35	347
35	358
36	368
37	374
38	379
39	387
40	395
41	401
42	413
43	419
Bibliography	429

1

"Ready?" the Spirit Chaser asked. The cameraman and priest behind him both replied yes. Austin looked to his left. Thai was leaning forward in a fighting stance. He grunted a yeah. Austin turned to his right, seeing Barrett close his eyes and nod. The Spirit Chaser issued his familiar mantra. "Let's do this." He kissed his crucifix and kicked the door open.

The group stood stock still, breathing lightly, quietly assessing the place. The L&D warehouse had been closed for a little over five years, but that didn't mean it was unoccupied. Austin stepped lightly as he approached the center of the large room, his crew following close behind. A black pentagram was painted on the concrete floor, and half-burned candles and empty booze bottles were strewn about. Austin's eyes flicked from right to left. Light from Gary's camera reflected off two green orbs in the distance. *A cat?* the Spirit Chaser wondered. At the same moment, a thunderous crack shattered the silence and reverberated through the expanse of the old warehouse. Barrett flinched. Thai tensed and turned slowly in a circle, searching for the source of the jarring noise.

"What was that?" Gary whispered.

Austin shrugged. Before he had become a world-famous paranormal investigator, he had worked in construction to get through college. To him, it sounded like someone had dropped a two-by-four on a concrete slab from four stories up.

"I don't like it," Luis said. The former Catholic priest thought it had sounded like the *strepitus* at the end of Tenebrae service.

Austin shivered and glanced at his hand-held thermal camera. Over the last ten seconds, the temperature had dropped fifteen degrees. The foul odor of rancid meat permeated the dark space. They all began to cough, but Barrett ran over to the wall and started retching. He had a sensitive stomach, and the dark entity's evil presence took full advantage. Austin followed him and put a hand on Barrett's shoulder. "You okay?"

Barrett flinched, then relaxed at his friend's gentle touch. Austin had never been demonstrative, at least not toward him. He turned his head. Even in the relative darkness, he could see the light from his thermal camera reflect off Austin's clear, blue-green eyes. The Spirit Chaser's brow was furrowed in concern and his usual cocky smirk was gone. "I'm fine," Barrett answered.

"Good," Austin pulled away—back to business. Barrett rubbed the shoulder that Austin's hand had formerly occupied and followed him back toward the group, taking care to breathe through his mouth.

"What now?" Gary asked. At six four, he was the tallest and strongest of the Spirit Chaser crew. Austin insisted that everyone on his team be in top physical condition. The ghost hunts put them in situations where they had to run, duck, crawl and, in some cases, wrestle. Being the camera guy meant Gary had to do all those things, plus lug around heavy equipment.

Thai's eyes were closed in meditation. He pointed to his right. "The entity is over there. I can sense its dark aura."

Barrett shook his head. "*Entities,* plural." Although the team members each had their special talents, as the lead psychic, Barrett was more in tune and more sensitive than the rest. His stomach twisted as he realized the beings were reaching out, trying to breach his mind. Austin turned to head toward them when Barrett grabbed his wrist. "They're strong; they're angry; and they want to hurt us. We need to get out of here. Now."

Austin motioned with his hand to stop filming, and Gary lowered the camera. "This is the final show of our highest rated season. We can't run out." Barrett knew he'd say that. Earlier that day, he'd had an unsettling premonition about the place. He spent the better part of the afternoon trying to talk Austin out of going, not that it had done any good. "You worry too much, Barrett."

"You don't worry enough."

Austin didn't reply. He waved the team over for a huddle. "There's more than one area of infestation here. I want to split up. Thai, Barrett, and Luis—you go check out what made that loud bang. Gary and I will investigate whatever is over there." He tilted his head toward the evil entities.

Barrett knew there was at least one demon lurking in that area. He didn't know what had caused the ear-splitting noise, but going to the other side of the warehouse was literally the lesser of two evils. *One will be hurt and the other one killed.* "No, I'll go with Gary. You go with Thai and Luis."

Austin narrowed his eyes. "Are you sure?"

"Positive." His internal warning systems were screaming at him, but he ignored them.

"Great. We'll regroup in twenty," Austin said. Luis powered up a second camera. Whenever the group split up, he shared filming duties. Thai, Luis and Austin strode off, with Austin leading the way.

Gary hefted his own camera onto his shoulder and walked with Barrett over to the right-hand corner of the building. The entities were snarling and hissing unintelligibly, but it was the demon that made Barrett stop in his tracks. The hairs on his arms and the back of his neck stood at attention.

"You hear something?" Gary asked. Barrett turned and nodded. Gary didn't have strong psychic abilities, but he was clairaudient—able to hear paranormal sounds. At least he wasn't psychically oblivious like Austin. On the sensitive spectrum, Austin was both blind and deaf. Barrett believed that was part of what made him so fearless.

Stay close, Barrett told his familiar spirits. A frozen finger trailed up his spine. He turned toward the evil entities. "What do you want?"

A single voice split into a dissonant, then harmonic chorus. "Get out," it/they laughed. This wasn't the first time Barrett had been told to leave by a spirit, but it was still unnerving. He shivered as icy breath slid over his neck. Malevolent tendrils reached out to him, darkening and confusing his thoughts. He stepped back and tried to clear his mind.

"No, you need to go," Barrett said forcefully. He put his fingers to his forehead. The demon growled, and an unseen hand grabbed Barrett by the shirt and threw him against the wall. His head hit the concrete with a hollow thud, and the impact knocked the breath out of him.

"Damn," Gary said and dropped the camera. He ran over, but stopped mid-stride as his feet lost contact with the ground. The entity lifted the two-hundred-and fifty-pound man as if he were a rag doll and suspended him in the air. Barrett watched as Gary, two feet off the ground, slowly spun in a circle.

Barrett pushed off the wall. The entity let go and Gary fell, landing on a pile of wood, PVC, and fiber board, detritus from when the warehouse was in operation. His awkward landing toppled a metal bucket containing screws. They clinked together noisily as they rolled out onto the floor. Then, silence. *Where are the guys?* Gary wondered. With all that noise, they should have come running.

For a split second, Barrett lost his concentration. Cracks formed in the mental barrier he had erected against the entities. He looked to his familiar spirits to see what was happening, but they were gone. The evil seeped into Barrett's consciousness. He closed his eyes for a moment and when they opened, the whites as well as the irises were the color of onyx. A deep, low-pitched growl rumbled from his core.

In a matter of seconds, his whole demeanor changed. Gone was the quiet, gentle man Gary had known. This creature in front of him was pure, animalistic rage. His mouth contorted into an ugly sneer as he snarled and hissed. The entity that now controlled Barrett leaped ten feet in the air and landed next to Gary. Then, just to show how powerful it was, it twisted its host's upper arm three hundred and sixty degrees. Gary winced at the sound of Barrett's cracking bone. The thing lunged toward the much larger, much stronger cameraman. Gary fumbled for his walkie-talkie. His eyes were wide with fear and his breathing was so rapid, he was panting. "I need backup."

Gary stumbled over some empty crates. He scrabbled backward, never taking his eyes off the thing. He found himself up against the wall with nowhere to go. The creature grunted and growled, so close to Gary, he could feel its cold, putrid breath on his neck. The larger man slammed his fist repeatedly into Barrett's nose, cheeks and lips. He clawed at Barrett's face with his fingernails, drawing blood.

It had no effect. The entity laughed at Gary's feeble attempt to harm it. It tilted its head, studying the frightened man for a moment. Not wanting to look into the creature's black, inhuman eyes, Gary's gaze swept down to its arm. The mangled appendage swung like a pendulum at its side. Turning his head to the side, he yelled in desperation. "Austin!" The lips of the Barrett-creature twisted up in a maniacal grin. Then it pounced. Even with a splintered humerus and mangled shoulder joint, it wrestled Gary to the ground.

Austin and the others had been looking now for fifteen minutes, trying to find what had made the loud crashing sound when they'd first entered the warehouse. He knelt down and pointed his flashlight along the floor. "I don't see anything that could have caused it."

"Yeah. Everything seems in perfect order," Luis said.

Austin rose, and Thai watched with horror as a shadow figure appeared right next to him. Wisps of black smoke floated around him. Thai opened his mouth to try to warn his friend, but nothing came out. It was like his lips were paralyzed. Austin turned his head directly into the figure. Thai finally managed the words, "Austin, don't," but it was too late. The dark, wispy smoke rushed into his mouth. His whole body jerked as he inhaled sharply. Austin exhaled, and the figure was gone.

He turned to face Thai. "What's wrong?"

"Are you okay?" Thai asked, his heart hammering in his chest.

"Yeah, why?"

He pointed to empty space. "There was a shadow figure standing right next to you. I could have sworn…." He shook his head. "It looked like it stole your breath."

Austin turned his head to the side and searched the air around him. "There was a shadow figure standing next to me? Damn! I hope we got it on film."

Luis glanced over at Thai. He didn't see the presence, but he knew without looking at the equipment that the temperature had dropped significantly. "I guess so. I had the camera pointed right at you."

"So, you're sure you're okay?" Thai asked. Shadow figures scared Thai almost as much as demons did.

"I feel fine," he said. At that moment, they heard Gary's panicked message for help over the walkie-talkie. "Roger that," Austin said. "C'mon. We've got to go." Thai and Luis ran after Austin, who was already several feet ahead of them.

Austin stopped short and Thai nearly slammed right into his back. "Holy shit," he muttered. Barrett, who was five nine and weighed about a buck forty, had Gary pinned to the ground. Gary was thrashing and kicking, trying to push him off. A string of drool slid down Barrett's chin and landed on Gary's chest.

Once Austin registered that Gary was in trouble, he took off toward the Barrett thing. He grabbed it by the waist and tried to pull it off Gary. The monster let go of Gary, slowly turning as his focus shifted. Austin couldn't believe what he was seeing. It wasn't

Barrett's eyes that were looking at him. There was no trace of sclera; the entire eye had been overtaken by black. His best friend was staring at him with pure hate. "Barrett?" Austin asked. The thing lunged at him, grabbing Austin's throat with its good hand and lifting him off the ground.

With all his strength, Austin tried to pull Barrett's hand away, but it wouldn't budge. Austin was fighting for breath and feared the creature invading Barrett's body was going to snap his neck. *One will be hurt and the other one killed.* Would Barrett kill him tonight? Or would Austin have to kill Barrett to save his own life? He didn't think he could do that. Dots appeared in his vision and the voices of the other guys seemed far off as he grayed out. The next thing he knew, he was sitting on the floor against a hard cinder block wall, gasping for air. Slowly, he pushed himself up.

Luis had pulled out his Aspergillum and was flicking holy water on Barrett. It acted like a holy whip and with each lash of the blessed fluid, a red laceration appeared on his skin. Thai grabbed Barrett by his good arm, and with Gary's help, pushed him to the ground. Luis sprinkled more holy water on Barrett, and red welts bloomed on his skin. The creature wailed as Luis chanted a prayer. His thrashing slowed. They rolled him onto his stomach. Gary ground his knee into Barrett's back to hold him in place and pinned his arms down. Thai sat on Barrett's legs.

"You okay, man?" Thai asked Austin. He was out of breath from trying to subdue a preternaturally strong Barrett.

Austin rubbed the sides of his neck and swallowed. His throat felt shredded, like raw meat. "Yeah, fine," he croaked.

"The spirits are really out to get you tonight," Thai observed. His eyes flicked down to the panting and grunting monster beneath him. "Both of you."

Luis looked at Austin. "We need to get him out of here. The evil here is too strong." The priest turned to Gary. "Do you think you can move him?"

"Yeah. As long as he stays like this."

Thai and Gary lifted Barrett up and half-carried, half-dragged him toward the exit. Luis continued to chant prayers. He turned and saw Austin lifting the camera over his shoulder. "Leave it, Austin."

"I'll be right there," he said. He picked up what equipment he could and followed them out.

Josie, the lead tech specialist, ran out of the tech trailer when she saw them approach. Her eyes grew wide and she took a step back as she saw their docile psychic growling and spitting like a rabid dog. "What happened in there?"

"No time to explain," Thai yelled over his shoulder as he helped Gary lift Barrett's thrashing body and pin him in the backseat of the Suburban. Gary and Thai sat on either side of him to hold him down.

Austin turned to Josie. His voice came out a hoarse whisper. "We left a lot of stuff behind. Don't go in there, JoJo. I'll come back at sunup to retrieve it."

"We don't need it. I got all the camera footage remotely in the tech trailer," she called out to him, but he was already running toward the Suburban. Austin hopped in the driver seat next to Luis, who had not stopped praying. The creature began speaking in tongues and screamed at Luis, but at least it wasn't trying to wreck the car. They drove to the closest sacred site, a protestant church. At that time of night, everything was locked up, but Luis knew that being on holy ground would work. There was a large wooden cross over the front doors, and Thai and Gary laid Barrett's semi-conscious form on the church's front steps.

Austin picked up the camera and began filming. "What are you doing, man?" Gary asked. Austin motioned for him to be quiet as he focused the camera.

Barrett's head was lolling back and forth, and he spoke in two different octaves at the same time.

Luis frowned at Austin, but decided to let it go. Right now he had more important things to worry about than Austin exploiting Barrett for the show. "Hold him down," he instructed Gary and Thai.

Luis placed his purple stole around his neck and kissed his crucifix. The demon saw the sacred object and began thrashing. "Don't come near me, you motherfucker," the Barrett thing yelled.

Ignoring the demon, Luis placed the holy symbol on Barrett's forehead. The hiss of searing meat could be heard, and when Luis removed the crucifix, its outline was burned into Barrett's flesh. He didn't waste any time with the Litany of the Saints or bible readings and went straight into the exorcism. "I cast you out, unclean spirit, along with every satanic power of the enemy, every spectre from hell, and all your fell companions." The demon spat on Luis. Its many voices laughed. The priest didn't miss a beat. He wiped his face with a handkerchief, then continued with the Rite.

When Luis began the Catholic Rite of Exorcism, The demon growled, "You're not a real priest. You're married to a whore. You have no authority over me." Ever since Luis had left the priesthood to marry, the demons tried to use it against him. Luis was used to it and didn't allow the verbal attacks to bother him. When the creature saw that Luis was unfazed, he tried a different tack. "Has your bishop authorized this? I doubt it." Luis didn't respond. That would be a mistake. He knew from experience that many a demon had been prayed out of a person by believers who weren't even Catholic.

The she-demon knew she was losing the battle, and her grip on Barrett was weakening. She proceeded to beg. "No Latin. Please, no more Latin." The Barrett thing writhed, then turned its head to face Austin. It spoke in a voice that didn't belong to Barrett or any other human. "This isn't over. I'm not done with you yet." Then Barrett's head rolled to the side and his eyes closed.

Auustinn, a woman with sable-colored hair giggled. He couldn't see her entire face, but from the glimpses he saw of her eyes and lips, he could tell she was beautiful. The alarm on his phone went off.

"Umm," Austin mumbled, as he stretched his arms over his head and opened his eyes. His schedule for the day was full. Meet with the crew at *Spirit Chaser Investigation* headquarters, then head over to the network studio for a television interview in the afternoon. TV appearances and interviews were nothing new, but he was kind of dreading this one. It would be the first interview since the season finale, and he wasn't looking forward to the questions that were bound to come up. He stretched, sat up, and put on his shorts and running shoes. This was his favorite time of day. Running relaxed and focused him. Once he was in the zone, there was nothing he couldn't do.

"Action," the director called.

Molly Lyons, camera-perfect in a grey and navy jacket and skirt, walked to the front of the studio. "Tonight we'll be taking a behind-the-scenes look at one of the highest rated shows on television—*Spirit Chaser Investigations.* The fascination with ghost hunting has reached a fever pitch. With devices such as EVP recorders and thermal cameras available and affordable, weekend ghost hunting has become a national pastime. All over the country, paranormal societies are popping up, dedicated to finding and confirming evidence of paranormal activity. Austin Cole, founder and lead investigator of *Spirit Chaser Investigations,* is here to explain why." She sat down on the stool next to Austin. "Thanks for coming in and talking with us."

Austin smiled at her and then into the camera. "Thank you for having me, Molly."

"So, as I was saying, it seems everyone is interested in ghost hunting these days. Why do you think that is?"

"There's no simple answer for that. Some have experienced paranormal activity in their own lives. Maybe they have had a loved one pass but still feel his or her presence. Others have experienced unexplainable events in their own homes—foul smells, cold spots, loud noises, inanimate objects moving on their own—and are looking for an explanation. And then, I think curiosity of what lies beyond the grave motivates some. I know I've always been fascinated with ghosts and hauntings, and I turned that fascination into a career."

"It's fascinating to a lot of people. Fifty percent of American adults say they believe in the existence of ghosts, and over twenty percent claim they have had contact with spirits. But I want to talk about *SCI* specifically. There are several ghost hunting shows out there. What makes yours so popular?"

"Austin!" a girl in the studio audience shouted out. The audience clapped and whooped. The camera panned out to the girl who'd screamed Austin's name. She and a group of teenage girls were holding signs that said, "We heart Austin". The camera took a close-up shot of her T-shirt, which was emblazoned with the words: Austin, I'd like to explore you in the dark.

Another camera showed a close-up of Austin smiling. This used to make him blush, but not anymore. He was used to the attention from his fangirls.

Molly tried to steer the show back to her agenda. "Yes, I'm sure you are the reason a lot of young, female viewers tune in. But you have widespread appeal in other demographics, as well. So, tell me, why do you think *SCI* is so successful?"

"While other shows are filming dust motes and calling them orbs, we're capturing full-body apparitions, doors slamming, and inanimate objects being moved by invisible hands. We only televise the clearest EVPs we record. If an EVP isn't clear enough for an average person to hear without prompting or suggesting, it doesn't go on the air. We've had spirits tell us to get out, call us by name, and curse us out."

"Yes, you do capture some incredible evidence. So, let's say you come to my house, set up your equipment, and capture evidence of a haunting—then what happens?"

"We won't tell you, 'Yep, it's haunted. Goodbye and good luck.' If we find evidence of spirits there, we have resources to help you deal with the problem. In some cases, we encourage the spirits to leave. In others, the occupants just want to know that they aren't in danger. We teach them ways to coexist with the spirits. Twice, we felt that the situation was so unsafe that the family needed to move out immediately. I remember one time in particular where the evil entity had killed the family's dog and was leaving scratch marks on their three-year-old son. The level of activity had increased to the point that dishes were flying out of cabinets and doors were slamming day and night. They could not stay there. Packing up and moving at a moment's notice is expensive and stressful, especially when you are already dealing with a haunting. We found a safe place for them, and our sponsors paid for two months' rent. Within twenty-four hours, they were out of the unsafe environment. We have a top-notch team, both in front of the camera and behind the scenes. And we keep in touch with the families. We do follow-up shows twice a season to let our viewers know how the families are doing. We couldn't do these things if we didn't have the resources and expertise that we do."

"You do have a talented and close-knit team. And you seem to work so well together. Do you believe that is part of the appeal?"

"I am so glad you asked me that. I've said it before and I'll say it again. The *SCI* crew members aren't just my coworkers; they're my family. That's not something you can fake for the camera. Just like any family, we have our squabbles and our disagreements, but we are always there for each other. The viewers see that, see how we have each other's backs, so yes, I do think that adds to the appeal."

"On that note, I'd like to ask you about your psychic." The studio audience went completely silent. "Everyone who has seen the finale is deeply concerned. How's Barrett doing?"

Austin took in a breath and said, "He's under treatment and has asked for privacy so he can focus on his health."

"We've heard rumors he won't be returning next season. Is this true? And, if so, do you have anyone in mind to fill his position?"

He knew the question was on everyone's mind, but it still pissed him off that he was expected to answer it. "First of all," he said more sharply than he intended, "I think it's premature to assume Barrett won't be back. We don't start filming again until September and that's months away. I won't even entertain the thought of replacing him. Not only is he the best sensitive I've ever met, he's like a brother to me. No one could ever fill his shoes."

Austin picked up his phone and looked at it for the fifteenth time that morning. No missed calls, no texts, no voice mails. He put it back down on his desk and ran his fingers through his hair.

"He hasn't responded?" Thai asked.

Austin shook his head. It had been a little over three weeks since the season finale of *Spirit Chaser Investigations,* and he hadn't heard a word from Barrett. It wasn't like Austin hadn't tried to get in touch with him. Derek, Barrett's boyfriend, had intercepted the last call and told Austin in no uncertain terms to leave Barrett the hell alone. The successful divorce attorney was ordinarily restrained and calm, but he'd taken that opportunity to rip Austin a new one. Austin let Derek rant for a bit but finally hung up on him when he realized he was never going to put Barrett on the line.

"Maybe he wants to be left alone," Thai suggested.

"Maybe he does, but that's not going to happen." He fished his keys out of his pocket and headed outside to his black Porsche.

Austin pulled into a parking spot at the outdoor café he knew Barrett often frequented. He had spotted Derek's gray BMW, so he knew they were there. He walked around the side of the restaurant and found Barrett sitting at a small outdoor table facing the street. His friend was thinner, and a dark, scraggly beard covered his usually clean-shaven cheeks and chin. He sported twin shiners from the broken nose Gary had given him in an attempt to subdue him, and his arm was in a sling. His warm, brown eyes were usually engaged and animated. Today they were vacant. The old Barrett was quite conscientious about his appearance, but you'd never guess it by his wrinkled long-sleeve shirt, baggy blue jeans, and flip-flops. His dress and demeanor were in stark contrast to Derek, his blond-haired, blue-eyed sharply dressed boyfriend. His tailored shirt and pants were perfectly pressed. Austin was sure the leather loafers on Derek's feet cost as much as one month's rent in his downtown loft.

Derek handed Barrett a spoon, unfolded the napkin, and placed it on Barrett's lap. He scooted the bowl closer so that Barrett could reach it. Barrett looked on, feeling useless and helpless with only one functioning arm.

"I was so glad they had your favorite. Sometimes broccoli-cheese isn't available." Derek rambled on about the soup. Barrett looked up from Derek's ministrations and his gaze fell on a familiar face. Austin was leaning against the railing, watching him. When he saw Barrett look his way, he waved and jogged toward him. Anxiety made Barrett's heart race. What the hell was Austin doing here? And after all that had happened, how was he supposed to act?

"I had to get Equal for your tea. I know you prefer Splenda, but they were out. Maybe for dessert we could split that raspberry torte I saw you eyeing. Barrett? Did you hear what I just said?" Derek looked up and noticed his boyfriend was pale as a ghost and staring out across the street. He turned his head to see why. When he saw Austin approach, he rose and stood in front of Barrett.

Austin shoved his hands in the front pockets of his jean shorts. "What's up, guys?"

Derek stuck his index finger in Austin's face. "I told you to leave us alone. What part of 'stay the hell away' don't you understand?"

Austin focused his eyes on Barrett. "I just want to talk," he said softly. The angrier Derek got, the calmer Austin became.

"You must have forgotten just how easy it would be for me to get a restraining order. Judge Collins is on my contacts list...."

"Derek," Barrett interrupted.

"There are some things I need to say," Austin said. He looked over at Barrett. "I owe you an apology."

"You owe him a hell of a lot more than that." Derek crossed his arms in front of his chest.

"Derek!" Barrett yelled. "I'm not thrilled to see him, either, but as long as he's here, we might as well hear him out."

Shit, Austin thought. *He really hates me.* Austin swallowed and approached the table. Barrett nodded, giving him permission to take a seat. Derek returned to Barrett's side. He poured two packets of Equal in Barrett's tea and stirred it with more force than was necessary, his eyes never leaving Austin. "You'd better make it good. I don't give a fuck that you're a famous TV star or America's heartthrob. If I don't like the sound of this apology or the tone of this conversation, I'll have you thrown out of here on your ass." Derek stirred the tea so vigorously that he sloshed some of it on Barrett. A bit of ice flew up and hit Barrett in the chin. "Oh, I'm so sorry." He took his napkin and wiped the cold tea from Barrett's face.

Barrett closed his eyes in irritation. He took a breath and calmly spoke. "Derek, stop fussing; I'm fine."

When Derek put the napkin down, Austin folded his hands together and leaned forward on the table. "I tried to call you, to check on you. I never got a response." His eyes darted over to where Derek was sitting.

"I know." Barrett stared at his glass of tea, then his gaze returned to Austin. "I told Derek I wanted to be left alone." Derek scooted closer to Barrett and put his hand on his knee. Barrett wasn't sure if he was trying to be supportive or staking his claim, but there was no way he could have any meaningful discussion with Austin if Derek was in attendance. He turned to face his boyfriend. "You know, I think I would like that raspberry torte and a decaf. Would you mind getting it for me?"

"Now? You haven't even finished your soup."

"Get a to-go box for the torte and we'll take it home. The soup, too."

"I don't know."

"Please. Just give us a minute."

Derek glared at Austin but stood up. "Fine. I'll be right back." He stormed off, but he continued to glance back in Austin's direction as he stood in line.

"Thank you," Austin said. "And thanks for giving me a chance to explain." He cleared his throat and his voice grew softer. "Look, I'm sorry about the warehouse. I wasn't expecting everything to go down that way."

Barrett narrowed his eyes. "Is that all you're sorry for?" Austin opened his mouth to answer but then closed it when he realized he didn't know what to say to make things right. "You are so focused on the show that you forget about everything and everyone else. You put the entire crew in danger. When that thing entered me, I lost all control." Barrett looked down at the table. He was unconsciously twisting the napkin with his hand. When he spoke, his voice was a whisper. "I could have killed you. How do you think I would have lived with that?" Barrett moved his hand from the metal table top to his lap so Austin wouldn't see how bad it was shaking.

"You're right. It was a stupid thing to do."

"It was much more than a stupid thing to do." Barrett took a sip of tea and stared into Austin's eyes.

Austin didn't want to rip the scabs off old wounds, so he changed the subject. "How are you doing?"

Barrett blew out his breath. "Well, other than the broken arm, nose and cracked ribs? I'm great. Thanks for asking." Austin winced.

Barrett nodded at Austin. "I see the bruises on your neck are fading. That's good. I'm glad I didn't do any permanent damage."

Austin swallowed. His hand unconsciously went to his throat. His fingers ran down the front of his collar, latching on to his crucifix. "Yeah. But what I meant was, how are you doing up here?" He tapped his temple.

Barrett inhaled audibly. "Derek has me seeing a shrink. He put me on medication for anxiety and depression. Luis referred me to Father Dempsey at St. Edward's Episcopal. He's been praying with me for deliverance. Apparently I'm no longer possessed, but I am oppressed. Derek hired a nurse to help me with bathing and meals while he's at work, but I know the real reason is he's afraid I'm going to overdose while he's out of the house. I drink too much. I can't sleep, even with the pills. And I'm scared shitless that it's going to come back and invade me again. Does that answer your question?"

Fuck, Austin thought. Everything he said just made things worse. "Has it helped? The therapy, I mean."

Barrett sighed. "I'm more functional than I was yesterday, which is ten times more functional than last week."

Austin nodded. "Father Dempsey's great. I've consulted with him for the show."

"Really? I thought you only worked with Catholic priests," Barrett said.

"You don't have to be a Catholic to know about demons."

"No, you don't. Unfortunately, I've had up-close, personal experience with one." Barrett lifted a not-so-steady hand and took a sip of his tea. "If nothing else, this whole experience has made me reevaluate my beliefs in heaven and hell. Now I'm like you. I don't ever miss a Sunday service. Honestly, I'm afraid to."

Austin looked down at his hands. Another awkward silence ensued. "Look, you just concentrate on getting better. The guys—we all miss you. We can't wait for you to come back."

Barrett looked at Austin as if he had grown three heads. "I'm not coming back to the show."

Austin leaned in. "C'mon, Barrett. Give yourself a little time. I know things seem out of control right now, but you'll get your bearings back." He squeezed Barrett's good shoulder.

Barrett shrugged out of his grasp. "You have no idea what you're talking about." His voice was shaking, and Austin didn't know if it was from anger or fear. "You can't keep doing this."

"Doing what?"

"Tempting fate."

"I don't believe in fate."

"You know what I mean. You walk into these places, knowing that there are likely inhuman entities lurking around, and you provoke them. You yell at them and command them to kick your ass. One of these days they will take you up on it. I know you think you're invincible, but you're not."

Derek appeared then, a to-go box and a Styrofoam coffee cup in his hands. The two men stared at each other in tense silence. Derek looked between them and finally spoke. "You ready?" he asked Barrett.

"Yeah. We're all done here." His eyes never left Austin's as he slowly rose from the table.

Austin stood up and shoved his hands back into his front pockets. "I'll call you in a couple weeks; see how you're doing."

Barrett pushed his chair back and allowed Derek to help him up. "Austin, my mind's made up. I'm not coming back."

Thai was sitting on the edge of Austin's desk in his office. It was a spartan place—a plain wooden desk with a lamp, a computer, pens and a notepad. It was simple and functional. He needed a place to sit and do the mundane computer work that came along with the show, but he didn't like to be tied to a desk and tried to spend as little time behind it as possible.

"Dude, we're running out of time. It's already June. September will be here before we know it," Thai said, taking a sip of his tea.

Austin sighed. This was the third time Thai had brought it up. Procrastination wasn't in his nature, but he hated the idea of looking for a replacement. He picked up his phone and pressed Barrett's name on the contact list.

After three rings, Barrett picked up. "The answer's still no."

Austin ran his hand through his hair. "That's not why I called. I need some names. We have to fill your position. I'm sure you know some psychics that are actually good."

"Not anyone I would feel comfortable recommending." Just because Barrett was pissed at Austin didn't mean he wanted *Spirit* to go down in flames. His friend John had some real talent, but he wasn't a team player. He would definitely try to be the center of attention and Austin "Control" couldn't have that. Matt was decent, but he embellished a lot. "Look, line up some interviews. I'll come in and give you my opinion on whether or not they know their stuff."

"I don't have time for that, and I wouldn't know where to begin."

"You found me, didn't you?"

"That was before we became famous. I don't need a bunch of carnival fortune-telling hacks turning up for a casting call. C'mon Barrett. You have to know someone. What do you think about Natalie Banks?"

"Natalie sucks."

"She has a great following."

"She's famous and she's got a great television presence; that does not equate to real talent."

"Okay, then who?"

Barrett sighed into the phone. "There is one person, but I haven't seen her in years. I don't even know how to get in touch with her."

"What's her name? I can find her."

"Casey Lawson. I grew up with her in Dallas."

Austin grabbed a pen and wrote her name down. "How is she at communicating with the dead?"

Barrett chuckled. "She doesn't have to seek out spirits; they come to her. Her abilities are second to none. She's tough. She won't freak out, but she'll let you know if you're about to do something stupid."

Austin ignored the pointed remark. "So you think she'd fit in?"

"I know she would with the other guys. You could learn to get along with her if you are willing to give up a little control."

"Fine. I'll give her a call." What other choice did he have?

"And Austin?"

"Yeah?"

"I haven't seen her in a long time, but that doesn't mean I don't consider her a friend. Do not screw her over." *Like you did me.*

"I won't." Austin said sharply. "Thanks for the info." He put down his phone. Austin pinched his bottom lip between his index finger and thumb, deep in thought.

"So what did he say?" asked Thai.

"Hmm?"

"I asked you what he said."

"Oh, uh, he gave me a name." He tore the paper with Casey Lawson written on it from the notepad and handed it to Thai. "Now we just have to locate her." He leaned back and crossed his arms behind his head. "How would you feel about taking a road trip?"

2

"So what did you do after that?" Tina asked.

Casey was sitting across from her friend, sliding a beer bottle cap across the table. They had agreed to meet at the Red Armadillo. The bar was small, old, and housed a jukebox that only knew how to play old country. It wasn't the hippest drinking spot in Shadow Creek, but it had two things working in its favor: Guinness on tap, and a great location. "What do you mean? Throwing Brandon and his shit out of my apartment wasn't enough?"

"Yeah, but that was nearly a week ago. By the way, I'm still mad you didn't tell me right when it happened." Casey had met her willowy, platinum blonde BFF a little over two years before when she'd applied for a job at the health food/new age store Tina owned. Tina was the classic hippie/Earth-mother type. She was only two years older than Casey, and they got along like a house on fire. But there was a reason she hadn't told her friend about her break up right away. Tina took the emotional pain of others and made it her own. There wasn't an anti-depressant invented that she hadn't tried, and she thought everyone belonged in therapy. She was a soft-hearted person and a sucker for every sob story she heard, extending sympathy to those who didn't need or deserve it. Like right now. Tina thought Casey was distraught about her breakup and needed emotional support. Nothing could be further from the truth. If the conversation continued, she would probably start feeling sorry for Brandon because he couldn't control his dick. "Has Brandon even tried to call you? Apologized? Begged to be taken back?"

Casey took a sip of beer and flipped the beer cap up into the air. She caught it with her left hand and rolled it between her fingers. "Of course not. He probably took his box of junk over to his girlfriend's house and never looked back. I'm sure they're living in domestic bliss as we speak. Well, she can wash his dirty underwear now. I'm out."

"Oh, honey," Tina said, her brow creasing in sympathy. "It'll get better."

"It's already better. When he moved out I lost two hundred pounds of grade-A turd. And I didn't even have to diet."

"You can make jokes all you want, but I know you're just trying to cover up the pain. You and Brandon were a serious couple for over two years. You don't just amputate someone from your life like that without emotional repercussions."

Casey sighed. Tina would never understand. It wasn't about quantity of time, it was about emotional investment, and Casey had invested about ten percent of her emotions into her relationship with Brandon. Well, maybe eight percent. If she were being honest with herself, she had stayed with him because it was easier and more convenient than breaking up. Finding out that he was doing the dirty with his co-worker was the impetus she'd needed to finally end their pathetic reign as boyfriend-girlfriend.

"Don't worry, I'm fine."

Tina narrowed her eyes at Casey. "That's what you said when you first moved here, too, and look what Robbie put you through."

Casey cut her off. "This is nothing like the situation with Robbie. That was different."

"Well, if you need to take some time off, I'll understand," Tina said, rubbing her forearm.

"I don't." Even if she did, she had bills to pay. Maybe Tina didn't get it because her parents subsidized her lifestyle, but taking mental health days was a luxury Casey could not afford. She knew there was only one way to re-direct Tina's one-track mind from her relationship and onto another subject. "So how are things with you and Todd?"

Tina threw her head back and gushed. "Wonderful. He's taking me out of town for Labor Day weekend. Things are really getting serious. It may be premature to say this, but I think there may be a ring in my future!"

Casey finished her beer and signaled the waitress to bring her another. "Congratulations," she mumbled. She was happy for her friend but wasn't really in the mood to hear about all the sunshine, roses, and rainbows that were the staples of her coupling with Todd. The waitress brought Casey her beer, and she concentrated on that. Now she had two beer bottle caps to play with. Tina was selecting the colors for her bridesmaids' dresses in her fictional wedding universe when the theme from *The Exorcist* began to play. Casey pulled her phone out of her purse. "Sorry, Tina, I've got to take this," she said, without even looking to see who it was.

Casey spoke into the device. "Hey, just a second. Let me go where I can hear you. Noisy bar."

She was walking toward the front door when a lanky cowboy in jeans and a black Stetson intercepted her. Casey's eyes were drawn to the gold belt buckle at his waist that was roughly the size of his head. "Hey, pretty lady, when are you going to let me buy you a drink?" The corner of his moustache pulled up in a grin.

"One of these days, Earl." She smiled at him and kept on walking. Earl had been hitting on her for over two years. He was a nice guy, and according to the old-timers, he had a thing for redheads. She definitely would have considered his offer to buy her a beer if he hadn't been dead for over ten years.

"Hello. Hello? Are you there?" the male voice on the other end of the line asked. Once she was outside, she answered.

"Okay," Casey said. "I can hear you now."

"Oh, uh, hi. Is this Casey Lawson?"

"Sure is. Who am I speaking to?"

"Yeah. This is Austin Cole from *Spirit Chaser Investigations*. We have a mutual friend. Barrett MacDowell gave me your name."

Holy crow! Casey hadn't heard that name in ages. "Geez, I haven't seen Barrett in five, no, it's been about six years. How's he doing?"

"Well, that's kind of the reason I called. He was my lead psychic on the show, but due to health problems, he's had to resign his position." Austin stood up and paced in his living room as he spoke to Casey.

"What kind of health problems?"

Did she really not know what had happened on the season finale? "He had an accident while on location last season." Austin blew out his breath. He really didn't want to get into the details of Barrett's departure from the show. He didn't like to think about it, much less talk about it.

"What kind of accident? Is he okay?"

Damn, she wasn't going to drop it. She didn't even seem interested in knowing why he called. "Yes, but he's still healing from his injuries. So, anyway, he told me you were one of the best psychics around and recommended you highly. When can you come in for an interview?"

"Hold up. You're speaking Greek to me. First off, what show? What are you talking about?"

He ran his hand through his hair. "Like I said, this is Austin Cole, the lead paranormal investigator from *Spirit Chaser Investigations*. You know, the number-one rated show on cable."

"Never heard of it."

"Never heard of it? Where have you been the past three years, living under a rock?"

Casey pulled the phone away from her ear and stared at it. No he didn't just play the "Do you know who I am" card. She blew out her breath and put the phone back to her ear. "I don't have cable, or a TV, for that matter. And even if I did, I wouldn't waste my time watching live-action Scooby Doo."

"You really don't have a TV?"

"No." Television was an unnecessary waste of money and with her credit, cable was out of the question. The only reason she had utilities was because they were all in Tina's name.

"Okay, that's really weird, but okay."

Casey's patience was wearing thin. "The channels without programming are an open invitation for a spirit to invade your home. As a paranormal investigator, I would think you would know that. Look, I don't know what Barrett told you, but I'm not interested. Not even a little. Sorry you wasted your time.…"

"Wait." Austin smiled into the phone, and tried for as conciliatory a tone as possible. "We got off on the wrong foot. Can we at least start over?"

Casey sighed. "Okay, I'm listening."

"I don't have to tell you how hard it is to find a psychic with any real abilities. Most of them are only half-assed or complete phonies. Barrett is the best I've ever met, and he told me you were better than he is."

"Well, at some things. I can communicate with the dead better than Barrett, but he kicks my ass in the precognition department. No, wait, we shouldn't even be discussing this. I'm not—"

Austin cut her off. "Do you at least have access to the internet?"

"Yes," Casey said, thinking of the store computer. When Brandon lived with her, she used his computer. She didn't miss Brandon, but she did miss his high-speed internet connection.

"Good. Before you say no to the interview, YouTube a few of the episodes."

"I don't know. I don't have time for anything else. My job keeps me pretty busy."

"You're a part-time psychic slash cashier at a new age slash health food store. You live in the apartment above the store because the store owner likes you and charges you very cheap rent."

Casey blinked. "Stalk much?"

He laughed into the phone. "No, but my friend Thai was in your shop the other day shooting the shit with you and Tina. You two really should be more careful about giving out all your personal information to a complete stranger."

Casey had a flashback to last Friday night. A friendly, good-looking dude in jeans and a Star Wars T-shirt had walked into the store, pretended to look around, asked a lot of questions, and hadn't bought a damn thing. She and Tina had both chatted him up, obviously way too much. Tina, at least, had an excuse. She was naturally curious, overly friendly, and too trusting. She was one of those people that was impossible to get away from. How many times had Casey witnessed customers backing away from her while she followed them out of the store, still running her mouth as they put their car in reverse?

Casey had mistakenly thought Thai was flirting with her. She felt her face get hot and knew if she looked in the mirror, it would be beet red. "You sent a spy? So you don't even do your own dirty work."

Austin chuckled. "Trust me, sweetheart, I'm not afraid to get down and dirty." Casey rolled her eyes. "But Thai has a particular gift that I don't possess. I wanted his assessment."

"This particular gift—could it be manners?"

"Ha—you're so funny. But, no." Austin ran a hand through his hair. "Thai has some psychic abilities, and he can sense a phony a mile away."

"So what was his assessment? Am I the real deal?"

Thai read auras and he could detect the gift in others. He'd explained it to Austin once. True psychics had a bright spark to their aura that others didn't possess. Austin didn't understand but he took Thai's word for it. According to his friend, Casey had the brightest psychic aura he had ever seen, like walking into the sun. "Well, sweetheart, if he thought you weren't the real deal, I wouldn't be wasting my valuable time talking to you right now, would I?"

Sweetheart. She'd given him a pass the first time he'd said it, but condescending male chauvinism was her hard limit. Casey didn't like to be rude to a total stranger, but with this asswagon, she was willing to make an exception. "I'm not your sweetheart. And I'm not your future employee either. It was nice talking to you, but I really should get back to cleaning the lint trap on my dryer. Good-bye...."

"Wait. We haven't even discussed salary. How does $40,000 sound?"

Casey laughed out loud. Between psychic readings and working at the shop she pulled in about $30,000 a year. Working for Tina was not difficult. She let Casey do what she wanted; it was almost like being self-employed. There was no way she would give that up for a few extra dollars.

"An episode," Austin finished.

Casey nearly dropped the phone. When she regained control of it and her voice, she asked, "And how many episodes do you do in a year?"

"The television season runs twice a year. Six episodes in the fall and six episodes in the spring."

Casey did the math in her head. Not wanting to sound too eager, she said, "I tell you what. I'll watch a few of your shows and I'll consider coming in for an interview."

"Fine," Austin said. "I'll call you in a few days."

Casey said good-bye and headed back into the bar.

Tina waved her over, motioning for her to hurry up. "Who was it?" Tina demanded. Geez, she was such a Nosy Nelly.

"Some guy. Does a ghost-hunting show. He heard about my psychic abilities and wants me to come in for a job interview."

"A show? Like on television?"

Casey nodded. "He called it *Spirit Chaser Investigations*, I think."

"No way!" Tina exclaimed. "I love *SCI*. Austin is *so* yummy!" Tina fanned herself with her hand and took a sip of her rum and Coke.

"You've heard of it?"

Tina frowned at her. "Casey, it's one of the most popular shows on TV. You really need to get out more." Tina slapped the table. "I can't believe my best friend just got called to interview with *Spirit*. Who'd you speak to? A producer?"

"That guy you thought was yummy."

"Austin?"

"Yeah. Arrogant as hell. Seems like a total dick."

"You spoke to Austin freakin' Cole? And he wants you to join *SCI*?"

"Yes, I spoke to Austin *freakin'* Cole." Tina squealed, took Casey's arms, and shook them back and forth. "Hey, don't get too excited. I haven't got the job yet." She wasn't even sure she wanted it. "As long as we're on the subject, would you mind if I watch a few episodes tomorrow at work? I want to know what I might be getting myself into."

"I'll do you one better. You're coming over to my house tomorrow afternoon. They're doing a *Spirit* marathon for Friday the Thirteenth. It'll be great!"

"Uh, I have to work."

"No biggie. We'll close early." Tina smiled and had a dreamy, faraway expression on her face. Casey didn't know what to think. Tina was unfazed by the possibility of losing her best and most loyal employee. Of course, Casey was her only employee.

3

Tina walked around her apartment, turning off all the lamps in preparation for the show. She flopped onto the couch with a bowl of popcorn and motioned for Casey to join her. The only light in the room came from the screen of her ginormous TV. Tina grabbed Casey's arm as the intro music to *SCI* began to play. "There he is! There he is!" She pointed at the TV screen. "That's Austin."

The camera zoomed in on Austin's face as he started his monologue. "I'm Austin Cole. My team and I spend our time exploring things that go bump in the night. If it can't be explained by modern science, we want to know about it. Cold spots, loud banging, disembodied voices—we're there. We rush in when others run away. Proving the existence of ghosts and entities in the spirit realm is what we do. We are *Spirit Chaser Investigations.*"

Tina had a fifty-inch flat screen, making it easy to see all the details. Casey could certainly understand Austin's appeal. Even in high definition, with up close and personal views of his pores, he was hawt. He had Hollywood good looks—high cheek bones, straight nose, blue-green eyes, and light brown hair. His skin was a golden brown, kissed by the California sun, and Casey imagined his wardrobe team had spent long hours and used bottles of hair gel to create his messy "I just ran a comb through it" style. His beard was perfectly groomed. It was short, more like bad-boy stubble than a filled-in beard, but so well-defined you could trace the margins with a Sharpie. Casey wasn't a huge fan of facial hair, but she had to admit he wore it well. A series of images were shown of him running through dark corridors, listening to strange noises, and challenging invisible beings to show themselves.

"Now what do you think? I told you Austin was a total babe."

"I said he was an arrogant turd. I never said he was a troll."

The words Barrett MacDowell, Lead Psychic, appeared on the screen. "There he is," Casey exclaimed as she grabbed Tina's arm and shook it. With his jet black hair and dark brown eyes, he was just as handsome as Casey remembered. In dark jeans and a turtleneck, he was the picture of casual sophistication. They showed him with his eyes closed, arms extended slightly away from his body, as he always was when he communicated with the dead.

"If I had known this was the Barrett you always talked about, I would have told you about the show sooner." Tina said through a mouth full of popcorn.

The camera showed a close-up of Thai. One half of his face appeared on the screen and on the other were bands of color. Beside his name was the title Aura Specialist.

Tina slapped her forehead. "I still can't believe Thai was in my little store and I didn't realize it."

"Yeah, if you're such a big fan, how did you miss that?"

"He was wearing glasses and a baseball cap. I told him he looked like the guy from *Spirit*, and he said he gets that a lot. He said his name was Alex, and I believed him." Tina shrugged.

In addition to Barrett and Thai, there was Luis, a Catholic priest; Gary, a cameraman; Josie, a tech specialist; and Bob, a Native American Shaman. Tina fast forwarded through the walk through and hit play when she got to the actual investigation.

Ominous music played in the background to increase the creep factor. "What was that?" Gary yelled. Casey heard a deep, animalistic growl as one of the team was thrown to the ground. The camera wobbled and a string of curse words was bleeped out. It happened so quickly, Casey couldn't tell what was going on. Afterward, she saw Thai and the rest of the crew gathered around Austin.

"Did you see that? Did you get that on camera, Gary?" he asked.

"Damnit, don't worry about that. Austin, are you okay?" Barrett asked.

"I'm fine. But whatever that was left its mark." Austin pulled off his tight-fitting white T-shirt to reveal three long scratch marks extending from his chest to his abdomen. Casey rolled her eyes. Of course Cole had to show proof of the attack; getting half-naked for the camera was just an added bonus for the viewing audience.

"Oh, Austin," Tina empathized. Casey eyed her friend, who was practically drooling. Austin was ripped, but not in a 'roid-user kind of way. He was lean and had the body of an underwear model. While Casey could appreciate rock-hard abs as much as anyone, she was more concerned with the number of scratches on his skin. Demons loved to mock the Trinity. The three angry marks screamed demon attack.

Casey mindlessly chewed her popcorn, her eyes glued to the screen. *SCI* was formulaic, like so many shows of its kind; still, Casey was hooked by the third episode. She continued watching long after Tina fell asleep. In the first few episodes, Austin would ask the spirits to show themselves. As the series progressed, he stopped asking and started demanding. By the end of the first season, he was knocking on walls with a wooden stick, yelling. "C'mon you f****** coward. Show yourself."

Casey shook her friend awake. "What?" Tina asked sleepily.

"Look at him. Has he lost his freakin' mind? Why would he taunt a potentially evil spirit like that?"

Tina rubbed her face. "That's Austin. That's what he does."

"He's gonna mess with the wrong entity one day and find himself in deep shit."

"He already has. But it was Barrett who paid the price. That's why he's not on the show anymore."

Casey turned the volume down, so she could hear. "What are you talking about? Austin told me he left because of some sort of accident."

"Well, I wouldn't call demonic possession an accident. It broke his arm and made him attack the other guys on the show."

"No shit?" Casey bolted upright. "Do you know what happened? Is he okay?"

"I have no idea. He's not doing TV interviews." Tina shrugged. "All I know is what they showed on last year's season finale and what they say in the tabloids." Tina pulled out a drawer on her coffee table and hefted out a stack of magazines. "Here," she said, handing them to her friend. All the magazines were about *SCI* and its stars.

"Seriously, Tina?" Casey said, appraising the stack.

"I told you I love the show. I will not apologize for my crush on Austin," she said defiantly, but Casey noticed her face turning red.

"How did I not know about this obsession of yours? I, like, see you every day."

"It's not an obsession," Tina disagreed. "You know I can't talk TV with you. You don't know anything about it." Casey began thumbing through them. The second one she pulled out was *People*'s sexiest man alive, and Austin was on the cover. Casey rolled her eyes and put that one down. On the next cover was a picture of Austin walking down the street in sunglasses, and over to the side, a smaller picture of Barrett with a frown on his face. The caption read: Bitter Feud Tears the *Spirit Chaser* Team Apart. Lead Psychic Vows Not to Return.

She flipped to the correct page and began reading. The article was titled, *The Real Reason Barrett Left*. Casey was disappointed by the lack of details. No mention was made of demonic possession or Barrett's health problems. In true tabloid fashion, the piece focused on sex and cheating. There were three pictures of Austin—at an awards show, going to a movie, and eating at a restaurant. He was with a different Hollywood starlet or supermodel in each one. There was also a picture of Austin and Barrett at an outdoor café.

Austin had his hand on Barrett's shoulder and Barrett had a pissed off scowl on his face. According to an unnamed source, Barrett and Austin were lovers. The source claimed that Barrett had issued Austin an ultimatum: Give up the women or give up me. Casey put the magazine down. Whether or not it was true was immaterial. The article didn't answer any of her questions. "I need to watch that final episode," she told Tina.

"It'll be on late tomorrow," Tina said, without looking up. She had picked up one of her other magazines and was reading. On the cover was a picture of a smiling Austin in an *SCI* T-shirt with the caption: *On Top of the World: Austin Cole Turns Tragic Childhood into Hollywood Triumph.* "Poor Austin," Tina said as she flipped the page.

"Yeah. Getting everything you ever wanted and more.... It's gotta be a complete hell."

Tina rolled up the magazine and smacked Casey on the leg with it. "Shut up, Casey."

Casey rubbed her leg where Tina had swatted her and sat up to check out the rest of the stack. Among the magazines she found *Spirit Chaser Investigations: A Complete Illustrated Guide.* On the first page was a breath-taking photo of Cole in jeans and a black V-neck sweater. He was leaning against a brick building with his arms crossed over his midsection and a relaxed smile on his face. The photographer had captured every last bit of hotness Austin possessed and infused it into the photo. Her eyes skimmed down to the bio underneath. The successful Spirit Chaser and CEO was twenty-nine, only four years older than she was, and had begun hunting ghosts with Thai, Barrett, and Josie in college. As his reputation grew, he was able to buy better and more expensive equipment. The guys were discovered by an entertainment company and picked up by a cable network just three short years before. That's when their budget exploded and they were able to hire the exorcist priest, the Shaman, and a professional cameraman. Casey studied the photograph. *So you've accomplished something. You're not just a pretty face.* Casey looked up at Tina. "What were you saying about the final episode?"

"Huh? Oh yeah. They always show it at the very end of the marathon. But," she smiled, "I recorded it."

"Great. Let's do it. Fire up the DVR. "

"I'll put it on for you, Casey, but I can't watch that one." She shivered. "The ending was … disturbing. Besides, it's way past my bed time."

Casey threw a pillow at her. "Fine, go to bed, you big chicken."

A serious, troubled expression passed over Tina's face. "I'm not a chicken, it's just that … well, you'll see."

Tina was right. It was disturbing. Especially since she knew Barrett. Casey found herself clenching the pillow in her lap and at times covering her eyes. An icy tingle trickled down her spine as she heard the inhuman voice speak out of Barrett's lips. The entity had so altered Barrett's appearance, he was almost unrecognizable. How could anyone go through something like that and be even half-way okay? She grabbed the remote as soon as the show ended and flicked the TV off.

Casey really needed to talk to Barrett and see how he was doing. Problem was, she had no idea how to reach him. Casey logged onto Tina's computer and pulled up a social media site. She hadn't been on in such a long time it took three attempts for her to remember her password. In the search box she typed Barrett MacDowell. As luck would have it, he had a fan site, and she was able to leave a short message and her phone number. Hopefully, he would get the message and contact her before Austin called back for an answer.

Casey rolled her eyes at her client. "Like I told you last week and the week before, I can't control who comes through. Your husband, Bill, doesn't want to talk, but your Aunt Gloria won't shut up." The deceased older woman was giving Casey a headache, muttering about how her niece, Sarah Sheffield, should never have inherited the silver tea service that had been in the family for five generations, and that Bill Sheffield was a lazy, good-for-nothing husband and why did she want to talk to him anyway?

"Well, can't you just go to the other side and find him or something?" the Widow Sheffield asked.

"Number one, I don't do that. If a spirit comes to talk to me, that's fine. But I won't open myself up to them. I could go looking for Bill and end up crossing paths with something else. Number two, even if I did find him, there's no guarantee it would actually be *him*. Demons can pretend to be anyone or anything, and they literally lie like the devil, so you can't trust anything they say anyway."

"Whatever." Mrs. Sheffield threw fifty bucks on the table and got up to leave. "Tell Aunt Gloria I didn't want that piece-of-crap tea service anyway. She wants cousin Maddie to have it, fine. Next time I see her, I'll stick it straight up her ass."

The bell jingled on the door as Mrs. Sheffield walked out in a huff. Casey cleared the small table at the back of the shop she used for her readings and grabbed her keys. As she was locking up, her purse began playing *Tubular Bells*. Casey grabbed the phone out of her bag. "Yeah," she answered without seeing who it was.

"Casey? It's Barrett."

Her eyes lit up and the corners of her mouth pulled up in a grin. "My long-lost buddy."

"Yeah, I didn't do such a good job of keeping in touch. I suck."

"Me, too. Life kind of got in the way," she said, as she walked up the stairs to her one-bedroom apartment.

"I got your message. I guess that means Austin tracked you down."

"Yeah, he did, and I have some questions about that for later." Casey threw her purse on the entry table and flopped down on the couch. "But first I want to talk about you. I saw what happened on the finale. It was awful." Casey paused for a moment. "How are you doing?"

"Yeah, that wasn't my finest moment." No it wasn't. Casey thought it was a crappy thing to do, televising what had to be the lowest point in Barrett's life. But she understood about ratings and the Almighty Dollar. "I'm better now, though," he told her.

"How did it get in your head?"

"She was strong. Very strong."

"She?"

"Yeah, the entity self-identified as female. She got in before I even knew I'd been attacked." An involuntary shiver went through Casey's spine. Barrett had always been careful. If an entity could get hold of him like that, then no one was safe.

"So, do you remember what happened?"

"Thankfully, no. I have vivid memories of everything that happened before we entered the warehouse. But after that, it's all kind of a blur. This is what I do remember: She put the darkest thoughts of violence and rage in my head." It had been like seeing his friends through someone else's eyes. He had been crazy-out-of-control-angry at Gary and Luis. But the level of hate he'd felt for Austin was off the charts. Not only did he want him to suffer a slow, agonizing death, he wanted to inflict the pain and watch every excruciating moment as he slipped closer and closer to the edge. Barrett exhaled. "Anyway, the next thing I know, I'm in the hospital with a broken arm, terrified of something I can't name or describe. You remember how I was in high school? When everything was hopeless and I was hating life?"

"Yeah," Casey said. For as long as she had known Barrett, depression had been a daily struggle. He was the typical high school loner, a bit of a weirdo who didn't fit into any of the usual cliques. He wandered around the halls with a sad, empty look in his eyes. The dark cloud over his head was what drew Casey to him in the first place. She was an outcast in her own right. Being the preacher's emo daughter who spoke to ghosts didn't win her any popularity contests. His vulnerability struck a chord with her. She wanted to take him home with her, like a stray puppy, and hold him until he felt safe and secure. But her comfort was not what he needed.

"That was nothing compared to the level of depression and despair I was feeling after the … *thing*"—he couldn't bring himself to articulate the word "possessed"—"attacked me. I found out later that the doctors placed me on a suicide watch." Barrett shook his head. "Weird. Sorry to unload on you. I'll save the confessing and emotional vomiting for my priest and shrink."

"No worries. I shouldn't have brought up a sore subject."

"No, Casey. You're one of the few people who've even asked how I'm doing. My boyfriend, Derek, wants to ignore it, pretend like nothing happened. He's afraid if we discuss it, I'll lose it or something. I think a few of my friends are even kind of scared of me." Barrett sighed. "Well, enough about me. What have you been up to, Ms. Lawson? Something fabulous, I'm sure."

"Not really. I've been working at my friend's store. It's a low-stress job and not taxing on the brain. I'm kind of at an in-between place in my life right now. Trying to figure stuff out." Casey paused and took a breath. "So, what's the deal with this Austin dude? He tells me you're the one who suggested me as a replacement. Why?"

"Because you're the best. And *Spirit* deserves the best. They're great people and I don't want some attention-seeking charlatan screwing things up for them."

"Well, if it's so great, why don't you want to go back?"

Barrett sighed and put his hand to his forehead. "That is a completely fair question, especially since I'm the one who gave Austin your name. But truthfully, I'm still in recovery mode. When Luis exorcised the she-demon, he got rid of my familiars, too. And I relied on them a lot." Unlike Casey, Barrett came from a long line of seers. The familiar spirits that helped him see the future and communicate with the dead had been in his family for generations. "I mean, I can still see ghosts, but I can't see the future anymore, and that kind of sucks."

"So ask them back."

"No, I don't want to do that. After the she-devil got in, I'm not itching to open myself up again."

Casey couldn't blame him. "Well, even without your familiars, you're still a million times better than most of the so-called psychics out there. And when you do get better, you're going to want your fantastic job back."

"No. I have my own personal reasons for not wanting to return that I'd rather not get into. It's a great job, Casey, just not great for me."

"Well, I haven't even interviewed yet. Once Austin meets me, he might say forget it."

"I know for a fact he has no one else lined up. The job is yours to refuse or accept."

"I don't know. I'm going to tell it like it is. Some people can't handle that."

"That's what makes you the perfect choice. Austin is very persistent, very charming, and very persuasive. It's nearly impossible to tell him no. And once he gets his mind set on something, he won't stop. The team needs someone like you to stand firm, because Austin can't see the danger and really doesn't understand it. He'll lead them all straight into hell without even knowing it."

4

C asey stared at her reflection in the airport bathroom. She took her kohl pencil and expertly lined her eyes. She could fix her upper and lower lids in less time than it took most women to apply a coat of lip gloss. Of course, she had been wearing her make up this way since she was sixteen years old.

She glanced down at her long, loose-fitting black skirt that had seen the inside of a washing machine a few too many times. Aside from being a comfy choice on the flight to LA, it was the nicest article of clothing she owned. "It'll have to do," she muttered to herself. She couldn't justify forking over money on an interview suit for a job that might not happen. At least she would get a nice meal and an overnight stay at a swanky hotel, courtesy of *SCI*, for her trouble. Casey hauled her overnight bag onto her shoulder and headed out to find a taxi.

As soon as she walked in the door of *SCI*'s main office, a perky young woman with short, black hair and cobalt blue highlights stood up. Casey's eyes were drawn to the diamond studs in her left nostril and lip. She was tiny, probably less than five feet, and cute in a pixie kind of way.

"I'm Josie," she said as she ran around the desk to greet her.

Casey stuck out her hand. "Nice to meet you, Josie. My name is Casey and I'm here to see—"

"I know exactly who you are. You're the new psychic." The words spilled out of her rapid fire. She took a sip from the venti Starbucks cup in her hand. "C'mon. Austin told me to let him know when you arrived." She took off down the hall and Casey had to jog to catch up with the highly caffeinated and enthusiastic young woman. "You're going to love it here. Austin is a really cool boss, and everyone gets along great," she gushed.

"Good to know," Josie led her to a two-story indoor gym in the middle of the building. The CEO, in basketball shorts and a T-shirt, was standing on a mat, balancing on one foot with his hands in the air. Thai was standing in front of him in the same position. Austin was shorter than Casey imagined, probably a little less than six feet. But he still towered over her five-foot-four frame.

When Thai saw Josie wave, he leaned over and whispered to Austin. They broke the pose and walked over to where Josie and Casey were standing.

Austin stuck out his hand. "Thank you for coming out. It's a pleasure to meet you. This is Thai, but I guess you two have already met."

Thai shook her hand. "You have an amazing aura. No hard feelings about the spying, I hope."

He had a charming, infectious smile, and even if she had been upset about being deceived, she doubted she could have stayed mad at him. "No, I understand. You needed to vet me."

"Well, I'm glad you'll be joining the team."

"Um, thanks." Casey shrugged. Everyone was acting like she already had the job.

Austin grabbed a bottle of water out of a standing cooler. "Want one?"

"Sure," Casey said. He threw it to her and she caught it.

"Let's go up to my office. We can talk there." She waited for him to slip on his shoes, then followed him up the stairs to a room with a large glass window that overlooked the gym.

Casey was surprised at the space. It was plain. No artwork hung from the dull, beige walls. In fact, the only decorations were a sign that said 26.2, a sign with the *SCI* logo, and a poster from the Ironman Triathlon from a few years before. The metal and wood veneer desk looked like it had come from a cheap office-supply store, and the two simple chairs in front of it belonged in a doctor's waiting room, not in an executive's personal space. She was expecting something more lavish from a famous television star.

"Have a seat." He motioned to one of the chairs.

Her stomach rolled over and she realized how nervous she was. Even though Austin was very casual about the whole thing, this was still the most important interview of her life, and she wanted to put her best foot forward. She took a sip of water to calm her nerves as he pulled the resume she'd sent him out of a file on his desk.

"We've already discussed your current position on the phone, one that you are massively overqualified for." He looked down at the piece of paper. "Went to high school in Dallas and attended OSU for three and a half years." His eyes narrowed and he looked up at her. "You never graduated?"

"Is that a problem?"

"Not necessarily. Most everyone here is degreed in something or other, but it's not a requirement."

"I'm not aware of any schools offering a bachelor's program in clairvoyance."

Austin smiled. "That's true. But looking at your transcript, your grades were good. It seems strange that you would spend all that time, money, and energy only to drop out the final semester of your senior year."

Casey didn't know what to say, so she just folded her hands in her lap.

He put down the folder. Casey looked up at him, staring at eyes the color of the Pacific Ocean. "Do you plan to go back?"

"Not anytime soon."

He jotted something down on a piece of paper then gazed into her eyes. "So, tell me about your abilities."

Casey absolutely hated these types of interview questions. She was sure Barrett had told Austin everything he needed to know, anyway. "Well, for as long as I remember, I've seen ghosts and other entities. They tell me what they want the living to know. I can also sense if a presence is good or evil, and know if a building has bad energy."

"Can you see the future?"

"No. Precognition is not one of my gifts. I'm clairvoyant, but I'm not a medium. I will not channel, open portals, or use spirit boards. I hope that isn't a problem."

"No, Barrett wouldn't channel, either. I am slightly disappointed your familiars don't allow you to see the future, though."

"I don't have familiars."

"What?" Austin sat up. "I thought every psychic had familiars." Even Bob, the Native American Shaman, had his spirit guides.

"Having familiars requires a lot of trust on my part. And I don't trust people—living, dead, or otherwise."

Austin's brow furrowed in confusion. "Then how do you communicate with the dead?"

Casey shrugged. "I have no idea. It's just something I've always been able to do. But I can assure you, even without familiars, I have no problem seeing and speaking to spirits."

"That's all I care about." He leaned forward and picked up a pencil from the desk. "Barrett told me you can read the minds of the living, as well." He paused, twirling it between his fingers. "So, can you tell me what I'm thinking?"

Casey internally cringed. It always came down to this. If she had a dollar for every time someone asked her to read his or her mind, she could have paid off her student loans years ago.

Casey shook her head. "No. That's not something I really like to do. It's an invasion of privacy."

"It's not an invasion of privacy if I want you to."

"Look, this never ends well. If I find out something you don't want me to know, you're going to be mad."

Austin smiled and shook his head. "I'm open. I'm inviting you in." He stood up and leaned against the desk with his arms crossed.

Casey looked up at the ceiling. "He was talking to me, not you. You're not welcome here." She looked over at Austin. "Don't say stuff like that."

"Stuff like what?"

"I'm inviting you in. A spirit could take that the wrong way."

Austin rolled his eyes. "Well, c'mon. I'm ready whenever you are."

"If you're sure...."

"I am."

She relaxed and her third eye opened. Austin was like most people who didn't understand how mind reading worked. They would deliberately think of other things, believing they were safeguarding the one thing they didn't want anyone to know. That was like surrounding it with arrows and a neon sign that said, "Don't look over here. This is my deepest, darkest secret."

As soon as her third eye entered Austin's mind, memories of a happy early childhood surfaced. He loved his mother deeply. Nothing about a father. There was sadness and regret over the loss of his sister. The people at *SCI* were his best friends and he considered them family. A four leaf clover appeared in her mind, and she knew he considered himself lucky and blessed to be able to work at something he loved, surrounded by his best friends.

Her third eye turned and examined his everyday life. He was a fanatic about fitness and sports, as well as eating healthy. No red meat, but he did eat fish and occasionally, poultry. She saw images of him running, doing yoga and eating lots of green stuff. Her third eye revealed lots of beautiful women surrounding him— not surprising. There were one or two girlfriends in his past, but most were not serious relationships. He was deeply religious—quite surprising—and judging by the images she saw of a crucifix and him kneeling to receive the Eucharist, Catholic. Considering what he did for a living, that was probably a good thing. A clock face appeared in her mind. Routine was very important to him. He was up every morning at six to run. He worked hard; he played hard; and he went to bed every night at ten o'clock unless he was on an investigation.

Then, her third eye took a peek at his innermost thoughts and desires. Ghost hunting was not just a job to him. It was his passion. Mentally, he was always at work. If he wasn't researching locations, he was watching footage of past investigations. He was constantly thinking of ways to challenge himself and make the show better. From what he showed her of his work ethic and determination, he was hands down the most driven person she'd ever met.

Her third eye turned again, and she spotted his most shameful secret. It was in the corner of his mind wrapped in the brown paper of guilt and tied with strings of self-loathing. For a moment, she considered unwrapping the package, but two things stopped her. First, although it would prove beyond a shadow of a doubt how great her abilities were, it would deeply embarrass him. She didn't mind messing with him a bit, but humiliating someone by divulging the one thing he wanted to hide from the world was cruel. And it probably wouldn't help her chances at getting the job. Second, she sensed that his secret revolved around Barrett. This was none of her business. She would never hurt her old friend by uncovering things she wasn't supposed to know.

"So, are you getting anything yet?" Austin asked.

She glanced down, her eyes flicking from side to side as she got a read on him. A small smile played on her lips, as she thought about how she would answer. "Um, yeah. You're thinking about knocking off early, as soon as this interview is over, and playing some hoops."

"Not bad," Austin said.

"But you were thinking something else when I first walked in. You wondered if I was wearing this long, flowing skirt to play up the whole gypsy, fortune teller angle. To answer your question, no I didn't. I *was* trying to dress up for this interview, when obviously I didn't need to," she said, as she stared at his flip flops.

"Well, you know...."

"Also, you were thinking that I have a pretty face but I need to work on my smile for television appearances. I look kind of mean and unapproachable. Oh, and yes, I am a natural redhead, just not this shade of red." She pulled on a few strands of her hair. "I did these highlights myself."

Austin looked down at his hands. "What I meant was...."

"That's strange. I thought I was interviewing for *Spirit Chaser Investigations*, not *Extreme Makeover*."

"Huh?" Austin asked, and Casey couldn't believe he had the nerve to look confused.

"You're thinking the camera would like me better if I dropped ten pounds, got a new, sexier wardrobe, and had my hair professionally done. You might even be able to capture a demographic that has so far eluded you—heterosexual males between the ages of eighteen and thirty-four." She paused in concentration, then added, "Oh, and a boob job wouldn't hurt, either."

"All right, I can see you know what you're doing. You can stop with the mind reading now." Casey could swear that under the tan, Austin was turning a dark shade of pink. She sat back and rested her hands on her lap. He cleared his throat. "So, how soon can you start?"

Austin pulled out a bunch of forms for her to fill out—the usual new-hire stuff. He excused himself but promised to return in case she had any questions.

She was looking over the job requirements when Austin stuck his head back in. "How are we doing?" There was a basketball tucked under his arm and he had exchanged his flip-flops for Chuck Taylors.

"What's all this about mental and physical training?"

"Um, yeah. The investigation team is required to maintain a high level of physical fitness. When we're not on location, we work out every day. When you're on my time you will eat well and stay strong. That means a healthy breakfast and lunch. If you're not a person of faith, then I expect you to spend time in mental exercise to strengthen your mind every day. Thai leads meditation if you're interested. If you do believe, a strong prayer life and regular worship is expected."

She wasn't wild about the nutritional part, but for what he was paying her, she could do it. The spiritual didn't bother her either, but the physical exercise was a different story. "Is this about television appearances again? Because I don't think you need to be a size four to talk to ghosts."

Austin blew out his breath. "No, sweetheart. These requirements are-for-ev-ry-one." He paused between each of the syllables. "I don't give two flying fucks about your dress size, but I am deeply concerned for the safety of the team." He pointed to his head. "It takes a strong mind *and* a strong body to combat evil entities. We encounter some pretty nasty creatures, and you'd better be able to haul ass away from them at a moment's notice. Do you have a problem with that?"

Sweetheart again? If he wasn't already pissed at her and she didn't need this job in the worst way, she would have called him on it. "When you put it that way, no."

"Fine. It was nice meeting you, Casey, and I look forward to working with you," he said in a polite and even tone, but underneath, Casey could tell his teeth were clenched.

"Likewise."

He turned and ran down the stairs. A moment later she heard the sound of a basketball bouncing and tennis shoes squeaking on a gym floor. An impressive string of swear words soon followed. Casey continued filling out her paperwork.

Down in the gym, Thai handed off to Austin. He threw the ball but missed the basket. Thai rebounded and scored. "So how did the interview go?"

"It was okay. I hired her," Austin said. Thai handed off to Austin again, and this time the ball went through the net.

"You don't sound thrilled about it."

Austin shrugged. "My gut tells me she's not the right fit."

Gary smiled. "You don't have a gut. So if you're getting the feeling she's wrong, that means she's perfect."

"I don't know." Austin sank another basket. "She seems kind of demanding." He picked up the ball with one hand and put the other hand on his hip. "I can't do this and I won't do that," he said in a high-pitched voice, as he mock-flipped his hair. He dribbled the ball a few times." I hope she's not some prima donna who needs her own private trailer and expects lattes to be delivered to her on location." He passed off to Gary.

"I talked to her for a while back at that shop in Shadow Creek," Thai said. "She seemed pretty down to earth to me."

"C'mon," Gary said. "Barrett recommended her. Give her a chance."

"Fine." Austin took a shot and missed. "But she better be tough. The last thing we need is a chickenshit psychic, afraid to do a walk through."

"I really don't think Barrett would have recommended her if that was the case. Besides, she's seen ghosts her whole life. Someone like that doesn't scare easy."

There was a soft rapping at the door and Josie poked her head in. "How'd it go?"

"Okay, I guess." She shrugged. "I got the job, but it was the strangest interview I've ever had." And that was saying something. Tina had interviewed her while watching a Lifetime movie.

"It was probably strange for Austin, too. We've had the same team for a while now, and with the exception of some of the technical crew, none of us had to go through a formal interview process."

Casey rose, grabbed her purse, and handed the paperwork to Josie. Rather than walk through the gym again, Josie took her out the front door of Austin's office, giving her a mini-tour of the building as she went. Once the two women arrived at the front door, Josie handed Casey an envelope. "Austin wants you to report for work in three weeks. I know that's not a lot of time, but hopefully this will help with moving expenses."

"Thanks," Casey said. She peered at the check. It was more than enough to move her small bit of junk three times over.

"Oh, I almost forgot," she ran behind her desk and pulled out a T-shirt. It was white and the letters *SCI* were written in neon green. "Welcome to the team. You're one of us, now."

5

"Ready?" Tina asked.

"Yeah." Casey's bags were all packed and loaded in Tina's car. She handed her friend a check.

"What's this?"

"Six months' rent. I don't want you to give my room away." Thanks to the generous moving bonus, she could keep her place in Shadow Creek.

"Casey, quit acting like things aren't going to work out. You're a talented psychic. *SCI* is lucky to have you." She tried to hand Casey back the check, but Casey wouldn't take it. "You're going to make so much money and have so much fun, you'll forget all about this place."

"Not true," Casey said. She took a look around the health food store one last time. Shadow Creek wasn't a mecca of culture and sophistication, but it had been a soft place to land after the drama of college. And Tina had been a lifesaver. Her friend had provided her with a job, an inexpensive roof over her head, and a good ear for listening. As much as Casey ragged on Tina for her soft-hearted ways, she counted herself lucky to have been one of the strays she took in.

"I expect weekly status updates."

"Of course. You know I can't go more than a few days without talking to you."

Tina walked over and gave Casey a big hug. "Girl, I'm going to miss you."

"Me, too."

"Well, c'mon. We don't want you to be late for your flight."

Once Casey had checked in at the hotel and put her bags away, she plugged in her new laptop. Now that she worked for *SCI*, she actually had to check her email on a regular basis. She opened her inbox and found a message from Josie.

> Casey,
>
> I just wanted to touch base with you about the schedule this week. We meet at SCI at nine am tomorrow for breakfast and introductions. Wear your work-out clothes here and bring a change of clothes. We have shower facilities on site. We're pretty casual. There's no need to dress up. I know you said you don't have a car. I'll send you an email with a list of apartment complexes near the office. My wife's a real estate agent, and if you want, we can help you with apartment hunting. See you tomorrow when all the fun begins.
>
> Josie

"Yes!" Casey pumped her fist. As a newbie from small-town America, she had been concerned about finding an apartment in the area without getting completely ripped off. Knowing a local real estate agent certainly helped.

Josie had included the itinerary for the next two weeks. Every morning was spent in physical conditioning, and the afternoons were reserved for mental preparations. After that, the six-member investigation team and tech crew would meet. In addition to getting to know how the investigations were conducted, Casey would have to learn how to work the equipment and get used to having a camera pointed at her. The television stuff kind of made her nervous. *You'd better get over that real quick.* In two weeks, filming for the new season would begin.

Casey was more of the loose-fitting skirt type than the tight-fitting stretch-pant girl. The idea of going to a store and putting down real money for workout clothes seemed sacrilegious. She picked up her purse and headed out the door. It might take a while to find workout clothes she actually felt comfortable wearing.

Casey pulled down the oversize T-shirt that mostly covered her ample behind and walked in the front door of *SCI*. At least the yoga pants were comfortable and loose-fitting. Josie jumped up when she saw her. "Hey, Casey. C'mon, I'll introduce you to the crew." She was already halfway down the hall and Casey had to run to keep up with her.

The massive black cameraman was standing by the door with a protein drink in his hand. He was so tall, Casey had to tip her head back to see his eyes.

"Gary, this is Casey, the new psychic."

He put down his drink and extended his hand. "It's great to meet you, Casey. Any friend of Barrett's is a friend of mine." His large hand swallowed up her small one.

"Thank you. It's great to meet you, too." She felt a tingle in her palm. "You're a sensitive," she observed.

Gary shrugged. "I hear things—noises, voices. But I can't see like you or Barrett. Almost everyone here has some kind of ESP, except Control."

"Control?" Casey asked.

"That's what we call him. Austin Control." Casey's eyebrows furrowed and Gary laughed. "You'll see why soon enough." At that moment, Luis walked over and Casey's stomach clenched. She knew first hand that clergy and clairvoyants didn't always see eye to eye.

"Casey," he enclosed both his hands around hers. "It is good to meet you. I've heard wonderful things about you. Your gift of discernment will be a great aid in our work."

"Thank you, Father."

"Please, call me Luis. I'm no longer with the Roman Catholic Church," he said with a kind smile. Behind the wry smile was a story, and Casey was interested to hear it. But having just met him, she didn't feel comfortable getting up in his business.

"Barrett has told me good things about you, too. He really appreciates everything you've done for him."

Luis smiled but wouldn't take any credit. "God did all the heavy lifting." He patted his chest. "I am just fortunate that He has put this calling in my heart." His expression darkened. "Barrett is in my prayers every day. We all miss him." The former priest sighed. "Maybe you can convince him to come up for a visit."

"Maybe," she said, not sure how Barrett would feel about that. "So, how did you get involved with the show?"

He lifted his index finger in the air. "It began with exorcism."

"Exorcism. Well, how did you get involved with exorcism? I mean, not all priests are exorcists, right?"

"Very few priests are exorcists, actually. I've always been interested in foreign languages, particularly the ancient languages of Mesopotamia. It was my area of study in seminary. One day, a colleague approached me to listen to a recording he had made. It was of a demon-possessed girl, and she was speaking in a strange tongue. I accurately identified it as Sumerian and was even able to translate a good bit of it. From that moment, I was hooked. At the time, the public opinion of exorcisms was very low. I asked to receive training to become the exorcist of the diocese and it was granted. Truthfully, no one else wanted the position." He shrugged and smiled.

Luis was kind, and much different than she thought he'd be. If it made him feel better to call what she did a "gift of discernment," she could live with that. Even her pagan friends would concede there was power in the words of Jesus Christ when they were spoken to dark entities. It would be good to have a priest on their side.

Casey joined Josie at the food table. There were no muffins or doughnuts. Not a slice of bacon in sight. Unfortunately, it was all healthy. She grabbed a plate and placed a hard-boiled egg, fruit and wheat toast on it.

At nine-thirty on the dot, Austin motioned for everyone to take a seat. Casey sat down next to Josie and turned her attention to the front of the room.

"It's great to see everyone back for the fourth season of *SCI.*" *Except Barrett,* he thought. Thai whooped and everyone clapped. Austin's eyes panned the room and when they fell on Casey, a pang of disappointment shot through him. He shook it off and continued. "Bob will be out most of this week. We've got a lot to cover today, so I won't waste your time with any silly speeches. Our new psychic, Casey Lawson, is here. We'll need to help her learn the ropes." All the heads in the room turned to stare at Casey. It was nerve-wracking to be the center of attention, but at least Cole (or should she say Control?) didn't make her stand up and introduce herself. "Let's meet downstairs in ten minutes." That said, he was out of the room in a flash.

As soon as Casey walked into the gym, she knew she was in trouble. Not having a car meant she walked everywhere when she lived in Shadow Creek. She thought she was in pretty good physical condition. But what passed for fit in Shadow Creek was obviously something completely different in LA. Everywhere she looked she saw hard bodies. Gary was the size of a professional linebacker. Thai looked like a ninja from one of those martial arts movies. Even the fifty-year-old priest was ripped. She turned to watch Josie take off her outer shirt. Her sleeveless tank revealed a Monarch butterfly tattoo on her right arm, just below the shoulder, and super-toned biceps. Casey crossed her arms in front of her, trying to hide her soft, jiggly upper arms with her hands.

Thai and Austin had their heads together. Austin nodded in Casey's direction and Thai walked over. "Josie, Austin wants you to be Casey's workout partner this week."

"Cool," Josie said.

Thai smiled at Casey. "Just follow along with Josie. You'll be fine."

After stretching out, Austin decided to take the crew to a nearby park for their run. He threw Josie the keys to his Porsche and opened the passenger-side door. Gary unlocked the Suburban and Thai hopped in the passenger side. That left Luis and Casey in the second row of the SUV. *Look at him; he's got his own chauffeur. Guess he's too good to ride with the rest of us peons,* Casey thought. Thai noticed her staring out the window and told her, "On Mondays, Josie and Austin meet with the tech team right after the run. That's why they take a separate car. Josie's the only one he trusts to drive his baby. She loves that car almost as much as he does." Gary turned the key in the ignition and they headed for Runyon Canyon Park.

Casey's cheeks burned. It was a good thing Thai couldn't read her mind. "Austin said Bob was off this week. Is he on vacation?"

"No," Thai said. "This isn't his only gig. He is the shaman for his tribe and has duties and responsibilities to perform there. He doesn't accompany us on every investigation, but he's definitely there when we need him to be."

Gary parked the car and Casey glanced out the window and stared at the uphill running trail. Did he really expect her to run on the incline?

The answer was a resounding yes. By the middle of the first hill, Casey was far behind the others. Walking was more Casey's speed. She ran, but she didn't push herself. The California weather was beautiful and she loved viewing LA from the vantage point of the trails. She came in dead last, but at least she finished.

After the run, Austin gathered the group together. "Get cleaned up and get some lunch. We'll meet up at one-thirty in the conference room." He hopped in the Porsche with Josie and they sped off.

Reluctantly, Casey pulled herself out of the hot shower. She wrapped a fluffy towel around her and shook out her long, wet hair. Josie was already dressed and waiting for her on the bench.

"You're back," Casey observed. "And already showered."

"Yeah. The meeting didn't take long. And riding in the Porsche, we made good time."

"What is the deal with his car anyway? Couldn't you get your own Porsche with what he pays us?"

"I do have my own. But the coolness factor is so much higher when I'm driving Austin Cole's Porsche with the SP1R1T vanity plate."

Casey stepped into the changing room to put on her clothes. "That's an awesome shower. I'm impressed. Cole spent some major money on a women's locker room for you."

"It wasn't for me."

"Then who was it for? You're the only female I've seen around here other than me."

"This is brand new. The day after your interview he called in a construction crew." She patted the bench. "This used to be a storage room."

Casey pulled the curtain back. "Wait, so where did you shower?"

"In the other locker room."

"The *men's* locker room?" Josie nodded. "Not with the other guys in there?"

"Not usually. But if I was in a hurry to get back to work, hell yeah, I did. There are separate shower enclosures and I just changed in the bathroom stall. It's not like the guys give a shit if I see their junk or not."

"But that didn't bother you?"

Josie shrugged. "I grew up with brothers who loved to walk around commando. Weenies and nut sacs don't really do anything for me. With the exception of Luis, the guys like to strut around like half-naked peacocks in the gym anyway." She smiled at Casey and shook her head. "I remember one time we had just got in some new digital recorders, and we were having trouble with the sensitivity levels. Now when Austin has something on his mind, he's got to discuss it right then. No waiting around. He called me into the locker room while he was showering. And, I shit you not, he turned off the water, hiked his leg up on the counter and toweled off his balls while we discussed the technical problems with the equipment."

Casey narrowed her eyes. "Funny, I don't have any trouble believing that story."

"Anyway, Austin thought you'd have a problem showering with the guys, so he built this." She gestured to the room.

"Yeah. I would have raised hell about that." She slipped her skirt over her head and pulled it down. "So, what's the deal with all the workouts and eating wheat grass, anyway? Does Cole really think he can stop an incorporeal being with a buff body?"

"He believes in the 'strong body, strong mind' philosophy when it comes to spiritual warfare. The weak and weak-willed are more susceptible to attack. That's why he wants us to eat right and take care of ourselves. See this?" She lifted her wrist to show Casey the band she was wearing. "It tracks how many steps I take a day, my heart rate, and how much sleep I get at night. He'll get you one, too, if you want."

"I don't think I want Austin to have access to all that personal info."

"He doesn't. This is strictly for self-monitoring."

"Seriously? Austin Control wouldn't access that info?"

"He may seem a little over the top, but he only wants to keep us strong and safe, physically and mentally. That's why he has the requirement for meditation or prayer. He and Luis, obviously, are

Catholic. Thai's Buddhist. Bob's a shaman with his tribe and Gary's some kind of Protestant, but I don't know which."

"Yeah, I figured he was Catholic from the crucifix around his neck." *And from reading his mind.*

"That's how he met Luis. Luis was the priest in his church growing up. When Austin was still a kid, Luis was trained as the exorcist for the diocese. They lost touch, but when Austin learned he'd left the priesthood for good, he invited Luis to join the team."

"So why'd he leave the Church?"

"The not getting married thing. Luis always wanted a wife and kids, but he wanted to serve the Church, too. He struggled with it for years and then he met his wife, Marie. He knew he couldn't do it anymore and decided to leave the priesthood rather than break his vow. Now that he doesn't have to go through the red tape of the Church, he does more exorcisms than he did before. He's still on pretty good terms with the bishop, and I think the church secretly approves of what he does. Evil is combatted and the Catholic Church doesn't come across as crazy and unenlightened. It's a win-win. He lives off what Austin pays and performs exorcisms in the off-season for free. He helps a lot more people this way."

"I imagine so," Casey said as she laced her shoe. "So, what about you? What are your beliefs?"

"I believe in God and heaven and hell. The things I've seen and heard make it hard not to. But I'm not super-religious. When I do go to church, it's with my wife, Liv. She's Presbyterian."

"And Austin doesn't have a problem with that?"

"I'm on the tech team. I'm not subject to the same rules as the investigation crew. But Austin lets me join you guys for training."

"Wait. So you don't have to work out every day?"

"No. I work out every day because I want to."

6

On Friday after work, Casey curled up on the overly soft hotel bed and called Tina to give her the *SCI* scoop, as she had promised.

"So, how great is it to work with the *SCI* team?" Tina squealed.

"Okay, I guess. The exercise regimen bites, but the television stuff isn't as scary as I'd thought it would be."

"So, tell me all about Austin."

"What about him?"

"What's he like in person? You have to give me all the details."

"I have no idea. I hate to disappoint you, but he's spoken about two words to me all week. When he wants me to know something he has Thai or Josie tell me."

"Really?"

"Really. He kind of ignores me and I'm just trying to stay under his radar."

"I thought with such a small group of people and spending so much time with one another you'd get to know each other pretty well."

"Josie and I have hit it off pretty well. We're going apartment hunting tomorrow. Thai's nice to me. Actually, everyone's been nice."

"I guess these things just take time."

"I'm not worried about it. As long as he pays my salary, I don't care what he thinks of me." Her words came out sharper than she intended. "Look, I've got laundry and some other stuff to do before tomorrow. I'll talk to you later." Casey said her goodbyes and hung up. She sighed. Problem was, she did want to fit in and she did care what he thought of her.

Josie and her wife swung by Casey's hotel early the next morning to begin the search for an apartment. Liv was just as petite as Josie, but she had a more conservative look. Her brown hair was neatly styled in a bob and she was dressed in a light-blue, button-down blouse and tailored navy slacks. There were no extra piercings on her face, and if she had a tattoo, it was well hidden.

"So, Josie tells me you want a place that's walking distance to work. There are a few, but they're kind of pricey."

Whatever the price was, it was still cheaper than buying a car, and she didn't want to rely on public transportation. When she got her debts paid off she could think about getting her own vehicle. "I don't need anything big. A small studio will work fine."

"Okay. The first one is super close. Just three blocks from *SCI*." It was super close, but it was also super small, and super expensive. There was no separate bedroom. Just a main living area, small kitchenette, and tiny bathroom. The shower had seen better days. She turned the hot water faucet on and a weak stream of tepid water filtered through. That was a deal breaker for Casey. There was virtually no storage space. The small closet would have trouble holding even her sparse wardrobe.

"Let's keep looking," Casey suggested.

As they drove to the next place, Liv told Casey, "I think you're going to love this one. It's been completely updated." It was five blocks from *SCI*, much bigger, and surprisingly, a lot cheaper. As soon as Casey walked in the door, she knew why. She strolled on by the state-of-the-art kitchen and living area with its newly refinished hardwood floors and over to the bathroom. Beautiful granite countertops, brushed nickel fixtures, and porcelain tile could not overcome this apartment's one major flaw. "Sorry, Liv. This isn't going to work."

"Gosh, I thought you'd love it."

Casey leaned against the doorframe and pointed into the bathroom. "It may be fine for someone else, but I just can't get past the dead guy in the tub."

"No shit?" Josie asked. She stepped by Casey and turned her head from side to side, trying to see what Casey saw. "So there's really a ghost here?"

"Unfortunately, yes." A man, approximately fifty years old and wearing nothing but boxer shorts, was hunched over in the tub. There was a pistol in his hand and a large, gaping hole on the side of his head. A steady stream of blood pooled on the tile.

Casey saw ghosts almost everywhere she went. She tried hard to avoid crime scenes, car wrecks, and hospitals. The grisly horrors in those locations made for strong psychic reverberations and unhappy spirits. This one was fixed in his death mindset. "Taking long hot showers is one of the few luxuries I enjoy. Watching this guy recreate his suicide every day in my bathroom would not be relaxing."

"Oh my," Liv exclaimed. "The listing agent never told me anything about this. What do we do? Do we call the police?"

"Nah." Casey looked at the floor and swept her eyes back and forth. She could see the man, Oliver Dunhee, when he was alive. He showed Casey snippets of his life. In her mind she saw him surrounded by guns and booze. She felt boxed in, trapped. There was an overwhelming sense of fear, too. He was scared of the police but more frightened of the people he worked for. Looking through his eyes she was overwhelmed by hopelessness. On that particular afternoon, he decided he wanted out, and made the permanent decision to blow his brains out. "He offed himself at least fifty years ago."

"Creepy," Liv said and shuddered. The women walked out and Liv locked up. "Well, I have one more place to look at. It's about ten blocks away from *SCI,* on the west side. It's not much larger than the first place, but it is cheaper."

The place was older, but it was well-maintained. As soon as they entered the small studio, Casey smelled coffee brewing and sensed a benevolent presence. In the small, dated kitchen was a thirty-something blond woman in a light-blue nightgown pouring coffee from an old silver percolator. She smiled at Casey. The woman wasn't traumatized, just happily reliving her daily routine. After stirring in creamer, she turned and walked through a wall.

"What do you think?" Liv asked.

There are certainly worse dead roommates out there, Casey thought. "It's perfect." Casey turned and faced her. "I'll take it."

Her good feelings over the weekend ended abruptly Monday morning. Austin upped the run to three miles, followed by strength training in the gym. By the end of the run she was dying, and if she weren't so stubborn, she would have sat out halfway through the intervals. Before breaking for showers and lunch, Austin made an announcement. "Lunch is on me. I've reserved a table at Marley's for twelve-thirty. After we return, we'll begin our regular afternoon routine before we go over some of the tech stuff. Meet with Thai in the gym for meditation or in Luis's office for prayer."

After a quick shower, Casey and Josie walked to the outdoor café. Not surprisingly, Marley's only served healthy fare. Casey was exhausted and starving. What she craved was a thick cheeseburger and greasy fries. Unfortunately, she had to settle for a grilled chicken sandwich with veggie chips. Austin sat at the end of the table flanked by Thai on his left and Luis on his right. They joked and teased in a light-hearted way that could only come from a long-standing friendship and a high level of respect and trust. Casey sat at the other end of the table trying not to feel like the newbie inter-loper that she was. Midway through the meal, Austin rounded the table, checking in with each member of the team.

When he got to Casey he said, "I can tell you're new to running. I know it's hard, but you've got to push yourself." Casey nodded, though she had no intention of pushing herself. "Once you get in the zone, it's the best feeling in the world." He patted her shoulder and started to move on when Casey spoke.

"About these prayer and meditation classes. Do we have to choose one or the other?"

He crouched down so that he was eye level with her. His brow furrowed. "I don't understand."

"Is it an either or thing, or can we do some prayer and some meditation?"

He narrowed his eyes. "You don't know what you believe?"

Yes. No. Maybe she really didn't. "I'd just like to try both, if you don't mind."

Austin rubbed his chin. "No one's ever asked that before. I guess you could do both. I mean, I spend most afternoons praying with Luis, but on Wednesdays I do yoga with Thai." Austin moved on, asking Josie how things were going in the tech lab. Casey crunched on a veggie chip. It wasn't much of a conversation, but at least he acknowledged she was there.

"A strong body is the first part of the equation," Thai began. "Good nutrition as well as plenty of rest and exercise is key. I think we all have that covered, so I'll move on to the second part." Bob joined them, but sat in a different area of the gym performing his own meditation rituals. The shaman had a young face, but the streaks of silver running through his long braid belied his age. "Desires are the fuel evil spirits run on." Thai continued. "Steering clear of obsessive desires will safeguard our bodies and minds. Strive for a balanced lifestyle of moderation and contentment. Evil spirits cannot invade a harmonious body. Avoid the extremes and stay on the Middle Way. Now, let's begin with some relaxation exercises."

The following afternoon, Casey went with Gary and Austin to meet with Luis. Luis's office was actually two rooms. The outer room looked like any other office, with a desk and a couple of chairs. The inner room looked like a mini chapel. The cross of Christ was prominently displayed in the center of the room. Luis opened, "Let us pray."

Gary and Austin knelt down and Casey followed their example. After a prayer of protection, Luis recited the Lord's Prayer. Austin and Gary joined in. Once the prayers were concluded, Luis read the lesson from the lectionary. It was the closest thing to a church service Casey had attended in years. On Wednesday morning, they were all back on the trail. Casey pumped her arms and willed her feet to propel her forward. She made an observation: Running sucks. She was sore from two days of back-to-back three-mile runs and the strength exercises were killing her arms. Austin wasn't making it easier on her, either. He didn't care that before last week the longest distance she'd run was to the mailbox and back.

He ran up beside her. "What's the problem, Lawson? Why aren't you keeping up?"

Casey looked at him like he lost his mind. "I'm not used to this much physical activity. You can't expect me to be as fast as the others."

"I realize that, but today you are really dragging. Are you hurt?" he asked.

Casey started to laugh. Every muscle in her body ached. "I'm sore as hell," she told him.

"That comes with the territory. Are you getting enough sleep, drinking enough water?"

"Yes."

"What did you have for breakfast?"

"Nothing," Casey said. She had never been a breakfast person to begin with. This morning she'd gotten up late and rushed out of the house.

Austin shook his head and swore. "You can't do that. Eating healthy is a necessity." He pulled her off the trail and motioned for her to follow him over to the Suburban. He took a jug of some kind of protein shake and poured her a large glass. "Drink this. You can skip strength training today and take a hot shower. That will help with the muscle soreness. Tomorrow we're doing a five-mile run. I need you to be in top physical condition by the time filming starts."

Casey took a sip. It was cold and thick like a shake, but with a funny, non-sweet taste. She made a face as she forced herself to swallow it down.

He leaned against the passenger side door. "I know this is hard, but I expect the best from you. Right now, you're not giving it to me. Luis is twice your age and can run circles around you. If you're not in peak condition, you will be a drag on the whole team. While we're on location, we have enough to worry about ourselves. You can't expect us to carry your water."

Casey's head snapped up. "Don't worry about that. I can take care of myself."

"I hope so. Right now I'm still waiting for you to start." He pushed off the Suburban and ran over to the trail. "You're doing great, guys," he yelled out to the rest of the team.

"Jerk," Casey said as she took a sip of water. She was mad at him, mostly because he was right. She wasn't putting forth the effort and the boss man noticed. So much for flying under the radar. She finished as much of the shake as she could stand and headed back to the trail. *He wants me to push myself, fine. I'll show him.*

When they got back to the gym, Casey did additional reps on the arm and leg machines. Now both her upper and lower limbs were screaming at her and she was sure she would pay for it this evening and tomorrow. But she was stubborn enough not to care.

After a long shower and a quick turkey sandwich, Casey headed back to the gym. *Yoga can't be too hard,* she thought. Josie had tech work to do, Bob was doing his own meditation and exercises and Gary was lifting weights with Luis. That left her alone in Thai's yoga class with Austin. Casey groaned and rolled her eyes as she entered the room. Neither Thai nor Austin were wearing anything above the waist. Casey pursed her lips. *Lovely.*

Before today, Casey thought yoga was like in-depth stretching. Boy, was she wrong. Her balance was for shit. And holding the poses for the time Thai expected was sheer torture. Casey was relieved when Thai had them lie on the mat for sitting poses. Unfortunately, these poses were no easier. By the time Thai had them move to a downward dog position, the muscles in her arms and legs were trembling and she was short of breath. Austin saw her struggling and came over. "Your hands aren't in the right position." He showed her the placement. Then, he gripped her hips and pulled her butt up higher in the air.

She frowned. "I thought Thai was running this class."

"He is," Austin answered.

"In that case, would you mind removing your hands from my ass? I'm sure Thai can correct me if I'm doing it wrong."

Austin put his hands up and walked back to his own mat. She heard him mutter, "Whatever floats your boat pose, sweetheart."

On Thursday morning, she was cursing herself for being so stubborn. She should have skipped strength training instead of attempting yoga. Now she could barely move. *One foot in front of the other,* she told herself.

"C'mon, Lawson!" Austin put his hands around his mouth and yelled. "Let's move it! Everyone's finished and you're still a lap behind." This chick was more trouble than she was worth.

Lawson? What was this, middle school track? Casey turned her head and narrowed her eyes at him. Her middle finger ached to flip him off. *Don't think about that jackass; think about that beautiful check he pays you.* She stared straight ahead, ignoring her aching calves and concentrating on breathing. Exhausted, she tripped and stumbled. After that, she gave up and walked the rest of the way.

She tried to catch her breath as she headed inside. "It's about time, sweetheart," Austin called out to her. Casey's head snapped up. Her brain told her to just keep walking, but her mouth just wouldn't let it go.

She turned and walked over to him, her hands clenched at her sides. "Maybe I wouldn't be moving so slowly today if you hadn't been torturing me all week with this crazy exercise regimen, which is pointless, by the way. After you get killed by a demon you can't outrun, your fans can take comfort in the fact that at the time of your death, your coronary arteries were clean as a whistle." She pointed her finger at him. "And don't call me sweetheart ever again." Thai had come back outside and was standing nearby, sipping on a bottle of water. She turned, speed-walking away from Austin.

"So that's how I get you to move. Make you mad." He watched her backside as she strode off. "I think you're right. You're mean as a two-headed snake. Sweetheart doesn't really fit. I should probably call you Sweet Cheeks instead." Casey stopped in her tracks.

Thai shook his head. "Not cool, man."

She turned around to face him, any bit of self-restraint long gone. "And maybe I should call you pencil dick."

Austin snorted, then walked closer. Now they were standing toe to toe. "No, but maybe you should try calling me Mr. Cole, the boss, or the guy who signs your checks."

Thai ran over and pushed them apart. "Let's take a breath and cool down." He looked at Casey. "Before someone gets fired."

Then he turned to Austin. "And someone gets sued for sexual harassment."

Casey turned and stomped toward the gym. She could feel hot tears threatening to spill onto her cheeks. She took a breath and willed them not to fall. Josie saw the upset on her face and walked over. "What's wrong?"

"Nothing," Casey said in a trembling voice.

"Listen up, everybody. After you finish your reps you can take the rest of the day off," Austin yelled. Then he looked over at Thai. "Meet me in my office," he said in a low voice. Gary arched an eyebrow and gave Luis a knowing look. Luis shrugged. Casey didn't know why he canceled the afternoon and didn't care. She was just glad she wouldn't have to see the son-of-a-bitch for the rest of the day.

"C'mon," Josie said to Casey. "I know what you need."

"What?"

"You are on testosterone overload. You definitely need a girls' day out."

"She's not that slow, Austin. You're not even giving her a fair shot," Thai told him as soon as they were in the privacy of Austin's office.

Austin leaned back in his chair. "I am giving her a fair shot. All she's giving me is attitude. Face it, Thai. Right now, she's a liability."

"It wouldn't kill you to be a little nicer," Thai answered. Austin's lips were pressed together in a scowl, and he was looking down and away from Thai, like he didn't hear a word he was saying. "Look, can we just cut the bullshit? This isn't even about her. This is about Barrett."

"No, man. It's not."

"Whatever." Thai turned from the window and crossed his arms. "Maybe you'd get better results if you tried talking to her.

When you're not completely ignoring her, you're yelling at her to get her ass in gear. She's actually pretty interesting once you get to know her."

"That's not true. I'm not ignoring her."

"Yes, you are, dude."

Austin sighed and ran his fingers through his hair. "Fine. We'll try it your way."

7

Josie punched a number on her cell. "Hey, babe, you want to meet Casey and me for lunch? Okay. Cool. See you there. Huh? Austin gave us the rest of the day off. Yeah. I'll explain when you get there." She turned to Casey. "Liv's off today. She's going to meet us. After lunch we can go shopping...." Casey shook her head. On a good day, she hated to walk into a department store. She certainly didn't want to today. "...Or we could head back to our apartment for chick flicks. Liv is the rom-com queen. She's got like every cheeseball romance ever made."

Casey nodded. "That's cool." She wasn't much for romance movies, but it still sounded better than shopping.

They climbed into Josie's blue Porsche and drove around the corner to a café that served soup, salads and sandwiches. Liv walked in the door shortly after they did. She took a seat at the table, placing her purse on the chair beside her. "So what's going on?" Casey sat quietly.

"Austin and Casey aren't getting along so well," Josie answered.

"What's the matter?" Liv asked Casey.

Casey knew she was in the minority opinion as far as Austin was concerned. But since Liv asked, she was going to give it to her straight. "I haven't even been here two weeks and he expects me to be running a marathon. Yes, I signed up for the exercise and eating regimen when I took the job. But he knew before I started I wasn't an athlete. And calling me out and making fun of me doesn't encourage me to move any faster."

"Don't take it personally. I promise you, he's way harder on himself than the rest of us," Josie said.

Casey huffed. "I'm sure he is."

Josie ran her tongue over her pierced lip. She debated on how much to tell Casey, or if she should say anything at all. The rest of them knew Austin's issues. Maybe it was time to give Casey the facts and let her make up her own mind. "Here's the deal. Austin has always been a hard-core health enthusiast. He met most of us at the gym in college. When Barrett joined our small-time ghost-hunting society, he began working out, too. But he never took it as seriously as the rest of us. Austin has always believed that the demons can only possess those with a weak will. If your body's strong enough, if you can discipline your mind, then you can deflect a demon attack. The idea that there are some places that shouldn't be messed with is not something he can accept. He couldn't process what happened to Barrett. He needed to believe that Barrett had done something wrong for the demon to get in. Sure, some people are more susceptible to possession than others, but I don't think Barrett could have done anything differently to prevent what happened, other than not show up. We all know the psychic is at greater risk because he or she has to open up to receive the information from the other side. But Austin didn't believe that. He doubled down after what happened to Barrett and we all had to increase our mental and physical training regimens. It's not your fault but, unfortunately, it is your problem. He's going to work you harder and expect more out of you than he ever did Barrett."

Liv leaned forward with her elbows on the table. "I've known Austin a long time. Almost as long as Josie. Before I got my real estate license I worked as a sous chef at Jean Claude's. Trust me, I know asshole manager dickwads when I see them, and Austin isn't one. Is he OCD? You bet. Is he trying to be a bastard son-of-a-bitch?

No way. He's got a good heart. Sometimes you have to look through his manly bullshit to find it, though."

"You, too?" Casey asked, incredulously. "I thought you'd be immune to his charm and sex appeal."

Liv laughed. "I'm not going to lie; the boy is fucking hot. I can appreciate beauty in the masculine or feminine form, and as far as masculine goes, he's the most gorgeous thing this side of heaven. But that has nothing to do with what I just told you. Maybe you don't know this because you haven't been at *SCI* that long, but Austin is one of the good guys."

Casey pointed at Liv and looked over at Josie. "Does it bother you that your wife has a crush on your boss?"

"Nah," Josie shrugged and squeezed Liv's shoulder. "She's always talking shit. I'm used to it." She smiled at Liv. "I know she only married me to get close to him."

Liv shook her head. "True, but you only married me for my tiramisu. C'mon. Let's get out of here. I'm in the mood for a chick flick."

"All right," Casey agreed. "But only on one condition. We don't discuss work for the rest of the evening."

Liv nodded her head. "That we can do."

They grabbed their purses and walked to the car. Watching a romance didn't sound great, but she knew if she went home right now, it was highly likely that she'd suck back a few beers, call Tina and beg for her job back. Then she'd wake up tomorrow feeling much worse than she did now. They passed by a homeless man, leaning against a store front. Josie bent down and stuffed some bills into his jar. He smiled and whispered, "Thanks."

Casey frowned. *Way to go. You just subsidized his next hit.* She started to say something then closed her mouth. How Josie decided to throw away her money was her business. But if she thought she was helping the guy, she was sadly mistaken. Casey blew out her breath. This thing with Austin was coloring her mood, and she didn't need to piss on everyone else's parade.

After the movie, Josie took Casey home. She talked herself out of calling Tina, but she needed to talk to someone. She could think of only one person who might understand.

"Hello," Barrett answered on the first ring. He was lounging on his couch. The TV was on but he really wasn't watching it.

"Sorry to bother you."

He sat up. "Casey, what's wrong? And don't say nothing. I know better."

Casey awoke extra early the next morning. She stood in front of the sink, staring at her reflection. The long, hot shower she had just taken hadn't done much to ease the soreness of her muscles. She grabbed a glass of water and sucked down three Advil. Barrett told her Austin was hard on everyone and to give it another chance. She wasn't a quitter, so she would try. "C'mon, Casey, you can do this," she told her reflection. "Don't let him beat you down." She splashed cold water on her face, grabbed her purse, and headed out the door.

When she got to the gym, the guys were already warming up. She slowly made her way over to where Josie was stretching. Every little movement made it feel like her muscles were going to rip in two.

Austin watched as she slowly limped through the gym. She winced as she sat down cross-legged on one of the mats, and he wondered if she would be able to get back up. He waved Josie over. "How's she feeling?" he asked, tipping his head in Casey's direction.

"Obviously, she's hurting."

Austin shook his head and crossed his arms. "Fuck. She's not going to make it one mile, never mind five."

"I don't know about that. It may take her all day, but she's determined to prove to you that she's not a quitter."

Shit. He'd given her that lecture about trying harder to motivate her, not to tear her down. If she went through with the run today she could really hurt herself. "Thai," Austin called out. "Call John and see if he can see Casey this morning." John was Austin's personal masseur, but he worked on everyone at *SCI* when needed. Thai pulled out his cell phone while Austin talked to the rest of the group. "All right, listen up. Meet me out on the track in five."

Thai ended the call. "He's on his way. He can see her in fifteen minutes."

Austin pulled Josie aside. "Take Casey down to the massage room. Let her know that everything's cool, and I do not expect her to run today."

"Why don't you tell her yourself?"

"I think it would go over better coming from you." From the moment he'd entered the room, she'd been avoiding all eye contact with him.

An hour and a half later, Casey stepped out of the massage room feeling like a new woman. John had worked all the knots loose. It was agony at the time, but now, she could actually stand upright and move faster than a snail.

"Casey, c'mon," Josie was waiting for her.

"What?"

"Thai and Austin are fighting."

"Huh?" An image of high school brawls that the vice principal had to break up popped into her head.

"About once a month, Austin challenges Thai to a match. Thai usually wins, but Austin refuses to give up. The rest of us place bets and watch the show. It's pretty entertaining." Casey was disappointed. She had hoped Thai had gotten sick of Control's shit and let him have it. The idea of a formal match wasn't nearly as exciting.

When she walked into the gym, Austin and Thai were facing each other. They bowed and assumed a ready stance.

Casey sat on the floor next to Josie. She knew next to nothing about martial arts, but it was still entertaining to watch the guys go at it. They would strike each other and make these short little yelps.

Thai kicked and Austin raised his arm to block. Austin punched, but Thai intercepted and spun Austin around. Austin managed to get free from Thai's hold, but Thai had him backing up, and Austin ended up running off the mat to get away from him. Thai let him gain a little ground then charged toward him with a yell. He tackled Austin and they both went down to the mat.

"It's over now," Gary said. Casey looked up at him and Gary explained. "Once Thai gets you on the ground, you're not getting up." Austin struggled, but Thai held him down. Casey could hear the guys grunting and breathing heavily.

"Tap out, asshole," Thai told Austin.

"Go fuck yourself," Austin gasped.

They struggled and fought for a few more moments. Then Gary stood up. "All right. It's over. Thai wins." The rest of the crew clapped and cheered. Especially Casey. A smile spread across her face. Thai extended his hand, and Austin allowed him to pull him off the mat. Casey heard Austin tell him, "Good fight, bro."

She was still grinning and laughing with Josie and didn't notice Austin approach. He knelt down and peered into her eyes. "How are you feeling?"

For the first time, Casey actually felt like he saw her. The gloating smile fell from her lips. "Good. Thanks for arranging the massage."

"That's what I pay John for. Thanks aren't necessary."

"Well, you didn't have to allow it."

"Casey, that's not how I work. If a massage helps out one of my crew, why not bring John in?" Austin stood. "We'll meet back in the conference room at one-thirty to go over the background information for our first episode. You all remember the Thompson estate."

There were a few groans, and Casey saw Luis and Gary exchange troubled glances. Casey couldn't help but wonder about the lackluster reaction. This was the first time she had witnessed this enthusiastic bunch not go into full orgasmic ecstasy over something their fearless leader said.

When they reconvened in the conference room, Austin was already waiting for them. A power point presentation projected onto a screen behind him.

"You guys all know I like to start the season off with a bang." He turned and pointed to the screen. "There it is. Full-on demon infestation." Austin depressed the clicker and an image of a large luxury home appeared on the screen. It looked brand new, but even in the static image, Casey could sense something was wrong with the place. Her third eye opened, revealing a dark mist overlying the upper floor.

"I know. I was there for Barrett's walk through," Gary said. "I remember him saying we shouldn't go near it. It's a very angry house. In its current active condition, it's too dangerous for an investigation."

"Active houses give us our highest ratings," Austin replied. It was like he hadn't heard a word Gary said. "No one lives here, so there is no urgency to do a therapeutic cleansing of the place. Our goal here," he said, as he laser-pointed to the picture of the home, "is to prove the existence of paranormal activity. With this house, it should be a walk in the park." Austin turned and spoke to Casey directly. "Even though Barrett did a walk through, I want you to do one of your own for our first episode. I think it will be the best way to introduce the new psychic. And with that, I'm going to ask you to go downstairs with the tech team. I don't want to say anything more in front of you that could influence your findings. JoJo has pulled some of Barrett's past walks—the unedited ones—so you know what to expect and what our expectations are." Casey nodded and got up to leave.

Josie sat her down in front of a monitor with a remote. She pressed the play button and stared at the screen. The episode was titled the Brown Sanitarium. She watched as Barrett spoke to the camera. It didn't seem too difficult. Barrett answered the questions Gary posed and made observations about the unseen inhabitants. Simple. The next location was a lively poltergeist house, and Barrett actually had to duck mid-sentence to avoid a flying vase. A moment later they were running from plates being hurled at them. *Okay. So maybe being nimble and athletic isn't such a bad idea.* Most of the other videos were similar in format, but without the editing, she could see that walk throughs took a lot longer in real life than they appeared to on television.

Her stomach rumbled as she finished the last of the video footage. The tuna fish on a bed of kale she'd ordered for lunch had been so unappetizing, she had just picked at it. It had been a week since she'd had red meat, and that was far too long. She stretched and peered out the window. The afternoon light was waning as the orangey dusk settled over the city.

"Later," she heard Thai tell Austin as he headed out the door. Casey grabbed her purse and followed him out. He held the door open for her.

"Great fight," she said.

He grinned. "Thanks. See you next week." He hit his key fob and it beeped twice as he opened the door to his bright yellow Corvette. "You need a ride?"

Part of her considered it. Thai was a nice guy and riding in his 'vette would be fun. But her stomach had already lined up a date with a cheeseburger, and that took priority over everything. "Thanks, anyway. But I have a few errands to run before I head home."

"Okay. See you next week."

Casey waved goodbye, then headed down the block.

Austin pulled out of the lot and turned right onto the busy street. Up ahead, he spotted a red-headed woman with pale skin in a long, loose skirt that flowed down to her ankles. Only his psychic would be covered up like that instead of enjoying the California sun. *It wouldn't kill you to be a little nicer to her.* Thai's words echoed in his ears. "No time like the present," he said to himself.

Visions of a thick, juicy burger and hot, salty fries filled Casey's mind. Maybe she'd even order a vanilla shake. She was lost in her fast-food fantasies when she felt someone watching her. She heard the sound of a car slowing down and turned her head. A black Porsche idled next to her. The driver's side window rolled down and Austin Cole lifted his shades and smiled at her. "Need a ride?"

"No, thank you." Casey said curtly. She faced forward and continued walking toward her gastronomic destination.

He couldn't just speed up and drive off like any normal person would. "I think we need to talk."

Casey blew out her breath. Her stomach was rioting, but it was her boss who was asking. She didn't need to give him another reason to be pissed off at her. He opened the passenger-side door, and she climbed in. "Where to?" he asked.

"In-N-Out."

"In-N-Out?" He raised an eyebrow.

"Yes. I'm hungry and I'm off the clock, so don't give me any shit about it. I have a personal policy against eating nutritious, whole foods on the weekends."

Austin scrunched up his nose. "Eat what you want, but can we at least go to a place with a more subdued atmosphere? It would be nice to actually hear each other speak."

"I thought we were going to talk on the way there. I don't recall inviting you along."

Austin took in a breath. "I'd rather be facing you and have a real conversation, so yes, I'm inviting myself along. And I know the perfect spot."

She turned her head and pursed her lips. "Fine, but nothing vegan. I have my mind set on a large, juicy, red-meat cheeseburger, and I will be very unsatisfied with tofu on a bean sprout bun."

"I promise, you'll love it. Jerome's makes a mean grilled cow."

The light changed and they headed toward Wilshire Boulevard. Casey's eyes were drawn to Austin's right hand as he gripped the knob and shifted into second, then third, gear. For some reason, she'd always found it strangely powerful and sexy to watch a man drive a stick shift. And, like everything else he did, Austin drove well.

Casey cleared her throat and leaned her head against the window. "Is this place far away?"

"Why? Are you in a hurry?"

"As you pointed out yesterday, I'm not a sweet person. And that was on a full stomach. Trust me, a hungry Casey Lawson is not someone you want to mess with."

"Noted. We'll be there in less than ten minutes. Do you think you can hold out that long?"

"Maybe."

"So, I guess you enjoyed the fight. Your smile lit up the whole room. Or maybe you enjoyed watching Thai kick my ass." His eyebrow shot up.

Casey tucked a strand of hair behind her ear. "I won't answer that on the grounds that I could get terminated for being truthful. But I will say this: I was impressed by your mad skills. I'm not really into martial arts, but you two looked like ninjas from a movie or something." Austin downshifted as he approached a red light. Casey studied his movements. They were automatic. He didn't have to think about it. His right hand just knew what to do.

As they waited for the green light, his head turned, and his ocean eyes bore into hers. "So you're not into martial arts, cable TV, running, or wheat grass. What are you into, other than cheeseburgers?"

Casey rubbed the back of her neck. *Survival.* How was she supposed to answer that? Struggling to pay off her debts didn't leave a lot of discretionary income for hobbies. "I like to read," she finally answered. In Shadow Creek, she wore out her library card. Books were free entertainment. "The first thing I bought with my *SCI* paycheck was an e-reader."

"An e-reader? Wow. You go all out. Ever think about getting a car?"

"One day. Down the road."

Silence with Austin was uncomfortable. Casey tried to think of something to ask him. It was kind of hard because she'd already read his mind on her interview. Then she thought of something. "Why do you believe?"

"Huh? I've been Catholic my whole life."

Casey shook her head. "Not that. I'm talking about ghosts. You don't have a psychic bone in your body."

"Thanks for pointing it out."

"What I mean is, you should be the biggest skeptic in the world."

"Blessed are those who have not seen and yet believe," he said with a grin.

"I may be a wayward Baptist, but I'm pretty sure that is a gross misrepresentation of that particular bible verse."

The light turned green and Austin shifted into gear. "Baptist?"

"I grew up in the Baptist Church. My dad's a minister."

Austin rubbed his chin. "Interesting."

"Not really. My dad doesn't approve of what I do or the choices I've made. I haven't seen him in a long time." She cleared her throat. "So, you didn't really answer my question."

"I got interested in the other side when I lost someone close to me." Austin stared straight ahead. "Audra, my sister, died when I was twelve. I was a shit little brother. Always messing with her stuff. The day she died, I'd stolen her diary and read it out loud in front of her friends." He shook his head. "She was so pissed at me. Then, she was gone." Austin bit his lip and glanced out the window. "For a while, I searched for proof of ghosts in order to find her. I wanted forgiveness, absolution. It was eating me up, not knowing if she was still angry with me. I spent a ton of money on fortune tellers, mediums, and palm readers. They were a joke. They couldn't get the simplest facts about her straight. Then, I met Barrett. Not only did he refuse to search for her, he told me I was lucky the hacks only took my money. A demon could pretend to be her and fuck with me hard. He said she'd already crossed. If she was still here, she would have contacted me long ago."

"I'm sorry. I didn't realize.…" At the time of the interview, when she'd read his mind, she'd known he felt guilty about his sister's death, but didn't know the circumstances.

"No big deal. Like I said, she died a long time ago. I did stop looking for her, but my fascination with ghosts never went away."

He pulled into the parking lot of a swanky-looking pub for urbanites. The place was packed, with a long line at the door, but all Austin had to do was remove his shades and the hostess was falling all over herself to find him a seat. "You don't have to do that," Casey whispered.

"Yeah, I do. You said it yourself. You're dangerous when you're hungry."

"I don't want to cut in front of all these people." The crowd was staring at them. Casey didn't know if it was her own guilt for being moved to the front of the line, or because she was in the company of the great Austin Cole.

"Relax. The owner's a friend. He has a table in the back reserved for me." Casey hoped it was true. The hostess led them to a booth with a nice view of the boulevard. Casey stared out the window, mesmerized by the lights of the city at night.

She was still looking out the window when the waitress brought Casey a beer and Austin a Perrier. "So," Austin said, and Casey faced forward. "It has been brought to my attention that I have been a total asshole to you, and that I need to issue you a proper apology." Casey stopped fiddling with her beer cap and stared into his serious eyes. "I'm sorry I've been so rude. I can understand why you don't like me."

"Austin."

He held up his finger. "Let me finish. I know I've been a dick in the past and will most likely be a dick in the future. But I don't go around trying to hurt people's feelings. We've always been a close team and it bothers me that you and I don't get along. I'm hoping we can put our contentious feelings aside and learn to work together." He put out his hand. "I'm asking for a truce."

"Truce." Casey took his hand and shook it. She wanted to admit that she hadn't been the easiest person to get along with either, but the words died on her lips. She wished the food would come, and not just because she was ready to eat her own hand. Austin's penetrating gaze put her on edge. She needed something to do, so she rolled the beer cap between her fingers.

Austin leaned back and draped his arm over the back of the booth. He arched an eyebrow. "So what do you like to read?"

"Romance, paranormal, paranormal-romance."

"Paranormal romance? What is that, falling in love with a ghost?"

"It can be, but I prefer other creatures. I get enough ghost stuff in real life. Basically, it's anything non-human—alien, werewolf, shape-shifter, vampire, demon."

"Demon? How could anyone fall in love with a demon?"

"Demons in books are not usually like the evil entities we encounter. They are often beautiful creatures and charming. They can even be good guys that are misunderstood."

Austin's face twisted in confusion and revulsion. "I don't care how charming or gorgeous they are. That's just sick. They're liars. They can pretend to be anything they want. How could anyone believe they were good?"

"I don't. And it's fiction, so I wouldn't get too upset about it." Just then, a couple of teenage girls cautiously approached the table. They were smiling, blushing and giggling all at the same time. One of them punched the other one in the arm and the one with the sore arm spoke. "A-a-austin? I mean, Mr. Cole? Could we have your autograph?"

He flashed one of his winning smiles at the girls, the kind that reached all the way to his eyes. "It's Austin. And I'd be honored." He took the napkin and pen she offered. "What's your name?" he asked.

"Mackenzie."

"And I'm Leah," the other girl added. "We love *Spirit Chasers Investigations*. We have every episode on DVR."

Austin's eyes darted to Leah's hand. She was holding a phone. "Would you like to get a picture?"

The girls looked at each other and squealed. "Casey, would you do the honors?" She nodded and Leah handed her the phone. Austin stood between the two girls and pulled them into a hug as Casey snapped a few pictures.

"Thank you," the girls gushed. As they were walking off, Casey overheard Mackenzie tell Leah, "You better send me that picture."

"I will. Just let me post it on my wall first."

Casey watched them walk away and smiled. "You have a nice smile." Austin told her. Despite every effort to stop it, her lips stretched out wider. She shrugged and gazed at the table top. "You should smile more often. It makes you look sweeter, even when you're hungry."

8

Casey got up early Monday morning and had just enough time to make one of Austin's disgusting protein shakes before walking to work. When she entered the gym, Thai was standing in the front of the room. The rest of the investigation team was sitting on mats facing him, but Control was nowhere to be seen. Casey leaned over and whispered in Josie's ear. "Where's Austin?"

"He's out of town. His mom got married this weekend and he went up for the wedding."

Relief flooded through her. She and Thai got along. Working out with him wasn't so bad. "How come I didn't know? Is it a secret?"

Josie nodded. "Kind of. It's a sore subject with him, so no one likes to bring it up."

"Why? Is the guy a jerk, or does Austin harbor latent fantasies of his parents reuniting?"

"No, and no. Lyle is a wonderful guy. Puts his mom up on a pedestal. But Austin is very close with his mom and he resents having to share her with anyone." Their heads snapped forward as Thai began to speak.

"All right. We have a lot of ground to cover today. Wednesday we head out for our first investigation. Let's start with a three-mile run."

Casey was wiping her forehead with a towel and walking toward the main doors when Luis caught up with her. There was a look of concern on his face. "I don't want to frighten you, but this is a very bad place we are investigating," he told her.

"Yes, that's what everyone keeps telling me."

"As the one with special sight, you put yourself at more risk than the rest of us. Would you allow me to say a prayer of protection with you and give you a blessing?"

Casey had always been a fan of blessings. She could use all the positive she could get. "Sure. I'd like that."

Luis smiled and patted her shoulder. A few minutes later, Casey was kneeling in Luis's office with his hand on her head. She closed her eyes, letting his lyrical voice flow over her like a calming stream.

On Wednesday, Casey and the crew boarded a plane bound for Ohio. Austin was waiting for them at the airport when they arrived, pacing impatiently. On the limo ride to the hotel, he briefed Thai on some of the logistical details of the location. Casey stared out the window and tried to think of a cozy fireplace on a winter day, a morning walk in the forest—peaceful things. As soon as they parked, Thai ran to the registration desk to pick up the room keys while the others grabbed the luggage. Stiff and tired from the plane ride, Casey stretched and walked around the lobby. Austin strode up to her. He bent over to look into her eyes. "How are we feeling?"

"I'm feeling fine."

"Not nervous?"

"Well, yeah, of course I'm nervous. But I'm not freaking out or anything."

"That's good. On most walk throughs, it will be just you and Gary. But this is your first walk through and this location is a special case, so Thai, Luis, and I thought it would be best if we tagged along for backup. If the house starts acting up, which is a strong possibility, I don't want Gary to have to worry about getting you to safety while he's filming, too."

Casey bit her lip to keep from telling him she could take care of herself. As much as she hated to admit it, his plan actually did make a lot of sense. "Okay."

"Now get some rest if you can. Do some relaxation exercises if you need to, and—"

"Austin. I know how to prepare myself mentally for what I'm doing tonight. I've seen spirits my entire life."

Austin stiffened. "Yeah, I guess so. Meet us down here at five tonight. It takes about a half hour to get there, and I want to arrive before it gets completely dark so that you can see the place in the daylight."

He walked over to speak with Thai, and Casey rolled her luggage to her room. Thai was into yoga, Barrett had his relaxation exercises, but for Casey, nothing put her in a peaceful state of mind like a long, hot shower.

The Thompson Estate was located on a two-acre lot in an upscale suburban neighborhood. It was a sprawling, red-brick two-story with a circular drive and a large wrap-around porch.

"Pull over," Casey instructed.

Austin grinned. "You need to throw up?"

"No. I want to walk the property first."

Austin chuckled. "I'm impressed. Barrett was already hurling before we turned onto the street."

"I don't get sick," Casey told him. Sometimes, if an entity was very evil, she would get a headache that made her nauseated. Barrett, however, had a sensitive stomach, and the spirit world exploited it.

Thai parked the car and they all got out. Gary pointed his camera and began filming. She touched a tree and then bent over to put her hand on the ground. Her third eye opened up. "This house was built on a Native American sacred site. Probably a cemetery or something."

"Ding, ding, ding. You are correct, Ms. Lawson. You win the prize," Thai joked.

Austin shrugged. "Lucky guess. You can't swing a dead cat without hitting a haunted house built on an ancient Indian burial ground." Casey walked all around the perimeter of the house as the twilight deepened. She looked up at the façade. Her heart sped up when she glanced at the upper left window. A black mist swirled behind the windows. It coalesced into a humanoid form and grinned toothlessly at her. *Leave, go!* Her third eye urged. She ignored it and her pounding heart, as she continued around the side of the house. When it was full dark, they approached the front porch. The light from Gary's camera was all they had to see by.

Austin bounded up to the front door, followed by Thai, Casey, and Luis. As cameraman, Gary brought up the rear. Austin kissed his crucifix and opened the door. Casey stepped into the foyer. Directly in front of her, a winding staircase with ornate wrought-iron spindles led up to a grand landing that overlooked the living room. Casey placed her hand over the round finial on the banister and felt a tingle through her palm. She dropped her hand and stepped away. "Let's check out the downstairs first."

Austin nodded and led her through the living room and den. This house was the complete opposite of what a haunted house should look like. It wasn't turn-of-the-century old, with creaking wood floors and a history of blood and violence. In fact, Casey knew no one had died here. It was new construction, with gleaming marble floors in the entryway, granite countertops in the kitchen, and state-of-the-art appliances. The house was fully furnished, as if the family had just stepped out for a few minutes. The absence of electricity and running water and the layer of dust on the furniture were the only obvious signs it was uninhabited. She glanced around and touched the fireplace to get a sense of what she was dealing with. The whole place was overshadowed by darkness, but the main living areas on the first floor were less affected.

They entered the kitchen next. On the counter was a spoon and a half-full cup of moldy coffee. "They left in a hurry," Casey observed.

"I could have told you that," Austin said, as he leaned against the counter.

Casey ignored his sarcasm and continued her inspection. She stopped short and pointed up to the ceiling. "The evil originated there."

"Two for two," Thai said. "The Thompson's son, Brad, and his friends, used to play the Ouija board in his bedroom, right above the kitchen. We believe they are the ones who inadvertently invited the spirits into the house."

That pissed Casey off. She hated Ouija boards. The occult device was mass produced, placed in a box, and sold next to Candy Land in the games section of most stores. They might as well have called it Portal Opening for Dummies.

Casey looked down and her eyes swept side to side. "That's not all of it. Brad is still affected by the spirits."

Casey's gaze flicked back and forth on the floor again. "What are you doing?" Austin asked.

Casey looked up, annoyed. "Reading the place."

"Barrett always closed his eyes and put his hands out like this." Austin splayed his fingers and put his arms out at forty-five degree angle.

If she was with *SCI* ten years from now, Austin would still be comparing her to Barrett. Her patience with him was rapidly waning. "Everyone's different. I like to keep my eyes open so I don't go into a trance state." She straightened her blouse and redirected her gaze to the floor. Her head snapped up and she spoke to Luis. "You've been exorcising Brad."

"Yes," Luis answered. "He underwent a full psychiatric evaluation. His doctors diagnosed him with depression and put him on medication. But still, he manifested symptoms that could not be explained by modern medical science. So he was referred to me."

"What symptoms?" Casey asked.

"He would levitate twelve inches off the floor and answer questions in Akkadian, a language of the ancient Babylonians."

"Nothing says demon possession like floating in the air and speaking in tongues," Austin joked.

Casey ignored his remark. "There is a weak connection between the kitchen and that bedroom." The moldy coffee cup slid across the counter and hit the floor. Casey and the others flinched as it shattered.

They stared at it for a moment, before Austin stepped around the remains of the mug. "I'm going to have to disagree with you there. Barrett says the portal goes from Brad's bedroom," he pointed at the ceiling. "To the spirit world."

"You didn't let me finish. Yes, the main portal is upstairs, but it is widening and extending down to the kitchen. This house has been empty for months, but with our arrival, the evil has awoken."

Casey headed over to the staircase. *C'mon, Casey. You can do this.* She gathered her courage and ran up the stairs. The guys followed. Midway up, she stopped and released her third eye. It was strong and not easily manipulated. She sent it to places she couldn't or didn't want to go. Brad's room appeared in her mind and she saw the dark mist swirling around the middle of the room. Shadow figures hovered around it, walking back and forth like guardians from hell. The room was small, but it packed a shit ton of evil per square inch. The shadow figures were speaking in a language Casey had never heard before. Her third eye translated it for her. Her eyes widened. "The portal terminates at another location," she blurted out. She turned to the guys. "You've been there before. Full disclosure—I've seen last season's final episode, so I know it's the warehouse."

Austin uncrossed his arms and leaned forward while Luis and Thai exchanged meaningful looks.

"What are you saying?" Austin pointed at the floor. "This house is somehow connected to the warehouse from last season?"

Casey nodded. "And there's a third location. But they don't want me to know about the other place. They're blocking me."

"What else?"

She closed her human eyes and let her third eye travel to the first doorway on the left. "I see a bedroom; a girl's room. There is a lot of activity there as well." Her eye showed her that Brad was scared to stay in his own room and would come and sleep on the floor next to his sister's bed. The little shit had opened a can of supernatural worms in his own room and then brought it down the hall to infect his sister's as well.

"Yeah, we already know about the sister's room," Austin told her. "Tell me what's going to happen tonight."

Casey's eyes darted side to side. A moment later, she looked up. Austin had positioned himself right in front of her and she found herself staring into those ocean eyes. "I told you I'm not great with seeing the future. What I can tell you is the kitchen, and pretty much the whole upstairs, are your hot spots."

Austin turned to Gary. "Okay. We'll set up static cameras in the entry pointing up the stairs, the kitchen, and the little girl's room, and we'll try to get one in Brad's room. Last time we were here, the house wouldn't let us open his door. We'll also put one in the upstairs hallway. Barrett got a bad feeling when he was there."

Casey ran down the stairs and sat in the living room, watching the guys haul the equipment into the house. She felt pretty useless not helping them but, on the other hand, she wasn't familiar enough with the cameras to know how and where they wanted them placed. Gary and Luis set up the downstairs while Thai and Austin handled the upstairs. Austin slung a camera bag over his shoulder and glanced over at her. "You want to come up with me and get a feel for the bedrooms while I set up?"

"No, thank you." She pointed at her temple. "I have a pretty good idea of what's in there."

"Suit yourself. But tomorrow night, we all go up together. No wussing out." He glanced down at her ankle-length skirt and ballerina flats. "Oh, and what you're wearing is fine for the walk through, but during the investigation, you'll need something you can run in. I have a tendency to piss these entities off."

Casey peered up at him innocently. "No shit? I thought you only pissed off the living." He frowned at her, then traipsed up the stairs.

9

Casey wrapped her arms around herself and shivered as she eyed the estate. The place looked freaking creepy in the twilight, but in the dark of night, it was downright evil. The shadows cast a grinning humanoid visage against the façade, and the two upstairs bedroom windows looked like sinister eyes. Casey thought if eyes were truly windows to the soul, then these windows must overlook hell.

Incorporeal, shadowy hands waved to them from the windows, beckoning them to come closer. Whatever was residing on the second floor seemed pleased that they were there. That made her heart race and her head throb. She was no stranger to ghosts—hell, she'd seen them for as long as she could remember—but she had actively avoided the darker side of the spirit realm. Now she was breaking every rule she'd ever made for herself by rushing headlong into a demon pit.

"Nervous?" Thai asked.

"No," Casey answered. What else was she going to say?

"Just remember to stick with the group. We'll be fine." Thai looked away as Austin began to speak.

"We'll investigate the downstairs first. Gary, Bob and I will check out the kitchen, dining room and master bedroom. Thai, Luis, and Casey will handle the formal living room and den. We'll regroup at one o'clock." Austin turned his head back. "Ready?" he asked his team. They all nodded in the affirmative. "Let's do this." Austin kissed the crucifix around his neck and pushed the front door open. The others followed, right on his heels.

Casey hustled out of the entryway and over to the living room as quickly as she could. The living room and den had a negative vibe, just as they had had this morning, but it wasn't overwhelming. She wasn't itching to go anywhere near the staircase, though.

Luis made a cursory check of the camera in the entry pointing up to the second floor. "What section do you want?" Thai asked her.

"I'll take the den." She knew that was the chicken thing to do. The den was the furthest from the stairs. Luis staked out the living room, and Thai stationed himself in the entry. Casey sat on the couch and pulled out her digital recorder.

"I know there are spirits here, harassing the Thompson family. Why are you here? What do you want?" she asked. A succession of disembodied voices and a low growl answered her. Casey froze in her seat. Her eyes darted from side to side as a shadow figure flew by her and ran toward the kitchen. Casey bit back a scream.

It took a few minutes for her heart rate to return to normal, but once it did, she realized ghost hunting wasn't as glamorous as it appeared. The television made it seem like non-stop action, non-stop paranormal activity, but that really wasn't the case. Most of the time she sat in the silent dark, holding a recording device out in front of her, waiting as the minutes slowly ticked by. Hell, if her nerves weren't wound tight from knowing that thing upstairs was waiting for them, she probably could have taken a nap. If she, who was extra sensitive, found it tedious, how boring must it be for someone like Austin? He had to be knocked on his ass to know that a spirit was hovering nearby.

At midnight, a loud bang in another room startled her so badly, she jumped an inch off the couch. It was followed by the guys' shouting expletives. "Holy shit, did you see that?" she heard Austin yell excitedly.

Casey stood up and Luis whispered, "Stay where you are. If there's anything we need to do, Austin will call for us." Casey tried to calm her pounding heart and resumed her position on the couch.

At one o'clock, Austin rounded everyone up. They went out to meet with the tech team in the trailer. One of the guys played the footage for them all. It turned out the noise they all heard coming from the kitchen was a pantry door slamming on its own. An unoccupied chair in the kitchen also skidded across the floor and Austin wanted to be sure they caught it on camera. He asked Josie to play it again, and Casey, and the others took that as a cue to leave.

She headed over to the "lounge," the name the crew gave to the second trailer they always brought with them on location. There were a couple of couches, a kitchenette with a refrigerator and microwave, and a bathroom. It was basically a place to chill out while on the investigation. Luis and Gary were already sitting there, having a snack. Casey used the restroom, grabbed a cup of coffee, and went back outside.

"So, how was it?" Josie was leaning against a tree, sipping on her own coffee.

"Okay, I guess."

"Did you see any creepy stuff?"

"I think most of the creepy stuff is upstairs. But here," she handed Josie her recorder. "I caught some growly stuff. I marked the time I heard it."

"Cool," Josie said. She exchanged Casey's used recorder for a brand new one. "I'll analyze this while you're in the house for the second part of the investigation." She started to walk toward the tech trailer, but turned back and said, "Be careful. As the psychic, you are the safety valve for the team. Don't let Austin pressure you to do something that puts everyone in danger. You don't have to prove yourself."

"Thanks, Josie. But this is the first investigation without Barrett, so yeah, I think I do have to prove myself."

Austin waved the team over and they joined him on the front lawn. "Bob, I want you to stay outside this time and see what you can find out from the Native American spirits residing on the property. The rest of us will check out the upstairs. Get your equipment and meet me by the front porch in five minutes."

Lucky Bob, Casey thought. She glanced over at Josie. "It's show time." She finished her coffee and headed over to the house. No way would she be the last one ready to go.

Austin waited for everyone to assemble, then he spoke. "Ready?" Everyone nodded. He kissed his crucifix. "Let's do this," he said as he opened the door. As soon as they entered, the sound of glass shattering echoed down from the second floor. Austin dashed up the staircase to investigate, Thai and Gary running after him.

Luis started up the stairs then turned back. "Coming, Casey?"

She took a breath and steeled herself. "Yeah. I'm right behind you."

Gary started filming when Austin entered the upstairs hall bath. Thai, Luis, and Casey hung back in the doorway. Bits of glass were all over the carpet. "Whoa, do you see this?" Austin asked the camera. Gary followed his pointed finger and began filming the tile, which was covered in shards of glass. "Check this out." Gary aimed the camera at the vanity. "That loud shattering was obviously the mirror breaking, but my question is, what caused it?" When they could find no source in the bathroom itself, Austin, Gary, and Thai walked into the bedroom on the other side of the bathroom. The rocker in the corner began moving on its own, slowly at first, then faster. So fast, the chair began to squeak.

"C'mon," Austin shouted at the air. "So you can make the chair rock. Is that the best you can do?" A doll flew off the windowsill and smacked him in the shoulder. Austin tensed as a low, sustained growl rumbled through the room. The bookcase in the corner fell over. "What the fuck," Thai yelled, as books landed on his feet.

Back in the bathroom, Luis was hunched over, staring down at the tile to study the glass shards. When he stood up, the mirror was hanging over the vanity, completely intact. His gaze returned to the floor. There was not a sliver of glass to be found. He met Casey's wide-eyed stare with one of his own. "Austin," he yelled as he ran around the corner.

Casey put her hand over her mouth and slowly backed out of the doorway and into the hall. This was too much; she needed a moment to regroup, so she stepped into the hall. But something was wrong here, too. It smelled wrong; it looked wrong. Even the air around her *felt* wrong. It was stagnant, stale, dead. This was a mistake. It was chilling to realize just how alone and vulnerable she was out here. She placed a foot in front of her, meaning to go back to the bathroom, but a dark, rolling mist surrounded her and she could no longer see the bathroom door. Her heart sped up and fear made her blood run cold. She heard Austin and the others, but their voices sounded distant. "Shit." She backed up as the black mist trapped her. It was pushing her down to the end of the hallway.

"Austin, you gotta see this," Luis exclaimed as he ran into the bedroom. Gary and Thai were staring at the rocker while Austin was hunched down, examining the bookcase. "Hurry," Luis exclaimed. "Before it changes again." Austin jumped up. This house had come alive and it was going to make for one hell of a show. He flew back into the bathroom.

"What happened? "Austin asked, rubbing his chin, as he studied the space above the vanity.

"I don't know. I looked away for just a second and when I turned back around the mirror was hanging back above the sink," Luis answered.

Austin made a circular motion with his hand, indicating that Gary should start filming. "I can't believe what I'm seeing. We all saw how the mirror was broken, and look now," Austin touched the smooth surface. He turned to face the camera. "It's just fine. Not even a scratch on the glass."

"Casey, what do you sense?" Austin asked as he stared at the mirror. "Casey?" He turned around, but she was not behind him. "Where's our psychic?" he asked Luis.

"She was standing right here when I went to get you."

"Damn it. Can't she follow the simplest instructions?" Austin turned around and exited the bathroom. Thai and the others followed.

"What the hell," Gary said. He could hear a low, guttural growl. He was looking for its source when he saw Casey standing at the other end of the hall, in front of Brad's room. He cocked his head to the side as he studied her strange, frenetic behavior. She would go to one corner of the space and push and pull on the air, then move to another side and do the same thing. To Gary, she looked like a psychotic mime trying to break out of an invisible jail cell.

Casey shouted at the air around her. "Be gone. You may not enter me." She swatted at the mist with her hand. Luis wrapped his purple stole around his neck and began to pray.

Thai's eyebrows were furrowed in concentration. "What's happening? What's going on?" Austin asked him.

"There are dark auras surrounding Casey."

"Auras? Is she in danger?" Austin demanded. He paced back and forth. It sucked being the only one who couldn't sense a damn thing.

"I don't know." Thai shook his head slowly. "I can't detect her energy anymore. The dark entities are overshadowing it."

Austin's eyes met Thai's as he registered the significance of what he'd just said. "Fuck!" Austin ran full speed toward Casey.

"Wait!" Thai cried out. Austin didn't stop until he was standing two feet in front of his psychic. Her eyes were trained on something he couldn't see and she held the cross around her neck out in front of her. Now he understood what Thai was talking about. Although he couldn't see the mist, he could tell when he passed through it. The air surrounding him was cold and heavy. Casey shouted into the air. "Leave me alone!" A dark sense of dread and despair came over Austin. He shook his head to clear his mind. "Focus. Get control," he told himself. His number one priority was getting his psychic to safety. Casey was still yelling as Austin grabbed her hand to pull her out of there. The heavy air pressed around him like he was walking underwater. It felt like fifty-pound weights were strapped to his legs. Entering the mist had been easy enough, but now that he was here, the evil didn't want to let him go.

Time seemed to slow down as he trudged along. Austin heard a low-pitched growl and felt cool breath on his neck. It made his skin crawl. Up ahead, he could see Luis making the sign of the cross and flicking holy water in his direction. Gary and Thai were shouting at him and waving, but their voices sounded muffled and far off. *This is nuts,* thought Austin. The hallway wasn't that long; he should be back to the landing by now. It felt like he was moving in slow motion. It took all his concentration to put one foot in front of the other. It all seemed so pointless. Why was he bothering to get them out at all? It would be so much easier just to lie down on the floor and let the mist engulf them both.

Horrific images passed through his mind in a dark, twisted cinematic presentation. He saw himself lying in bed in his loft in LA. He sat up and poured a glass of whiskey. There was a prescription drug container on his bedside table next to the bottle of booze. He emptied it out, pouring the small white pills on the table. Then he scooped them up and swallowed them all. That image faded, and a new one appeared. He was standing on a chair in the middle of his room. A rope with a loop was hanging from the ceiling. Austin grabbed it and put his head through it. Then he kicked the chair out from under him. His legs were jerking as his face went from red to gray. Then, his body stilled. The third and final image was of him picking a pistol up off a table. Even though he had never handled a firearm before, he knew it was a Beretta. He studied the gun. It was beautiful. His mouth watered as he thought about placing the cool, metallic barrel against his tongue. He shoved it down his throat and pulled the trigger. The loud concussion was the last thing he heard before he came back to himself. "No!" he shouted. It was the dark entity messing with his mind, but damn if it didn't feel real.

While he had been out of it, he'd lost his grip on Casey. Panicking, he stretched his hands out in the dark mist until he found her arm. This time, he picked her up and threw her over his shoulder to keep from losing her again.

Just as he wondered if they'd ever get out, the oppressive energy let go, like a rubber band pulled taut and then released. He fell forward as he was shoved back into real time. To keep from falling, he threw out one hand to brace himself, and held onto Casey with the other. As soon as he had his feet back under him, he took off, flying past his team and heading down the staircase. Only when they were safely out of the house did he put Casey down. Austin bent over at the waist with his hands on his knees, catching his breath. He looked back at the door he had just run out of. It all seemed surreal. Just a few moments ago they had been trapped inside.

"What the fuck was that?" Casey screamed. At first, he thought she was asking what kind of presence it was, but it made no sense for the psychic marvel to be asking the psychic dud his opinion. Then he turned to face her. She had her hands on her hips, and if looks could kill....

He pointed at his chest. "You're mad at me? You were being attacked. I had to do something."

The rest of the team filed out of the house. Luis approached them.

"Luis and I had things under control. I could feel the entity loosening its hold when you decided to pull your caveman act and carry me out like a sack of potatoes. I am not a damsel in distress. You don't have to rescue me!"

He stood with his feet apart and glared at her. "You're welcome."

"Is there a problem?" Luis asked.

"Yeah," barked Casey. "He-man here thinks he has to protect the poor, helpless little girl. I'm part of this team, Austin. You need to treat me like you treat the other guys."

His hands clasped the back of his neck, and he pivoted 180 degrees, exhaling and taking a beat before speaking again. Man oh man, did this chick know how to piss him off. He stuck his index finger out as he spoke. "Look, sweetheart, I wasn't protecting the *girl*, I was protecting the psychic. In case you missed it, I've already lost a damned good one this year, and I don't want to lose another. And if you want to be treated like the rest of the guys, then grow up and start acting like you're part of the team instead of getting up on your feminist high horse."

Casey felt her cheeks get hot. She couldn't speak for a moment. She clenched her fists and pursed her lips. When words finally came to her, she blurted them out. "That's a nice little lecture you have prepared, but we both know it's a load of bull. You wouldn't have thrown Barrett over your shoulder and carried him out." Her voice came out high-pitched and squeaky. She sounded like the nagging, whiny baby he had just accused her of being instead of the calm, self-assured woman she felt like most of the time.

"I wouldn't have had to." Austin stepped closer, and now they were standing toe to toe. His voice was raised and he bent down so he could more easily yell in her face. "Barrett was smart enough not to wander off on his own." His face was turning red and the veins in his forehead were popping out. That made her feel a bit better, knowing that she got under his skin, too.

They stood there, glaring at each other, until the priest broke the silence. "All right, that's enough. I think the negative energy is affecting both of you. Calm down and relax."

Casey stepped back and thought about it. Her anger at Austin was irrational. And as much as she hated to admit it, the arrogant a-hole had saved her bacon. Knowing the evil spirit was playing with her emotions, she let it go. Luis put his hand on her shoulder. "Casey, you've got to stay with the group. We had nothing under control. If God had not restrained the enemy, you would still be trapped." She opened her mouth to protest, but shut it quickly when she realized he was right.

He looked at Austin. "My son, what you did was really stupid. You couldn't see the danger, but that didn't mean it wasn't there."

Austin took a few calming breaths as the last of his fury receded. He looked over at the priest. "What do you mean?"

"You were in there for so long. It was pulling you toward Brad's room." Luis gave Austin a knowing look.

"How long?" Casey asked.

"Over an hour." That revelation shut them both up. She glanced at Austin and the shocked expression on his face mirrored her own. No way had it been over an hour. It seemed like ten minutes, tops.

"You *both* need to realize you're on the same team. Don't let the enemy get a foothold. If it controls your mind, it controls you." Luis squeezed Austin's shoulder, then walked away.

Josie and Gary ran up to them. "Austin, you got to see this," Josie shouted animatedly. "We caught that shit—whatever it was—on tape."

Gary glanced over at Casey. "Maybe you should see this alone first. It's kind of shocking."

Austin crossed his arms and shook his head. "No." He looked Casey in the eye. "She's part of the team. I'm sure she can handle it."

They walked over to the tech trailer. It was filled with monitors showing the inside of the building from different angles and locations. Casey studied a static image of the hallway they had been trapped in. Although the dark mist had dissipated, the memory of it was strong, and Casey shivered. Josie sat down in front of the monitors and began pushing buttons. "Check this out. You're not going to believe it."

Austin leaned over her shoulder and squinted into the screen. A dark gray haze was covering Casey and him. Then he saw what Josie was talking about. Black vines extended out of the mist, twisting and lengthening, reaching out toward the two of them. The vines stopped about a foot away from Casey's head and body. It looked as if some kind of force field was surrounding her, preventing the dark ropes from coming any closer.

The hair on the back of Casey's neck stood on end. It was one thing to feel the evil presence surrounding them; it was quite another to see it captured on film. While it was unnerving to see herself under attack, what she saw it doing to Austin scared the hell out of her. The evil tendrils were twisting and pushing into his skull. A shadow creature darted behind him, and a blurred, featureless face replaced Austin's for a few terrifying seconds. He shook his head and the faceless creature was gone.

Casey glanced at Austin. If he was disturbed by the footage, he didn't show it. He rubbed his beard and asked Josie to replay it. Casey turned away. She didn't need to watch it again.

"This is good. Really good." He smiled broadly at Josie. "I'll check back with you later." Austin walked out of the trailer, and Gary and Casey followed. He cupped his hands over his mouth. "Hey, everyone. We got some excellent footage. Let's get back to the hotel and get some rest. We'll regroup this afternoon to go over what we saw and plan out our next move."

"Are you fucking out of your mind?" Gary asked Austin, echoing Casey's thoughts exactly. Austin dropped his pencil on the notepad and ran his hand through his hair. The team was sitting in the hotel conference room after watching the videos from last night's investigation. They had amassed over two hours of loud bangs, cold spots, and movement of inanimate objects, even a full apparition. But Austin still wasn't satisfied. He wanted to return to the Thompson estate.

"We'll discuss tonight's investigation later," Austin deflected. "Right now, I want to hear from Bob. Did your spirit guides reveal anything to you?"

"Yes," the shaman replied. "Once I found them. They were cowering over in a corner on the northwest side of the property. My people are not your problem. Were they upset that the Thompsons cut down all the fruit trees on the north side lawn? Of course. But they aren't haunting the place. Hell, they're too scared of what inhabits the upper floor to come near the main house."

Luis arched his eyebrow and Gary had an "Oh shit" look on his face.

Austin rubbed his chin and turned to Josie. "Well, what about EVPs? Did you get anything we can use?"

"Let me first say that you guys kept the tech team busy last night. We're still going over some of the digital recorders. But I want to play back something Casey caught on hers."

She cued the recording. Three voices hummed together in a dissonant chord. It was musical. Creepy, but musical. Casey tilted her head to get a better listen.

Josie stopped the recording. "Okay, I want you to pay attention to this part. The voices stop singing in unison and they each start speaking at once. At first I couldn't understand what they were saying, but then I was able to separate out the voices. Two of them are speaking in some kind of tongue or language that we don't understand. I'm giving a copy to Luis to see if he can tell what they're saying. But I was able to isolate the one voice that was in English." Josie pushed the play button.

"Auuustinnnn," a melodic female voice whispered. "Auuusstinn." The voice became more firm and insistent. "Auusstinn, come seeee meeee." Then a disquieting, high-pitched feminine laugh.

A chill ran down Casey's spine. She looked up at their fearless leader. Instead of being freaked out—the normal response—his eyes lit up and an incredulous smile broke out on his face. "Play it again!"

Josie did and he whooped after it was finished. "How cool is that? She called me by name." Casey glanced around the silent room. No one else seemed to think it was awesome sauce. Thai stared quietly at his coffee cup and wouldn't look her in the eye. It was then that Casey noted he hadn't said a word the entire time.

"The rest of the recording is just growls and junk. But the voice. That's an intelligent haunting if I've ever heard one," Josie said.

"That's it. We're going back in," Austin said.

"No way," Gary said. "Count me out."

"Me, too," Casey said.

"Guys, this is the best footage we've gotten in a while. Houses like this don't come along very often. They are the reason people watch *Spirit Chasers*. I know if we returned we could get even more proof."

"You don't need any more proof. We've got enough material to make the Thompson Estate a two-hour *Spirit Chaser* movie," Gary stated. He looked around the table. "Who here thinks the Thompson Estate is haunted?" Everyone's hand shot up. "Okay, now. Who thinks we should go back in tonight?" Austin's hand shot up. A moment later, a reluctant Thai lifted his right hand in a half-hearted gesture.

"Well, you're outvoted, Austin."

"Fine, Thai and I will go by ourselves."

Gary shook his head in disbelief.

"You've riled the demons up." Luis tried to reason with him. "You've taken this house from a low simmer to a rolling boil. It's not safe to go back in."

"It's not up for discussion. The equipment is still there; we have to go back for it."

Casey looked at him as if he had grown three heads. "It was trying to get inside your brain, trying to control you. That doesn't worry you the tiniest bit?" She pinched her index finger and thumb together.

He shrugged. "If I felt any different, I guess it would."

"Just because you don't feel it doesn't mean it's not affecting you," Luis told him.

"This is what I mean about him," Gary turned to Casey. "The boy has no fear." He turned to face Austin. "Look, I'll *buy* new equipment. That one tripod was kind of rickety anyway."

"But there could be footage on *that* camera we haven't seen yet. JoJo said her monitors blacked out about thirty minutes after we left last night. That means one of two things: Either the camera malfunctioned, or something shut it off. I want to know which."

"Did you ever think that maybe that thing drained the battery?" Luis asked. "It wouldn't be the first time the demonic stole our power."

"Of course that's occurred to me. But guys, there is also the possibility that we caught something else on that camera." He looked around the room. They stared at him, stone-faced. He realized he hadn't convinced anyone of anything, so he tried a different tack. "Look, now that we know the danger, we can avoid it. If your will is strong, you can defeat it." He slapped his palm on the table and stood up. "It can't affect you if you don't let it."

"Barrett wasn't weak-willed. Barrett was as strong as they come," Gary replied seriously.

"We're not talking about Barrett here," he said sharply. He blew out his breath and checked his tone. When he spoke again, it wasn't harsh. "That was a different situation." He crossed his arms in front of him. "I know I can shut it out before it gets to me."

Casey shook her head. "Barrett warned me you'd try something like this. He told me I had to stop you from doing stupid shit because you couldn't stop yourself. Enough, Austin."

"It's not up to you." His eyes settled on Casey. "Any of you."

"I'm telling you—hell, we're all telling you—how lucky we were to get out alive and unharmed, and you want to go back in? That's way past cray-cray. That's a death wish," she said.

"Casey's right," Luis agreed. "Look, the Thompsons have moved out. There's no immediate danger to the family. In a few months, when things settle down, we'll come back. I'll perform an exorcism and Casey and Bob can seal the portal. But right now, we need to stay away."

Austin shook his head. "Do what you want. I'm going back in. In case you didn't notice, I get paid to do the stupid shit."

10

L ater that night, they gathered back on the front lawn at the
Thompson Estate. Casey supposed she could have stayed at
the hotel; she wasn't going back inside, and her presence
wasn't needed tonight. But she couldn't stay away. She needed to
watch the train wreck with her own two eyes.

Austin wanted to wait to go in at nine o'clock, full dark. He said
it would make for a more dramatic television effect. Casey supposed
it didn't matter. Going back into that house at any time of day was
insane.

Casey needed to talk to Thai. She saw him in the back field,
stretching out on a yoga mat. As she walked past the tech trailer,
she caught a snippet of loud conversation. Luis and Austin were
engaged in a heated discussion.

"Did you hear what I just told you, son?"

"Yes, Luis, perfectly. But it really doesn't change anything."

It took Casey a moment to catch on. Apparently, they were discussing the other two voices on the EVP she had captured. Luis had
been able to translate them and didn't like what they had to say.

"Son, they've marked you. You are in grave danger. And that
she-demon, she thinks you belong to her. Is any of this sinking in?"

"Look, I won't be in there long. Just long enough to grab the
cameras; then we're out."

They continued to argue, and Casey walked away. At this point, whatever happened to Austin was on him. She just didn't want him to take Thai down, too.

As she continued over to the back field, she could see Thai lying face down on the mat. She waited until he came out of the pose to speak to him. "How are you?"

He smiled at Casey. "Honestly? Terrified. I'm just trying to clear my mind before we go in. So, did you need something?"

"I just wanted to talk." She smoothed her skirt underneath her as she sat on the overgrown grass. "Thai, you don't have to do this."

He wiped his face with a towel. "Yeah, I do." He didn't look at her as he spoke. He stared off in the distance to where the new moon was rising.

"If Austin is pressuring you...."

Thai turned his head toward her and spoke sharply. "He's not."

"Then why did you agree to this? I don't need my psychic abilities to tell me you don't want to go back in."

"Nobody goes in alone. That's the *SCI* way."

"No," Casey said, her voice rising. "That's the I-can't-tell-Austin-no-so-I'm-going-to-get-myself-killed way."

Thai said nothing for a moment. When he finally spoke, his voice was very soft. "Look, Austin and I go way back. I seriously can't remember a time when we weren't friends. He will do this, with or without us, and I couldn't live with myself if he went in alone and something happened to him."

"So, you're willing to risk your life for his stupidity?"

Thai shrugged. "It wouldn't be the first time. Barrett and I used to joke that Austin is like a two-year-old who wants to play on the freeway. He can't see the danger; it just seems fun to him. It's up to the rest of us to keep him from getting mowed down. He's run right into a shadow figure without even knowing it. If he goes in alone, he's a sitting duck."

"Hey, Thai!" They both looked up. Austin was standing in the distance, waving both his arms.

Thai rolled up his mat. "Wish me luck," he said with a smile.

"You're going to need it," Casey said. She watched him as he jogged over to where Austin was standing.

Casey walked back over to the trailer when Luis stopped her. "Come pray with us."

"Huh?"

"Are you or are you not a Christian? We need to pray for the safety of Austin and Thai. I've enlisted Gary and a few of the tech guys, but the more people we have praying, the better."

Was she a Christian? Good question. In her short life, she'd been through hell and held out hope for heaven. With her upbringing, she definitely identified more with Christianity than any other religion, but it had been a few years since she'd darkened the door of a church. There were things about her father's beliefs she definitely disagreed with. However, when she did pray, it was to the Father, Son, and Holy Spirit.

Casey knelt down next to Gary and clasped her hands together. She closed her eyes as Luis began his entreaty.

"Dear Lord, We implore you to watch over and protect Austin and Thai. You are a gracious and merciful God, and protect your children even when they act foolishly and arrogantly. Send your guardian angels to their aid, restrain the Evil One, and carry both Austin and Thai to safety. In the name of the Father and the Son and the Holy Spirit. Amen."

Luis made the sign of the cross, then immediately began reciting the Lord's Prayer. Casey opened one eye in time to see Austin and Thai approach the front of the house.

"Are you sure about this?" Austin asked Thai. "I don't want a repeat of the warehouse. I'm cool with going in by myself."

"Shut the fuck up, man."

Austin smirked at his friend. "We get the cameras; we leave. In and out." Thai nodded.

"Ready?"

"Yeah, man."

"Let's do this." Austin kissed his crucifix as both men strode up to the front door. He held his right hand out to turn the knob but suddenly stopped. He looked at Thai, and Thai looked right back at him. There were times he'd had to kick a door down because the ghostly inhabitants didn't want him there. A few times an ornery spirit had turned a lock to keep him out. But in all his investigations he had never seen this.

With a slow creak, the leaded glass front door opened by itself. The massive chandelier in the entryway flicked on and began to sway. It made an eerie plinking sound as the crystals rubbed against one another. "Oh, great," Austin said. "They sent the welcome wagon."

Thai sensed an increase in activity the moment Austin's foot crossed the threshold. The house was thrumming with energy and coming to life. He could hear creaking and groaning as more lights blinked on. Long-silent appliances resumed their chores. Thai could hear the clothes in the dryer begin to tumble and smelled coffee brewing. A television in the den flicked on, filling the room with white noise. The upstairs bathroom mirror shattered again, and a light bulb exploded. Thai blinked, and his heart sped up. Having light would have been a good thing if he didn't know that the power to the house had been shut off months ago.

"This is some crazy shit," Austin said, a goofy grin on his face. "Damn it, I should have brought in my hand-held camera."

"Austin! In and out. Remember?"

Austin started up the stairs, and Thai went to follow him when a bureau in the entryway skidded across the marble floor, blocking the staircase and separating the two of them. The front door slammed shut. Austin glanced back at a terrified Thai. "It's cool, man. I'll get the cameras upstairs and you grab the one in the kitchen. I'll be right back." Before Thai could protest, Austin was gone.

Goosebumps broke out on Thai's skin. He could hear the sound of footsteps on a hard floor in a distant room. Turning his head to the side, he peeked into the kitchen. Three dark auras were growling and walking in a slow circle around the kitchen table. Thai jerked his head back and squeezed his eyes shut. "Fuck this shit!" He backed into the corner of the entryway, as close to the front door as possible, crossing his arms in front of his chest. "Austin!" he yelled. "Hurry the fuck up!"

As Austin reached the landing, the hall light on the second floor blinked on. Dark shadow figures surrounded him, like wisps of black smoke. He couldn't see them, but when he turned, they turned, and when he stopped, they stopped.

He headed toward the first bedroom and tripped on the footboard as he walked in the door. The furniture had been completely rearranged. The bed was turned at an angle and the bookcase was now sitting on top of it. The books that had spilled all over the floor the night before were now neatly organized on the shelves. He heard squeaking as the rocker began moving back and forth, and the doll that was thrown at him the night before was sitting in it, grinning at him. He wished he could stay and film some of this, but Thai was already yelling for him to hurry. He grabbed the camera and headed out of the bedroom into the hall.

Austin thought he heard something, but then he turned and the sound was gone. A familiar image flashed in front of his eyes. For a moment, he could have sworn he was standing in the living room of his LA loft. Even though he saw no one with him, he knew he wasn't alone. Very weird. Austin shook his head to clear his mind. After slinging the camera bag over his shoulder, Austin rounded the corner and headed for the landing. Thai blew out his breath, relieved to see his friend standing there. Finally, they could get the hell out of there. Austin placed one foot on the top stair, starting to descend, when something grabbed him from behind and threw him down the hall. He landed on his back, the wind knocked out of him and at least five feet from his starting point.

"Austin!" Thai cried as he saw his friend being snatched away. He tamped down his fear and jumped over the bureau that was still blocking the stairs. As he started to climb, he felt a dark presence pushing him back. He scrambled back over the bureau. His heart was hammering in his chest and his breathing was ragged. He backed up, pressing his body into the wall closest to the front door. All the electrical went out at once, plunging the house into total darkness. It was disquieting when the lights and the appliances came to life without any juice to power them, but the sudden absence of electricity was worse. Thai blinked. The sound of heavy breathing was close. He moved his head back and forth, trying to see in the pitch black. Directly in front of him, a pair of glowing red eyes appeared. *Oh shit, oh shit.* "Leave now." It growled its hot putrid breath in Thai's face. He screamed as warm piss ran down his leg.

Upstairs, Austin grunted and pulled himself up to a kneeling position. He reached for the crucifix around his neck. It wasn't there. When the entity had thrown him down the hall, it must have snapped the chain. He spotted the sacred object lying on the floor right next to Brad's room. Slowly, he inched toward it and was about to grab it when the lights went out.

Outside, the others watched as the lights in the house suddenly died. Casey had been kneeling when the house came to life. Now that it was dark and quiet as death, she rose to see what happened. Luis was still deep in prayer, but Gary was standing, facing the house with his arms crossed, transfixed by the strange goings on. Casey walked toward Josie, who was pacing back and forth by the tech trailer.

"How long have they been in there?"

Josie stopped pacing and glanced at her phone. "About fifteen minutes."

"Shit. That's too long." Casey shivered.

Austin was on his hands and knees, patting down the carpet to find his crucifix in the dark. He switched on his penlight so he could see. A door creaking got his attention. He looked up. For the first time, the house was giving him a glimpse of Brad's room. He stood up and peered in. It looked like an ordinary teenage boy's bedroom. Sports posters covered the wall and there was a dark blue comforter on the bed. Nothing was out of place. The only thing he noticed was that he could see his breath. He checked his thermal camera. Outside, it was seventy degrees, but in Brad's room, it was forty-six.

He put one foot out, dangling it over the threshold, about to enter, when light from the moon glinted off something on the floor. His crucifix. He snatched it up. His mind cleared and he remembered Thai. He needed to get out of there.

"Some other time," he said to Brad's room. The door slammed shut. Austin ran down the hall, clutching his crucifix. He grabbed the other camera on the landing and yelled to Thai. "Open the door. I'm coming down."

Thai fumbled with the knob. "Now, Thai. C'mon." Austin yelled as he hauled ass down the stairs. Thai's eyes widened in fear. The shadow figures were on Austin's heels. He yanked at the knob harder and flung the door open. *Run*," yelled Austin, and Thai did. Austin's feet hit the entryway and he paused for just a moment to grab the camera there. He added it to the camera collection he was already holding when the door started to close. *Oh no you don't, you bastard.* Running full speed, he shouldered the door open and ran out into the front yard. The door slammed shut and an angry growl issued from the left upper floor.

Austin whooped and held the three cameras up in the air. "Success!" he yelled. Josie, Gary, and Luis ran over to talk to an ebullient Cole. Casey headed the other direction. She walked into the lounge, where she saw Thai go.

Thai could hardly believe he was safe in the lounge bathroom. With shaking hands, he took some paper towels and cleaned up as best he could. He wished he had brought a change of clothes, but at least he was wearing dark jeans. As he turned the faucet to cold and splashed water on his face, he stared at his "scared shitless" reflection in the mirror. There was a knock on the door, and a female voice asked, "You okay?"

Thai gripped the sink and took in a breath. "I'm trying to take a piss, Casey." *Correction, past tense. You took a piss ten minutes ago. .*

"Sorry, Thai. I just wanted to make sure you were all right. You looked kind of upset when you ran out of the house."

The door flew open. Casey took a step back as Thai walked through. "What happened in there?"

A humorless laugh escaped from his lips. "Nothing. Everything. I don't want to think about it and I sure as hell don't want to talk about it." He sighed and rubbed the back of his neck. "All I want is to get back to the hotel and forget this night ever happened." She nodded and patted his shoulder. Her eyes followed him as he walked over to the Suburban and climbed in.

On Monday afternoon, when the crew returned to *SCI*, they gathered in the conference room to watch the unedited episode before the edited version ran on cable. Josie explained it was an *SCI* tradition. Thai was conspicuously absent.

As it turned out, Austin was right. The cameras had caught some additional and disturbing footage. The one in the little girl's room showed the furniture rearranging itself in real time. Still, as she thought about Thai, Casey wondered if it was all worth it.

Gary had filmed Austin's dramatic departure from the house and everyone agreed it should be the last shot of the episode. Casey studied his face as the slow motion film captured Austin shoving the door open and running out of the house like he'd just conquered Mt. Everest. As Casey watched Austin lift the cameras triumphantly into the air, she started to believe that maybe, just maybe, he was invincible.

11

"So, are you going? Please say yes." Josie cajoled. It was Friday afternoon and Josie was sitting in Casey's office, waiting for her to get her things together so they could leave.

"I don't know." Casey shrugged. "Football's not really my thing." Spending an afternoon with a bunch of drunk guys eating wings and yelling about touchdowns and fumbles didn't sound like loads of fun. Thai liked to host football parties at his place on Sunday afternoons. It was another *SCI* tradition. When Thai showed up for work on Tuesday, he was all smiles, and back to his usual happy self. Whatever it was that had him so freaked out on Saturday night, he had managed to get past it.

Josie shook her head. "You don't have to watch football. Most of the girls don't. Liv will be there, and Thai's girlfriend. Sometimes Luis's wife makes it. And there's usually one or two other women there, too." Casey filled in the blanks. The other women were with Gary and Austin. That thought was even more depressing. She would be the pathetic single woman hanging out with all the happy couples. "It'll be fun," Josie insisted. "We can chill out on the balcony while the guys watch the game."

"Thai has a girlfriend? How come I'm just finding out about this?" She had to admit, she was a little disappointed.

"He doesn't advertise it. He likes to keep his private life private."

Josie shook her arm and Casey groaned. "Fine, I'll be there. Text me the address."

Casey knocked on the door and Thai welcomed her into his Asian-influenced apartment. The furniture was sleek, modern, and highly varnished. There were pops of vibrant color in the throw pillows and draperies. A painting of a bonsai tree hung on one wall, and a decorative mirror on the other. A statue of Buddha sat on a small, ebony table.

Thai put his arm around a young woman standing next to him. "Casey, this is Anna, my girlfriend." He smiled broadly, his face full of pride. Casey was touched and impressed by his obvious affection for her.

"Nice to meet you," Casey said.

"You, too." Anna had dark, shoulder-length hair that was perfectly straight and smooth as silk. Her smile lit up her whole face. She was slender and looked stunning in a short, black pencil skirt and loose-fitting dark-pink blouse. Casey was a tad envious. She'd always wanted to wear a pencil skirt, but it just wasn't feasible, unless she planned to have her hips surgically removed.

"So, who are you rooting for?" Thai asked.

Casey pursed her lips. She had no clue who was playing. After glancing over at the big screen TV she answered. "Chargers?" and shrugged.

Thai put his fist out for her to bump. "Excellent! Can I get you something to drink?"

"I'll take a beer."

"What kind?"

"What do you have in a bottle?"

"Guinness, Bud, Heineken."

"Guinness, please. It's good for you. Ha ha," she finished lamely.

"Right." Thai walked over to the tub filled with ice and he dug out a Guinness. "You are a woman of impeccable taste. You know your beer and you know your football."

Casey raised her index finger to disagree. "Actually, drinking beer enables me to sit through a football game."

Thai's brow furrowed. "Oh. Well, as long as you root for the Chargers, that's cool." He popped the cap off and started to throw it away.

"Here. I'll take that."

As he handed her the beer and the bottlecap, Gary, Luis and his wife appeared at the door. "Welcome, welcome, fellow Chargers fans," Thai called out and ran over to greet them.

Anna closed her eyes and placed her fingers on her forehead. "He's out of control."

Casey smiled. "Thai's a great guy."

Anna nodded. "He's amusing, so I keep him around."

"How long have you two been together?"

"February will be two years."

Luis's wife walked over. "I'm Marie. You must be Casey."

"Yes, nice to meet you."

"Where are the kids? You know they are welcome here anytime," Anna told her.

"At my sister's. Matt had homework and the girls wouldn't be interested in football. I appreciate it, but with this crew, I would be afraid my kids would learn some new, colorful vocabulary."

Anna laughed. "Yeah. I hadn't thought of that."

Marie pointed to her temple. "I never thought of that either until I had children."

Austin burst through the door then, holding the hand of a tall, gorgeous blond. He pulled her into the room. Casey didn't want to, but she couldn't help but stare. She recognized her from one of Tina's magazines. The woman had flawless skin and her mascara and subtly applied eyeshadow perfectly framed her peridot eyes. She rocked a sleeveless silk blouse with a silver and black beaded necklace, and her jeans fit her so perfectly, they looked like they were drawn on. Austin was wearing his usual T-shirt and shorts, but even with his casual attire, they made a striking couple. He kicked off his flip flops and headed over to talk to Thai while the blond walked up to Anna and gave her a hug.

"Casey, this is Tish." Her name wasn't followed with the designation "Austin's girlfriend." Casey wondered if that was an oversight on Anna's part, or by design.

"It is so great to meet you." She put her flawlessly manicured hand to her chest. "I would *love* to be able to read minds."

Casey got that a lot. It took too long to explain that she really didn't *like* to read minds of the living, and that she mostly used her gifts to communicate with the dead. She told Tish, "It's nice to meet you, too."

Austin leaned over and spoke to Thai in a low voice. "Did you invite him?"

"Yeah. Of course. Derek, too." Thai shrugged. "He said no." Austin took a drink from his water bottle and flopped down on the couch in front of the TV.

"Who wants to watch football?" Anna asked. None of the women said anything. "Who wants to suck back martinis and gossip on the balcony?" Tish, Casey, and Marie all raised their hands. "Great. Josie and Liv are already out there."

Anna led the women past a small herb garden and over to a moderate-sized, outdoor seating area. Liv waved and Josie jumped up to give Casey a hug.

"I'm so glad you came," she whispered in her ear. Anna went in to make the martinis, and Marie joined her. When they came back, they passed out the glasses and Anna handed Casey another Guinness.

Casey nursed her beer and listened as the women discussed their jobs, their interests, and their relationships. Marie was a stay-at-home mom of three pre-teens, Anna was a clothes designer for a major label, and Tish was a model for a high-end clothing line. Anna and Tish were in a deep conversation about their shared interests. Then Tish told the group of women about some party she and Austin had attended the night before. Casey opened her mouth to ask how long Tish and Austin had been dating. Then she thought better of it. She barely knew Tish. She flipped her beer cap between her palms.

"What about you?" Tish asked her. "Are you seeing anyone?"

"Uh, no." Casey snatched the beer cap out of the air and placed it on the table.

"Don't get any ideas, Tish. She's new to town. Give her a chance to acclimate," Josie warned.

Anna pointed at Tish. "You gotta watch that one. She thinks she's Little Miss Matchmaker."

Tish put down her martini glass and put her hand on her hip. "I'm a great matchmaker. What about Gary and Shonda?"

"You mean Shonda, Gary's ex?" Liv asked, and the other women chuckled.

"Hey, I just get couples together. It's not my fault if they don't stay together."

The door flew open. In two quick strides, Austin appeared next to the women's table. "Liv, you made my favorite. You are the most awesome woman on the planet!" He came over to the table, wrapped his arms around the petite brunette, and kissed her on the forehead. Liv blushed.

"Liv can make vegan cuisine and a few other Austin-approved dishes that don't taste like baked dog turds. She uses her culinary skills whenever we get together like this," Josie informed Casey.

"I think it's only fair that Austin have something he can eat," Liv replied.

"Thank you, Liv." With his right arm still around her, he pointed at her with his left hand. "Isn't she a sweetheart?" Casey couldn't help but notice that he sounded sincere when he attached the endearment to Liv.

He moved over to Tish and put his arm around her. "What are you doing out here?" she asked.

"Commercial break. But at half-time I'm going to run upstairs." He rubbed her arm and arched his eyebrow. "You want to join me?"

"Not on your life," she said, and smacked his hand away.

"Hey, I was only kidding." He kissed her on the temple and ran back inside.

Curious about the strange exchange, Casey asked. "What's upstairs?"

"Austin's haunted loft," Anna answered.

"Seriously?" Casey asked.

Tish nodded. "He knows I won't go within ten feet of his place." She shivered.

"So why aren't we investigating his loft for the show? I would think it would be great for ratings," Casey asked.

"We already have," Josie answered. "Over the years, he's brought his work home with him, if you know what I mean. The spirits there are the leftover flotsam and jetsam of past investigations."

Casey drank a couple more beers, listening to the women talk. It seemed like the second half of the football game passed more quickly than the first. She was kind of sad to say good-bye to the women. Thanks to their company, she'd had a much better time than she ever imagined she would. On the way out the door, Tish called out to Casey. "When you're ready to meet someone, let me know. I know lots of great guys … or girls."

"Thanks, but I'm not really looking."

"C'mon babe," Austin said, wrapping his arm around Tish's waist. Casey watched him blow a kiss in her ear as they walked out the door.

12

Casey strode confidently onto the set. With this episode and the rest of the season, the walk throughs would be her own. She wouldn't have Barrett's impressions of the place looming over her, or Austin constantly comparing their clairvoyant styles.

Thai and Austin watched from the tech trailer while Gary followed Casey into the building. The old two-story wooden structure had a colorful past. If what the owners claimed was correct, it had been a speakeasy in the twenties with heavy mob ties, and in the thirties, a brothel where a young prostitute had been murdered. On paper, it was the epitome of what a haunted hotel looked like.

Casey inspected the first floor. The waning sunlight from the front windows cast eerie shadows along the dark wood paneling. Every once in a while, she would stop, lower her eyes to the floor, and look from left to right. She paused at the stairwell, then walked up. With every step she took, the wooden risers creaked.

She paused at room 215. She grasped the old iron door knob and turned it clockwise. The hinges squeaked so loudly, it sounded as if the door was in physical pain. She stepped inside, lowered her eyes, and swept them back and forth.

"What do you see?" Gary asked.

She turned toward Gary. "Nothing. And I mean nothing. This place isn't haunted. "

Austin pinched his bottom lip between his fingers. He turned to Thai. "What the fuck is she doing?" Thai shrugged.

Gary continued to film. Usually he didn't like to give the psychic any leading information, but she was so adamant, he thought he should prompt her to look harder. "Well, guests have reported hearing knocks and bangs, and the owner saw a partial apparition in the main room downstairs."

Casey crossed her arms. "An apparition? I doubt it. More likely, he was seeing the shadows on the walls. There are no intelligent spirits here. No residual haunting, either."

"Then how do you explain all the noises?"

"Something mundane rather than paranormal. I could make this hotel unhaunted real fast. Buy a new furnace and a can of WD40."

"Fuck!" Austin threw down the headphones, leapt out of his chair, and began to pace. Thai closed his eyes and rubbed his face while Josie suppressed a grin and turned away. "What the hell are we supposed to do now?" Austin asked Thai. He didn't answer, but they all turned back to the monitor when Casey spoke again.

"I think we ought to just pack up and go," Casey glanced out the window. "The burger joint down the road has probably served more ghosts than this place."

Austin blew out his breath. He picked up his phone and began dialing. "What are you doing?" Thai asked.

"Damage control."

Austin had met Natalie Banks two years before on the talk show circuit. They were on a paranormal panel together. After the interview, the attractive thirty-five year old invited him up to her hotel room for a drink. Although he was a teetotaler, he'd followed her up to her suite like a horny teenage boy. He spent the night and they shared a cab to the airport the next morning. But she made it very clear to Austin that if he ever needed anything, to give her a call.

"Done," Austin said, and put down his phone.

"What's done?" Thai asked.

"Natalie is flying out tomorrow. She's going to do a walk through of the hotel and give us her opinion."

Thai shook his head. "Austin, I know you're upset about what Casey said, but I don't think bringing in a psychic to undermine her is going to help the situation. Or improve your relationship with her."

"She's not going to budge. You heard her. We can't air an episode if the psychic doesn't even believe."

"I thought you wanted a real psychic, not a phony. Do you want her to tell the truth or do you want her to boost the ratings?"

Austin blew out his breath. "Both," he said, and walked out of the tech trailer and over to the hotel.

On his way over, he ran into Casey. "Sorry about that," Casey told him. "But I have to call it like I see it."

Austin shrugged. "You win some; you lose some. It's better we know now."

Casey blinked. She never thought Control would be this relaxed about it. She half-way expected him to be pissed off at her for doing her job. "So what are you going to do?" she asked. "Find another location?"

"It's too late for that. This episode airs in two weeks." Austin shrugged. "We'll throw something together. Maybe end the episode with more footage of the Thompson place. It won't be our highest rated show, but it'll work out." He rubbed his chin. "Look, I don't expect you to sit in on the investigation after what you've found—or should I say, failed to find. You can go back to LA. We've got it."

"No. I'll stay with the crew. Maybe I'll hang out in the tech trailer with Josie. Learn the behind the scenes part of it."

Austin mentally cursed. "At least take tomorrow off. You've been working your ass off. Go into town and do some sightseeing or something. In fact, you don't have to be back here until Friday night. We aren't doing the investigation until then."

"Why the delay?"

Austin rubbed his beard. "Technical issues."

"And it's really okay?" She narrowed her eyes.

"Yes. Go." He waved his hands to shoo her away.

Casey shrugged. Hell, if he was going to give her the time off, she'd take it.

The next morning, Austin met Natalie at the airport. She was dressed in a short, fitted V-neck black dress that didn't leave much to the imagination. Her long, auburn hair was swept up in a loose French twist. She kissed Austin on the cheek in greeting. "It's been too long, Austin. What have you been doing with yourself?"

"Well, you know. *SCI* keeps me pretty busy." He stuffed his hands into his jean pockets.

Natalie nodded. "Yes, darling. I know too well. I'm so busy with the late night show, I barely have time for anything else." She placed her long, blood-red fingernail on his chest. Austin sighed. He'd forgotten how hands on she could be. "So tell me about this place," she purred.

"Just your standard, hundred-year-old hotel with all the requisite cold spots, footsteps and doors slamming."

"Sounds charming," she smiled. "Maybe you and I could meet for drinks after filming?" She ran her finger up his arm and winked at him.

"Maybe," Austin said, noncommittally. He opened the limo door for her and she climbed inside. He climbed in beside her and the driver pulled away from the curb.

"You know, when I heard that Barrett resigned, I thought about applying for his job. But then, poof!" she snapped her finger. "Almost instantly, the position was filled." Natalie put her hand on Austin's knee and patted it. "You must have interviewed at light speed."

"Actually, Barrett recommended someone before he left. I liked her and hired her."

"I can understand taking Barrett's recommendation, but still, shame on you for not calling me first." She smacked him on the arm. She stared seriously into his eyes and her voice dropped an octave. "Is she any good?"

"Yes, the best," he said curtly. He shifted in his seat, suddenly feeling defensive.

Natalie's hand crept higher up his thigh. "I'm surprised to hear you say that. I mean, this is only the second episode of the season and you're already calling for someone to fill in." She squeezed his leg. "Is there a chance this walk through could turn into something more permanent?"

Austin coughed. "Uh, no. Like I said on the phone, our psychic is ill and we're on a tight filming schedule. When I realized she couldn't do it, I called you." He scooted away from her and gently lifted her hand off his leg. "I really appreciate you dropping everything to help us out, but this is a one-time deal."

"Does Casey know about Natalie?" Gary asked Austin while he did a final check of his camera.

"No," Austin answered. Gary frowned at him. "She won't care. I'm sure she'll be fine with it."

Gary raised his eyebrows. "Then why don't you tell her?"

"I will, eventually. But for now, I'd prefer she doesn't know."

Gary shook his head. "And how do you expect to keep it a secret from her? She'll find out at the screening."

"I realize that. I'll tell her before then. Let's just get this walk through over with and get Natalie on a plane out of here."

Gary shook his head. "What?" Austin asked.

"There's no way in hell I'm going to follow Ms. Banks around without Casey's blessing."

Austin rubbed his chin. "You're right, Gary."

"Good, then you'll tell her?"

"No, but I'll film the walk through with Natalie myself. This is my decision and I'll take responsibility for it." Austin picked up the camera and went out to find Natalie.

Austin turned his head, staring at the strange, beautiful woman across the room. Her lips were burgundy silk and her eyes were dark and fathomless. The rest of her features blurred together. For some reason, he couldn't get a good look at her entire face at the same time. The temptress giggled and smiled. She was teasing him, but there was another disquieting emotion buried deeper. An undercurrent of danger and malevolence.

His dream woman was dressed in a gauzy white gown that flowed about her as if she was standing in the middle of a violent wind. Austin blinked and she was beside him, curled up next to him in bed. *She moves impossibly fast.* The woman crept on all fours until she was positioned over him. She was a large, wild cat and he was her prey. His breath caught in his throat and his heart sped up as he realized she wanted to kiss him.

A loud crack of thunder jolted him awake. He bolted upright, startled and breathing heavily for a moment. When he realized it was just a thunderstorm, he rubbed his face to wake up and walked over to the hotel window. Arcs of light, like white veins, lit up the still-dark sky. He blinked. The boom of thunder came right on its heels. The rain pelted down so hard he could hear it thumping on the metal balcony furniture. *Shit,* he thought. *Guess I'm running indoors today.* He got dressed and took the elevator down to the hotel gym.

He stepped on the treadmill. Running on a moving conveyor belt was about the most boring thing in the world. He hated watching TV or even listening to music when he ran. For him, it was all about being outdoors, observing nature or listening to the sounds of the city and people watching. Being trapped indoors on this treadmill gave him too much time to think.

Up until this year, he had lived most of his life without regrets. But over the last several months, he felt weighed down by guilt. And now, he'd just added to it. Austin didn't need to be psychic to see that Natalie's walk through was a bunch of bullshit. She was an actress, and not a very good one. He was regretting ever bringing her in. And he still hadn't told Casey about it.

Speak of the devil. Casey walked through the gym door. She climbed on the only other treadmill available, the one right next to Austin, and started off at a walking pace to warm up.

He stared straight ahead and increased the speed. Perspiration dotted his forehead. He lifted the hem of his shirt and wiped his face. Casey looked over at the time on his machine. Fifty-five minutes had elapsed. "I never told you thank you," she said.

"Huh?" Austin asked, confused.

"For the day off. And for excusing me from the investigation tonight. I mean, it makes sense. None of the viewers would buy it if I'm trying to capture evidence in a place I've declared wasn't haunted."

"Yeah. That's true," he said awkwardly. Even though she was hard to get along with, she didn't deserve to be second-guessed. He cleared his throat. "Speaking of days off, I know how much you love running, but I thought you'd be sleeping in today," Austin remarked. She'd tied her long hair up in a ponytail and skipped the makeup. Without that raccoon black shit around her eyes, she didn't look so mean.

His voice came out even and without effort. Casey wondered how anyone could be running so hard and not be completely out of breath. She shrugged. "Yeah, well, if I don't do some kind of exercise this weekend, running three miles on Monday is going to kick my ass." She flipped open her reader case and set it on the machine in front of her. "This isn't so bad. I've got air-conditioning and a book to read." Casey bumped up the speed of the treadmill to 3.2 MPH and increased the incline to 2.0.

"You know, I bring the crew out to run because I like us all being together and I think running out in the fresh air is good for the soul. But if you prefer to stay back at *SCI* and use the treadmill, that's fine by me."

She stared up at him. "Really?"

"Yes, really. As long as you stay strong, I don't care how you do it. So, what are you reading? Paranormal romance?"

"You got it."

"Ghosts?"

"Actually, no. It's called *Obsidian,* and it's about aliens."

Austin left her alone to read and concentrated on the investigation tonight. Natalie had seen so much stuff on her walk through and Casey had seen nothing. If Natalie was right, they would have a great show. If Natalie was wrong, then Casey was justified, but the ratings would tank. He wasn't sure what he wished for.

Austin slowed his treadmill down to a walking pace. Casey was just getting into a good run. He waited for the belt on his machine to stop, then stepped off and sat on the floor for some stretches. Fifteen minutes later, his red-headed psychic climbed off her machine and headed for the door. He finished his floor work then walked out himself.

It was still pouring, so rather than leave, he walked over to the hotel restaurant for some breakfast. He'd fasted last night as he always did before an investigation, and now he was starving. As he entered, he saw his psychic sitting by herself. A large glass of water and a cup of coffee were sitting in front of her.

Fuck, I can't get away from her. She looked up from the menu and waved him over. He waved back. *It's your guilty conscience,* he told himself as he forced a smile.

"You can join me if you want." She motioned to the empty seat in front of her.

"Um, sure. Thanks," Austin said, as he took a seat.

"Look, about the walk through...." He was going to tell her about Natalie. Get it over with. But when he saw steely blue eyes peering up at him from behind the menu, he wussed out. They were sort of getting along. He could wait to drop that bomb on her until they returned to LA. "I mean, how do you know when a place *is* haunted?"

"How do you mean?"

"Is it a feeling you get? Do you have to see or hear the ghosts first to know?"

"It's both. Yeah, I get that classic chill up my back when spirits are around. But for me, they always show themselves. I seem to draw ghosts out of hiding."

"Ready to order?" the waitress pulled out her note pad. Austin motioned for Casey to go first. She had planned to order bacon and pancakes, but she felt self-conscious with Mr. Healthy Lifestyle sitting in front of her. "I'll have a spinach omelet and a bowl of fruit."

"That sounds good," Austin said "I'll have the same." The waitress nodded and Austin asked, "What do the ghosts look like? Are they see-through?"

"No. Semi-opaque is probably the best way I can describe it. Their skin has a bluish cast that has a luminous, ethereal quality."

"Wow. That's almost exactly what Barrett says. He told me something once that I thought was fascinating. I always assumed ghosts wandered around, looking the way they looked when they died— sickly, bloody, old—but he said that's not usually the case."

"Yeah. They only look like that if they're stuck in that death mindset. It's usually someone who can't get past their death to move on, or someone who keeps reliving how they died," Casey said, thinking about the dead guy in the tub of that apartment Liv showed her. "Ghosts aren't the happiest beings to begin with, but those stuck in their death mindset—they're pretty pathetic. Thankfully, it's rare to see them that way. Most try to dress and look the way they did in happier times."

"Wait. You said ghosts aren't happy. Why is that?"

"Because it's a piss-poor state of existence. Most have unfinished business or can't let go of the past. Some are scared for what waits for them beyond this world. Others are jealous and feel cheated that they are no longer one of the living."

"So, have you ever met a happy ghost?"

"Yeah. My Gran. She's totally fine with her death and has a purpose for hanging around."

"Really?"

"Yeah. My dad's an only child. She's waiting for him to pass, then she'll join him in crossing over."

"Interesting." Austin rubbed his chin. "I know one thing. Even if I don't have any unresolved issues, I would still come back."

Casey narrowed her eyes. "Why? What would be the point?"

"I would at least want to tell my friends and family goodbye and let them know I was okay. I wouldn't want to leave them wondering. Like I did with my sister."

The waitress brought their plates and they finished their breakfast in silence. Austin charged the bill to the room, then stood.

"Austin, I could have paid. I didn't invite you over so you could buy my breakfast."

"Relax. I charged it to *SCI*. Think of it as a business expense. The rest of the crew certainly does." He stretched and yawned. "Well, I'm going to go lie down. I need to get some rest before the investigation tonight."

"Yeah, I'm going to finish my coffee and go back to my room to rest, too." Casey's eyes followed him as he walked over to the elevator banks. She stared at him until he disappeared behind the metal doors.

13

The investigation was just as uneventful as Casey predicted it would be. She sat in the tech trailer with Josie, watching the guys staring at dark space. They didn't capture a single usable EVP, and the orbs were easily explained away as floating dust motes. Discouraged, the crew packed up and went home.

After their work out on Monday morning, the crew met in the conference room at *SCI* for the viewing. They lingered outside the doors as Josie fiddled with the projector. "Find a seat. Episode two plays in five minutes," she announced. The crew filed in the room.

It's now or never, Cole, Austin told himself. He made a beeline for his psychic. Casey stood and began walking toward the screening room when Austin grabbed her arm. "Wait, Casey, there's something I need to tell you."

"Can't it wait until after?" she asked.

He rubbed his chin. "Well, it's kind of about the screening. I sort of got a second opinion on the walk through."

"I don't understand." Her forehead furrowed in confusion.

Austin rubbed his hands together. "You know how you said the place wasn't haunted?"

"Yeah."

"Well, I called in someone else for another opinion."

"What! Who?"

"Natalie Banks."

"What?!" Casey exclaimed. Natalie was one of the more famous phony psychics and probably made a mint from her 1-800 infomercials and late-night TV special programming. While Casey was sure she had no real psychic abilities, she obviously knew how to read people. It was infuriating to think about all those she had swindled over the years, pretending to have spoken to their deceased loved ones. And she usually got at least some of the facts right, leading the more gullible to believe her. But as Casey's Gran always said, even a blind hog finds an acorn once in a while.

Austin put his hands out. "Calm down, Casey. If you just watch the entire episode, you'll see...." But Casey was gone. She took a seat, crossed her arms, and waited for the show to begin. She threw her left leg over her right thigh. Even in the dark, Austin could see her left foot was tapping the air non-stop.

Gary leaned over and whispered in Austin's ear. "So, she's fine with it, I see." Austin glared at him. Gary shook his head and muttered, "Um, um, um."

Casey watched, her fury rising, as Austin filmed the charlatan repeating *her* walk through. Natalie's head lolled from side to side and her eyes closed as she supposedly went into a trance. She placed her hand on the doorway. "I'm sensing an angry, threatening presence." She walked over to the stair well and turned to Austin. "It's stronger here. I'm going up."

When she got to the first door on the right, room 215, she stopped. With a doleful expression on her face, she turned to face Austin. "There is so much despair and sadness here."

"What's causing it?"

"Shh. You hear that?"

Austin shook his head.

"You don't hear that knocking sound? There is a dead soldier in a revolutionary uniform trying to get my attention."

Casey huffed. It took all her willpower to stay seated. Natalie couldn't even get the timeline of the hotel right. "The war created a lot of unhappy spirits. And the dead are hostile to the living. They want to destroy this place and anyone inside is in grave danger. This place should be torn down. It's not safe."

"Tear down a hundred-year-old hotel? That seems pretty extreme," Austin told her.

"Well, that would be my first choice, but if the owners don't want to do that, I could cleanse the place and cross the dead over." Casey blew out her breath. This was too much. She had put up with a lot of shit because the paycheck was so good, but no more. Her self-respect could not be bought. She stormed out of the screening room, the soles of her flats clacking on the hard floor. Gary gave Austin an "I told you so" look.

"What the fuck?" Thai asked. "I thought you told her." Josie crossed her arms and glared at him. Luis and Bob were staring at him in disbelief.

"Pause the film. I'll be right back," he instructed Josie. He ran after the pissed off redhead. "Wait, Casey, we need to talk."

Casey walked into her office and tried to slam the door, but Austin grabbed it before she could. She stood behind her desk, facing the wall. Hot tears gathered under her eyelids, and she took in a few deep breaths to try to calm herself. This was worse than that day at the track. She was never going to be a great runner and she couldn't care less what he thought of her athletic abilities. But insulting her psychic gifts by bringing in Natalie? That hurt worse than if he'd slapped her across the face and called her a stupid bitch. Mostly because that was exactly what he'd done. *Damn it, Casey. Don't cry in front of this asshole. Don't you dare give him the satisfaction.* She was pissed off and hurt, not sad. So why the hell was she crying?

"I'm sorry," he said softly. "I didn't think it would bother you."

For a long moment, it was silent. Austin walked over and sat on the edge of her desk. "Casey? Say something."

She didn't turn to face him, but waited until she thought she could speak without her voice quivering. As she dabbed at her eyes with her fingers, she asked in a low voice, "How in the fuck could you think it *wouldn't* bother me?" She took a tote bag out of a desk drawer and started clearing her desk.

He backed out of her way as she stormed across the room, grabbing her belongings and putting them into her bag.

"You know, Austin, I am confident in my abilities," she said as she cleared off the top of her cabinet and unloaded it into her bag. "I know what I'm doing." She turned around and pointed at her chest. "I know my shit, and I am a damn sight better than Natalie Banks. If you had concerns, the mature thing to do would have been to *talk to me.*"

Austin nodded. "You're right. I was totally in the wrong." He leaned against the wall, his eyes darting back and forth while she packed her stuff. It was almost like watching a tennis match.

She didn't acknowledge what he said but continued to pack her bag. "Look, I know I'm not your first choice; I'm not Barrett. But I don't deserve to be mocked this way. Since I started, exactly how many times have I been incorrect in my communications with the spirit world?"

"No times. Now, Casey, if you'd just let me—"

She began shaking her head vociferously. "That's right. Zilch. Zero. Nada. But you let that damn late-night-tv-psychic-wanna-be come in and try to make me look like an idiot."

"That's not what I was trying—"

"Well, you could have fooled me." Her voice rose and broke without her permission.

"I'm sorry, Casey. I should have at least run it by you...." His voice died off as she bored holes into him with her eyes. "What I mean is, I never should have let Natalie in on the investigation at all. It was really stupid, and I'm really sorry, and it won't ever happen again."

Casey swung the large tote over her shoulder. "You're right about that. Cause I quit." She stomped toward the door.

Under his breath Austin muttered. "You know what? Fuck it." He strode over to her, grabbed her by her shoulders, and spun her around.

Her bag fell to the floor as he pushed her against the wall and planted his lips firmly on hers. Her eyes widened in surprise. *Da-amn. He has strong lips.* So strong, she could feel her toes curling. Casey was too stunned to protest. He took that as a green light and weaved his fingers through her hair without releasing any pressure from her lips. Not once did he try to stick his tongue down her throat, but that didn't stop it from being one of the most powerful kisses Casey had ever experienced.

She tried to remember she was totally pissed off at him, but another thought crept into her head. *I haven't been kissed like this since college.* Brandon had been a terrible kisser. He never took any time because he was always in a hurry to get down to business. The shock wore off. Her senses returned and she pushed him away with both hands. She glared at him as she wiped her mouth with her hand. "What the hell was that for?"

"To get your attention. You weren't listening." He paused, and in a softer voice said, "And I wanted to." His serious ocean eyes bore into hers. "Now, this is what's going to happen: You're going to go back to the screening room and watch the rest of the episode. If you still want to quit after that. I won't try to talk you out of it." He tipped his head toward the door. "C'mon."

Casey pursed her lips and they stood in a silent stand-off for a few heartbeats. "Fine." She hefted the now-full tote onto her desk. "But I mean it. After this episode, I'm out." She arranged her blouse and smoothed her hair.

He took her hand and led her toward the door. It was a simple gesture, and not anything she would have thought seriously about with anyone else. But this was Austin Cole, and that kiss put a complex spin on everything. Once they were out in the hall he released her hand, and she followed him back into the screening room.

"All right, JoJo. Roll film," Austin instructed. Casey took a seat and Austin plopped down next to her.

A clip of the investigation played. Most of it was time-lapsed, since they'd found nothing. After that, Austin appeared back on set by himself. The camera zoomed in on him standing in front of the hotel. "As you just saw, we found nothing paranormal on this investigation." He glanced back at the old hotel. "But that doesn't mean we didn't learn anything."

The next clip was of Casey's original walk through. After it played, Austin resumed his monologue, slowly approaching the camera. "I messed up big time because I didn't trust my psychic when she told me the truth. Instead, I brought in someone else who told me what I wanted to hear. Next time, I'll know. I won't ever doubt my psychic again."

The end credits rolled and Thai whooped. "Who's up for drinks and wings?" The rest of the crew stood up and followed him out. It was quiet with only Casey and Austin in the screening room.

Austin turned toward her. "So, what did you think?"

Casey shook her head. "Honestly, I think I'm in shock." She narrowed her eyes at him. "Did I just see Austin Control admit on air that he made a mistake?"

Austin pulled at his bottom lip. "Yeah, I think you did. One I will pay dearly for, I'm sure. This is really going to piss Natalie off, and frankly, I'm even more afraid of her than I am you." He glanced down for a moment, then his gaze returned to her face. "So, will you stay?"

Casey observed the contrition in his serious ocean eyes. She finally nodded and said, "Yeah, I'll stay."

A smile spread across his face. "Great. C'mon. I'm taking you out for a drink." He took her hand and pulled her to her feet.

"You don't have to do that. The on-air apology is penance enough."

Austin rolled his eyes. "This isn't penance. I'm going out for a drink." He continued to hold onto her hand. "And I would like it if you joined me."

"What about Tish?"

"What about her?"

"Shouldn't you call her?"

"For what?"

"You know how the tabloids are. Even though it's perfectly innocent, they'll twist it into something else. Give her a heads up. You don't want any misunderstandings."

Austin chuckled. "Tish and I aren't together like that. We've been friends for a long time, and when she's in town, we go out. But we aren't dating. She's in Milan or Paris or wherever right now, and I'm sure she's hooked up with some guy there."

Casey gave him a sideways stare. "I don't know what you're up to. If this is your attempt to charm me into submission, or take a fat chick on a date...." She shook her head. "I don't like to be played."

"You're not fat."

True that. Although she would never admit it, his Draconian torture methods were making positive changes to her body. She stepped on the scale that morning and it read 135, a number she hadn't seen since her junior year in college. Of course fat was a relative term. Compared to most of the women Austin dated, she was five inches too short and ten pounds too heavy. She would always have a genetically large ass—Thanks, Mom—but now, at least, it was toned and perky rather than jiggly and flabby. And the best thing about being a card-carrying member of Austin Control's boot camp was that her inner thighs didn't slap together anymore when she walked. Bonus.

"Casey, I'm not playing you." He tipped his head toward the door. "C'mon. First round is on me."

14

To avoid the others, Austin drove them to an out-of-the-way bar. It was more like something you'd find in Shadow Creek than outside the city limits of LA. Rudy's Bar was an old, wooden building, filled with neon beer signs and a jukebox playing an odd mix of classic country and rock from the seventies and eighties. Austin bypassed the bar stools and the front counter, and led her to a secluded table in the back corner. Casey took a look around. The place was bigger than it appeared from the outside. There was even a small parquet wood floor for dancing. She stared at him in confusion.

"What?" he asked.

"Why'd you bring me here? This doesn't seem like a place you would frequent."

"I come here when I don't want to be recognized. Now, what'll you have?" he asked.

"Whatever they have on draft. And bring me a bottle of Guinness."

"A draft and a bottle?"

"I'm thirsty."

He came back a minute later with three beers. She took a sip from the frosty mug, then popped the top off the bottle and started rolling the beer cap between her fingers. Austin sat across from her and opened his own bottle.

"So, why'd you do it?"

"Do what?"

"Bring in Natalie."

Austin rolled his eyes. "Oh, we're back to that conversation. You know, Casey," he shrugged, "I fucked up. I don't know how many times I can tell you I'm sorry, but—"

"No. This is not about an apology. I want to know why."

Austin leaned forward and held his beer bottle with both hands. He started peeling off the label. "You remember the day of the initial investigation when you said nothing was there?"

"Yeah. It was the truth."

"Casey, it may be the truth, but it makes for really lousy television. And really lousy television makes for really lousy ratings. If Natalie said it was haunted, which she did, it actually gave us a reason to investigate."

"This is what I just don't get about you. It's all or nothing. You're either frolicking with demons or searching for ghosts where none exist. There are some truly haunted places out there that aren't actually portals to hell. So, why waste your time investigating this bullshit hotel?"

"This bullshit hotel seemed legit."

"Seemed legit? Or the owners wanted the great Austin Cole seal of approval? I'm sure it's good for their business if you declare it to be haunted. How much did they pay you?"

"Damnit, Casey, that's not how I work." He ticked off points with his fingers. "Several employees and guests witnessed strange phenomena. The thermal cameras detected wild temperature fluctuations, and the local paranormal society captured some impressive EVPs. We had to check it out."

Casey didn't have much faith in the local investigators: enthusiasts who spent their weekends tracking ghosts with devices they spent all their spare change on. But they were a strong fan base, and Austin respected them. Deep down, Casey knew Austin was a hard-core paranormal investigator, not a sell-out. It wasn't about pleasing others. He truly got his rocks off on haunted houses. "I'm sorry. I shouldn't have said that; it was wrong."

Austin blinked. Then he pulled out his phone and held it up in front of her. "Would you mind repeating that? I need to get this on video."

She pushed the hand with his phone down. "I realize you have the locations all lined up for the fall season. But when you have a new place in mind, why don't you let me scout it out first? If I think it's an authentic haunting, we'll bring up the entire crew. It will save us time, money, and embarrassment."

Austin considered it. "Maybe. But I want to go with you."

"What was that little speech you gave about trusting your psychic from now on?"

He pointed his beer bottle at her. "I'm not the one with trust issues." He returned to peeling the label off his bottle of beer. "I just like being in control."

Casey grabbed his bottle cap off the table and looked at it. "O'Doul's? You're not even drinking real beer?"

"It is real beer. It just doesn't have alcohol."

"So, you're a Catholic who doesn't drink?"

Austin inclined his head to her bottle. "And you're a Baptist who does."

"Never?" Casey asked as she flipped the beer cap into her other hand.

"Only the blood of Christ on Sunday morning. Like I said, I like to be in control."

"That's right. Austin Control. Let's see. You always eat healthy; you don't drink; you work out every day; and you never miss church. So, what are your vices? Other than the obvious."

"The obvious?"

"Practicing necromancy."

He nudged her shoulder with his finger. "Actually, I pay you to practice necromancy."

Casey shook her head. "Your avoidance tactics won't work. C'mon. I know you have a pet sin. Everyone does."

"Okay," he said rubbing his chin. "I am easily tempted by beautiful women. Especially when they're naked in my bed."

"Filthy fornicator," she teased. "So, tell me, how do you reconcile that with your Catholic faith?"

"I don't. You asked me what my pet sin is, and I told you." He shrugged. "The spirit is willing but the body is weak." He leaned in and whispered, "Like you said, everyone has a pet sin. Wanna confess yours?"

Casey leaned back in her seat. "I'm not Catholic, and you are not a priest."

"C'mon. I told you mine."

"Nope." She played with the beer cap and finished off her draft. An upbeat country song began to play.

Austin tilted his head toward the dance floor. "Okay, then how about a dance?" She took a sip from her bottle of Bud and shook her head.

"Why not?"

"I told you I don't want to be played," she said seriously.

"Case, this isn't a set up. I just thought it'd be fun. C'mon." He grinned and tipped his head to the dance floor.

Casey stared at the neck of her beer bottle. "I don't know how to."

"No way! A Texas girl that doesn't know how to two-step?"

"Have you forgotten? My father is the Reverend Luke Lawson of Holy Spirit Baptist Church. I was brought up believing that dancing was a sin and roughly equivalent to a vertical dry hump." She rested her elbows on the table and narrowed her eyes at him. "So tell me how this television star from Los Angeles knows how to two-step."

"I didn't always live in California. I was born and raised in Huntsville, Alabama."

Casey smiled. "I thought I detected a southern twang. You lose it for the camera, but when you're mad, it comes out."

The side of his mouth turned up into a half-grin. "You know, I can't really picture you as the daughter of a Baptist minister. What was that like, growing up a preacher's kid?"

Casey shrugged. "I didn't think it was much different from any of my friends' families. Of course we never missed church. Sunday morning, Sunday evening, and Wednesday night—every single week. It wasn't until I was about eight that it became a problem."

"What happened?"

"I started talking to deceased residents in our small, Texas town, and my dad went ballistic. He told me there was no such thing as ghosts, and I was making stuff up. When I was a few years older, he stopped calling me a liar and started telling me I was in league with the devil for practicing witchcraft. At that point, I didn't care what he said." Casey stood up. "Now I'm going to get another beer. You want anything?"

"Stay here. I'll get it."

"You bought last round."

"And I can buy this round, too."

Casey shrugged and sat back down. She watched him as he strode to the bar in jeans that sat just right on his hips and a T-shirt that accentuated his well-defined biceps. She might be immune to his bullshit charm, but she was quite susceptible to lust. *You've seen his type, and it's not you. It's okay to look, but don't get any ideas.*

Austin placed another draft on the table in front of Casey. "So, was that when you became friends with Barrett?"

Casey took a swallow of beer. She was confused for a second, still thinking about what lay underneath his tight fitting T-shirt, and then she realized he was continuing their conversation from before. "Uh, yeah, it was about the same time. I had finally found someone who believed me. He understood, because he had daddy issues, too."

"His parents didn't believe him, either?"

"Oh, I don't know whether they did or not. I was talking about his sexuality, not his sixth sense. Our psychic ability was our common bond, but a great friendship grew out of that." The alcohol was loosening her lips, and she knew she was telling Austin way too much, but she couldn't seem to shut up. "When I was rebellious and out of control, he reigned me in. When he was down, I picked him up. Back then, I didn't know why he was so sad. He's always been a private person, kind of shy. I had such a crush on him back then. I tried to kiss him my sophomore year. It was pretty awkward. By my junior year, I realized he liked boys as much as I did. Then he left for college, and unfortunately we lost touch with one another. But I was older then, and more confident. I knew my dad was wrong about my psychic abilities and just figured he was wrong about everything else, too. He thought I was a shameless sinner, and I was determined to prove him right. When I turned eighteen, my dad invited me to leave for good, and I took him up on his invitation."

Austin didn't say anything but looked into her steely blue eyes. She stared back. Her mind was going places it shouldn't. He smiled at her and Casey felt her face get hot. She wasn't sure if it was the alcohol or the intense gaze from the sex magnet sitting across from her. A romantic rock ballad from an eighties hair band began to play.

Austin extended his hand. "You can't say you don't know how to dance to this." He tipped his head toward the dance floor. "You just hold hands and rock back and forth."

Casey eyes flicked to his face. "Ocean eyes," she mumbled.

"What?"

"Nothing, I was just talking to myself." Finally, she offered up her hand and he took it, leading her to the dance floor.

"You know," Austin said as he put his hands on her waist, "It wasn't that I didn't believe you, or that I doubted your abilities. I wasn't going to like anyone who wasn't Barrett. It's stupid, really. I thought I was betraying him by being nice to you."

"But it was his decision to leave." Casey stared down at the hands that were firmly gripping her midsection. It had been too long since she'd been handled this way.

"Yeah, well, some shit I pulled helped him make up his mind."

She tried to maintain some space between them, but as the song wore on, she found herself moving closer to his chest as she wrapped her arms around his neck. As much as she hated to admit it, leaning into him and swaying to the music was more than a little pleasant. Geez, why did he have to hold her so tight and smell so good?

The song ended and they slowly pulled apart. "What now?" Austin asked. "Do you want another beer, or do you want me to take you home?"

She looked up into the blue-green sea of his eyes and carefully weighed what she was about to say. With her index finger she traced the angle of his jaw, down his neck, and over his T-shirt, stopping at the center of his chest. Her steely blues heated up as she stared up at him. "Are those my only options?"

Austin raised an eyebrow. Casey nodded. When he saw she was serious, he entwined his fingers in hers. He leaned over and blew warm breath in her ear. "Let's get out of here."

The city lights seemed to blur into one another in Casey's beer-buzzed eyes. She was surprised when he didn't take the turn-off into town. He placed a call, and in less than a minute they had reservations at a luxury hotel five minutes from the bar. Her un-focused eyes studied his movements as he expertly shifted gears. Austin pulled into a parking space, popped his trunk, and grabbed a duffel out.

"What's that?" Casey asked.

"My overnight bag."

"My, you come prepared."

"I was a boy scout." He winked at her and grabbed her hand. "Don't worry," he said. "I have an extra toothbrush for you."

"I wasn't worried," Casey said. Good dental hygiene was the last thing on her mind.

Austin placed the key card in front of the door. The light turned green and he turned the handle. He stepped back and allowed Casey to enter. He hadn't spared any expense. The suite was beautiful. It was decorated in a modern palette of dark browns and powder blues. The lighting fixtures were high end and elegant. Tasteful artwork adorned the walls. Austin stepped into the oversized, luxury bathroom and flicked on the light. While he put his overnight bag on the counter, Casey stared longingly at the frameless glass shower. It had one of those cool, rain-shower heads and multiple sprayers along the wall. Austin stepped past her and walked over to the king-size bed.

"You want another beer?"

The buzz she felt at the bar was quickly fading, but she shook her head. If she was going to do this, she wanted to remember it. He removed the comforter and sat down on the edge. He patted the space beside him and Casey joined him.

With his index finger, he lightly traced the side of her face and took her chin between his finger and thumb. He moved both hands to the side of her head, and stared into her eyes as he pulled her closer. His lips touched hers, lightly at first, then his arms encircled her, and he pressed more firmly. This time her lips parted and his skilled tongue explored her mouth. Casey relaxed and let go of her misgivings. Tomorrow they would have to go back to work and maintain a professional relationship. Sleeping with her boss was probably a huge mistake. But as long as she was royally screwing things up, she was determined to enjoy it.

She slipped her hand under his T-shirt, rubbing her fingers up and down the hard lines of his back. He stopped kissing her long enough to slip the shirt over his head, then picked up where he left off. Now she could explore those amazing pecs up close. His hands slipped down to her neck and she exhaled as he began trailing kisses from her chin to her collar bone. His beard tickled her neck, and she giggled. Liking her response, he nuzzled her neck with his chin until she wiggled and cried out.

His lips never left her face and neck as one by one, the buttons on her blouse popped open under the direction of his experienced fingers. She pulled her arms out of the sleeves and suddenly felt self-conscious in her very plain, white utilitarian bra. The fact that she wasn't wearing Victoria Secret lingerie didn't seem to bother him. He placed his mouth on the hollow of her neck. She leaned back, allowing him room to move down the center of her chest. When he pressed his lips against her cleavage, she felt a spark that tingled through her body all the way down to her toes.

One at a time, he slid the bra straps off her shoulders and began pressing light kisses along the tops of her breasts. Casey felt her lower abdomen clench and warmth spread as the flesh between her legs began to throb. His hands went to her back and in what had to be world-record time, his expert hands unlatched the three hooks of her bra. It joined her blouse on the floor.

Austin laid her down on the bed and twirled his tongue around her right nipple as his fingers lightly stroked the left. Her breathing was erratic as he continued to lavish her nipple with attention that was long overdue. She rubbed her hands down his sides until she reached his jeans. She put her hand against his zipper and traced her fingers along the outline of his erection. He gently moved her hand away and kissed the top of it. "Not yet. I want to take my time," he whispered. He kissed her earlobe and blew a long warm breath in her ear. Casey exhaled audibly.

Wanting to be fair to both breasts, he switched sides, flicking his tongue over her left nipple while tweaking the right with his fingers. Casey arched her back, pressing her chest up to meet him. He slid the tip of his nose between her breasts, warming her skin with his breath.

When he was satisfied that he had coaxed every last bit of pleasure from her sensitive peaks, he continued down, tracing his tongue in a line between her breast bone and her lower abdomen. He paused at her navel, swirling his tongue and dipping it into its shallow recess. One hand went up to caress the side of her breast and down her rib cage as the other hand dipped into the elastic waistband of her skirt.

Her eyes flew open. This morning when she got dressed she hadn't expected to end up in the bed of the sexiest man alive. She had chosen very practical, very worn, and very comfy granny panties. It was bad enough he had seen her in her sensible and supportive bra. There was no way she could allow him to see her in underwear that would probably scare his cock into a flaccid state. It might be better if he didn't see her ass or thighs up close, either.

She grabbed his hand and pulled it out of her pants. After turning off the lamp, she slid down her skirt and panties in one quick movement. Taking her cue, he slid out of his jeans and underwear. He lay next to her, his naked form against her side and his erection pressing into her hip.

He lifted her arm over her head and traced his fingers along her side from the side of her breast down past her hip. While he kept her mouth occupied with his tongue, his other hand ventured down to the apex of her legs. He ran his finger up and down, stopping this time to nestle his fingers into her wet warmth.

While his fingers caressed the sensitive skin between her legs, she explored every inch of his toned back and buttocks before reaching in front to massage those well-defined abs. She moved lower and he groaned. His tongue plunged deep into her mouth as his fingers circled her most sensitive spot.

Casey heard his breath hitch. He pulled his lips and hands back and raised up on his knees. In a low voice he said, "Be right back." Casey saw the light flick on around the corner. She leaned over the bed to get a better view. In the stark light of the bathroom fluorescents, she could see the delineation of every muscle in his perfectly sculpted body. He was rummaging through his overnight bag. "Can't ever find the little bastards when you need them," he muttered. A moment later, Casey heard the sound of ripping paper and then the light went out. Austin returned to the bed, this time positioning himself over her.

Casey reached between them and guided him in. He pushed gently until he felt her relax around him. Then he moved his hands to her rib cage and lowered his weight onto her body. She wanted him closer, so she locked her ankles around his back, trapping his hips between her thighs. He wrapped his hands behind her shoulders, drawing her closer to him. His strong lips claimed her mouth as he slid into her soft wet, heat. Slowly, he pulled all the way out. He repeated this agonizing routine over and over.

Austin was surprisingly quiet in bed, and for that, Casey was thankful. With his filthy mouth, she hadn't known what to expect. When Brandon wasn't trying to talk dirty to her—awkward—he had been grunting and moaning like a rutting pig. Austin made a few gasps and little hums. It was just enough for Casey to know what he liked and when he was getting close.

She unlocked her ankles and planted her feet flat on the bed. He picked up the pace, and she matched his rhythm, pushing against him as he rocked into her. A sheen of sweat glistened on their skin as arms and legs tangled together and slick abdomens pressed against one another. Austin grabbed her ankles and hooked them over his shoulders. His thrusts grew faster and more desperate.

"Are you close, baby?" he whispered. "I'm not going to last much longer."

Shit. Casey thought. It was their first and probably last time together. She never expected him to be concerned with her pleasure. "Umm," she mumbled. He took it as a yes, as she hoped he would. She studied his face and carefully watched his body language. His head and eyes were staring straight ahead as he pushed in and pulled out. His crucifix dangled down, lightly skimming her chin each time he plowed into her. She wondered what he was thinking, or if he was thinking at all.

Casey heard his breath catch as he plunged into her one last time. He arched his back and gripped her hips. Then he relaxed and wrapped his arms tight around her. He rested his forehead against hers, and lay there until his breathing returned to normal. After kissing her on the forehead, he pulled out slowly. Then he reached for the light switch, peeled off his condom, and chucked it in the trash. Casey blinked as her eyes adjusted to the light. She couldn't help but stare at his tight, naked ass as he strode over to the bathroom. A moment later, he returned with two towels. He handed her one as he cleaned himself with the other. She covered her midsection with the towel and rose. "I think I'll just take a shower, if that's okay with you."

"Of course, Sweet Cheeks." Austin reached out and gently squeezed her ass. Casey's eyes widened, and she turned to look at him. There was no derision in his gaze. His eyes drifted up from her backside and settled on her face. By the smoldering look in his eyes and the way his lips were parted, she knew he'd meant it as a compliment.

She walked into the bathroom and shut the door behind her. While the shower heated up, she sat on the toilet to pee. "Holy shit!" she muttered to herself. She stood up and gripped the vanity. "You just fucked Austin Cole," she told her reflection.

15

Casey walked out of the well-lit bathroom and into the darkness of the hotel suite. "There's a T-shirt on the dresser if you want it," Austin told her. *He does come prepared,* Casey thought. She slipped it on and he pulled back the covers for her. She slid in beside him. He was lying on his stomach but reached an arm across her and pulled her close. He kissed her on the forehead. A few minutes later, she heard his breathing grow steady and even as he fell asleep. She waited a few more minutes before extricating herself from his embrace. As she pulled off his T-shirt and slipped on her own clothes, her gaze turned to a sleeping Austin. She placed the T-shirt on the bed next to him and lightly kissed his temple before quietly opening the door.

Casey was having a coffee with Mrs. S., her deceased roommate, when she heard her phone buzz. It was only seven-thirty in the morning and there were three voice mails and two text messages. She pulled up the messages and quickly saw that they were all from Austin.

Where r u? R u okay?

She texted him back. *I'm fine. I'm in my apartment.*

If u wanted to go, u should have told me. I would have taken u home.

I didn't want to wake you. I took a cab.

Do u want me to stop by? I could bring breakfast and take us to work.

Oh, fuck no, Casey thought. Last night when the others left, she had been super pissed at him. And if today she showed up to work in his Porsche? Geez, they would totally get the wrong idea, which would actually be the right idea. But that was beside the point.

Thanks for the offer, but I'm headed out the door now. I'll just see you there.

Ok.

Casey pulled her hair up into a ponytail and grabbed her purse. "I should just act natural. Pretend like nothing happened. Right?" Mrs. S. nodded in agreement.

His black Porsche was already parked at *SCI* when she arrived. She took a breath and walked in. Austin stood up from his desk when he heard the door open.

She was headed over to her office when she heard him call out. "Casey, can I talk to you?"

Casey froze. *Might as well get this over with.* She tried to smooth her features as she slowly turned. "Okay," she said in as nonchalant a tone as she could manage. Austin was leaning out the door of his office. She walked over and stopped in front of his doorway.

Austin leaned on the corner of his desk. "You want to come in?"

Casey leaned on the doorframe with her arms crossed. "I'm good right here." She looked down at the floor. "Is there something you needed?"

Austin rubbed his chin. "I just wanted to talk." She lifted her head. "Is everything okay?"

"Everything's fine," she said.

"Then why are you avoiding me?"

"I'm not avoiding you."

"Really? Then why won't you come in my office and talk to me?"

"Look, Austin, let me just get it out there." She ran her fingers through her ponytail. "It was a mistake. You're an adult. I'm an adult. Let's just forget last night ever happened."

Austin blinked. "What? Why?"

Casey's eyes widened. "Are you serious? We work together. I think that's reason enough."

"It doesn't have to be."

"I just started here. I don't need everyone talking about me behind my back."

Austin stood up. "Case, we're not like that here."

"Everyone's like that everywhere."

"No, you're wrong. We're close, like a family."

"That makes it even worse. In normal families, you don't fuck your sister."

Austin crossed his arms. "I think you're overreacting, but fine. You're the boss."

"No, *you're* the boss. That's why last night never happened."

Casey turned when she heard Thai and Gary's voices. She put her finger to her lips, and gave Austin a warning glare. Then, she rushed off to the gym.

Fifteen minutes later the entire crew had arrived and was warming up.

Thai looked over at Casey, then asked Austin, "Is everything cool?"

"What do you mean?"

"Well, she's here, so I guess she didn't quit. But she doesn't look too happy."

Austin glanced over at Casey. When she saw him looking, she averted her eyes. He cleared his throat and looked straight ahead. "Things are okay."

"I hope so. The last thing we need is tension on the team."

Barrett raised his glass and toasted Casey. "So, I saw the old hotel episode last night. And of course, you nailed it." He had called her that morning and invited her out to lunch.

Casey blushed, but clinked his glass anyway. "Thanks. I know you would have read it the same way."

"Probably. But I wouldn't have had the nerve to be so blunt," he said with a smile.

"You're the diplomat, not me."

He swirled his glass of wine around. "So, things are going better?"

"Definitely getting better," she said. Austin wasn't giving her shit about her running anymore and they were both safely back in the coworker/friend zone. "How about you?"

"Definitely getting better." He echoed Casey's words. "If anything, I'm going stir crazy hanging around the house." He pushed his hand through his thick black hair. "I really just need to get a job."

"So do it." Barrett laughed at her. "What's so funny?" she asked.

"I've been at *SCI* for so long, I don't know if I could do anything else." *Or if I'd even want to.*

"I have a great idea." Casey leaned forward. "Come with me to Thai's house tomorrow."

"Thai's house?" His brow furrowed. "Ah, okay. Sunday football."

"You said you need to get out of the house." Casey leaned back. "I went a couple weeks ago. It was fun."

"You? At a football party? I don't believe it."

Casey nodded. "Believe it. Of course, I didn't actually watch the game. I was out on the balcony having drinks with Anna and Josie and the other football widows. Please, Barrett." She gave him her most adorable smile.

Barrett shook his head. "I don't know, Casey."

"Everyone misses you. They'd love to see you. You could bring Derek."

"Uh, no. He's out of town, but even if he wasn't, he can't stand.... He wouldn't come, anyway."

"Even better. You can be my date." Barrett's mouth turned up in a half-grin. "If you drive, I won't have to take a cab." Casey poked him in the arm. "C'mon. You know you want to."

He held up his hands in surrender. "All right, I'll go."

Barrett picked her up, and they arrived shortly after the game had started. By arriving late, he could avoid any awkward pre-game chit chat with Austin. They walked in, and Thai looked up from the couch. "Hey ... Barrett?" Thai said with surprise. Austin's head popped up from the seating area. Thai slid his feet off the coffee table and stood up. He gave Barrett the standard bro hug. "Go on in there. I'll grab you a beer."

Barrett approached the living area. Gary was lounging on the recliner and Luis on the love seat. Austin was sitting on the couch. He moved over so Barrett could take a seat, but Barrett turned and sat next to Luis. Austin stared at his hands.

Casey headed out to the balcony. Josie ran up to her. "Hey, girl. We were beginning to think you were a no-show."

"Barrett wanted to arrive fashionably late."

Her eyes widened. "Barrett's here?" Casey nodded. "I've got to go say hi." She waved over to the table. "Liv, Barrett's here."

Liv followed Josie and Casey into Thai's apartment. They nearly ran into a beautiful dark blond with a light beer in one hand and a protein water in the other.

"Whoa." She caught herself before her drink spilled.

"Oh, hey, Cheryl," Josie said. "This is Casey, our new psychic."

"Nice to meet you. I'd shake your hand, but mine are full, as you can see."

"Babe, you coming, or what?" They heard Austin call out.

"Well, I'm being summoned. Talk to you later." She walked over to the living room and handed Austin the protein water. Then, she sat next to him on the couch.

Casey felt all the breath leave her lungs. She should have prepared herself for this.

"What's wrong? You look like you've seen a ghost. Wait, is there a ghost here?" Josie asked.

Casey shook her head. Josie and Liv ran over to talk to Barrett. Casey casually meandered over to the living room and leaned against the wall, sipping her beer. When she was sure no one was paying attention, she snuck a peek at the couple. Austin had his hand draped across Cheryl's shoulder, and she was leaning into him. She was simply gorgeous. Sultry dark eyes, straight nose, and plump, rose-colored lips. She had a nice rack and wore a tight-fitting, scoop-neck shirt to accentuate it. In fact, her entire ensemble screamed high-end fashion-forward boutique. Perfect. Casey looked down at the comfy, yet frumpy, ankle-length skirt and knit top that belonged on a middle-aged woman. Who was she next to this dream woman? Wholly inadequate, that's who. A twinge of jealousy coursed through her, and she tamped it down. She hated that she felt this way. *Grow up, Casey. Put your big girl panties on. He's Austin Freakin' Cole. Not an Augustinian monk.* She returned to the kitchen and sat at the bar.

"Casey?" Liv asked. "You okay?"

"Um, yeah." Casey shook her head. "I'm sorry, my mind was somewhere else."

"Then let's go back to the balcony." Casey was grateful to get out of there.

"Should we ask Cheryl if she wants to join us?" Anna asked.

"Nah," Josie said. "She wouldn't come, anyway." She leaned over and whispered in Casey's ear. "She's one of those strange chicks who actually digs football."

Casey leaned over to see what Anna had in her hands. It was an album, and Anna was showing Marie pictures of flowers and wedding venues.

"You and Thai are getting married?" Casey asked with surprise.

Anna laughed. "I forgot Thai is so-closed lipped about everything. Yes, we're getting married on New Year's Day. Just a simple service. Then we're hosting a reception. Look for the save the date. I'll be sending it out in the next few weeks." Casey sat back and rolled her beer cap between her fingers while the other women discussed the wedding plans.

During half-time, the guys gathered in the kitchen. Barrett was leaning against the counter and Austin walked over to him. "Good to see you, man. How are things?"

Barrett stared at him for a moment. There was a part of him that deeply missed his friend. Hell, he deeply missed all the guys. "Great," he lied. "Everything's great."

"If you ever want to come up to *SCI*—shoot some hoops, or hang out with the guys—you know you're always welcome," Austin told him.

"Um, thanks." Barrett scratched the back of his neck. "If you'll excuse me, I'm going to grab another beer." Austin nodded, and tried to hide his disappointment. He couldn't even talk to Barrett for a moment before polite conversation mutated into a mountain of awkward. The door from the balcony swung open and Casey walked in, followed by Liv. They headed to the kitchen, and Casey grabbed another beer, but not before her eyes met Austin's. She quickly averted her gaze. *Damnit,* Austin thought. She was the one who thought their encounter was a mistake, so why was it he felt like an asshole for bringing Cheryl over?

Staying for the rest of the game was suddenly the last thing he wanted to do. He needed to find Cheryl and get the hell out of there. Austin walked out of the kitchen and down the hall. Cheryl was coming out of the bathroom.

"You ready to go?"

"It's only half-time. You don't want to stay?" she asked.

He leaned over, blew warm breath in her ear, and whispered, "What I really want is to get you horizontal underneath me." He kissed her on the mouth and grabbed her hand. "Let's go." Austin stared straight ahead and walked with a purpose to the front door. "Later, Thai."

"You leaving?"

"Yeah," he said. Cheryl waved at Anna and the other women as Austin pulled her along. He didn't notice, but both Casey and Barrett's eyes followed him as he walked out the door.

The following week, Austin approached Casey in the *SCI* gym. She was jamming to her playlist and reading as she ran on the treadmill. He tapped her on the shoulder, and she turned down the music and looked over at him.

"When you get done here, can you meet me in my office?"

"Yeah, sure. What's this about?"

"I'll tell you when you get there. Finish your workout. There's no rush."

Casey nodded and watched him leave. She ran for ten more minutes then headed to the locker room for a quick shower. No way was she going to meet with him all sweaty and disgusting. She smoothed her hair before knocking on his door. This would be the first time she'd spent any time alone with Austin since the day after their one night stand. Her stomach knotted in nerves. *Hey Austin, I don't really know what to say or how to act around you, because every time I see you, I picture you naked in my mind.* Unfortunately, she had never come across a greeting card that covered this type of situation.

"Yeah," Austin said from behind the door.

Casey slipped in quietly. He glanced up from his computer monitor and cleared his throat. He looked as uncomfortable as Casey felt. "Have a seat." Casey sat down and Austin began speaking. "So, here's the deal. We have a major problem. The house we were slated to investigate for the mid-season finale mysteriously burned to the ground."

"Really? What happened?"

"It's listed as an electrical fire, but we'll probably never know for sure. Barrett told me once that angry houses with lots of activity sometimes took themselves out of existence."

"Yeah. Usually, they don't like the way a homeowner is remodeling, or the place has a negative and violent history. Those houses are usually very hostile to the living."

"Well, this place was all that and more. So, now we have to find a suitable replacement." He leaned back and stared at Casey. "I was thinking about what you said. How it would be better if you went up and scoped out a place before bringing the entire crew in case it was a total bust."

"Yeah."

"I have a place in mind, and on paper, it sounds great. But I want to know for sure before we go up there. I've contacted the local authorities. The place is old and falling apart. They are planning to demolish it early next spring. We only have a small window of time to do the investigation."

"So, what's the plan?"

"We'll leave for Georgia tomorrow. That gives us an extra day to check the place out before we meet the others in Missouri for this week's investigation."

Casey needed clarification. "When you say we, who are you talking about?"

"You and me, of course."

"Oh." *Great.*

16

A winding, dirt road led up to an old, abandoned farmhouse. The white paint was peeling, and it was surrounded by a picket fence that was half-standing, half-falling. To Casey it looked like no one had lived there in years. Over to the right of the house stood a barn that must have been red at one time, but weather had faded it to a dark pink. The enclosure for the cattle was mostly gone, and the metal door was hanging crooked and looked as if a stiff breeze would knock it all the way off. She stared out the window at the house.

"We aren't trespassing, are we?" Casey asked as Austin cut the ignition to the rental car.

"Nope," he answered as he opened the car door and stepped out. "I make every effort to get permission from the owner before we see the property. In this case, no living owner exists, and no one has taken ownership of the place. To me, that means we are welcome to take a look."

Casey got out of the car and started to move forward. She stopped, tilted her head to the house, and stared.

"You sense something, don't you?"

"Yes," she said. "There are spirits here, but they don't seem malevolent."

"Spirits with an 's'? As in more than one?" Casey nodded as she followed Austin up the crumbling concrete steps and onto the front porch. The screen on the door was ripped, and the frame had obviously been painted over many times with a black, high-gloss paint. It looked like it was overdue for another coat. He kissed his crucifix. "Hold this," he said, shoving the camera into her hands. The screen door squeaked as he opened it. He tried the knob. It was in the locked position, but he could tell by the way it gave when he pushed on it that the frame had shifted away from the latch. With a few hard shoves, Austin was able to gain entrance to the house.

The door opened directly into the living room. Rat droppings littered the floor and what furniture was left was covered in dingy sheets. Dust and cobwebs covered every available surface. Casey coughed and was thankful she didn't have allergies.

They walked through the living area to the kitchen, and then to the bedrooms. Austin turned the camera on her. She gazed down, her eyes moving from left to right. Austin hung back and let her do her thing. When she got a reading, she took off and he followed her. In a corner of the last bedroom, she met the occupants whom she had sensed were there the moment she and Austin had pulled up to the house. Three teenaged girls were standing huddled together, a mixture of fear and suspicion on their faces. Casey was terrible at placing fashion with a time period, but their simple cotton dresses with flowery designs reminded her of the flour-sack dresses she had seen in old pictures of her great-grandmother.

"What do you see?" Austin asked from behind the camera.

"Three very frightened young women from sometime in the early twentieth century." She tried smiling at them in a kind, non-threatening manner. "We aren't here to hurt you. We just want to talk to you."

"What's going on? What do they look like?" Austin asked impatiently.

"The youngest wears her hair in long brown braids, like Laura on *Little House on the Prairie*. She looks about fourteen. The other two are close in size and age, maybe eighteen or nineteen. One has blond hair combed up in a tight bun and she seems kind of stern, like a no-nonsense grade school teacher. She's tall and big-boned. I think she's the oldest. That's the vibe I'm getting from her. The third is acting shy, hiding behind the other two. She wears her dark hair in a bun, but she is more petite and feminine in form than the blond."

Casey knelt down on the dingy floor to put them at ease, and motioned for Austin to do the same. He continued filming, but sat cross-legged on the floor across from Casey. The youngest approached first. Knowing Austin was filming, Casey spoke out loud. "The young one with the braids is Imogene." She was frightened, but curious. Ghosts communicated in different ways. Instead of creating words and phrases in Casey's head, Imogene gave her an inside look into her own thoughts and memories. "She lives here with her middle sister, Prudence, and her oldest sister, Gladiola. They were left to run the farm after their parents passed away." Casey could see from her memories that the sisters worked very hard to keep the farm going. They plowed, fed the pigs and gathered eggs. Then Imogene showed a picture of all three of them exhausted and sick. Their cheeks were rosy and they were listless and shivering. The next image was of the sisters' tombstones. "The three of them died of a fever," she told Austin. The next thing she showed Casey was another family moving into the house. Imogene drew a line between the new owner and a picture of her father so that Casey knew he was a relative. "After they died, their uncle moved in." It was clear Imogene did not like her uncle. She showed pictures of him drinking out of a bottle, yelling at his wife, and beating his children. Imogene showed herself cowering in a corner and Casey could tell she was afraid of him. "He was not a nice man. He was an abusive alcoholic."

Gladiola pulled Imogene back. The eldest sister spoke. *What do you want with us?* Gladiola was a verbal communicator; she formed actual words in Casey's mind.

For Austin's benefit, Casey answered aloud. "We've heard reports of a haunting here and we came to see."

There were some young hooligans here a few weeks back, but we scared them off. They threw a rock and broke the window in the kitchen. If you've come to tear up what my daddy worked so hard to build, we'll run you off, too.

"We're not here to harm you or disturb your house." She flicked her hand in Austin's direction. "Austin and I are part of a ghost-hunting TV show." Casey smacked her head as she realized they probably had no idea what a television show was. "What I mean is, we record proof of the existence of spirits like yourselves. Would you be willing to let us come back with a few of our friends and record sounds you make and have you move objects for our motion picture camera?"

Imogene nodded excitedly. She showed Casey a memory of the three of them sitting around, their chins in their palms, looking utterly bored. Then an image of happier times with their parents and other people who used to come and visit. Casey felt the weight of Imogene's loneliness.

Prudence peeked over at Austin, then quickly averted her gaze. Casey couldn't get a read on the enigmatic middle sister. She was catching a deceitful vibe from her, but without any true malice.

Gladiola spoke next. *I suppose. As long as your friends don't write bad words on the barn or break my mama's collectibles.* Gladiola let her guard down a little bit and Casey could feel her unease drift away. *We can bang some pots and move things around so they know we're here. Can't we girls?* Imogene nodded while Prudence clapped her hands together and danced around in a circle.

"What's going on? What are they saying?" Austin asked.

"They said yes. We can come back. They will cooperate fully to make it an exciting show."

Casey spent the next hour fielding questions from both the living and the dead. Austin kept the camera rolling the entire time.

"What do they look like?" he asked.

"Gladiola is the oldest and she wears her hair up in a bun—"

"No. What I mean is, do you see them like you see me?" He pointed to his chest.

"Yes, but their skin is luminous. They shimmer." She grabbed Austin's hand and ran it through Imogene's. "Do you feel anything?"

He looked at Casey. "It felt cold for a second. What was that?"

"Imogene's hand," Casey answered. Prudence moved around Gladiola and closer to Casey and Austin. She poked his shoulder, then ran to stand behind Gladiola. He shivered and she giggled.

The girls had never met anyone like Casey, and they wanted to know why she talked to them while everyone else ignored them. Casey explained that she was a clairvoyant and she could see and communicate with spirits. She pointed to Austin. "He can't see you, either. If you want to say something to him, just tell me and I'll pass on the message."

It was then that Prudence revealed herself. She wasn't a verbal communicator like Gladiola, but she communicated in a slightly different way than Imogene. Rather than let Casey read her mind, she showed Casey images of what she was trying to express. When Casey saw the first image from Prudence, she wondered if she had been wrong about the girls not knowing about television. She was showing Casey a commercial from a cologne ad of a man and a woman making out in an elevator. His shirt was off, and she was running her fingers up and down his chest while he kissed her. She gave Casey a look that could best be described as "Bow-chica-row-row."

Casey threw her head back and laughed. "What's so funny?" Austin asked.

"Prudence thinks you're...." The word that was about to come out of Casey's mouth was sexy, but then she saw the panicked look on Prudence's face. She pointed at her sister Gladiola and shook her head. Then she took her index finger and put it to her mouth in a shushing motion.

"Prudence thinks you're handsome," she said. Prudence gave Casey a thumbs up. The girls grew up in the last century, were unmarried, and were definitely innocent. But at least one of them wasn't naïve or unworldly. Prudence then showed Casey images of Times Square, the Eiffel Tower, and a trolley in San Francisco— all places she had traveled to in her spirit form. Then she showed Casey an image of a very distracted Gladiola, knitting in the rocker, with no idea that Prudence had ever left the farm. Prudence made a key with her finger and turned the lock on her lips. Casey nodded her agreement.

Austin stood up and walked around the room. He was admiring an old cuckoo clock and reached out to touch it when Gladiola swatted his hand. He didn't feel the slap but felt a cold rush of air on his hand. He rubbed his fingers together. "What was that?"

"Gladiola says you can look but don't touch."

"Okay." Austin looked up into the air, speaking in the exact opposite direction of where Gladiola was standing. "I'm sorry. I won't do it again."

Imogene pointed to Austin and showed Casey two pictures: one of her uncle and one of Santa Claus. "He's a nice man," Casey assured her.

How long have you been married? Do you have any children? Gladiola wanted to know. Casey didn't even know what Austin was to her— friend, boss, one-night stand, complete pain in the ass—there was no way she could explain it to the prim and proper older sister. And she certainly didn't want to talk about it in front of Austin. *Not yet,* she answered in her mind so Austin wouldn't wonder what they were discussing Imogene loved to sing and tried to teach Casey *Camptown Races,* one of her favorite songs. Casey played along even though she couldn't hold a tune. After a few minutes, Prudence joined in. She didn't say much, but Casey could see a mischievous twinkle in her eye. Imogene insisted they play Ring Around the Rosie. Even Gladiola joined in. When the song ended, they all fell down, laughing.

Austin peeked at Casey over the camera. She was sitting cross-legged on the floor playing some hand slapping game with one spirit, while invisible hands weaved her red hair into a neat braid down the center of her back. He wished, not for the first time, that he could see what she saw. Even just hearing one side of the conversation was quite entertaining. It reminded him of when he was a kid and he would spy on his sister's slumber parties. "Do I want to know what you're talking about?"

"Just girl stuff," Casey told him. Imogene giggled.

Austin filmed them for another hour. He glanced out the window at the setting sun. "I think we better get going. It'll be dark soon."

The girls couldn't hide their disappointment as they walked their guests to the front porch. Imogene showed her a sad memory of when her cat died. Gladiola tried tempting them to stay. *Wait until after supper, at least. You haven't lived until you've had my pot roast.*

"Thank you. We appreciate the invitation, but it's getting late." She had no doubt that if they stayed, the ghost would try to prepare a meal for them. Prudence said nothing. She was standing with her hands behind her back, moving her foot back and forth across the floor and whistling.

Casey and Austin said their goodbyes and headed over to the rental car. Austin turned the key in the ignition. It didn't start. He tried again. Still nothing. He got out of the car and pulled the phone out of his pocket. "Son of a bitch," he muttered, as he kicked the tire. "Stupid rental piece of shit."

Gladiola frowned and put her hands on her hips. "Uh, Austin, watch it with the language. Gladiola doesn't like potty talk."

Austin tipped his head. "Sorry, ma'am," he said to the barn. "I didn't mean to offend."

Gladiola nodded her head.

Austin pushed a few buttons then stared at his phone in disbelief. "No battery? What the fu ... dgesicle?" He nodded at Casey. "Check yours."

Casey pulled out her phone. There wasn't even enough juice to power on. "It's dead."

Austin got out of the car and leaned against it, staring at his worthless device. "It was fully charged this morning. Your ghost friends must have drained all the power." Prudence turned and wouldn't look Casey in the eye. Austin started pacing and ran his hand through his hair. "This is great. We need to get to the location. This will put us behind schedule. And with no signal, I can't even call a tow truck." His voice rose with his increasing irritation. "What are we supposed to do now?"

Imogene ran to hide behind her big sister. Gladiola put her hands on her hips. *Tell him we did not drain the power from his little telephone box. We opened our house to you, and this is the thanks we get?*

"Calm down, Austin. You're offending Gladiola."

Austin blew out his breath. It seemed he had spent the better part of the afternoon apologizing to a ghost. "I'm sorr—" he began.

"Wait," Casey said, and turned him to face the oldest sister.

"I'm sorry I accused you of stealing my battery supply. I'm just frustrated with the situation. Will you please forgive me?" Austin turned to Casey to see what Gladiola had to say.

I forgive you. I'm going to start supper. Prudence, you can help peel potatoes. Imogene, put out a couple of extra plates.

Casey relayed Gladiola's message and the two living beings followed the sisters back into the house. Casey sat down on the floor, leaned against the fireplace, and pulled out her fully charged tablet. She opened it up and started reading.

"How is it you have battery on your tablet and our phones are dead?"

Casey shrugged and continued to read.

"Hey, I know. You could email Thai. He checks his phone all the time." Austin pulled his arm and fist toward his body. "Yes! Help is on the way."

"Sorry to burst your bubble, but I never set up email on my tablet. Not that it matters, but we don't have a wi-fi connection."

Austin growled in frustration. He started pacing again. "I guess I could hike to town and get someone to come out and tow the car."

Casey looked up at him. "I don't think that's a good idea. It's getting dark. Winfield is a small town. All the service stations would be closed by the time you got there."

"Well, I can't just stand here doing nothing."

"Relax, Austin. Do your yoga breathing or something."

He stopped mid stride and turned to her. "How can you be so calm? We have no electricity, no running water and no contact with the outside world."

"I am not a mechanic; therefore, I cannot fix the car. I cannot create an internet or phone connection out of the thin air. There's nothing I can do about any of this, and neither can you, Austin Control. We ate before we came and there's bottled water in the car. At least it's not freezing cold, and we do have a mostly intact roof over our heads. The spirits here are friendly. It could be a lot worse."

Austin frowned at her. "I suppose."

"Just pretend you're on one of your investigations. It's not like you don't love a haunted house."

Austin sighed. He nudged her leg with his shoe. "Move over, Case."

She scooted over, and he sat next to her, looking over her shoulder. "What are we reading?"

"It's called *Opal.*"

Austin followed along for a bit. "What's the deal with this Daemon dude?"

"He's an alien."

"And that makes him cool?"

"Well, you can't transform into a light being, can you?"

"No, but can he capture ghosts on film?'

"Probably. He's a big fan of paranormal investigation shows. You and he would probably have a lot in common."

Austin frowned. "So you fantasize about this Daemon?"

Casey smiled and didn't try to deny it. "Sometimes guys in books are better."

Gladiola entered the room then. *Supper's ready.* Austin and Casey walked into the kitchen and sat down at the table. Imogene had put out five dinner plates. Casey could see things the way the ghosts remembered them. The oil lamps were lit and the sisters were flitting around, filling water glasses and taking pots off the stove. Austin sat staring into the relatively dark kitchen, hearing the sounds of cabinets opening and drawers closing, but unable to see any of the preparations. Casey nudged Austin and he followed her lead, picking up his fork and knife. The living pretended to eat their air dinner so as not to offend the dead, and after the meal, they all headed back into the main room.

Austin ran out to the car to retrieve the bottled waters. Although Casey could see the living room through the girls' eyes—neat and clean with time-worn but well-taken care of furnishings—in reality, she knew the place was dusty, and the sheet-covered couch was probably critter-infested. She and Austin elected to return to the floor by the fireplace. Casey arranged her skirt as she watched the sisters complete their evening routine. Gladiola went to the rocker and took out her knitting. Prudence sat on the couch next to the oil lamp and pretended to read from the family bible. Casey caught her looking over the pages, checking out Austin more than once. Imogene went over to the piano and began plucking out a tune. Although the sisters were aware they were dead, they continued to perform the same nightly tasks they did when they were alive.

Casey rocked her head back and forth to the music. "What's going on?" Austin asked as he took a sip of water. He could see the rocker move but couldn't hear the piano.

"Imogene's playing the piano and singing. I don't recognize the song, but she's got a great voice."

Austin smiled. "As much as I hate being off the grid, I have to admit, it's kind of nice to slow down like this. For one night, I have no emails or texts to answer, and no computer work."

Casey picked up her tablet and Austin read along, this time without making any extraneous comments. At some point, Casey drifted off. She woke up with her tablet in her lap and Austin nuzzling her neck.

"What are you doing?" she asked.

"Reading about Kat is fine, but I'd rather be kissing Casey." He leaned over and pressed his lips against hers. It didn't take long for Casey to wake up and respond. She gripped the back of his neck and opened her mouth as he slid his tongue in. Geez, she had missed those strong lips. She was so distracted that at first she didn't notice the ghost trying to get her attention. Prudence nudged her foot and Casey sat up straight. Shit. She'd forgotten where she was.

"Where are the others?" Casey asked. Prudence showed an image of them asleep in their beds. Then she curled her index finger toward herself and Casey stood up.

"What's going on?" Austin asked.

"I'm not sure, but she wants us to follow her." Prudence led the way with an oil lamp in her hand. Casey guided Austin so he wouldn't trip. The light from the moon was strong and bright, but with no windows in the hall, Austin couldn't see a thing.

Prudence opened the door to another bedroom. She swept her hand across the bed and smiled broadly. Casey didn't want to be rude, but the idea of lying down on a moth-eaten bed spread that may or may not have roaches and rat droppings was not appealing. Prudence sensed her hesitation and pulled back the coverlet, revealing clean sheets underneath.

"Whoa," Austin said, when the bedspread folded down by itself. "Who did that?"

"Prudence. She's offering us her bed."

Austin's lips pulled up in a naughty grin. He kicked off his shoes and lay down with his hands behind his head. "This is pretty comfy. Thanks, Prudence."

He grabbed Casey by the waist and pulled her down with him. "C'mon, Sweet Cheeks. Check it out. It sure beats sleeping on the hard floor against a stone fireplace."

"I don't know. Who knows what's been living in that mattress. We might be safer on the floor."

"Pretend we're camping." The bed was lumpy, but at least it was soft. Casey relaxed against it and tried not to think about bed bugs and other things.

"Now, where were we?" Austin rolled onto his side and placed his palm against her cheek. He stared into her eyes then he ran the tip of his nose down her neck.

"Austin, we have company."

"Prudence?" He asked, but he didn't stop nuzzling her with his beard.

"Uh-huh." Casey sighed.

"Well, is Prudence as uptight as her sister?" Austin sucked on her earlobe, exhaling warm breath.

Prudence threw her head back and laughed. She showed Casey an image of Las Vegas show girls doing the can-can. The ghostly dancer at the end of the row was Prudence. "No. Definitely not." Casey turned her head away and tried not to giggle while Austin tortured her with light kisses against her neck.

Austin winked into the dark. "Well, then, Prudence. Hope you enjoy the show."

Casey knew she should tell him no—this was not the time or the place—but her mouth couldn't form the words. He slipped his T-shirt off and positioned himself over Casey. Prudence reached out and traced her finger along his bare back. Austin shivered. "It's kind of drafty in here."

"Yes, it is." Austin's lips returned to Casey's neck and Casey mouthed the words *naughty girl* to Prudence. The ghost girl shrugged in an "I couldn't help myself" gesture. She stood at the edge of the bed looking on, while Austin and Casey got it on. It wasn't anything Casey wasn't used to. Having a dead audience to the act of sex was just a fact of life most of the living had no knowledge about. Ghosts, she'd learned, missed the activities that the living engaged in. Thanksgiving wouldn't be Thanksgiving if at least one dead relative didn't show up. The same was true for sex. At least Prudence stayed back and watched quietly. Her ex-boyfriend, Robbie, had a dead uncle that was a total creeper. He'd always had a beer in one hand, rubbing his incorporeal member with the other, while she and Robbie messed around.

Austin unbuttoned Casey's blouse and pressed kisses in a line from the hollow of her throat to her stomach. He paused to caress her navel with his tongue. She reached down and unzipped his jeans. He growled as she stroked his erection.

He stood up and pulled his wallet out of his jeans, then removed his jeans and boxer shorts. In the moonlight, she studied his naked form. Geez, he was all kinds of male gorgeous. She could have stared at his profile for hours. Austin rummaged through his wallet until he found the small square he was looking for. He ripped it open and rolled it on.

Austin stared down at her with a wicked grin. He had a new appreciation for flowy skirts. His hands moved down as he slipped his hand up her skirt. He pulled it up and it billowed up over her chest and neck. Casey raised her hips off the bed as he slid her panties all the way down. She pulled away so that she could unhook her bra, remove her blouse, and pull the skirt over her head. Then, her hands were in his hair and her tongue in his mouth.

Austin wasn't in the mood to take his time. His fingers dove between her legs as he continued to attack her mouth. He wanted to be inside her already, feeling her silky walls squeezing against him. He straddled her, and in one thrust pushed himself all the way in. "Damn, Case," he muttered and closed his eyes. Being inside her now felt better than it had the first time. Casey arched her back and brought her throat up to meet his lips. He lifted her rear, squeezing it each time he rocked into her. When his breathing grew ragged, he pulled out and flipped her over onto her stomach. He hauled her up on her knees and applied soft kisses along her tailbone as his hands caressed her bottom. His gentle touch caused the muscles in her rear to clench and release. She closed her eyes and audibly sighed. "You like this?" he whispered.

"Uh-huh," she said, but it came out more of a moan. With his finger he traced a line along her tail bone, which set her nerve endings on edge. She wiggled to get away from his tortuous touch, but he held her firmly and caressed the end of her spine again. The moonlight outlined the soft curves of her ass. "You are so beautiful, Sweet Cheeks." He pressed his lips to her lower back and continued to rub her rear until she was raising up, pressing herself into his pelvis. He positioned himself to take her from behind.

"I hope you're ready, babe." He groaned and pushed into her faster. Their weight shifted the bed. The frame was squeaking with every thrust, and Casey hoped it wouldn't fall apart under the stress. The old mattress probably hadn't seen action like this in years, if ever. At least there was no headboard to bang against the wall. A gasp escaped from Austin's throat. He suddenly stilled, grabbing her hips, and holding her tight against him as he came. It was strong and it was hard. He shuddered as the final waves of his climax flowed into her. Afterward, he encircled his arms around her waist and rested his cheek against her back.

Austin pulled out and they both lay on their backs breathing hard. She was sweaty, dirty, and smelled like sex, but she couldn't have cared less. She rested her arm above her head and looked up. Prudence was standing beside the bed, mouth open, staring at the two of them. *Little perv*, Casey thought. Austin kissed Casey on the forehead. "Be right back," he told her. He rolled off the condom and left the room to dispose of it. Prudence followed him as he walked down the hall to toss it out a broken window. Casey slipped on her underwear and blouse. She smiled as she thought about the voyeur ghost. Austin even had fangirls among the dead.

When he came back into the room, Casey was sitting on the edge of the bed. She handed him his boxers. "Why did you do that? What if Gladiola had woken up and seen you naked in the hallway?"

"Would it have been better for her to find a used condom in her sister's bed?" Prudence's mouth flew open and Casey was sure if ghosts could blush, her cheeks would be scarlet right now.

"Still, you could have at least put your pants on. You could have given her a heart attack."

"Well, she's already dead, so it wouldn't have killed her." He pulled his underwear on, then pulled Casey down on the bed next to him. "And she obviously sleeps like the dead if our activities didn't wake her up. Speaking of ... do we still have company?" He bent one of his legs and rested one arm under his head.

"As a matter of fact, we do."

"You mean my cock of epic proportions didn't scare her off?" Prudence giggled.

"No, your average-sized penis didn't frighten her at all. In fact, I think she's crushing on you. She has this crazy, love-struck look in her eyes." Prudence opened her mouth in shock, then pursed her lips together. She wagged her finger at Casey and dashed out of the room. Austin didn't see her go, but definitely saw and heard the door slam.

"Now she's gone," Casey announced.

She rested her head on his shoulder, using it as a pillow. He rubbed his fingers up and down her arm. "You know, you're a damned good psychic, Case, but you're an even better lay."

Casey frowned. She wasn't quite sure how to answer that. Finally, she said, "Um, thanks. You don't suck, either." She patted his thigh, then rolled over on her side. He wrapped his hard body around her soft one, legs and arms tangling together as they both fell asleep.

17

"Case, Case. Wake up," Austin was shaking her. Casey blinked as she opened her eyes to the bright sunlight. "I got it to start."

"What?" Casey sat up groggily and tried to focus on what he was saying.

"The car. It's running. Get your stuff, and let's go." He grabbed her hand and yanked her out of the bed. She pulled her skirt on and slipped on her shoes.

"Hurry," Austin said.

"Okay. Geez," she said, as she fastened her bra.

The sisters were standing on the front porch.

Imogene showed Casey a piece of paper. On it was written. "We'll miss you."

Casey patted her cheek. "We'll be back, I promise."

Are you sure you can't stay for breakfast? It wouldn't take me long to scramble some eggs and bake some biscuits.

"I'm sure. But thank you for all your hospitality."

Prudence stood with her arms crossed. Casey spoke to her through her mind.

Are you still mad at me for telling Austin you like him?

Prudence turned her back to Casey.

If you forgive me for telling Austin about your secret crush, I won't tell him how you messed with the car. Casey showed Prudence an image of her from the night before disconnecting the battery cables. Then she showed a second image of Prudence reconnecting them early this morning. Prudence's eyes grew wide. Casey smiled and winked at her.

The first thing Austin did was plug his phone into the car charger. After they had been on the road for about an hour, they stopped for breakfast at a mom and pop diner. Austin ordered an egg-white omelet with wheat toast and a bowl of fruit. *Screw that noise,* Casey thought. She ordered a stack of buttermilk pancakes with a side of bacon, extra crispy.

While Casey was finishing up, Austin pulled out his phone.

"Yeah, Thai? My car wouldn't start so we had to stay overnight at the location. And my phone was dead. Yeah, I think it will work out. We saw some pretty great stuff. Yeah, yeah, of course I got it on film."

"Well, at least it wasn't a total loss if you got some footage," Thai told him. "You must have been going nuts, stuck out in the boonies without a working phone. That had to have sucked."

His eyes flicked over to Casey, who was currently in a bacon coma. Her eyes were closed and she hummed a little as she chewed and savored her meal. Even though he wasn't a fan of the greasy meat, the way she ate and enjoyed her food was kind of adorable. "It wasn't too bad," he told Thai, as he shifted in his seat. "But, anyway, we missed our flight this morning. I thought we'd just get a hotel room here tonight. Can you book us a flight for tomorrow?"

"Sure thing. We can get the equipment set up and interview the family."

"Yeah. Do it." He ended the call, but continued to watch Casey eat.

"What?" she asked.

"Just wondering." He extended his arm over the back of the booth. "What's it like?"

"What's what like?"

"Communicating with the dead. You make it look so easy."

"It can be, sometimes. Ghosts like Gladiola and my Gran are simple. They speak words into my mind. It's more challenging with those like Imogene or Prudence who show me pictures. It's kind of like a puzzle you have to put together. It can be frustrating when I can't understand their meaning."

"Does that happen often?"

"I wouldn't say often, but there are plenty of times that a ghost has to show me something several times before I finally catch on."

"For instance?" Austin prompted.

Casey pushed her plate aside. "Okay, you know Tina, right? My boss at the health food store?" Austin nodded. "Well, her grandfather died about a year ago. For over a month after he passed, he kept showing me a picture of his wife, Rose, a fireplace, and a gold circle. Every single night he would come to me in my dreams with those three images. At the time, Rose was still alive, so I didn't know what to make of it. Then, about six months later, Rose died. Tina and her mom were cleaning out the house when Tina's mom found Rose's wedding ring among the ashes in the fireplace. I didn't know it was missing and neither did Tina, but apparently the grandmother had lost the ring years ago. I was bummed that I never got it back to her, but at least Tina's mom has it now."

He stared at her intently. "What?" she asked, suddenly feeling self-conscious. She picked up her napkin and wiped her mouth in case she had a piece of food stuck there.

"What you do—seeing and talking to ghosts—it's amazing." He reached over and touched her hand. "*You* are amazing."

Casey cleared her throat and smoothed her hair. His words of praise were discomfiting. She wasn't sure how to respond. Rather than acknowledge his statement she asked, "Don't you think we should get going?"

His hand was still on hers, tracing a light circle with his fingers. "Hmm?"

"We're done eating. Let's go."

Austin stood up. "Yeah, okay."

Austin drove until he found a hotel near the airport. When they pulled into the parking lot, it was close to noon. They walked up to the registration desk, and Austin turned to flash Casey a wicked grin. "One room or two?"

She pursed her lips. "Two," she said definitively.

The grin fell from his face. "Then two it is." They finished registering and the clerk handed them the key cards. The elevator doors opened, and Austin motioned for Casey to enter first. She pulled her rolling bag and stood on one side of the elevator and he took the other. Both of them stared at the carpet during the ride up to the eighth floor. It was a long, silent trip. Casey wondered if an elevator could move any slower. Finally the bell dinged and the door opened.

They made the short trek down the hall to their rooms. Casey took out her key card. She was almost safely to her room when she heard him speak. "Everything okay?" His voice was unsteady, unsure.

She turned to him, forcing her lips to stretch into a smile. "Yeah, fine."

Austin rubbed his chin thoughtfully, considering how to phrase what he wanted to say. "It's just that, I thought we were getting along. Yesterday, too. But just now … I mean…." He rubbed his hand through his hair. "I guess what I'm trying to say is, I don't want things to get weird between us again."

"I don't want that, either. Believe it or not, I don't spend my weekends planning out how I can piss you off on Monday morning, Austin."

He leaned against the door frame. "Okay. Then why two rooms?"

Casey exhaled. "Ah, geez, is that what this is about? Look, if I were Thai, we wouldn't even be having this conversation."

"True. But you're not Thai." The corner of his mouth turned up in a half-grin. "And I've never been as thankful for that as I was last night."

Casey wasn't smiling. "Look, you said you don't want things to get weird again, and I agree. But that means this," she pointed back and forth between the two of them, "whatever it is, has to stop. Don't take this personally, but I don't want to be your back-up plan or your booty call." Casual hookups might be just another day in the life Austin Cole, but for Casey, the potential to get hurt again was a risk she wasn't willing to take. Though she would never admit it, she didn't like the inequity of power that gave him. Austin's eyes widened but he didn't say anything. Casey stared at her shoes. "Look, all I really want is to take a long hot shower and go to bed. Neither one of us got a decent night's rest. I'll see you tomorrow morning at check out, kay?" Before he could say anything else, she walked into her room and shut the door behind her.

Casey stood under the spray until the scalding-hot water ran cold, then reluctantly stepped out. She pulled a strand of her wet hair to her nose and sniffed. Geez, it felt great to be clean and not smell totally obnoxious. She wrapped a fluffy, hotel towel around her middle and picked up her phone. There were three missed calls, two text messages and one voice mail—all from Austin.

"I can't deal with this right now," she muttered. She threw the phone on the bed then slipped on her underwear, a T-shirt, and some boxers. After she was situated under the covers, she grabbed her phone and called Tina.

"Hey, girl," Tina answered. "I was just thinking of you, but I'm sure you already sensed that. I've been watching *SCI*."

"Again?"

"What do you mean 'again'? My best friend is lead psychic, and it's chock-full of super-hot guys. What else would I be doing?"

"It's the weekend. You could be hanging out with Todd. Remember him, the guy you're engaged to?"

"He's fishing with a buddy. That means I have some time to myself. So, what are you up to?"

"Well, we're in Atlanta right now. Tomorrow morning we fly to Missouri to meet the other guys on location."

"Who's we?"

"Austin and me. He wanted my opinion on a haunted house here in Georgia."

"Well, isn't that cozy?" Tina teased.

"It's not like that." Except it kind of was. At least last night.

"So you two haven't hooked up again?" Tina asked.

Casey's face was flaming. She opened her mouth, then shut it. What the hell was she supposed to say? Unfortunately, her protracted silence was confirmation enough.

"You totally did. Damn, girl. I'm impressed. Nailing the sexiest man alive for the second time. So what? Are you two a thing, now? Should I be looking for your picture on the magazines at the checkout line in the grocery store?"

"Uh, definitely not. It was a mistake both times. Not going to happen again."

"That's a shame. Your mistakes are the highlight of my existence."

There was a loud, persistent knock on the door. "Hey, Tina, someone's at the door. Let me call you back."

"You'd better. I'm expecting a complete report with lots of details."

"Later," Casey said and ended the call.

She groaned and crawled out of the bed. She opened the door partway and peered out.

"Hey," Austin said. He had changed into basketball shorts, a T-shirt and flip flops. His hair was still slightly damp from a recent shower. She inhaled his clean, masculine scent. It short-circuited her brain and made her want to throw him on the bed and lick whipped cream off his chest.

"Hey," she answered softly.

"I tried to call you. Didn't you get my messages?"

"Um, yeah. But I just got out of the shower. I haven't had a chance to call you back."

He rubbed his beard and his eyes narrowed. "Can I come in? I think we need to talk."

No, Casey thought. *'Cause if you're coming in, clothes are coming off.* "I'm really tired. Can't it wait until the morning?"

"I don't think it can."

Casey exhaled and moved to the side to let him enter. Beyond the king-sized bed, there was a small seating area with an upholstered chair flanked by a leather love seat. Austin took a seat in the chair. Casey started to sit on the bed facing him, then, realizing how that looked, moved over to the couch. Now she would have to turn her head to speak to him, but it was still preferable to sitting on the bed.

"You want something to drink? I've got a fully stocked mini-bar with bottled water," Casey offered.

Austin shook his head. He leaned forward with his elbows on his knees, rubbing his hands together. "I've been thinking. What you said earlier, about the booty call? It bothered me—a lot. I don't want you to feel that way. I know I don't think of you that way."

Casey rested her cheek on her hand. "Is this the little speech you have prepared for all your one-night stands?"

Austin's head jerked up. His lips were pursed and the words that followed had a sharp edge. "I never said that. That's *you* calling it a one-night stand. Although, technically, you'd be incorrect since we've now done it twice."

"Relax, Austin. I'm not some psycho stalker chick who's going to boil bunnies on your stove. I'm grown; you're grown. You don't have to let me down easy."

"Who says I want to let you down at all?"

Casey chuckled and shook her head.

"What? You don't believe me?"

"Please, Austin. You're only here because I'm convenient."

"You wound me," He put his hand to his chest. "You know, if I just wanted to get laid, I could go downstairs and pick up someone at the bar. I meant what I said last night, Case. You and me, we don't always see eye to eye." His voice lowered and she felt his eyes and his words undress her. "But when things are good between us, they're really good." He arched his eyebrow suggestively.

Casey stood up and walked over to the sliding glass door. "Be serious, Austin. This can't continue." She leaned against the wall and peeked out the curtain so she didn't have to face those ocean eyes. "The first time, I admit—I was curious, and so were you. I will take total responsibility for that. But last night, you were bored, and I was the only live vagina in the room."

Austin stood up and pointed at his chest. "You think I didn't want to?"

"I think if your phone had been working, we would have been on a plane out of there on our way to the next location. You would have hooked up with Cheryl, or Tish, or one of your other devastatingly gorgeous women when we got back to LA. You're Austin Freakin' Cole. Beloved by all. I'm just Plain Jane Casey from East Texas."

He shook his head and pivoted on his heel. "I just don't get you, Case. From day one, you've been busting my balls, knocking my ego into the dirt. And now, you act like you're not good enough, or something. I'm having a little trouble getting my head around this version of Casey with low self-esteem. If anyone should be insecure, it should be me."

"You?" Casey huffed. "Insecure? That's ridiculous."

"I'm a frickin' ghost hunter who can't see ghosts," he blurted out. He sat back on the bed staring at his hands. Casey didn't know what to say. Talking to the dead was her normal. It was not something she appreciated because her "gift" had only made her life harder. But ghost hunting was everything to Austin. He'd made it his life's mission to prove the existence of something he couldn't even see. "You can interact with the dead," he continued, his tone softer. "You see them just as plain as you see me. Thai can see auras and Luis can exorcise demons. Bob has his Native American spirit guides. Hell, even Gary can hear the dead. But me, I'm just a workaholic asshole with a type-A personality. You guys are the talent."

Casey uncrossed her arms and walked over to him. "What kind of messed up bullshit is this? You're the driving force for the show. I'll admit, I was skeptical at first; I thought you did it all for the money and fame. But I was wrong. We help terrified people expel ghosts and reclaim their homes. We help the dead find peace and cross over. You don't settle for anything less than the very best from us and yourself. Because of you, we're the best damned paranormal investigators in the country. *SCI* couldn't exist without you."

"You really think so?" He pulled at his bottom lip.

She stared up in confusion at this altered version of Austin. The unsure one who was seeking her approval. "Of course. I wouldn't have said it if I hadn't meant it."

"Thanks, Case." He gently punched her shoulder.

"You're welcome." She sat on the couch and he plopped down next to her.

"Then can we end this pity party and agree that we're both awesome?" He looked at her, his mouth slightly open, a mixture of amusement and arousal.

Casey narrowed her eyes at him. "That depends."

"On what?"

"On what you want."

He leaned over and ran his nose along her neck and blew his warm breath in her ear. As he leaned forward, she found herself leaning back into the seat cushion. "What I want right now is to throw you down on the bed and pull your panties off with my teeth."

She pushed him away gently and sat up. "I'm serious, Austin. What happens when we get back to LA? What happens when we get back to the office?"

"Sweet Cheeks, I don't know what to tell you, or what you want me to say. I'm married to my job right now and even if I wasn't, I'm not sure I'm ready for a relationship. With anyone."

Casey felt her face get hot. The last thing she wanted was for Austin to think she was jealous. "That's not what I meant. I'm not looking for a relationship, either. But that doesn't mean I'm okay with sleeping with you today and then you sleeping with two or three other girls later this week. I told you, I don't want to be played."

Austin rubbed his chin. "I know that. I don't want to get played, either. I'm telling you the truth. I don't know what's going to happen down the road. But for the foreseeable future, I want to spend as much time between the sheets with you as possible." His hand glided up her thigh as he nuzzled her neck with his chin.

She leaned back and pushed his hand away. "Can we have a real, serious conversation for a moment? You may mean what you say and you might even try. But eventually, you're going to want someone else."

"How can you be so sure of that?"

"Because I've seen the girls you usually date. I'm not your type."

"I think you're exactly my type."

Casey rolled her eyes. "You date supermodels, not girls who enjoy cheeseburgers. And besides, you don't exactly have the reputation of being a one-woman guy."

He pulled back. "Is that what you think? You shouldn't believe everything you read about me in the line at the supermarket. Yes, I've dated a lot of women. That doesn't mean I'm always looking for my next score."

She crossed her arms and bit the inside of her lip. If she said she didn't want what he offered, for as long as he offered it, she'd be lying through her teeth. She cleared her throat. "Will you at least end things with me before you sleep with someone else?" Heat rushed to her cheeks. *Did I really just say that? That sounded so clingy and pathetic.*

He had the decency not to grin. His eyes bored into her own. "If it makes you feel better, I promise. But I'm telling you, that's not going to happen anytime soon." His statement did nothing to make her feel better. "You and I have a common bond. I'm a ghost hunter and you talk to ghosts. Can't you understand how great it is to be with a woman who I can talk to about *SCI*? Tish and Cheryl are great women, but they couldn't care less about ghosts." He rubbed the top of her hand with his fingertips. "You fascinate me." She looked into his eyes, unconvinced. He stroked her cheek and stared into her steely blues. "Casey, you are a beautiful, sexy woman." He grasped her face with both hands and moved over her, transitioning from an upright position to a horizontal one. He was smiling down at her as if he had won something. Something Casey knew would cost her much more than it did him. It felt like she had ceded what little power she had to him.

He moved to kiss her, but she placed a hand against his chest. "Okay, but let's make it quick. I'm in the middle of a good book and I want to get back to it."

He opened his mouth in surprise. "Um, sure."

Casey smiled. Power regained.

Austin invited himself to spend the night in her room. He went back across the hall to gather his things and came back to Casey's room to take a shower. As he let the hot water rush over his back, he thought about her insecurities. At work she seemed so confident, but today he had seen a fragile side to her he never knew existed.

Then, he thought about their activities that afternoon and began having insecurities of his own. "Hurry up and let's get this over with so I can get back to my book," was not something he'd heard before. During the act, she seemed into it, but she never got super excited. Was she holding back, or was it something else?

When he had told her they were great together in bed, she had never agreed. Maybe he was reading too much into it, but he was still thinking about it after he crawled in bed beside her. "It was good for you, right?"

Casey looked up from her e-reader. "Huh?"

"You know, the sex."

"Yeah, sure."

Yeah, sure? "That doesn't sound convincing."

"It was good, Austin. Sex with you is always good." She continued reading.

Good wasn't exactly a glowing endorsement. "It's just that, I was thinking back. You are so calm. Always so calm. Most chicks start thrashing and screaming. You orgasm quieter than anyone I've ever known."

Casey put down her reader and looked at him. "What's this about?"

He put his hand on her leg. "I don't know. You'd tell me if I was doing something wrong, wouldn't you?"

Casey smiled and shook her head.

"What?"

"Nothing. Never mind. Everything's great, Austin."

"No." Austin propped himself on his elbow facing her. "There's definitely something more to it than that. I want to know what it is."

"It's not important."

"If it's about you, then I disagree. It's very important."

"You're not going to let this go, are you?" Austin shook his head. Casey blew out her breath. "Okay. Here it is: You know those girls? The ones who need about thirty seconds of foreplay, a couple of quick thrusts, then they go off like a bottle rocket?"

"Yeah."

"Well, that ain't me."

"Wait." Austin said, pausing to ponder what she just said. "So, you've never?"

"Not with you." Casey shrugged and gave him a little smile.

Ouch. His eyes grew wide as all the air left his lungs. "Seriously?" She nodded.

Austin impaled his heart with an invisible sword. "You're killing me, Sweet Cheeks." He ran his hand over his face. "I don't think this has ever happened to me. At least not since I turned eighteen."

Austin sat up and leaned against the headboard. He blinked as he mulled over what she said. *Not with you.* "So, I guess it was your ex who made you see stars?"

"Brandon? Hell, no." Casey picked up her reader and found her bookmark.

"How long were you together?"

"About two years."

"Two years? And he never?" Casey shook her head. "Why did you stay with him so long?"

Casey laughed. "That is a very good question, but not for the reasons you're thinking."

"So who was it?"

"Who was what?"

"The guy who made you see stars."

Casey turned to him and raised her eyebrow. "Are we really going to have a conversation about my sex life?"

"Yes, I want to know about this guy that could whip you into a frenzy."

Casey put her reader down. "His name was Jake. He was a guy from college. Really cute and super popular. Kind of reminds me of you. A real player." He frowned at her. "Anyway, I was curious and he was willing. So we ended up together." Casey blushed. "What can I say? Mind blown."

"Did you love him?"

"No. We only went out a few times."

Austin propped his head up with his hand. "Really?"

"Really."

"And you didn't love him?"

"No. I know the difference between sex and love, even when it's really good sex."

"So, have you ever been in love?"

Casey cleared her throat. "I thought we were talking about sex."

"We were. But now I'm curious. So, have you?"

Casey's gaze flicked over to the corner of the room. "Once. A long time ago."

"What happened?"

She turned back to face him. "We broke up."

"No kidding. I mean what happened to break you up?"

She looked over at him. He had rolled up on his side with his arm propped on his chin, waiting for her to begin. "Fine." She put down her reader. It wouldn't kill her to give him the abbreviated version of their ill-fated love story. Maybe then he'd drop the subject. "Robbie got messed up. Got into drugs. I tried to get him help, but every time I'd think he was doing okay, he'd go to a party or meet up with some old friends. Then boom. He was right back into that lifestyle." She looked off into the distance, her voice wistful. "There was a time I really loved him; even believed we were soulmates." *Stupid, so stupid.* "But he stole from me over and over; he lied to me over and over. That got really old." Casey took in a deep breath, more than ready to change the subject. "Your turn. I want to know about all your girlfriends."

Austin arched an eyebrow. "So it's going to be quid pro quo?"

"It's only fair."

"Okay." Austin ran his hand through his hair. "I would like to say I've been in love twice, but the older I get the more I realize that what I thought was love in high school was really infatuation mixed with lust. Stella was the older sister of my friend, Adam. She was the first girl to let me slide into home plate. It wasn't until I got to college that I started hooking up on a regular basis. Then, I met Misty. She was the real thing. I was crazy in love with her. She was beautiful, with gray-green eyes and dark brown hair. No doubt she was the sweetest girl I've ever met. We dated most of my senior year and a little bit after that. But then, *Spirit* took off and it all blew up in my face."

"So you broke up with her to date supermodels."

"No," he said sharply. For a moment Casey thought she might have actually hurt his feelings. "She broke up with me."

"Oh." *Even the irresistible Austin Cole has had his heart trampled on.* "So, what was the deal? She didn't want to do the whole long-distance relationship thing? Got sick of the fangirls?"

"No. She was more than willing to follow me around while we were filming. And, no, she didn't enjoy the girls throwing themselves at me all the time, but she was willing to put up with it. But it was the stuff that always seemed to follow me home after an investigation that she couldn't deal with. I think she was a little bit psychic, nothing like you or Barrett, but she could detect a chill wind in the air and knew if a spirit was around. One day I went out to get us some coffee and bagels and when I came back, she was gone. I checked my phone, and sure enough there was a text telling me it was over."

"She broke up with you in a text? That sucks."

"Tell me about it." He rubbed his chin. "I knew that she didn't like the loft. She had been telling me for a while that she was seeing stuff, but I kind of blew her off."

Casey sat straight up in bed, facing him. "C'mon. You're Austin Cole, the Spirit Chaser. You're telling me your girlfriend told you your place was haunted and you didn't investigate?"

Austin shrugged. "It's like the cobbler's kids are the ones without any shoes. I was busy as hell with *SCI.* I didn't worry about it. Anyway, I called her as soon as I got her text. At first she wouldn't talk to me, but I kept calling and calling."

I bet, Casey thought.

"And calling. Finally, I got her to speak to me. Apparently when I left to get the bagels, something attacked her. I tried to meet her somewhere, give her clothes and stuff back to her, but she didn't want anything to do with me or my place."

"Wow. I'm sorry." She patted his arm. "That's rough."

"At the time, it hurt, but I went on." He shrugged. "And, like I said, *SCI* kept me so busy I didn't wallow in it. But after that, I decided to do things differently. If I met a girl, we'd go back to her place or get a hotel room. That's the real reason I keep an overnight bag packed in the trunk of my car. I don't want to scare anyone like that again."

Casey narrowed her eyes at him. "I really must see this loft of yours."

"Ordinarily, I would say no way. But something tells me it wouldn't freak you out."

Casey's eyes returned to her reader, and Austin snuggled next to her and looked over her shoulder.

"*Opal*?" he asked.

"Yes," Casey said. They read in silence for a bit.

"Did she just...."

"Yes, she saw stars."

"What the hell? He makes it look so easy."

"He's an alien."

"So?"

"So, you're not an alien, or a fae, or a vampire, or even a were-wolf. You're a mere mortal, Austin. You don't have a magical penis."

Austin's mouth flew open and he glanced down at his crotch. "What? You're kidding." He sat up in bed. "Well, that's a crap hand I've been dealt! I can't see spirits or talk to ghosts; I can't tell the future or read people's minds. I thought I'd at least be blessed with a magical dong. Fuck!"

"You have such a shitty life," Casey said seriously.

"Tell me about it," Austin sighed.

Casey turned off the light and rolled on her side. "C'mon, let's get some sleep. That alarm is going to go off pretty early tomorrow."

"Case?"

"Um?"

Austin scooted next to her. "As long as we're going to be seeing each other, I want to tell the crew."

Casey's eyes widened and her jaw dropped. She was thankful he couldn't see her reaction in the dark. "I don't think that's a good idea."

"Case, I'm not a real PDA kind of guy. I'm not going to go around sticking my tongue down your throat during an investigation or pull you onto my lap in the conference room. But I don't want to have to pretend like I can't stand you at work. And I don't want to have to worry that if I do look over at you, someone might suspect something."

He had a point. Acting like mortal enemies or completely ignoring each other around the crew could be just as telling as holding hands and kissing. Plus, she had called Tina right after it happened the first time, even though she had sworn him to secrecy.

Casey sighed audibly. "All right. But we wait until we're back in LA to say anything. I don't want to do this on location and screw up the investigation. And I want to tell Josie myself. Make sure I'm nowhere around when you tell the guys."

"Got it. Business as usual during the investigation. And, Case?"

"Yeah?"

"Can I ask you something?" He paused for long enough that Casey got nervous wondering what was going to come out of his mouth next. "I mean, if you're not getting off, why do you do it?"

Casey felt a rush of heat go to her cheeks. No guy had ever been so up in her business. She shrugged. "I don't know. For me, it's different I guess."

"How? I want to know."

Seriously? "It's relaxing. Like a massage. That's not a bad thing."

Austin rubbed his beard. "I see your point, Sweet Cheeks. That could be a good thing."

"Now can we please be done with this conversation and get some sleep?" She leaned over and turned off the lamp.

He yawned. "Night, Case."

"Night, Austin." He pulled her over to him and tucked her head under his neck. She could feel his warm breath on her cheek as he exhaled. A smile played on her lips. Lying in bed with Austin's arms wrapped tight around her didn't suck.

18

Casey went straight to Josie's office their first day back. She wanted to get her confession out of the way first thing, before she lost her nerve. "I knew it. I just knew you two would get together." Josie got up, walked around her desk, and gave Casey a big hug. "I'm so happy for you. You guys are perfect for each other."

Casey sighed in relief. "Thanks." She was afraid Josie would think it was terrible or might be hurt she hadn't told her sooner. Tina would have dropped a shit-ton of guilt on Casey if she had kept her in the dark for so long.

"I can't wait to tell Liv. She had a feeling this was going to happen."

"Wait a minute—you two talked about me and Austin?"

"Of course. If you think about it, it really makes sense. All this tension between the two of you was really pent-up sexual frustration."

Casey laughed. "I don't know about that. I really couldn't stand him at first. And I'm pretty sure the feeling was mutual."

Josie shrugged. "Things have a way of working themselves out. Now, if we could just get Barrett and Austin back on track, everything would be hunky-dory in *Spirit* land."

Casey rested her chin on her hand. "I know. You could tell when we were at Thai's a few weeks ago how miserable they both are. Why can't they just cut the crap and talk to each other?"

Josie took a sip of her protein water. "Because they're dudes. Underneath all the macho male posturing are hurt feelings on both sides. At this point, I don't know if either one of them knows how to start the conversation. But maybe you and I can figure out a way to help them."

"How?"

"I'm still working on that part. But when I have an idea, I'll let you know."

❧

Austin passed the basketball to Gary. He made the shot and high-fived Austin. "Good game." The guys started over to the showers when Austin stopped them. "Hey, I wanted to tell you something."

They all turned to face him. Thai picked up the ball and tucked it under his arm. It was silent for a moment as they waited for Austin to speak. "Casey and I have been seeing each other."

"Seeing each other?" Thai arched an eyebrow.

"We're dating now. Exclusively."

Gary wiped his forehead with a towel. "How did this come about?"

"I don't know. When we got stuck at the old farmhouse that night … things happened." Austin shrugged.

Thai stared at his friend and shook his head. "You two can barely tolerate each other. Now you're telling me you're in a relationship? That's insane."

Gary shook his head and laughed out loud. He put out his hand and Austin slapped it. "I think it's great, man. Casey's good for you. She keeps you grounded. And she don't put up with none of your bullshit."

"Thanks, man," Austin said.

"She makes you happy?" Luis asked. Austin nodded. Luis patted his cheek. "Treat her well, my son. A good woman is more precious than rubies. Now, I've got to get home. Marie's parents are coming for dinner." He headed over to the lockers, and Gary followed.

"Congratulations," Bob said before joining the others.

When the rest of the crew left the room, Thai spoke up. "What the fuck are you thinking?"

"What?"

Thai rolled his eyes. "Don't play dumb, man. Dating our psychic."

"You're the one who wanted me to be nicer to her."

"Nicer to her isn't code for fuck her."

"What the hell's your problem?"

"What the hell's my problem?" He pointed to his chest. "I'm not the one shitting where I eat."

Austin pursed his lips. Why was this such an obstacle for everyone? Most of the couples he knew met through work, human resources guidelines be damned. The *SCI* team members were the most important people in the world to him. Why wouldn't he want to date someone in his inner circle? "I don't get why you're so pissed off. I thought you'd be happy for us."

"Why would you think that?" Thai dropped the ball and it bounced over to the wall.

"You and Anna are getting married. You're always telling me I should grow up and get serious."

"Yes, I remember giving you that advice, but I never imagined you would test the waters with someone we *work* with. Look, man, I know how you are. You don't have time for a girlfriend. You're too wrapped up in *SCI* right now. Casey may act like one of the guys, but she's a real girl with real feelings. And you are way too focused on work to give her the time and attention she deserves. Everything's great right now, but when the infatuation stage is over and you want out, what happens then? She'll be hurt and you'll be pissed. You think that won't affect the dynamics of our team? You're Austin fucking Cole. You could have any girl you want. So why do you want to screw over *SCI* for a piece of ass?"

A muscle in Austin's jaw twitched and he clenched his fists. He didn't know what made him angrier; Thai telling him he was stupid as fuck for dating a coworker, or him assuming that Austin couldn't keep it in his pants. "Damnit, Thai, I don't tell you who you can date. I'm a grownup, and so is she. Neither one of us would do anything to screw up things at work. So back. The fuck. Up."

They stared at each other for a tense moment. "All right," Thai backed down. "I'm sorry. I was out of line. But I'm warning you, don't screw this shit up."

After the morning run, Casey headed over to Josie's office. "Just the person I wanted to see. Operation Bromance is a go."

"Huh?" Casey asked, as she flopped down in one of the chairs.

"You know. Getting Barrett and Austin to kiss and make up."

"Oh, yeah. You've thought of a way?"

"Tony just gave his notice. He took a job in New York as lead tech guy. That means we have an opening," she said as she raised a pierced eyebrow.

"Josie, you're a genius," Casey said. Her eyebrows furrowed. "You knew about this before, didn't you?"

"Tony told me he was going on the interview but didn't know if he was going to take the job. We'll all miss Tony; he's a hard worker and a great team member, but if we're going to lose him anyway, we might as well bring Barrett back into the fold."

"What if he says no?"

Josie gave Casey a pointed look. "Don't be such a Debbie Downer. You're killing my buzz." She leaned back in her chair. "You said it yourself; he's going stir crazy at home and needs a job. This is perfect."

"And if we got those two together every day, they'd have to speak to each other. It's worth a shot."

"Right," Josie said. "So pull out your phone and give Barrett a call."

The next investigation was a single family home in rural Minnesota. After stopping at the hotel to drop off their luggage, Gary, Josie, Austin and Casey drove over to the Morrison House for the walk through. Gary attached the mic to Casey's collar. "I'm going to go check the camera one more time. Come over to the front of the house when you're ready."

Austin had been standing to the side, but when Gary left, he approached her. "There's something I need to tell you. During the interview with the family I found out this is their dream house. The Morrisons sank their life savings into this place."

"And this is pertinent information because …"

"They can't afford to move. So, they really don't want to hear that they need to leave."

Casey blew out her breath. "Why are you telling me this? I will do the walk through and give them my honest assessment. I don't really care what they can or cannot afford."

Austin put up his hands. "Just letting you know."

Casey walked toward the house, then spun around and faced Austin with her arms up. "Who does that? Who spends their life savings on a place without checking out whether it's haunted or not?"

Austin chuckled. "Just about all our clients."

Casey facepalmed. "That is so stupid. They probably spent a thousand dollars or more on a home inspection for the electrical and furnace, but it didn't occur to them to spend fifty bucks to have a psychic check the place out?"

Austin rubbed his chin. "I know. It doesn't make sense to me, either. But the family is deeply religious and made a point of telling me they read the bible every day. Consulting a psychic goes against their beliefs."

"So, what do they think I am? A Sunday School teacher?"

"Their opinion has changed somewhat now that they are in dire straits."

"That's the stupidest thing I've ever heard. It pisses me off." She crossed her arms."So they didn't want to bring in a psychic. Surely they know someone who's sensitive enough to tell them the place is bad news?" Austin shrugged.

"Geez, they could at least pray for discernment. They read the bible every day, but they don't bother asking Jesus to help them choose a home. Unbelievable." Casey sighed and walked across the front lawn.

Casey entered the house first, and Gary followed her with the camera. She paused in the living room, her eyes darting backing and forth across the floor. Casey paused near the sofa. "What do you see?" Gary asked her.

"There are a few dead here. I see a young woman; she's a mother. There are two young spirits hovering around her. She's standing in front, holding them back with her arms. She's trying to protect them."

"From us?"

"No. She's wary of us. But she's scared of something else."

Casey continued down the hall, her flats clacking on the hardwood floor. She stopped in the mud room, beside the back door. Gooseflesh appeared on her arms, and if Casey had her thermal camera with her, she knew it would register a temperature drop. She wrapped her arms around her midsection and shivered. "I don't like this. This is not good."

"What is it?"

"There is a very bad man here." She pointed out the window. "He likes this part of the house and the back patio. This is his place. He's very dark, very powerful."

"Human or inhuman?"

"He was human when he was alive but very evil. He's been damned but he's made friends with some low-level demons and they let him do what he wants."

"Could he be responsible for the banging noises and the doors slamming?"

"Oh, yeah. He's responsible for a lot of things. He's definitely strong enough to move objects around. And he can manifest. He has a real physical presence in our world. He drains the energy from the living and that makes him even more powerful."

"How does that affect the living?"

"All kinds of ways." Her third eye revealed to her the hell the inhabitants of this house were going through. In her mind she saw two young girls huddled together as a dark presence overshadowed them. The next vision was of a woman with a terrified expression, lying in her own bed wide awake. "Paranoia—although it's deserved. Depression, anxiety, stomach problems, headaches." Casey began swatting the air. She spun around and pressed down firmly on her skirt. "Stop it. Stop it now. Leave me alone." She spoke into the empty space beside her.

"What's going on?"

"He's touching me. He doesn't like women, and by nosing around, I'm making him angry."

"What's happening?" Austin spoke into the mic that went to Gary's earpiece. "Is she all right?"

"Austin wants to know if you're okay."

"Yeah, I just need to get out of here." She shoved the air around her, as if invisible hands were trying to grab her. As soon as she left the mud room, she smoothed her skirt down.

Gary followed her down the hall and stopped when she paused in front of one of the bedrooms. "I understand now," she said to someone Gary couldn't see as she opened the door. They entered a lavender-colored room with two beds. She looked into the camera. "Remember the woman in the living room, the one with the kids?"

"Yeah."

"She's afraid of the bad man. She was married to him and he murdered her. The only reason she hangs around here is to protect the living from him. There are two beds in here, and based on the décor, it doesn't take a psychic to know this room belongs to two girls. But only one bed is used. That one." She pointed to the one farthest from the door. "The living are terrified at night. They sleep together, not that anyone in this house gets much rest." They left the room and Casey pointed to the master suite. "He bothers the mother, too. He has a real problem with females in general."

Casey motioned for Gary to put down his camera. "I think we're done."

They walked outside. Austin was already waiting for them on the front porch. He bent down to look into Casey's eyes. "Everything okay?"

She pulled the elastic band around her hair tight. "Yeah. Fine."

He stuck his hands in his front pockets and nodded toward the house. "You seemed kind of upset back there."

Casey shook her head. "All in a night's work." They walked back to Austin's car. "I want to run something by you."

"Yeah?"

"I'd like to meet with the family before the investigation tomorrow night."

Austin arched his eyebrow. "Why?"

"I need to see the family dynamics before I come to any decision about this house."

"You mean you might advise them to stay?"

"Maybe. It depends on what I hear from them."

Austin pursed his lips and crossed his arms. "Do I need to give you a customer service lesson first?"

"Come again?"

"The people who call us for help are our customers. That means we have to treat them with respect. You have very strong opinions and your filter isn't always on. Even if they say things you disagree with, or have beliefs you don't hold, you have to be nice. Can you do that?"

"Austin, just because I'm brutally honest most of the time doesn't mean I am utterly lacking in the tact department. I can turn on the nice when I need to."

He narrowed his eyes at her. "All right. I'll set up a meeting tomorrow afternoon before the investigation."

She smiled. "Just don't send them a survey."

It was after midnight when they completed the filming for the walk through. Austin pulled into the hotel parking lot. He killed the engine and turned to Casey. "I have a ritual I follow. The night before an investigation, I abstain."

Casey arched an eyebrow.

"I need to keep focused and my mind clear. I've learned over the years that the spirits will go after you if your head's not in the game. The best way I know to stay sharp is with fasting and prayer. And by fasting, I don't just mean food and drink."

Casey narrowed her eyes. "Really?"

Austin feigned offense. "Yes, really. I'm not completely enslaved by my carnal side."

"You know, that's actually a great idea. I've been doing that myself, just not deliberately." Casey reached for the door handle. "Well, I better go in and reserve my own room."

He reached over and grabbed her hand. "No, Case. That's not what I meant. I want you with me in my bed. I want to hold you tonight. It just can't lead to anything else."

Austin grabbed her hand as they walked toward the main doors of the hotel. "Pfft," Casey huffed and rolled her eyes. "Like I'd even want to. You sure think highly of yourself, Mr. Cole. Assuming I wanted to get naked with you. Geez."

"You do want to get naked with me. Admit it. I've got game." He grinned at her.

"Hah," Casey scoffed. "Is that what you call it? If you weren't a famous television star, you'd probably never get laid."

"What? I charmed your panties off, and you're my harshest critic. Or maybe you just want me for my body."

Casey pursed her lips together. "You aren't hideous looking, but that's as far as I'll go."

Austin stopped in front of the hotel room and pulled out his keycard. He shook his head. "Hold it," he said, dropping his gym bag. "There's no way I'm going to get through the rest of the night if I don't get this out of my system." He took Casey's shoulders and turned her toward him. He gazed into her eyes for a moment, then captured her lips with his own. She put her arms around his neck and returned the kiss. They held the kiss for as long as Austin dared. He pulled back, breathless, and rested his forehead against hers. "That's better."

Casey took a long, hot shower and came out of the bathroom in her usual boxer shorts and T-shirt. She left the light on and the door cracked in order to see her way to the bed. Austin was sound asleep, still holding his rosary in his hand. She picked it up and placed it on his bedside table, then crawled in bed beside him. He awoke when he felt the mattress shift as she climbed in. She felt his hand wrap over her waist as he pulled her close. A contented hum rose from his lips, as his hand slipped under her shirt and his fingers caressed her rib cage. Up and down, over and over. So tender, so sweet. His hand never climbed any higher to her breasts or any lower to her underwear. He lay there with his eyes closed as he gently rubbed her side. It was both comforting and comfortable. Before long, his breathing became even as he fell asleep again.

Casey continued to stare at him in the dim light of the hotel room. His dark lashes framed his closed lids and Casey thought he looked much younger and more innocent than she knew he ever was. She tucked her head into his chest and wrapped her arm around him. A pleasant fluttering rolled through her stomach as she thought about the complex and contradictory man who lay beside her. Devout Catholic who dabbles in the occult. Fiercely loyal and won't speak ill of his friends but drops F-bombs as nouns, verbs and adjectives in every other sentence. Won't let alcohol touch his lips, but has no problem with sex outside of marriage. Sinner and saint, residing in the same body.

She relaxed into his side with a sigh. It should always be this simple. They were both here because they wanted to be. Not because of fear and obligation. Not because it was easier than breaking up. She turned her head and stared at him.

Here, in the dark, she could allow herself to be hopeful. Here, in the dark, she could wish for things that would never come true. It might be fleeting; it probably wouldn't last. But this, she knew, was how a relationship should feel.

19

The following afternoon, Casey and Austin were sitting in the living room discussing the findings of the walk through with Mr. and Mrs. Morrison.

"The good news," Casey began, "is that I think we can help you take back your home. The bad news: it's not safe for your family until he's gone."

"Why not?" Mr. Morrison asked.

"He was an evil man when he was alive. From what he's shown me, he's murdered one man, and beat his wife to death. She's the female ghost I was telling you about. She died protecting the children. He hates women; he thinks they're stupid. He loves to scare and intimidate them."

Mr. Morrison sighed. "I don't want my wife and girls living in fear, especially when I'm away on business, but it's hard for me to believe things are this serious. I haven't noticed anything."

"Well, you aren't here as much as your family is, and you're a male. He goes after them when you're not here. If you do nothing, within a few months you will start to see him, too. He's too powerful to stay hidden."

"This can't go on for a few months." Mrs. Morrison shook her head. "I don't want to stay here one more night."

"What if our minister came over and blessed the house?" Mr. Morrison asked Casey.

Austin squeezed Casey's leg. She looked over at him and plastered a smile on her face. "I understand you have deeply held religious beliefs. I'm all for doing a house blessing after the evil entity is gone. It will keep him from returning and offer protection against other paranormal intruders. But, right now, a blessing could actually make things worse. It will make him angry and he will act out in more noticeable ways."

"Like how?"

"Like going after your daughters." Mrs. Morrison's eyes widened. "My concern is for their safety. While I did my walk through, he touched me in an inappropriate way." Austin blinked. He was facing forward, but when she said that, his head jerked to the side to face her. She could see the concern in his eyes. She patted his leg to let him know she was fine, then continued talking to the parents. "He has bad intentions, especially toward your older daughter. And he is strong enough to manifest in our world, so he can definitely..." Casey paused, trying to think of a way to get her point across delicately, and continued, "do things to her."

Mrs. Morrison began to shake, and a few tears rolled down her cheeks. Mr. Morrison put his arm around his wife, and Casey handed her a tissue. She dabbed her eyes. "The girls are terrified. They can't sleep because he stands outside the bedroom walking back and forth. He jiggles the doorknob and beats on the door. When Ron is out of town, I let the girls sleep with me. A couple of nights ago, I woke up, and he was standing over me. He touched my cheek and I could feel something cold pressing down hard on my throat. Then this white mist came between us and he left. If he had stayed, I don't know what he would have done."

Mr. Morrison rubbed his wife's upper arm. "If you get rid of him, will the other ghosts leave, too?"

"Probably. But they're not the problem. For now, I want them to stay. I believe the white mist your wife saw was the female ghost.

At night, she stands in front of the girls' bedroom door, keeping him out. So far, she's been able to redirect his negative feelings toward herself. But he's strong. She won't be able to keep him out forever."

"I know it's frightening," Austin told them. "But this is your house. Not his."

"What do you need me to do?" Mr. Morrison asked.

"I want you to take your wife and daughters to a hotel. Then, come back here tonight. This spirit needs to know you will stand up to him. We'll be with you, but you are the owner and you need to let this entity know who's in charge." He rose and looked at both of them. "It's time to take back your house."

Austin shut the front door behind them, and took Casey's hand. "He touched you inappropriately? Why didn't you tell me?"

"I didn't think it was that big of a deal. The only reason I brought it up was to impress upon the parents how serious the situation was with their daughters. He's just scaring them now. But I know he can and will do a lot worse to them."

Austin stopped and turned to face her. "What exactly do you mean by 'touched me inappropriately'?"

Casey pointed at her butt. "He fondled my rear and tried to reach up my skirt."

"Are you sure you're okay?"

"Austin, it wasn't the first time a ghost tried to feel me up, and it probably won't be the last. It takes more than a phantom molester to upset me." They continued walking to the car. "I'm glad Mr. Morrison believes his wife, even though he hasn't experienced anything. It could have gone the other way."

"Yeah, that's happened to us before. Same situation, too—a woman-hating ghost, husband that never saw anything, religious family. But that husband didn't want us to help. Said his wife was nuts and if there was a problem they'd just pray about it," Austin pressed the key fob to unlock the car.

"So, what happened?"

"The wife called us and asked if we could come see her house. I tried to talk to the husband when we arrived, but he didn't want to hear anything I had to say. He actually ordered us off the property. I didn't feel right about leaving the wife there. She was terrified, couldn't sleep, and absolutely at her wits' end. Her husband worked nights, so I told her we'd be there the next evening after he left for work. This was long before we had a television show on cable, and we did the walk through and the investigation on the same night. Josie ran the cameras back then. She was filming Barrett on the walk through when the bully ghost started playing with her hair and stroking her cheek. Barrett commanded it to leave her alone. When Barrett talks to these creatures, he means business. It stopped touching her immediately."

"Yeah," Casey agreed. "Barrett taught me that. You've got to be firm with them and mean what you say, or they'll take it as a sign of weakness."

"No joke. He's told some of them to leave so forcefully, I wanted to run out of the house myself. So, after the walk through, Barrett tells me the ghost goes after women and is a bully. He also thought the ghost took cues from the way the husband treated his wife."

"Nice," Casey said.

"Yeah. Unfortunately, he was probably right about that. I knew we could handle a bully. I had this whole speech prepared, too. I was going to tell him 'leave now or we'll kick your ass. If you pretend to leave, but really stay, we'll kick your ass. If you leave and come back, we'll kick your ass again.'"

"Yeah, I think I've heard you deliver that speech before."

Austin smiled. "So, anyway, we walk in the door and I stroll over to where Barrett said he was standing. I start to explain the situation to him when, all of a sudden, Thai and Barrett bust out laughing. I ask, what's so funny, and Barrett tells me the ghost took off as soon as I walked over to him. Barrett scared him enough during the walk through that all it took was three strong men walking in the door to get him to leave. What a freaking coward. I sometimes wonder about the wife, though. If she's still with that same guy, she's probably not any better off."

"Well, don't expect such an easy time with this spirit. He's mean as shit and entrenched in that house. As far as he's concerned, it's his place. He's not going anywhere."

"I'm not giving him a choice in the matter."

"I'm serious, Austin. He's not a demon, but he's still a really bad dude. Proceed with caution."

Austin put a finger to her lips. "I'm serious, too, Case. He's terrorizing that mother and scaring little girls. Now you tell me he played grab-ass with my woman." Austin took a breath and calmly told her, "I'm gonna fuck him up."

It was a cold and cloudy night, and the crescent moon cast very little light. Casey joined the rest of the crew in the lounge. "Here's the plan. Gary and Bob, you're with me in the back of the house and patio. Luis and Thai, I want you to get some EVPs and other evidence on the female spirit and the two children. I think the best place for you to be is in the girls' bedroom and master suite. We'll meet at the front of the house in ten minutes. The crew stood up to leave.

Casey approached Austin. "What about me?"

"What about you?"

"Where will I be?"

"Uh-uh. We can handle this. You don't need to go in."

Casey shook her head. "I'm going with you. He's already pissed at me. I would make excellent bait."

Austin shook his head. "No, Case. I don't want you anywhere near this woman-hating bastard."

"I bet you never told Barrett he couldn't go with you on an investigation because it was too dangerous."

His jaw twitched. *Actually, I did once. But he didn't listen to me, either.* "This isn't about me being overprotective. This is about your safety."

"At least let me talk to the female ghost. She's developed a healthy fear of men from being married to that cruel jackass. Do you really think she'll open up to Thai or Luis?"

Austin rubbed his chin. She had a point. "Fine. But at the first sign of trouble, you haul ass out of that house and over to the tech trailer. Don't wait for us. Just go. Got it?"

"Sure. No argument there."

They lined up in front of the house. Austin looked back at his team. "Ready?" They nodded. "Let's do this." He kissed his crucifix, and they all entered the Morrisons' home. They split up and went to their respective areas. Bob, Gary, and Austin headed to the back patio and Casey, Thai, and Luis remained in the house to try to communicate with the female ghost.

"I'll take the master suite. You go check out the girls' room," Thai said to Casey. Luis stood in the hall between the two rooms, ready to film anything that happened. A few moments later, Casey heard Thai call out. "Luis, come here. You need to see this." Luis took the camera and went into the master bedroom.

Casey sat on one of the twin beds. A white mist appeared over her head. It gradually materialized into a solid humanoid shape and Casey introduced herself. "Hello. My name's Casey. If you don't mind, I'd like to record a conversation with you."

Why?

"We are trying to help the family who lives here now. The bad man is bothering them. But I guess you know that." The woman nodded. "What does he want?"

This is his house. He hates the family and wants them to leave. The ghost's eyes were wide with fear. She glanced over her shoulder, as if she thought someone was watching her.

"What will happen if they don't leave?"

She whispered. *This is his house. He will hurt them.* She folded her hands, begging. *Please, tell them they must go!*

There was a loud thump at the door and it squeaked as it slowly opened. The woman transformed into her mist form and floated up through the ceiling.

Austin and Bob were standing on the patio. Bob was pointing to where he had seen the man before he dematerialized. "So, you don't see him now?" Austin asked.

"Not anymore," Bob told him. "He took off as soon as we got close."

Coward, Austin thought. "Do you think he's gone for good?"

Bob shook his head. "He's not the type to leave that easily. This entity is intelligent. He's probably assessing the situation and looking for weak points to attack."

"Let's try and capture some EVPs," Austin told Gary. "Bob, keep looking around the yard and let me know if he shows back up. Maybe the others will have better luck with the female ghost."

A dark mist rolled into the room and Casey's heart sped up. "You aren't welcome in this house."

A sinister, disembodied laugh echoed all around her. Casey heard a clicking sound, and she panicked as she realized it was the lock of the door engaging. She made a run for it, but the entity was too fast. Two hands materialized out of the mist, grabbing her wrists. She came to a jarring full stop. It felt like she had ran into a cold brick wall. There was pressure on her throat, as the being lifted her off the ground by her neck. She flailed her arms and kicked her feet, but all she connected with was empty air. He snarled and pinned her up against the wall. She tried to yell for help, but with the pressure on her neck, all that came out was a muted whisper.

"What was that?" Luis asked.

"I don't know, but it came from the girls' bedroom." Thai ran out of the room and grabbed the doorknob. It wouldn't budge. He banged on the door with his palm. "Casey, are you okay? Casey?"

She could hear Thai. She fought with all her strength, but the evil man only held her tighter. He grinned, obviously enjoying her struggle.

"Hang on, Casey. We're going to get you out." Thai backed up a few steps, then ran forward, slamming into the wooden door with his body. He ran back and did it again. Then Luis took a turn. Little by little, the door began to give.

Gary's head snapped up. "What's that noise?"

It sounded like someone was pounding a sledge hammer into a wall. Austin didn't hesitate. He ran full speed into the house and Gary and Bob followed. By the time they got to the master suite, Thai and Luis had broken through the door. They raced into the room and found Casey shoved against the wall with her feet dangling a foot above the ground. She was gasping as she desperately tried to pull at an invisible force around her neck. Her hands dropped to her sides as her eyelids fluttered shut. Austin grabbed her around her waist and pulled. He couldn't budge her. Something powerful was keeping her body fixed to the wall. Thai jumped on the entity's back while Bob grabbed its hand and peeled its fingers off Casey's throat. Gary ran over and grabbed her right hand and Luis her left and pulled with all their strength. The dark being finally released Casey and glided away. The sudden reversal of force caused the whole group to tumble to the ground.

Austin sat up and pulled Casey onto his lap. He lifted her head off the floor and patted her cheeks. There was a blue-gray cast to her lips and her skin had taken on a ghostly pallor. He leaned over her face and felt a shallow breath on his cheek. *Thank God.* "Casey, wake up. C'mon, Babe. Open your eyes." He tapped on her cheeks.

Casey sucked in a deep breath, then coughed. Her lids felt like they weighed a thousand pounds, but somehow she managed to open them. Thai leaned over, holding on to his sore shoulder. "Is she okay?"

"I think so." Austin sighed in relief as his own heart restarted.

Their voices seemed far off, but their faces appeared ridiculously large as they loomed over her. She blinked to focus her eyes. "Luis, get me a bottled water," she heard Austin yell. The priest nodded and ran out of the room. Her vision was beginning to clear. Casey placed her palms down on the floor and pushed herself up. "Easy," Austin warned.

"I...." She tried to speak, but it came out a croak. Her throat burned, as if she had swallowed hot coals. Luis ran back into the room and handed Austin the bottle. He unscrewed the cap and pressed the opening to her mouth. It hurt like hell to swallow, but the cool liquid did ease the burn.

"Not too fast. You'll get sick," Austin warned. Casey crawled off his lap and slowly rose. "Careful."

"I'm fine," Casey said, but Austin's eyes didn't leave her face and he didn't let go of her. "I want to go back to the lounge."

"You okay to walk?" She nodded and leaned against him as he led her out of the house. He pushed the door open to the trailer and sat her on the couch. Gary handed her a baggie with ice. She rested her head against the back of the couch and placed the cold ice pack on her neck. Austin sat in front of her, his elbows on his knees and his hands folded under his chin. "I know it probably hurts to talk right now. Just rest."

Josie bounded up the steps of the lounge and flew through the door. "Casey, are you okay?" Casey had closed her eyes again, but she gave her friend a thumbs up. Josie approached Austin and spoke in a low voice. "I got the playback of the entity attacking Casey from the static camera in the girls' room if you want to check it out."

"I'll check it later, JoJo," Austin replied, without taking his eyes off Casey. He took her hand and rubbed the top of it.

"I know you want to see it," Casey whispered.

Austin shook his head. His voice was low. "It can wait. I need to know you're okay." Ocean eyes stared into her own with deep concern.

She smiled as she gently waved him away. "I'm fine. Go on."

Reluctantly, he stood up. He motioned to Thai to come sit with her, then followed Josie to the tech trailer. "I'm so sorry, Casey. I never should have called Luis away." Thai said as he took a seat.

Casey shook her head and whispered. "It wouldn't have mattered. He locked me in. There was nothing you could have done." Casey took a sip of water and cleared her throat. "I was talking to the woman. She told me he wants the family to leave and will hurt them if they don't. That's all I got from her."

A few minutes later, Austin returned to the lounge. His lips were pressed together and his eyes were focused and serious. "Listen up," he said in a calm, detached voice. Thai knew that voice. Underneath the placid demeanor, Austin was ten shades of pissed off. "At twelve-fifteen we meet in front of the house. We're going to take this motherfucker out. His reign of terror ends tonight."

Austin took Casey by the elbow and pulled her to the side. "How are you feeling?" Even though she would be staying back with Josie, Casey insisted on meeting with Austin before the team went in.

"I'm fine; don't change the subject." She pursed her lips. "Promise me you won't mess around with this ghost. He doesn't have a sense of humor." Her voice was getting a bit stronger.

"I'll take that under advisement." He winked at her and jogged over to where the guys were standing. She hesitated, then went back to the tech trailer.

Austin approached the front door with the rest of the all-male crew. Mr. Morrison followed right behind. "Ready?"

"Ready," Thai answered for the rest of them.

"Let's do this." Austin kissed his crucifix and opened the door. He leaned over to Thai. "You're my eyes. Show me where the son-of-a-bitch is."

Thai looked around then walked to the back of the house. "Over there. On the patio." They followed Thai to the back door. The shadows elongated, stretching out and defying the laws of physics to conceal the evil lurking there. As they approached, the whole team felt the cold, negative energy the being put off. Bob narrowed his eyes at the evil creature on the other side of the glass. Gary and Luis shifted on their feet. They could sense something was wrong, but didn't know what. Mr. Morrison blinked and took a step back. Even he could feel it.

Austin opened the back door and looked over at Thai to see where to go. "Five feet in front of you and a little to your right," Thai told him.

Austin strode up confidently to the unseen being. "Listen, asshole. I know you think this place is yours, but we have the true owner here and he wants you gone." Austin turned to Mr. Morrison.

"Get out," he said, just as they'd rehearsed. "And don't come back." The living always held the power in these situations, although most of them didn't realize it. If they ever started exerting that power, Austin and the crew would be out of a job.

Thai saw the spirit's dark aura approach the group. Austin couldn't see him, but he felt a cold rush of air in his face. "He doesn't like you at all," Gary told him.

"What do you hear?" Austin asked.

"The guy's yelling at you. Cussing you out."

An invisible force pushed Austin back into Thai. Austin regained his balance and walked right back where he was standing. "I don't like you either, motherfucker. You're a big, evil tough guy when you're trying to scare little girls, but let's see how well your act works against six grown men."

Gary covered his ears. "He's yelling at you."

Austin opened his mouth wide and began screaming, too. The entity jumped back. It moved away from Austin and over to Bob. Bob stood his ground. The being growled, then took a whack at the patio furniture. The metal table flew up in the air and landed with a crash on the concrete. The cushions from the loveseat flew, tearing apart. Stuffing slowly floated to the ground.

Austin shook his head. "Temper. Temper."

The ghost used its full force to slam into Austin. A wall of cold dense air pressed against him and Austin took a step back. He regained his footing and stood toe to toe with the entity.

Austin looked at Gary. "What's he saying?"

"He's taunting you. 'You can't make me leave. As soon as you're gone, I'll be right back.'"

"Is that so?" Austin took a step forward, shoving into the spirit with his open hands. The dark edges of the mist floated back.

"Do it again, Austin," Thai said.

He stepped forward and shoved harder. The entity took another step back. "It's working, keep going." Thai joined Austin, and Bob stepped forward, too. Mr. Morrison and Luis walked up, and soon they were all pushing back on the entity. They kept moving forward, forcing the entity into the backyard. Finally, they were standing on the edge of the property.

"Get the hell out of here, you asshole," Austin said.

Thai saw the dark aura pass through the back fence. Gary heard him issue a parting shot at Austin as he went.

"It's gone," Thai announced. He lifted his palms up. The air felt lighter all around the back patio.

"Good," Austin said. "Let's keep it that way."

With Mr. Morrison's permission, Luis went from room to room with a crucifix and holy water, blessing the house. Bob poured black salt along the perimeter of the backyard. With a sage torch in his hand, he walked the property to close off the backyard and keep the entity from returning. Austin headed over to the front of the house. Casey was standing there, speaking to an unseen being. Austin quietly moved closer so he could hear what she was saying.

"Thank you for everything you've done. The family is grateful that you protected the girls."

The woman nodded and asked, *He's really gone?*

"Yes, he's really gone. You and your children are safe."

The dead woman and her deceased children smiled and waved at Casey. Then they turned toward the light. Casey stood there for a minute, watching as the woman and her children blended into its white glow. Austin approached and put his arm around Casey's waist. "Did they cross?"

"Yes. They're gone now."

"You know, I'm sorry for what she went through, but I'm sure glad she was here. Even though her husband killed her, she came back to protect this family from him."

"She's brave."

"I hope I would do something selfless like that. She postponed her own happiness to help them."

Casey's brow furrowed. "Are you kidding? That's exactly the kind of thing you would do. You wouldn't hesitate to take a bullet for anyone on the team. We all know that."

Austin pulled at his bottom lip. *I doubt Barrett would agree with you, Case.*

While the crew was doing the post-investigation clean-up, Gary walked around the back of the house to the tech trailer. He found

Josie inside and handed her his digital recorder. "I need you to play this back on the big machine."

"What did you hear?" she asked, as she took it from him and adjusted some dials on the sensitive equipment.

"I'm not sure," Gary told her. "I think I must've misunderstood."

But he hadn't misunderstood. Josie stared at him wide-eyed after the playback. "Have you told Austin?"

"Not yet. I wanted to make sure I was hearing it right first."

"What do you think he'll say?"

Gary cocked his eyebrow. "You know Control. He'll probably think it's cool."

Josie replayed the recording. The threat was crystal clear. *This isn't over, Spirit Chaser. I'll be back. And you'd better pray to your God that I finish you before she gets her hands on you.*

20

They took an elevator up to the eighteenth floor, then Austin led Casey down the hall to another elevator. He removed a key and placed it in the lock.

"Your own private elevator?" Casey asked.

"All the penthouses have one." The doors opened to the twentieth floor and Casey and Austin were standing in front of his dark wood and iron front door. "Last chance, Casey. You can back out if you want."

Casey pulled the strap of her tote bag up on her shoulder. "I'm not backing out."

"Okay, here it is. Home sweet home," Austin said, as he opened the door to his loft and stepped aside so Casey could enter. Windows extending from the floor to the soaring twenty-foot ceiling covered one wall. The place was sleek and modern. She stepped into the spacious living area. The décor was straight out of a design magazine, all dark wood and metallic finishes. A large abstract of the backside of a naked woman was prominently displayed on the one living room wall. *That figures,* Casey thought. She glanced over at the state-of-the-art kitchen with its stainless appliances, quartz countertops and custom mahogany cabinetry. Something in the kitchen growled at her, but she ignored it.

It should have been a wealthy bachelor's industrial man-cave. Instead, the place was funky with paranormal detritus. The ceiling groaned. Her eyes drifted skyward. Shattered bits of troubled souls and twisted emotional energy cast a depressing gloom over the living area. She placed her bag with cleansing materials on the floor. "I can't believe you live here like this."

Austin shrugged. "Nothing here ever bothered me. I wouldn't even know it was haunted if Barrett and the others hadn't told me."

"What exactly did Barrett say?"

"He said my loft was unclean. At first, I thought he was making a crack about my housekeeping abilities. I took great offense to that. For a guy, I'm very neat."

"Yeah, you actually are."

"I have to be. The housekeeping staff is scared to come up here."

Casey put her hands on her hips as her eyes swept the room. "This may take a few hours. Is there somewhere you can go?"

Austin nodded and fished his keys out of his pocket. I'm headed over to *SCI* anyway. Thai and I want to go over some footage someone sent us. We'll probably shoot some hoops after that. He leaned over and planted a kiss on her lips. "Have fun. Call me if you need anything." He headed out the door.

Casey lit a bundle of sage, let it burn for a moment, then blew it out. She walked all around the living room waving the smoke in the corners, making sure to reach the ceiling. "All bad things must leave. Only goodness and light are welcome here." She repeated the process in the bathroom and hallway, then continued to Austin's bedroom.

She frowned when she opened the door. Three female ghosts were standing there, giggling. The first had short, straight hair, heavily made up eyes, and a long string of pearls. She wore black shoes with a small heel, and her short dress had fringe that covered the tops of her knees. The second was dressed in an elegant, long white gown and oozed Hollywood glam. Her ruby red lips were pressed around a cigarette holder. Casey recognized her from one of the *SCI* episodes she had watched at Tina's house. The third was a Madonna wanna-be from the early eighties. Casey took note of the large bow on the side of her head, her black and white striped shirt, ripped fish-net stockings and ankle-length black boots. She was smacking on chewing gum and fiddling with the tulle on her skirt.

"All right, ladies. It's time to go," Casey told them, waving the sage around the room.

"Aw, c'mon," the flapper said. "We're not causing any trouble."

Casey pointed at the door. "I said out."

The Hollywood glamour queen approached Casey. "I don't think Austin would appreciate how you treat his guests. He'll have something to say about this when he gets home."

"In order to be a guest, you have to be invited," Casey told her. She blew ghostly smoke into Casey's face, but followed the flapper out.

The Madonna look-alike dawdled. "Who the hell are you, telling us we have to leave?" She blew a bubble with her gum and Casey poked her finger at it, popping it.

"Someone who doesn't take attitude off ghosts. Now get!" she said, waving the bundle of sage in her face.

The ghost grabbed her purse. "Fine." She caught up with the other two. Casey overheard them griping about her as they floated down the hall.

"Austin's new girl is a pain in the ass," the Madonna ghost said in a thick Jersey accent. "He could do so much better."

"What does she have that we don't?" the flapper asked.

"A pulse," answered the glamour queen. They floated through the wall.

Casey shook her head. After she finished cleansing the room, she walked into the kitchen. "Oh, dear," she muttered.

A retro Sunbeam toaster, sitting on the counter, growled at her. Its electrical cord was pulled taut as the old appliance strained to pull itself out of the wall socket and closer to Casey. It looked like a dog trying to break free from its leash. "Yeah, I know you're a big tough guy, but you've got to go, too." She took holy water out of her bag and went to work.

※

Austin and Thai walked in to find Casey lying on the couch, reading. She sat up when they came in the front door. Austin pointed at the foyer. "You redecorated?"

"A little bit."

On the entry table, she had placed a statue of Mary and a bible. On the wall above it, she'd hung a wooden cross. "Every time you enter, say a prayer to keep the evil out. Do this in the foyer, before you enter the loft space. Now come check out your new place." Casey took his hand and led him into the living room.

Thai breathed in deeply. "Wow. It's so light and bright in here." He looked up and pointed. "You got rid of that funk on the ceiling."

"There was funk on my ceiling?" Austin asked.

"Yes. Globules of twisted psychic energy. It was dripping negativity down on the room," Casey explained.

Austin walked into the kitchen. He stared at the clear space on the countertop and two air fresheners plugged into the wall socket. "What happened here?"

"I couldn't save your toaster. It was fucking evil."

"Damn. No wonder it always burned my toast."

Thai leaned against the counter. "I told you not to bring it home."

"What are you talking about?" Casey asked.

"Bryant Antiques and Collectibles. We investigated the store the second season. There was this cursed doll wreaking havoc on the place. Luis exorcised the doll and its porcelain head exploded when he expelled the demon. The shattered bits flew everywhere.

Mr. Bryant walked away from the contents of the store, didn't want anything to do with it, but Austin saw the toaster and had to have it."

"It was cool." Austin said defensively. "It reminded me of my Granny's."

"Maybe," Thai said, "or maybe the demon *wanted* it to remind you of your Granny's."

"I'll buy you a new one," Casey promised. She pointed at the wall sockets. I replaced the fragrant oils with sage and incense. Leave them plugged in for a week. I cleansed the place with sage and put up some barriers, but you should also have Luis give this place a proper blessing. Otherwise, these entities will just come back and bring their friends."

Thai smiled and clapped his hand on Austin's shoulder. "Guess who's hosting the Super Bowl party this year, my man?"

To thank Casey and celebrate his newly cleansed loft, Austin wanted to stay in and prepare dinner for her. She was surprised to learn that he was a pretty good cook until he explained very few places prepared food as clean as he liked it. Casey headed off to the corner grocery to pick up salad and salmon for dinner. While in the check-out line, she glanced at the magazine rack. On the cover of a gossip rag was a picture of her with Austin's arm wrapped around her waist. Curious, she snatched it up and flipped to the article. *The Spirit Chaser Dumps Supermodel to Date SCI Psychic.* There were pictures of the two of them holding hands, running together, and having dinner at Bo's restaurant. There was also a picture of Tish with a scowl on her face. Casey rolled her eyes. It wasn't even a recent photo, and Tish's frown was taken completely out of context. She began reading. The article mentioned how she and Austin were often seen out together and that on last week's episode Austin had called her "Babe." Casey had wanted Austin to delete that scene from the episode, but he overruled her. She was still thinking about it after she returned from the store and helped Austin with the dinner prep.

"Does it take that much concentration to slice cucumber?" He stood beside her, seasoning the salmon for the grill.

"Huh?" she asked.

"You've said about two words to me since you got home."

"Sorry." She put down the knife and looked up from the cutting board. "Did you know that we're on the cover of a magazine?"

"That's nothing new. It's amazing when we're not."

"No, not *SCI*." She pointed between the two of them. "You and me."

"No, but I'm not surprised." He continued seasoning the fish. "Was it a good picture?"

"It doesn't bother you?"

"It doesn't matter if it bothers me or not, the paparazzi are going to post their photos. At least that one sounds accurate. Why? Does it bother you?"

"I don't know. Maybe." She had mixed feelings. "It's weird having the world know about your private life."

He patted her hand. "It goes with the territory, Case. I'm actually kind of glad. Maybe they'll stop posting pictures of me with Rhonda."

"Rhonda?"

"Rhonda Everson. From *Galaxy Girls*." Casey's expression was blank. "You have no idea what I'm talking about, do you?" Casey shook her head. "It's a popular television sitcom about two twenty-something aliens trying to make it as waitresses in New York. Anyway, we went out a few times last year. No big deal. But for months after, they posted photos of us together. She's married and has a kid now, but the tabloids still try to make it look like I'm trying to break up her marriage and get back with her. Her husband's a nice guy. I see him from time to time at charity fundraisers and awards shows. I know he knows it's all bullshit, but I still feel like a dick every time I see him."

Casey thought back to that picture of Tish. Austin hadn't seen her in a couple of months, and she was dating someone in Paris. Yet the tabloids portrayed Casey as the woman who broke them up.

They sat down at the kitchen bar to eat. "I was thinking, now that this place is de-spooked, you could spend the night." His eyebrow hitched up a notch.

"I'm one step ahead of you." Casey nodded to the entryway. "I brought my overnight bag. My toothbrush, too."

Austin smiled. "I'm rubbing off on you."

Casey shrugged. "Maybe. Or maybe I was a girl scout."

While Austin was putting new linen on the bed, Casey began washing the dinner plates. Austin came up behind her, wrapped his arms around her waist and blew warm breath in her ear. Casey smiled and tilted her head to the side. He took the opportunity to run the tip of his nose up and down her neck.

"Almost done?" he whispered.

Casey turned in his arms and wrapped her hands around his neck. She pressed her open mouth against his, closed her eyes, and lost herself in his warm embrace. His lips rocked her to the core, and she felt her knees turn to jelly. Most men just wanted to get to it. Not Austin. He treated the kiss as if it were the main attraction, not just a prelude of things to come.

Casey cupped his cheek with her palm and lost herself in his ocean eyes. He lifted her up, cradling her ass in his hands, and she wrapped her thighs around his waist as he carried her to the bedroom. He threw her on the bed and kicked the door closed with his foot.

21

*B*arrett could hear Austin and Thai discussing their strategy for that night's investigation of the L&D Warehouse. A wave of stomach spasms doubled him over. He turned away and gritted his teeth, waiting for the pain to subside. In all the years they had been doing this, he had never seen a place so thoroughly infested with evil entities. On his walk through the night before, he'd seen two shadow figures and a strong demonic presence as well. It tried to take over his body, but he shut it down. Still, Barrett saw enough of the creature's thoughts to know what it wanted.

"Later," Austin called out to Thai. Thai nodded and waved as he headed out the door. Now it was just the two of them in the quiet gym.

"Can we talk?" Barrett asked.

"Sure, man," Austin took a sip from his bottle of water and sat down on the mat next to Barrett. He bent his legs up and leaned against the wall. "What's up?"

"I had a premonition. You've got to cancel at the warehouse."

Austin rested his arm on one of his legs and exhaled. "This is the finale. We've been advertising this investigation for half the season. C'mon."

Barrett shook his head. "You don't understand." He pointed to his temple. "I've seen images in my head." Flashes of inhuman screaming, fighting among the team members, and preternatural feats of strength passed through his mind. He shook his head to clear them out. "They were violent images.

And the demonic presence spoke to me. She told me, 'One will be hurt and the other one killed.' Austin, she was talking about you and me."

"A she?"

"Yeah."

Austin tilted his head back against the wall. "I'm not afraid of what they—or she—says. They're always threatening to hurt us, and they never deliver. We'll be fine."

"This was different. It wasn't a spirit spouting off during an investigation. This premonition was a warning."

"Well, maybe your premonition is wrong."

"When have you ever known my premonitions to be wrong?"

Austin looked down at his hands. He didn't have an answer for that. In all the years he'd known Barrett, his ability to see the future was spot-on. "So which one of us dies?" the corner of his mouth curled up in a half-grin.

"Austin, this is serious."

"I know. I'm sorry." He rubbed his chin. "So, do you know?"

"No," Barrett said. "She didn't tell me that part."

"Seems kind of vague for a premonition."

"I don't get to choose. The spirits show me what they want me to see."

"Exactly. You're only getting bits and pieces, not the whole picture. You can't expect me to cancel the finale for a bad feeling you're having."

"No." Barrett shook his head. "No. She said it plain as day. 'One will be hurt and the other one killed.'"

Austin stood up and leaned against the wall. "Look, Barrett. I can see you're upset by what you saw. Why don't you sit this one out? You've done the walk through. The guys and I can handle the rest."

"You're already a man down. Bob won't be there."

"I realize that. But it will be okay."

"No, Austin." He stood up and faced his friend. "This is not about me being scared, although I am terrified. This is about life or death." He looked into the eyes of the man he had been best friends with for over six years, searching for any sense of understanding. He ran his hand through his hair. Shit. Austin wasn't going to budge. He was running out of options. "Are you really going to make me say it? Out loud?"

Austin narrowed his eyes. "Say what? Dude, you've lost me."

Barrett closed his eyes and bit his lip. Was he willing to permanently change, possibly wreck his friendship with this man? He felt like he had no choice. "Austin, I love you."

"I love you too, bro," Austin said.

"No," Barrett said seriously. "Not like that. I'm in *love* with you." Austin took a step back.

Neither of the men spoke for several long seconds. Austin stared at Barrett, his eyes flicking back and forth over his face. "No, dude. You're scared for us and you're confusing that for something else. You're in love with Derek." Except, deep down, Austin knew it wasn't true. From the time they first started hanging out in college, he would sometimes catch Barrett staring at him when he thought Austin wasn't looking. He never said anything, never tried to make a move on Austin. But, still, underneath the platonic male bonding, underneath the joking and bravado, the emotion was there. Even now as his friend stared at him, he felt it. Barrett's gaze was intense but not smoldering. Austin knew when someone was checking him out, and this was definitely not lust. This was a very deep connection Barrett felt for him. A connection Austin didn't share.

Barrett blew out his breath. "I'm not saying this because I have any hope that you will return my feelings."

"No, dude." Austin turned away. "I don't need to hear this."

"I know that's not going to happen. I am telling you this because I want you to know if anything happens to you.…" The words died on his lips. He paused for a moment, and finally exhaled. "Please, if you care about me at all, if you care about me as a friend, don't do this."

Austin turned to face Barrett, pressed his lips together, and sighed. "You know I care about you, Barrett. But I'm not canceling." Austin crossed his arms in front of his chest. "Show up at the location tonight or not." He turned to leave. "I won't judge you either way."

"Wait." Austin turned back to face Barrett. "I'll be there."

Austin nodded at Barrett, walked out the gym door, and didn't look back.

"No. I'm sorry I didn't listen to you. I'm so sorry, man." Austin bolted straight up in bed. Casey's hand was on his arm. She was staring at him.

"Are you all right?" she asked, rubbing his back.

Austin's heart was pounding in his chest. *You're letting a little night-mare get to you?* But this was more than a nightmare; it was a memory. He much preferred dreaming about the gorgeous brunette. Austin took in a breath before answering. "Yeah." Casey turned on the bedside lamp. He stared out the windows and realized it was still dark outside. "What time is it?"

Casey picked up her phone. "Two forty-five. You were yelling in your sleep."

"I was?" Austin said. *What did I say?* He wondered, but didn't ask.

"Yes. Do you remember what you were dreaming about?"

"Not really," he lied. He shook his head. "I don't know. I don't want to talk about it." He pulled the sheets off his legs and got up.

"What are you doing?" she asked.

"I gotta get out of here for a little bit. I think I'll go for a run," he said, as he pulled on his shorts and a T-shirt.

"Wait. Give me a second to get dressed, and I'll go with you."

Austin sat back down on the bed and stared into Casey's eyes. "I appreciate the offer, Case, but I really just want to be alone."

His eyes were so serious. And so sad. "Okay. I understand."

He grasped her chin between his thumb and index finger and kissed her softly. "Go back to sleep. I'll be here when you get up, with the coffee made." Casey lay back down and Austin covered her with the sheet.

Casey drifted off, and the next thing she heard was the sound of Austin's phone ringing. Bright sunlight filtered through the blinds. "Hey, Mom," she heard Austin say. She rolled over. Austin was back from his run and sitting on the edge of the bed talking to someone on the phone. "Yeah, okay, seven-thirty sounds good. And I'll be bringing a friend. No, not Barrett. Or Thai. Her name's Casey." His end was quiet for a moment. "Yes, that Casey." A pause. "I know. I want you to meet her. Love you. See you tonight."

He put the phone down. Casey crawled over to him from behind and wrapped her arms around him. He put his own arms over hers and turned his head to the side. "Sorry to wake you."

She kissed his cheek. "Feeling better?"

"Yeah." Even though nothing was resolved with Barrett, the anxiety from the nightmare he felt in the dark of night did not seem so bad in the light of day.

"So, you were talking to your mom."

"Hmm? Yeah." He sounded distracted. "I haven't seen her in a couple of weeks. She invited me out to dinner with her and the new hubby. I told her I was bringing you with me."

Casey bit her lip. "Are you sure it's okay? Maybe your mom wants some one-on-one time with her son." She was more concerned with what meeting his mom actually meant.

"No way. She's excited to meet you. You'll love my mom."

Casey finally settled on a knee-length plum dress with two-inch silver heels. It was the only dress she owned that she felt was formal enough for the occasion. Casey took out her pencil and began to line her eyes.

Austin yawned. He was still tired from the lack of sleep the night before. He was lying on the bed, still in his boxer shorts. Casey wished he'd start getting ready. He hadn't even taken a shower.

"Can I ask you something without you getting mad?"

"Maybe," she answered. "No promises."

"Why do you wear all that black shit around your eyes?"

Casey turned to face him. "I like all that black shit around my eyes." She thought of something. "Why don't you have any tattoos?"

"Huh?"

"You're the only guy under forty-five I know who doesn't have a tat." Even Casey had a small one on her ankle. It was of her third eye.

"I don't know." He shrugged. "I never wanted one. Too permanent." He rubbed his stubble. "I just think your beautiful blues would stand out more if you didn't hide them underneath all that black."

"Wrong. They'd just get lost in the paleness of my face." Casey blew out her breath. "Will you get up? We need to leave," She glanced at her phone. "In forty-five minutes."

Austin sat up. "What's got you so pissy?"

She pulled her hair back in a clip, decided it looked stupid, and pulled it out. "I'm a little nervous about meeting your mom. I want to make a good impression. What if she doesn't like me?"

"Like you? Case, she'll adore you."

"I don't even know if I should be intruding on a family dinner."

He got up and circled his arms around her waist. "C'mon, Babe. I want you there. You're not intruding. Besides, I need backup with my stepdad."

"Wait a minute. Austin Control will walk right into a demon-infested house without blinking, but he's scared to have dinner with his stepdad?"

"Scared isn't the word I'd use. But if I have to be subjected to this dude groping my mother and sticking his tongue in her ear over dinner, so do you. I'm not doing this alone."

A few heads turned and Casey heard a few whispers as she walked through the crowded restaurant on Austin's arm. She felt self-conscious in the shorter dress and heels, but it looked more sophisticated than her usual ankle-length skirt and ballerina flats.

Austin's mother and stepdad stood up when they approached. June Cole Hanson was an attractive, full-figured woman. In her four-inch heels, she was almost as tall as her son. She had a classically beautiful face and appeared confident and secure in her fitted royal blue and black designer dress, which flaunted her curves in a tasteful way. Her light-brown hair fell in soft waves just beneath her shoulders. Casey noted she had the same ocean-colored eyes as her son.

"Mom, this is Casey."

Casey stuck out her hand. "It's nice to meet you, Mrs. Hanson."

His mother wouldn't take her hand, but instead, walked around the table and gave Casey a hug. "Call me June. And the pleasure is mine." She turned and gave Austin a kiss on the cheek. Austin grinned sheepishly and put his arm around his mother's shoulder.

"Love you, Mom." He said adoringly. Casey smiled.

"I'm Lyle," Casey turned to the man who had stolen Austin's mother from him. He was slightly shorter than Austin and his silver hair was thinning on the top. He offered his hand and Casey shook it.

"Nice to meet you," she said. After the greetings, they all sat around the table—Austin across from his mother and Casey across from Lyle. Under the table, Casey squeezed his hand. Although he had exaggerated about his stepdad, Casey could see what he meant. Lyle was very affectionate. If he wasn't holding June's hand, he had his arm around her shoulder. His chair was scooted right next to hers and a couple of times during dinner he leaned over and kissed her cheek just for the heck of it. Casey thought it was adorable. It wouldn't be so bad to grow old with a guy who was that devoted to you.

"So, Casey. We just love seeing you on *SCI*. We're obviously huge fans of the show," June said. Lyle nodded in agreement. "Watching you do your walk throughs is amazing. You are so talented."

Casey blushed. "Well, I don't know if it's a talent. I've always seen ghosts."

"That's what Barrett says, too. We're so glad you joined the team. You let me know if this one gives you any trouble," she said, inclining her head to her son. While they waited for their food, Mrs. Hanson told stories of Austin as a wild, energetic little boy. She got a little teary eyed when she mentioned Austin's sister.

After dinner, the waitress approached. "Shall I bring a dessert menu?"

"I don't know where I'd put it," Lyle said.

Casey and Mrs. Hanson both shook their heads. "I'm saving up for Thanksgiving pie," Austin told her.

After the waitress walked off, June leaned in closer to her son. "Actually, I wanted to talk to you about that. Lyle has surprised me with a trip to Hawaii. We leave the Monday before Thanksgiving and won't be back until the first weekend in December."

Austin choked on his water. "But you just got back from your honeymoon. You're leaving again?"

"Yes, sweetheart."

Austin's mouth hung open in shock. "But you always have Thanksgiving at home."

"I know, dear. I told Lyle this is a one-time trip. He can't whisk me away every holiday."

Lyle kissed the top of her hand. "I know you've always wanted to go to Hawaii."

June smiled and blushed. "Yes, I have." She patted Lyle's hand then returned her attention to her son. "Don't worry. We'll have Christmas dinner at our house."

Austin stared down at his plate. "Yeah. Well, I hope you two have a great time."

"What are your plans for the holidays?" June asked Casey.

"I'll probably just hang around LA."

The waitress returned with the check. Lyle reached for it, but Austin grabbed it first.

"C'mon." Lyle put out his hand. "Let me pay, Austin. You are our guests."

Austin pulled his wallet out and handed over his credit card. "I think I'd like to buy my mother's dinner. You understand, don't you, Lyle?" They sat in tense silence while the server ran Austin's card. As soon as she returned, Austin scribbled his signature on the receipt. "Ready, Case?" He stood up and pulled out Casey's chair.

"It was nice to meet you, Casey. I hope we'll see you at Christmas," June said.

"Thank you for inviting us. It was nice to meet you, too."

"Love you, baby." Austin's mother kissed his forehead. "I'll call you when we get back in town."

"Love you too, Mom," he grumbled.

Austin was silent on the car ride home. He gripped the steering wheel so hard his knuckles were white. The car jerked as he shifted into third, and Casey flinched.

"Easy," she said.

"Sorry."

"So what's bugging you?"

"Nothing."

"Bull. You don't ever drive your baby like this."

At the stoplight, Austin ran his fingers through his hair. "Thanksgiving and Christmas are the two times a year I give myself permission to eat what I want. My mom's an incredible cook, and I look forward to her spread all year long. Excuse me for being a little disappointed."

"Okay, I'm going to ask you one more time. What's bugging you?"

Austin blew out his breath. "I never knew she wanted to go to Hawaii. I would have taken her anytime she wanted. But, no, Moneybags swoops in and looks like Mr. Hero and I look like the dickhead son who didn't have time for his mother."

"That's not true. This isn't a competition, Austin."

"Isn't it?"

"He's her husband, but you're her son. Nothing can change that. Quit giving Lyle such a hard time."

"A hard time is what he's probably giving her right now. If they weren't married, I'd have poked his eyes out for the way he was ogling her at dinner. She's not a piece of meat. She's my mother."

"He treats your mom like a queen. You should be happy she found someone who adores her."

Austin muttered something incoherent under his breath. The light changed and he shifted into second. Casey didn't try to engage him. He was either going to work this out in his own head or stew about it and get more pissed. Nothing she did or said was going to affect his mood either way. After driving for a few miles, he finally spoke. "So you're really not going anywhere for Thanksgiving?"

"Uh-uh."

"So what *are* you going to do?"

"I don't know. I haven't given it much thought." For the last few years, Thanksgiving had just been another day to her.

"Maybe we could spend it together. You and me. Do you know how to cook a turkey?"

"Yeah, sure, if you like your bird dry and burnt."

Austin sighed. "I'd be willing to try to cook for Thanksgiving, but there's no way it would compare to anything my mom made. I guess it's take-out for us." Austin pulled up in front of Casey's building. He grabbed his overnight bag, and they walked up to her apartment.

When Casey finally rolled out of bed the next morning, Austin had returned from his run and was already showered. He was sipping on a protein water and looking at his computer when she walked into the living room.

"Hey, sleepyhead."

"Um," Casey grunted and stumbled over to the coffee maker. "Morning, Mrs. S." She nodded at her incorporeal roommate, Mrs.

Sobelevsky, who was standing in her housecoat and slippers with a mug in her hand.

Austin glanced up from his computer screen. "You have a ghost here?"

"Yeah," Casey said as she poured water into the single-serve machine.

"People with ghosts in their own apartments shouldn't throw stones at my loft."

"That's different. Your spirits filled the loft with negative energy." Casey inhaled deeply and smiled. "Mrs. S fills my apartment with the aroma of fresh-brewed coffee."

Austin's gaze returned to his computer screen. "Your friend Tina called. She's nice. And funny. We had an interesting conversation."

Casey was immediately wary. "What kind of conversation?"

"Did you know your mother's been trying to reach you?"

"Yeah." She had a ton of missed calls from her.

Austin shook his head. "So why haven't you called her back?"

Casey took her filled coffee mug and scooted on the couch next to Austin. "She'll just tell me she wants me to come for Thanksgiving, and Christmas, and Easter and probably Arbor Day, too. She's always bugging me to come home for a visit."

"So why don't you?"

Casey shrugged. "There's nothing for me there."

Austin frowned and handed Casey her cell. "Give Tina a call."

Casey entered her passcode and selected Tina's name from her contact list.

"Hey, girl. So you have company?" Tina giggled.

"Yeah, I heard you two had a nice chat this morning."

"Yes, *early* this morning. Like he-must-have–spent-the-night early this morning. I guess that means things are good?"

Casey looked over at Austin. His gaze had returned to his computer. He was pulling his bottom lip and staring intently at something on the screen. "Yeah. Things are good."

"I nearly dropped the phone when Austin answered. It's still hard for me to wrap my head around the fact that my friend is dating a famous television star."

"So how are things with you?"

"No, Casey. Don't deflect."

"That's not it."

"Oh, so he's in the room with you right now."

"You got it."

"I actually called for a different reason. Look, I know you don't want to go home, but at least text your mom and let her know you're alive. I don't like being put in the middle. She probably thinks I haven't given you the message."

"No. I'm sure she knows better than that. I'll give her a call. I promise. So seriously, how are things with Todd?"

"Wonderful," she gushed. "Terrible," she added with dramatic emphasis.

"Why terrible?"

"He wants me to go with him to Kentucky to meet his folks over Christmas, but I can't find anyone decent to mind the store. I had to fire Kara."

"Kara? You mean my replacement, Kara?"

"That's the one."

"Why?"

"Because she's an incompetent dipshit. Lazy, too. Her boyfriend was hanging around all the time, distracting her from getting her work done. You should have seen the deposits. It took me over an hour to fix her mistakes." Tina blew out her breath. "So, now I'm stuck here."

Casey looked over at Austin. "Maybe not. We finish shooting on the sixteenth. I could probably fly up and fill in for the week before and after Christmas." Austin's head popped up from behind his computer screen. "But I have to leave before New Year's Eve. I've got plans."

"No, Casey. You're a famous television star now. I would never ask you to work at so mundane a place as the store."

"Stop it, Tina. I don't have plans for Christmas, anyway, and it will be fun to come back for a visit."

"You're sure you don't mind?"

"I wouldn't have offered if I did."

"Thanks, Casey, you're the best. I can't wait to tell Todd."

"You're welcome." Casey sighed. "I better call my mom and let her know not to put a place setting out for me for Thanksgiving. Talk to you later." Casey ended the call and started to dial her mom when she felt a strong male presence directly in her path. Ocean eyes stared down into her own.

"So you're going to Shadow Creek for Christmas?"

"Yeah. Tina's going out of town and needs someone to work at the store."

"But what about my mom? She's doing Christmas at her house."

"Geez, Austin. I'm sorry. I didn't realize I was invited. I figured she was just being polite."

"Of course you're invited."

"Let me call Tina back." Casey picked up her phone. "She's going to be so disappointed. She really wanted to go with her boyfriend for the holidays."

Austin grabbed the phone out of her hand. "No. Don't. We can do Christmas dinner with my mom before you leave. You've already committed to Tina."

"Are you sure? I don't want to upset you or your mother."

"Case, that's not why I'm upset. As long as we spend some time with my mom before Christmas, I'm okay with it. What bothers me is that you haven't seen your family in three years. They invite you for Thanksgiving, and you say no, but you eagerly agree to go out of state to work for Tina over Christmas. Do you know how fucked up that sounds?"

"I know it's fucked up. But that's just the way things are. Alone for the holidays beats miserable any day of the week. Just being around my dad gets me wound up. Raw, uncensored truth flies out of my mouth. It's not pretty. And think about it this way: I don't want to ruin their Thanksgiving, either."

Austin rubbed his chin. "How's your mom's cooking?"

"She's a great cook. Why are you asking?"

"We could go to your parent's place together. I could help keep that mouth of yours in check."

"No. Bad idea." She stared up at Austin, who was standing with his feet planted and arms crossed. He was not going to give up. Casey exhaled. "Why would you even want to go?"

"I'd like to see where you grew up. And, of course, sample your mother's cooking. It's a hell of a lot better than hanging around LA eating take out."

Casey gave him the side-eye stare. "What are you up to?"

"Nothing," Austin said. "I just thought it would be nice if you visited your family. And, maybe, while we're there, we could visit a haunted house. I heard about one not too far from San Antonio."

"I should have known." Casey shook her head.

"Look, I was going to go see this house over our winter hiatus anyway. I just thought you might want to tag along. We'll check out that house and eat a great meal with your family, all in the same trip."

Casey thought about it. She did miss her mom. But the real question was, did she miss her enough to put up with her dad? "Fine." She grabbed her phone out of Austin's hand. "I'll call her."

He punched Casey in the arm. "C'mon Sweet Cheeks. This will be fun. Road trip." He started whistling *Over the River and Through the Woods*.

Aces, Casey thought.

22

Sarah Lawson was thrilled when her daughter called and told her she was coming for Thanksgiving. "And, Mom, I'm bringing someone with me."

"That's great. Is it your friend, Tina?"

"No, Mom. He's someone I work with."

"Ooohhh," Mrs. Lawson said. "Well, what's his name?"

"Austin."

"Well, that's wonderful. I better change the sheets in the guest room for him. Gosh, it's been so long since we've had company in this old house."

"Mom, there's no need for that. We can stay at a hotel and just drive in for dinner."

"Nonsense. The guest room and your old bedroom are just sitting empty. You can't come all the way out here from California just to stay for a few hours."

"I don't know. I don't want to upset Dad."

"Why would that upset Dad? Casey, we both miss you so much."

"Hang on just a second, Mom." She muted the phone and told Austin, "She wants us to stay at their house."

"Great," Austin said. "Tell her yes."

Casey brushed her bangs out of her eyes and exhaled. "Okay, fine."

⚘

Per Casey's plan, they arrived at the Holy Spirit Baptist Church right on time for Wednesday night services. There was no time for introductions. Casey found her mother sitting up front with her bible on the pew and her hymnal open. She smiled at them, peering over her readers, and scooted over to make room. Casey heard a few whispers and saw a few elbow jabs as some of the congregation reacted to Austin's presence. Who knew bible believing folk in a small town in Texas would be avid fans of a ghost-hunting show? Her stomach fluttered with nerves. *What if one of the parishioners told Dad?* The organist began playing the opening hymn, and Reverend Lawson motioned for everyone to rise. He glanced down at his daughter and smiled when he saw her back in his church, singing hymns, just as she had when she was a little girl. During the sermon, Casey watched Austin. He sat in rapt attention as her father spoke of being thankful to the Lord in all circumstances. And when it was time for prayer, Austin displayed the same reverence he would have in the Catholic Church. At the close of service, they filed out and waited on the church steps as Reverend Lawson greeted his flock.

Casey stood by her mother and Austin observed them together. Mrs. Lawson kept looking at her daughter—smiling, giving her frequent hugs, and whispering in her ear. Casey might have her dad's features, but she definitely got her red hair and steely blue eyes from her mom. Unlike Casey's dyed and highlighted reddish-brown hair color, Mrs. Lawson's hair had faded with age to an orangey-blond with streaks of silver. She was the same height as her daughter, but about fifteen pounds heavier. They both wore long, ankle-length skirts and a cardigan over a blouse. Mrs. Lawson's makeup was minimal. A light, rose-colored lipstick and a bit of dusty pink blush on her cheeks. Casey had no color on her cheeks, but had coated her lips in dark maroon, and her eyes were lined in that black shit she was so fond of. They were similarly attired, but Mrs. Lawson came off as a respectable preacher's wife, while Casey looked more like an emo gypsy.

Austin stuck out his hand as Reverend Lawson approached. He was a tall, thin man, with hair that had at one time been dark brown but now had streaks of silver running through it. "Pleased to meet you, sir. I really enjoyed your sermon." Casey rolled her eyes and mouthed the words "Suck up." Austin ignored her.

"Thank you. It's good to meet you, too. We're so glad you could join us for Thanksgiving."

He turned to his daughter and awkwardly wrapped an arm around her. She bristled, but allowed it. He planted a kiss on her forehead. "It's good to see you, Casey."

Rather than lie she said, "Thanks for having us. I've missed Mom's cooking."

"Speaking of ... are you two hungry? Should I fix you something when we get home?" Mrs. Lawson fretted.

Casey shook her head. "Mom, we're fine. We ate on the way here."

"Are you sure? Austin, if you're hungry, you have to speak up."

Austin rubbed his stomach. "No, ma'am. I'm good. I'm saving up for tomorrow. Casey told me what a wonderful cook you are."

Mrs. Lawson blushed and Casey mouthed the words, "Double suck up."

It was a short, ten-minute drive home from the church. "Why don't you two go into the den? I'll bring us some iced tea, and we can all sit and visit."

Casey groaned. "Mom, we've been in the car all day, and we're exhausted. Can't we just talk in the morning?"

"Of course." Mrs. Lawson smiled to hide her disappointment. "Austin, let me show you to your room."

"Good night, sir. Good night, Casey." He pressed a chaste kiss to her cheek and followed Mrs. Lawson up the stairs.

Casey started to grab her bag, but her dad picked it up before she could. "Here, I'll help you."

"You don't have to."

"I got it," Reverend Lawson said.

She opened her bedroom door and was transported back in time. The pink and white striped curtains her mom had made to match her Hello Kitty bedspread still hung from her windows. The desk was untouched, and her trophies from middle school baton competitions sat on the bookcase. The only things missing were the posters of the Backstreet Boys she used to have hanging on the wall. Mrs. Lawson had replaced them with some of her own framed needlepoint.

Her dad placed the bag on the foot of the bed. He put his hands on his hips and thought about what he wanted to say. "We've missed you. We're both so glad you decided to come home."

Casey laughed humorlessly. "Decided to come home? Dad, you kicked me out."

"Casey, I..." he started. He rubbed his chin. Finally, he spoke. "Love you. Good night." He pressed a small kiss to her forehead and left.

She walked over to the bookcase. Her entire collection of *Little House* books was still there, along with some G-rated romance books. She picked one up and plopped down on her bed. After reading for a half hour, she heard her doorknob turn, and gazed at the door as Austin slipped inside her room.

"It's about time," Casey said, as she put the book on the bedside table.

"I wanted to make sure your parents were in bed first." He knelt down next to her and looked around the room. "This is so not you."

"Believe it or not, at one time it was."

"No way. When?"

"I guess I was about eight."

"I can't ever imagine you liking pink." He pointed to the bed-spread. "And Hello Kitty? I would have thought Wednesday from the Addams family would be more your taste."

"Well, of course. But you try and find an Addams Family bed-spread at the thrift store. Impossible." She traced the outline of the cat with her finger. "When I was in high school, I wanted to dye it black, but my mom vetoed that."

Austin's arms encircled her and he pressed his mouth against hers. She could feel the corners of his lips pull into a smile. "I'm glad. I'm going to have fun doing you in your childhood bed."

Casey wrapped her fingers around his neck and pulled his mouth to hers. After a moment, she told him, "You'll get no protests from me." She flipped off the lamp and Austin crawled in beside her.

He pressed his strong lips to hers and kissed her until they were both out of breath. He took a condom package out of his pants pocket then removed them. She flung her blouse and skirt to the floor and pulled the tie out of her hair. Her long, wavy hair fell down over her shoulders. Austin crawled on top of her, pulled her arms over her head and pressed kisses along her throat and breast bone.

Casey flipped him over so that she was straddling his hips. She leaned over and captured his mouth with her own while she un-hooked her bra. Her long, red tresses fell over her breasts. Austin pushed her hair over her shoulder. "We'll have to be quiet," he warned.

Casey hooked her fingers in his boxers and pulled them down and off in one fluid motion. "No worries. I'm not a screamer," she whispered. Austin lay back and let Casey drive. Afterward, he rolled her over onto her side and grabbed a Ziplock baggie from his pants pocket.

"Is that really necessary?" Casey asked, watching him put the used condom in a baggie and place it in his pants pocket.

"Casey, your dad is a Baptist preacher and we are engaging in premarital sex in his home. There's no way I'm going to throw this in the trash for your parents to find."

"You could just roll it up in some toilet paper. It's not like my mom sifts through the garbage."

"Nope. I'll take care of it. Your mom is a sweet lady. She shouldn't have to deal with my used sperm, even if it's in the trash." He stood up and slipped his pants back on.

"You're not leaving, are you?"

He leaned over and kissed her forehead. "I think I've pushed my luck being in here this long." He put his hand on the doorknob, then turned to face her. "Night, Sweet Cheeks."

"Night, Control."

Casey awoke to the smell of coffee brewing. She would have lingered in the shower, but she didn't want to leave Austin downstairs alone with her parents. She got dressed and headed straight for the kitchen. Mrs. Lawson gave Casey a quick kiss on the cheek. Her father was already sitting at the breakfast table, reading the paper.

"If you're looking for Austin, he went for a run," her mother said. She had set out a pan to fry bacon and was heating the skillet for pancakes. "He was up before the chickens this morning."

"Yes, he's an early riser." Casey grabbed a mug, filled it with coffee.

"I think I startled the life out of him this morning. I was in the kitchen seasoning the turkey when he walked in. I don't think he expected anyone to be up that early."

Casey finished her coffee and helped her mom with breakfast preparations. While Casey was setting the table, Austin returned. "Umm, smells good." He walked over to the sink and washed his hands.

"How was your run?" Reverend Lawson asked.

"It was a lot colder than I'm used to, but the scenery was beautiful."

"That was the cold front that blew through last night. It's not usually this cold in November. Maybe later I could take you for a tour of the property."

"I'd like that, sir."

Everyone took a seat and Mrs. Lawson began passing around the sausage, eggs, biscuits, and gravy. Austin tried a little of everything to be polite, but Casey noticed he filled up on the eggs, the healthiest food her mother served. He leaned back and rested one of his arms around the back of Casey's chair. "That was delicious."

Mrs. Lawson glanced at Austin's arm, casually wrapped around her daughter's shoulder. "So, do you two have some news to tell us?" She peered up at Casey hopefully.

"Sarah." There was a warning in his voice.

"You told me not to bombard them with questions last night. You didn't say anything about over breakfast."

"What's going on, Mom? Spit it out."

Mrs. Lawson's eyes lit up in excitement. "It's just that you've never brought a young man home before. I thought you might have some good news to share."

"Is that what you think?" Casey started laughing, then snorted. "No." She pointed to herself and Austin. "Don't go planning a wedding. We're just sleeping together." The smile fell from Mrs. Lawson's face and her eyes grew big.

Austin moved his hand under the table and stared down at his plate. He went from white, to dusky pink, to tomato red in seconds. He leaned over to her and whispered, "Knock. It. Off."

She ignored him and continued, "It was really cute how you put us in separate bedrooms, but as soon as you were in bed, Austin snuck in my room and boinked my brains out on my Hello Kitty comforter."

"Casey," her father said, sharply. "That's enough of this sinful talk."

Casey threw down her fork. It clattered on the china plate and her mother jumped. "What? She asked me a question about our relationship status, and I told her the truth. Thou shalt not lie. That's a sin too, Dad."

Reverend Lawson opened his mouth to respond but closed it as his dead mother entered the room. She was wearing the same faded pink house dress that Casey always remembered her in. Casey's eyes followed her semi-translucent form to the table, where she took a seat across from Austin. When her dad finally spoke, he was calmer. "I would remind you of the commandment to Honor thy father and mother as well," he said, never taking his eyes off Casey's Gran.

Casey would have liked to say something more, but out of respect for her grandmother, she didn't. Instead, she stood up, shoved the chair under the table, and stomped out the front door, letting the screen door slam behind her. She paced on the front porch and wished for a cigarette. She didn't smoke, but this would have been a great time to light up. It would have aggravated her dad even more.

Austin appeared a moment later with her coat. "Let's walk," he said, but he didn't look her in the eye. She slipped her arms through the sleeves and they headed for the woods. The dead leaves crunched on the ground under their footsteps. Casey blew on her hands to warm them up. When they were out of earshot, Austin stopped. "What the fuck's your problem?"

"Austin, I'm twenty-five years old. I'm not going to ask my parents for permission to have sex." She pulled her hand through her hair. "It's all an act, anyway. I'm quite sure they know I haven't saved myself for my wedding night."

"It's one thing to assume your daughter isn't as pure as the driven snow. But to shove the fact in their faces? You just gave your dad a visual of my giant cock thrusting into his daughter's helpless vagina."

"It's average."

"What?"

"You said your cock was giant. Actually, it's average size."

"Whatever, Casey." Austin put his hands on his hips and pivoted on his heel. "Your dad and I were getting along, and now he's probably ready to light up my ass with his shotgun. And your poor, sweet mother. Did you see her face when she thought we were here to announce our engagement? A simple no would have sufficed. You didn't have to destroy her by making it sound like we're just friends with benefits."

"Well, that's what we are," Casey said.

His brow furrowed and he rubbed his chin with his hand. "Yeah. I guess we're just *fuck* buddies." His jaw twitched as he looked at her a moment more, then he turned around and headed back to the house.

"Hey, where are you going?"

"I'm going to try to smooth things over with your dad."

"You don't have to apologize to him."

He turned around to face her, but continued walking backward. He lifted his arms in the air. "Somebody needs to."

Casey waited a few minutes, then headed to the back porch. She sat down on the swing and, a moment later, felt a presence next to her, moving it gently back and forth.

"What's up, Gran?"

I should be asking you that. You sure love stirring the pot.

"If you came out here to give me a lecture…."

No, I came out here to spend time with my favorite granddaughter. Her incorporeal hand tried to pat Casey's knee, but passed straight through her leg.

"I'm your only granddaughter."

Technicality. She shrugged. It was then that Casey noticed the mixing bowl in Gran's lap. *For Thanksgiving dinner. Everyone loves my cornbread dressing.*

"I'm sorry about earlier, Gran. I'm embarrassed that you had to hear that argument at the breakfast table."

Nonsense, dear. I like your guy; he's hot. I'd be hitting that every night, too.

"Gran!"

What? I'm dead, not blind. I'm just glad you didn't have this discussion tonight at Thanksgiving dinner. I don't think your brother and his wife would have appreciated it.

Her brother Seth had followed in his father's footsteps. He was a youth pastor, and his wife the organist, of a large church in Dallas. Seth was even more self-righteous and sanctimonious than her dad was. Casey chuckled. "I could see Seth's face turning blue from having a coronary while Lisa rushed to cover the boys' ears."

Gran chuckled. *If he survived, he'd be calling down hellfire and brimstone on your sinful derriere. I love Seth dearly, but he's so uptight. Not at all like your man. He's a keeper, that one. And he's completely devoted to you.*

Casey rolled her eyes. "Austin is completely devoted to Austin."

Gran put down her paring knife. *Have you seen the way he looks at you?*

"Yeah. Like I'm the flavor of the month. He'll grow tired of me soon enough." *Or at least he'll grow tired of my shit.*

I wouldn't be so sure about that. Gran sighed and returned to her peeling. Casey stared off into the distance. Things with Austin were complicated, and thinking about their last conversation put knots in her stomach. Gran's voice tore her away from her thoughts. *Anyway, before I came out here I was with your mom in the kitchen. She was whisking the eggs so hard I thought they were going to fly out of the bowl. And she mumbled something about you just getting here and now you'll probably up and leave. Maybe you should go reassure her. Offer to help with the green bean casserole or something?*

"Yeah, I probably should." Casey started to tell her Gran she'd see her at dinner, but she had already vanished.

Through the cracked door to her father's study, Casey spied Austin and her father. They were deep in discussion but, thankfully, there were no raised voices and her father's shotgun was nowhere to be seen. Casey crept past the door silently and walked into the kitchen. Her mom was facing the counter, cutting up a stalk of celery. She came up behind her and gave her a hug. "I'm sorry, Mom. I was out of line."

Sarah Lawson turned and scolded. "Yes, you were." She turned and hugged Casey back. "But I forgive you."

"And I'm sorry I haven't called or visited. I'd like to help you with dinner, if that's okay. I've really missed you, Mom."

Sarah Lawson cupped her daughter's cheek. "Me, too. Now let's put it behind us and try to have a drama-free Thanksgiving meal. Can you grab a casserole dish from the cabinet?" Casey bent down and pulled one out. "It'll be so good to have both of my babies home this year."

"Well, if it isn't the prodigal sister returned!" Seth said as he walked in the front door. He leaned over and gave Casey a hug. Her nephews ran past them into the den.

"Ha ha," she said. Ordinarily, she would have flipped him off, but she hadn't seen him in over three years, and she didn't want to upset everyone any more than she already had.

Austin stuck out his hand, "Nice to meet you. I'm Austin." He wanted to greet Seth first, before Casey decided to introduce him as her boy toy or something.

"Seth. Nice to meet you. And this is my wife, Lisa."

"Pleased to meet you, Austin. Those two blurs that ran into the den are our sons, Cameron and Caleb." Austin recognized the Mario Brothers theme song playing in the other room.

"Well," Reverend Lawson said. "I was going to show Austin around the property. You want to join us?" he asked his son.

"Sure thing. Let me just grab my coat."

The men were gone for over an hour, and Casey didn't have a chance to speak to Austin before dinner. When her mother announced it was time to eat, he deliberately avoided Casey, choosing instead to sit next to Casey's nephews. Gran materialized in the chair across from Austin and gave Casey a mischievous wink. It was Seth's turn to say grace, and he took his typical time about it while everyone sat quietly with their stomachs growling. He droned on and on, thanking God for everything from family and food to God healing one of his flock from an ingrown toenail. Casey opened one eye to peek over at Austin. He was sitting with his head bowed, listening respectfully.

Finally, the prayer concluded, and Casey's mom began passing the serving platters around. Austin was quiet, only speaking when asked a question by one of Casey's family. Too quiet. *Geez, he's really pissed.*

"That was delicious, as usual, Sarah," her father said.

Mrs. Lawson smiled. "Thank you, dear. But I had help." She looked over at the other two women at the table.

"Well, you all did a fine job," her dad smiled at Lisa and glanced over at Casey. She averted her eyes.

"How about you guys go on in the den? The girls and I will clear the table. After that, we'll make coffee and bring you each a slice of pumpkin pie," Mrs. Lawson said.

Seth held his stomach. "Why don't you wait a little bit, Mom? We're stuffed."

"C'mon, Austin." Luke Lawson clapped his hand on Austin's shoulder. "It's a Thanksgiving tradition for the menfolk to watch the football game while the womenfolk put up the leftovers."

"I think you mean it's tradition for the menfolk to fall asleep in front of the television, while the women continue to slave in the kitchen as they have all day," Lisa teased. Austin followed Seth and Mr. Lawson into the den, without even glancing in Casey's direction.

It was a completely sexist tradition, but this year Casey didn't mind. She wanted to be alone with her thoughts, and she could do that more easily as she washed the dishes on auto pilot. She hated that Austin was angry with her and she hated even more that it was all her fault. After the last plate was cleaned and put away, Casey excused herself. "I'm going to bring Austin his pie."

She headed to the den with a slice of pumpkin pie for Austin and a cup of coffee for herself. All three men were snoring as the football game droned on in the background.

She tapped Austin on the shoulder and he awoke with a start. "Sorry, I didn't mean to frighten you."

He rubbed his face. "It's okay."

"I brought a peace offering," she said, handing him the plate and fork.

"Um, thanks," he said curtly.

"Can we go outside and talk?"

Austin said nothing but nodded his head and followed her out to the back porch. Casey put her coffee cup down on the railing. "Look, I'm sorry about this morning. This thing with my dad, well, it's been going on for a while. I had no right to put you in the middle." Austin put his pie plate down and stood there, staring at her with his arms crossed.

"Geez, Austin, say something. At least cuss me out."

He tried to remain serious, but she could see the corners of his mouth pulling up in a grin. He rubbed his beard. "What am I going to do with you?"

"Rip off my clothes and spank my bare bottom?"

He grabbed her by the waist and pulled her over his lap as he sat down on the porch swing. He raised his hand like he was going to smack her hard, then, at the last moment, tapped her lightly on the rear. "You should be careful what you ask for, Sweet Cheeks. I'll be sure to grant your request as soon as we get back to LA." He pulled her up so she was sitting next to him instead of on top of him. "It's not entirely your fault. I mean, no, you shouldn't have announced it, but I shouldn't have snuck into your room last night, either. This is your parents' home, and we both know better. Look, I'll make a deal with you. If you make peace with your dad before we leave on Sunday, I'll forgive you and your big mouth."

"You drive a hard bargain."

He grabbed the pie off the railing. "Your dad's not a bad guy. He really loves you."

"He has a funny way of showing it. Everything I do is wrong in his eyes."

"I don't think so. He loves you, and he's very proud of you. He *is* concerned for your spiritual welfare. And, rightly so—the way you act sometimes, I'm sure you're going to hell." He gave Casey a lopsided grin and she punched him in the shoulder. "Actually, he's concerned for both of us. He's seen the show and thinks we are putting our immortal souls in peril."

Casey's eyes grew big. *Oh shit!* "He's watched *Spirit?*" Austin nodded. "What did you tell him when he said you were risking your soul?"

"I told him he didn't need to worry, that I was a good Catholic boy. He would have bought it, too, if you hadn't blurted out what you did at the breakfast table this morning. By the way, I apologized for our disrespectful behavior in his home and assured him it would not happen again. I left out the part about it not being entirely my fault because his daughter has an irresistible bootie."

"That was probably a good call," Casey said.

Austin swallowed a forkful of pie. "He accepted my apology, but he's more concerned about us communicating with the dead. I told him that a certain amount of danger goes along with what we do, but I assured him that we never forget who and what we are dealing with. You should be glad he cares. My dad didn't give half a shit about me until *Spirit* took off. Then he wanted to be my best buddy. Funny how having a millionaire son can suddenly turn a person into an attentive parent," Austin said, taking another bite of the pie. He closed his eyes and tilted his head back. "Man, your mom can cook. I haven't had homemade food like this in so long."

"Yeah, well, Mrs. Smith made that pie, not Mrs. Lawson. But the rest is all her. She is a very good cook."

Austin licked his fork and patted Casey's leg. "C'mon. If we're going to check out that location tomorrow, we need to get rested up. It's about a four-hour drive."

Everyone was having dessert in the den when they walked in. Austin stepped into the room and said, "We're going to turn in. Dinner was delicious, Mrs. Lawson."

Mrs. Lawson laughed and said, "You are most welcome." She stood up. "Thank you for bringing Casey home." She gave Casey and Austin both a hug and a kiss. "You come for dinner anytime you want."

They walked upstairs and Austin paused in front of Casey's room. He grabbed her waist and pulled her close. His mouth closed over hers and she felt the firm pressure from those amazing lips all the way down to her toes.

"So, I guess I'm forgiven?" Casey asked as she traced the side of his cheek with her finger.

"Yes." He leaned in, tickling her nose with the tip of his own and rubbing his beard against her cheek. She shivered as he blew his warm breath against her neck. He kissed her once more then pulled away. "See you in the morning, Sweet Cheeks." He slapped her on the rear and walked down the hall to his room.

They left at five the following morning. At first Casey was in an upbeat, chatty mood, despite the early hour. As they got closer to San Antonio, a feeling of intense dread came over. It was a hollow, sinking feeling in the pit of her stomach. A red light appeared in her mind and she saw the image of a foot slamming down on a brake pedal, a clear warning from her third eye. Casey shifted in the car seat and rubbed her forehead. "How far are we from this place?"

"About fifteen miles."

Casey blinked. She had never known an evil presence that could affect her from that far away. "How'd you say you found this location again?"

"Someone emailed me," Austin told her. She would never believe him if he said it came to him in a dream. Hell, he didn't even believe it himself.

The closer they got, the worse Casey felt. *Avoid! Stay Away!* Her third eye was frightened and that only added to Casey's unease. "Maybe we should stop for lunch first."

"Case, I promise I'll feed you when we're done. We're almost there."

They drove a little farther. She ran every excuse she could think of through her mind, trying to come up with a reason to bail on this house. But she couldn't come up with anything she thought Austin would go for. If she couldn't avoid, maybe she could delay. "Can you pull over? I need to go to the little girl's room." He sighed, but turned in at the nearest gas station. Casey wasted as much time as she dared, then finally left the bathroom. Austin was leaning against the car. He smiled when he saw her emerge, but he was pacing, and she knew he was growing impatient with her.

"I thought you fell in. I was about to have the lady in the store go check on you."

"Real funny," she said as she opened the passenger side door. Casey knew this was more than just apprehension. She couldn't shake the feeling that it was all inevitable. Things were in motion that were too powerful and too evolved to stop. *Let's just get this over with.* She was speaking to herself as much as she was telling her third eye.

As soon as Austin pulled into the dirt road of the property, Casey's blood ran cold. This was the darkest place she'd ever encountered. The bright, Texas sun didn't shine on this place. Shadow figures appeared in front of her, then suddenly vanished. Tormented ghosts wandered the property, in search of a way out. She closed her eyes, said a prayer, and clutched the cross around her neck.

Austin parked in front of a dark, three-story edifice. Casey stepped out of the car and stared up at it. Her vision went white as a stabbing pain ripped through her skull. She bit back a moan, realizing that this hulking evil masquerading as a house, was the third location. The portal from the warehouse joined the one in Brad's room at the Thompson House, and terminated at this site. What were the fucking odds?

In its heyday, it must have been a beautiful mansion, but now it was a dilapidated gray monstrosity that reeked of evil. The paint was peeling and dull from weather exposure. The ivy and hedges were overgrown and weeds grew up between the stone pavers in the courtyard. The stone gate surrounding it was falling down. The glass in the windows was intact, but so dirty, you couldn't see through it. But what really bothered her was the number of spirits walking around the property. She guessed there must be at least sixty or seventy ghosts in the front yard alone. The dead noticed her presence and approached the car. Casey backed away from them and hoped Austin didn't notice her strange behavior.

"I've done some research. This place is called Enchanted Hill Manor, built in 1910." *Enchanted Hill Manor?* Casey wondered. It was too innocuous a name for the terror that overshadowed this nightmare of a house. Only the darkest of fairy tales could even begin to describe the ancient evil that inhabited this place. Casey looked over at Austin. He had taken out his phone and was snapping pictures. "I won't tell you any more about it, because I don't want to taint your walk."

But Casey didn't need him to tell her anything, because the evil permeating the place shouted out its violent and demonic history. Her third eye showed her the first owner of the place. He went mad and stabbed his wife at the dinner table. The second set of owners had seven children and five of them died of mysterious illnesses before their tenth birthdays. The other owners didn't fare much better. There were bankruptcies, floods, disputes with the townfolk—no one who ever lived here prospered.

The west side of the house sat on a naturally occurring portal to the spirt realm. It was active and the dead were constantly passing through it. Satanic rituals had been conducted on this sight for a number of years. With her third eye, she saw a group of teenagers sitting at the table in the courtyard, smoking cigarettes and planning a séance. Now the place—the earth, the air, everything around it—was warped and foul. Casey turned to face the house. She heard a disembodied voice. It was female and eerily familiar, not originating from any specific direction, yet floating like the wind all around her.

Auustinn, you've come. Then, she cackled. It echoed in Casey's ears and made her aching head throb.

As if answering her call, Austin took a step forward. "C'mon, let's go check it out."

Fuck no. Casey grabbed his arm. "There's no need. This place is old and falling apart, but there are no ghosts here. Nothing evil here, either. It just looks spooky." She strained to keep her voice steady.

"You're kidding, right?" His jaw dropped as he stared at her. He turned back to the house with his hands on his hips. "I just knew this place was haunted. I can't believe I was so wrong," he muttered under his breath.

Casey chuckled, but it sounded phony even to her own ears. "Austin, you wouldn't know a haunted house if it walked up and bitch slapped you. Trust me, if you investigate this location, it's going to be just as boring and uneventful as the old hotel episode. C'mon. You owe me a cheeseburger," Casey smiled at him. She leaned against the Porsche because her head was spinning. The dead were touching her face, grabbing at her clothes. Normally she would walk around a spirit rather than through it, but there were too many. Shivers ran down her spine as she passed through their ice-cold forms and shoved discarnate beings out of the way to get to the car door. Austin stood facing the house for a moment more, and Casey was afraid he might go in anyway. "Austin, c'mon," she said, in as normal a voice as she could manage. Finally, he turned back and climbed into the driver's seat. She stared straight ahead, trying not to flinch, as the spirits banged on the door and the windows to get her attention.

As soon as Austin pulled up at the restaurant, she jumped out of the car. "Gotta pee," she yelled back. "Get us a table."

"But you just went," he said, as she ran off.

Casey fell to her knees as bile rose up in her throat. She vomited violently and repeatedly. *If you don't get it together in a minute, Austin's going to know something's up.* Finally, she pulled her head out of the toilet, convinced there were no stomach contents left to bring up. She splashed some cold water on her face, popped a couple of Excedrin, and exited the restroom.

There were two glasses of water and two menus on the table. Casey sat down and Austin leaned over. "Mind telling me what the fuck's going on?"

With trembling hands, Casey opened the menu. She stared at it instead of making eye contact. "What are you talking about?"

"Not haunted?" He held out his phone and put it up to Casey's face. "Then why is Barrett blowing up my phone with texts in all caps, warning me to stay the fuck away from the place we just left?"

Casey closed her eyes and mentally swore. *Barrett and his stupid remote viewing.* She was actually pissed at herself. She should have had the foresight to contact Barrett and let him know that she'd convinced Austin the place wasn't haunted.

Casey shook her head. "If I even hinted the place had ghosts, you'd have run straight in. That place is evil. As evil as I've ever seen."

Austin placed his hands on the table. "Even better. It will make a great season finale."

"No. Don't make light of this, Austin. I'm not kidding." Casey leaned in, across the table. "You don't get it. It's not a place for the living. It's too dangerous."

"You mean like the Thompson House?"

"Even worse." *She was calling to you.* "Some places are too evil. Some places should be left alone."

"We'll take extra precautions. I'm not afraid."

Casey grabbed his wrist. "*I* am afraid." She paused. "You have no idea. I … I'm terrified for you."

Austin leaned forward and folded his hands. "Case, it's not like you to be so over dramatic. It's just a haunted house. It can't hurt me."

"It's much more than a haunted house. It *will* hurt you." *She wants you in the worst way.* "Promise me you'll forget about that place." Tears burned her eyes as fear welled up in the pit of her stomach.

"Casey."

She tightened her grip on his wrist. "Promise me." Her voice was barely a whisper, but the intensity of her directive was so strong, Austin couldn't hold her gaze. He looked down at his hands.

"Okay, Case. Don't get upset." He put his hand over hers and rubbed it gently. "I promise."

Austin and Casey spent Saturday at Casey's parent's house. She was still recuperating from her headache the day before, and neither one of them felt like going anywhere. Mrs. Lawson made turkey sandwiches in the afternoon from the leftovers and, after they ate, the four of them played a game of Monopoly. It was nice for Casey to catch up with her mom, and her dad didn't bring up the past or her recent behavior, so it was a pleasant afternoon.

Early Sunday morning, Casey and Austin were sitting at the kitchen table in her parents' house. She was having a cup of coffee and he was drinking a protein water. "Sure you don't want me to come with you?"

He kissed her on the forehead. "I would love for you to come to Mass with me, but I think you should go to church with your parents and talk to your dad." She walked him to the front door and watched him drive off. *Might as well get this over with.* She put her cup in the sink, then willed her feet to move in the direction of her father's office.

Casey put up her hand up and rapped softly. "Come in," she heard from behind the door. No matter that she was a grown woman, when she walked into her dad's study she reverted to a scared little girl. With tentative steps, she closed the gap between herself and her father.

"Sit down," Reverend Lawson motioned to the chair in front of his desk.

Casey sat. "Dad, I'm sorry for how I acted. What I said was rude and disrespectful."

Her father steepled his fingers under his chin. Casey cast her eyes down to the neutral carpet. *Everything in this house is beige. Everyone in this house is beige. I am being suffocated by earth tones.* She thought of the faded old hand-me-downs she wore as a kid. Her mother was the epitome of frugality—clipping coupons, saving butter and cool whip tubs to use as Tupperware, and patching ripped jeans. The furnishings in their home were simple, functional and plain.

"I forgive you," he said. Casey stood up to leave, but her father motioned for her to stay seated. "I hope you have already asked God for His forgiveness." Casey squirmed and nodded. "Austin is a fine young man, Casey. Very respectful. We had a good conversation yesterday."

Casey picked at her fingernails. "That's nice."

"I like him; I just don't like what he does for a living. You can't expect me to approve of how you two place your souls in eternal peril."

"Geez, Dad, really?"

"Yes, really. The bible forbids communicating with the dead for a reason."

"It's not like I seek them out. They come find me."

"That's no excuse. Casey, I know you think you're helping the dead. But there is no such thing as ghosts. The bible says the dead know nothing."

"The bible says, the bible says ... is that your answer to everything? Dad, I've seen the dead as long as I can remember. I wasn't practicing witchcraft at age three."

"Not consciously, but you are unknowingly speaking with demons. Maybe if you ignored them, they would leave you alone."

"Ignoring evil doesn't make it any less real." Casey tipped her head to the side. "And how has that worked for you?" Reverend Lawson blinked. He opened his mouth to speak, then shut it quickly. "You know, when I was younger, and I saw your eyes track the dead, I thought it was my imagination. There's no way my father could tell me not to speak to ghosts when he sees them as clearly as I do."

Her father leaned back in his chair and crossed his arms. "All right, Casey. Yes, I can see them. But I don't interact with them. I pray and they leave me alone. These beings aren't like Casper. They're demons."

Casey shook her head. "That's not true. Gran is not a demon." Casey thought of Gladiola, Imogene and Prudence. Evil? No way. "She's your mother. And if you'd bother to speak to her for two seconds you'd know she's only sticking around to keep an eye on her only son. As soon as you die she's going to cross with you. Did you ever think that maybe they leave you alone *because* you ignore them?"

Reverend Lawson stood up. "No. No." He paced back and forth. "I don't know where I went wrong with you. I brought you up in the Church. I taught you right from wrong. I taught you about God's love and sacrifice. And now...." He folded his arms in front of him. "You are my child. I love you. But I don't even know if you're saved."

Casey rose. "Daddy, I don't believe everything you do. I believe in God and I know the devil is real. But I don't believe that all the spirits I see are evil. And I don't believe that a righteous God would send me to hell for using a gift he gave me. If I don't use my sight, if I squander my talents, that's just as wrong."

Reverend Lawson shook his head. "Gift? It's not a gift. It's a curse. I pray for you, Casey. Every day, I pray for you."

Casey rose out of the chair. "Good. I can use all the prayers I can get."

"Casey, I—"

"I gotta go. I need to get ready for church." She hurried out of the room.

23

Mrs. Lawson wanted to fix Casey and Austin lunch before they started driving back home, but Casey overruled her. "We have to be back at work on Tuesday. We need to get going."

Casey's father shook Austin's hand. "It was nice meeting you. Hope we see you again."

"You can count on it, sir." He climbed into the driver's seat and gave Casey a moment.

Mrs. Lawson gave her daughter a hug. "Don't wait another three years before you come to see us, young lady."

"I won't."

"And call me once a while."

"Yes, Mom," Casey said, returning the hug.

Her father opened the car door for her. "I love you, Casey. Remember that."

Casey nodded and climbed in the Porsche. "See that wasn't so bad." Austin said. Casey narrowed her eyes at him. Once they got onto the main road, Austin pulled some sheets of paper out of the glove box and handed them to her.

Casey stared at the page with lab values and ranges. "What's this?"

"I had a physical a couple of weeks ago. As you can see, I'm in great shape on paper."

"You're in great shape in real life. Why are you showing me this?"

He'd been wanting to have this conversation for a while, even before she told her parents they were just hooking up. She had been too keyed up on the ride to Texas, but now, with Thanksgiving behind them, he had her undivided attention. "I want you to trust me, Case. I know I slept with a few girls before you but, as you can see, I'm clean."

"I know. I didn't think you were messing around on me. What's this all about?"

"I want to renegotiate things." He should have known this present arrangement wouldn't work out. When something was important to him, when it really mattered, he couldn't half-ass it. It was all or nothing.

"Renegotiate?"

"Yeah." He ran his fingers through his hair.

Here it comes. He wants to break up. He wants to date other people. Her heart began to race and her stomach twisted in knots. *I don't want this. I don't want to lose him.*

"Case, I don't want to be your friend with benefits. I don't even want to date you exclusively. I want more." He placed his hand over hers. "I was hoping you would consider me your boyfriend. Your serious boyfriend."

"Boyfriend?" A warm flutter replaced the tense knot in her belly.

"Yeah. I want to see where this goes." His feelings for her went beyond affection. She had grown on him. Sometimes it was in a cancerous tumor kind of way, but most of the time, being around her made him feel like he'd come in first place at the Boston Marathon.

Boyfriend. She smiled at the thought of going out on dates and holding hands in public. Exchanging corny-sweet gifts and never spending a holiday alone. The hearts and flowers stuff Tina was always swooning over. She placed her fingers against the glass and stared out the side window so he wouldn't see the stupid grin on her face. "And that would make me your girlfriend."

"That's how it usually works. So do you agree?"

"Um, yeah. Sure. We could give it a try."

෨

Austin was at his desk, uploading the pictures of Enchanted Hill onto his laptop. His phone buzzed. It was a text message from Josie.

I'm finished with the interview.

What do u think?

I think we should hire him.

Bring him up here and let me meet him.

Austin sighed. He hated that Tony was leaving. Even though it was a good opportunity for him, Austin couldn't help but feel betrayed. *Face it, dude. You just don't like people leaving you. Period.* A few moments later, Austin heard a soft rap on his door. He opened it and his eyes widened in surprise. "Barrett."

Josie was smiling so broadly her face hurt. "I just found him wandering around on the streets and asked him if he'd like a job."

Barrett tried unsuccessfully to suppress a smile. "Yeah, she really had to twist my arm."

Still grinning, Josie said. "I'll leave you two to talk." She backed out of the room and shut the door.

Austin was stunned speechless for a moment. He ran his fingers through his hair and motioned for Barrett to take a seat. Then, he pushed his own chair from around the desk and sat facing him.

"So, tech specialist?" Austin finally managed.

"Yeah. It's time to get back to work."

"That's a little below your paygrade, isn't it?"

"I don't think so. It actually seems kind of perfect to me."

"Don't you want to join us on the investigation team? I can tell the producer we need another psychic. We *are* the network's cash cow. I can get pretty much anything I want."

"Nah, I'm good with behind-the-scenes. Besides, that would be stealing Casey's thunder."

"Are you sure, man?"

Barrett nodded. "I'm not the psychic I used to be. I can see what's happening right now, even from great distances, but I've lost all my precog abilities."

"That sucks."

"I thought so, too, at first. Then I realized it's not so great to see the future when all you see is bad shit headed your way."

There was so much Austin wanted to say, but none of it sounded right in his head. Barrett seemed comfortable around him for the first time in months. Maybe he should just keep his mouth shut and enjoy the moment. "So, you're back."

The side of Barrett's mouth kicked up in a half-grin. "I'm back."

To celebrate Barrett's return, Austin took everyone to Marley's for lunch. Thai and Austin were sitting on either side of Barrett, giving him a rundown of the current season. They were cutting up, teasing each other, and talking shit. Casey shared a secret smile with Josie. Josie gave her a thumbs up. The gang was back together.

Thai looked over at her. "What's your opinion?"

Casey swallowed the bite of apple in her mouth. "My opinion of what?" She hadn't been paying attention to the guys' conversation.

"Shadow figures. My grandparents always believed they were human once, but were mean and cruel while they were alive. In death, they become malevolent creatures, roaming around and bothering the living."

"They're not human," Casey said unequivocally. "Shadow figure is just another name for demon."

Barrett shook his head. "I agree they're evil and they're inhuman, but they're a step down from demons."

"They may be slightly different entities, but they are just as dangerous as demons and can kill you just as dead."

"Then I guess Austin's just plain lucky," Thai said.

Barrett leaned forward. "What are you talking about?"

Thai pointed at Austin. "At the warehouse. I saw one steal his breath. I expected him to get sick or something."

Austin shrugged. He remembered Thai freaking out about it, but he hadn't felt a thing, and simply blew it off.

"You must have been mistaken. If it actually stole his breath, it would have made him ill at the very least. Probably with some chronic side effects," Barrett told Thai.

"Yeah," Casey said. "Whatever you want to call them—demons, shadow figures—they're bad news. You can't have that kind of close contact with one and walk away unscathed."

"I'm telling you, it stole his breath," Thai insisted. "Let's go back to the office and look at the footage."

"Maybe some other time," Austin said. He doubted Barrett wanted to relive anything about the warehouse. "We need to focus on the last investigation before Christmas." He glanced at Casey. "We've had a lot of requests for interviews. I'll be sending you on the talk show circuit during the break."

"What about you?" Casey asked. "You're the one everyone wants to see."

"I'll be visiting the families from last season for the *How Are They Doing Now* episode."

"Well, can't Thai come along?" The thought of going on television by herself made her uneasy.

"No way. I'll be on my honeymoon," he told her.

Austin looked into her eyes. "Don't be nervous, Case. I know you can do this." He stood up. "Well, I hate to break up the reunion, but I've got to get back to review some footage." He threw his keys and Josie caught them. "You drive. See you later," he said to all of them, but his gaze was on Casey.

Her eyes followed him as he walked out the door. Barrett scooted over next to Casey. "So, you and Austin?" he asked, with his eyebrow raised.

Casey blushed and looked at her hands. "Well, yeah, we're sort of dating."

"It's a hell of a lot more serious than that. You can lie to yourself, but you can't lie to me." He pointed to his temple. "I've seen inside your head."

Casey smacked his upper arm. "Hey, it's rude to pry."

"I wouldn't call it prying when you're broadcasting it in IMAX digital."

Casey frowned. *Shit.* She'd tried to keep that from him. But lately, her thoughts had drifted to Austin without her permission. "So, how long have you known?"

"For a little while." He tipped his head toward her. "I was waiting for you to tell me."

Casey exhaled. "I'm sorry. I didn't know how to bring it up."

"I'm not trying to embarrass you or make you feel bad. Austin's a great guy. And you are good for him in ways you don't even know." He squeezed her hand. "I'm truly happy for you both."

"It's not a big deal." She shrugged.

"Don't downplay it on my account. You're not fooling me. Either one of you."

24

Asmile played on her lips as the plane lifted off the tarmac. Austin squeezed her hand. "Happy to be going back?"

"Yeah. It'll be good to see the girls again." Casey knew of all the episodes they'd filmed this year, the one featuring Gladiola, Prudence, and Imogene would be her favorite.

At first, the three young women were nervous when they saw all the guys setting up the cameras and walking through their house. But they relaxed after Casey assured them they were nice and were just here to see what the ghosts could do.

The ghosts did not disappoint. Gary captured some of the most remarkable footage of intelligent hauntings they had seen all season. Austin asked them to move a chair. The chair moved. Austin asked them what their names were. An invisible ghost finger wrote Imogene in the dust on the table. And when Austin recorded their voices, on playback you could hear Imogene playing the piano and all three of the girls singing *Camptown Races*.

As soon as the filming ended, Casey and Barrett walked over to speak with the sisters. "This is my friend, Barrett. He can see you, too."

"Hello, ladies. It's a pleasure to meet you." He bowed his head toward Imogene and Prudence, but he took Gladiola's ghostly hand

and kissed the top of it. For the first time, Casey saw the matronly sister giggle like a school girl.

With a serious expression on her face, Casey turned to Gladiola. "Imogene wanted me to talk to you." Imogene ran behind Prudence, hiding behind her skirts.

What about?

"She's unhappy here. She wants to cross and be with your parents. The only reason she stays here is because she doesn't want to leave you alone."

Gladiola's smile twisted into a frown. *This is my home. I'm not leaving. If she wants to cross over, let her go.* Gladiola made a shooing motion with her hands. Casey turned to Barrett for help. He put out his hands in a "Relax, I got this" gesture.

"Ms. Gladiola, may I say something?" Gladiola nodded and motioned for him to speak. "This old homestead is falling apart. In a few more years there will be nothing left to stay here for. Now this may be presumptuous of me to say, but you don't seem particularly happy to be here, either." Imogene peeked out from behind Prudence's skirt.

Gladiola bit her lip. *No, I guess I'm not. But this is all I know.* A silvery shimmer rolled down her cheek. She brushed the ghostly tear away.

Barrett took her hand. "It's okay to be frightened. It's normal to be scared of the unknown. But don't let your fear prevent you from being happy." Casey envied Barrett's people skills. He always knew what to say—to the living and the dead.

Gladiola turned back and looked at the house. Then she turned to Imogene. *This is what you want?* Imogene nodded her head vigorously. *All right.* She turned to face Barrett. *I don't know how. I don't know what to do.*

"You just walk into the light. You do you see the light, don't you, Ms. Gladiola?"

Yes. It's behind the barn.

"That's right." He smiled and reached out to her. "I'll walk with you." She took his arm and let him lead the way. Imogene skipped ahead of them, her braids bouncing as she went. As soon as they approached the light, Imogene waved and blew them a kiss. One moment she was there; the next she was gone. Gladiola took a bit longer. She fussed with her dress until Barrett told her, "You look beautiful, Ms. Gladiola. Heaven is blessed to have you." She gave a small wave, turned, and stepped into the light.

Casey faced Prudence. "Your turn...." she began but grew quiet. While Imogene and Gladiola were crossing, Prudence had changed out of her flour sack dress and black lace-up boots and into white denim capris, a turquoise blouse, designer sunglasses and purse. "You want to stay?" Prudence nodded. She showed Casey pictures of New York, London, Los Angeles and a few other places she wanted to visit. "All right. Suit yourself."

Austin walked up to them. He put his arm across Casey's shoulder. "Have they crossed?"

"All but Prudence. She has some sightseeing to do." She turned to face Barrett. He was staring off into the empty space that had recently been occupied by Gladiola's spirit. "Thanks for your help."

"Um? Oh. No biggie. It was kind of nice to stretch my psychic muscles again."

To celebrate the mid-season finale, Austin wanted to give back to the fans. He rented out a local bar, and fifty lucky winners were invited to attend a special screening of the *Farm Girls* episode.

The crew sat at folding tables on the side of the room to take pictures with the fans and sign autographs. The line to spend a moment with the Spirit Chaser was the longest. It snaked through the bar and out the front door of the establishment.

"Thanks for watching the show," Casey told the last fan at her own table as she handed him an autographed photo.

Josie was sitting with her. She tipped her water bottle over to where a group of young women were smiling and laughing. "It looks like Austin's babes are out in full force." Austin had morphed into Spirit Chaser, Rockstar edition. He posed for a picture with one of his adoring fans, then turned to flash Casey a sultry smile. Ocean eyes bored into her with intense heat.

"It must get old, always watching those women flirting with him," Josie observed.

"They can flirt all they want. He's coming home with me tonight." Casey said confidently. Secretly, she loved this incarnation of Austin. This was his reward for working so hard and giving a thousand percent to the show—sharing his non-stop enthusiasm for all things ghost with his die-hard fans.

"Rawr!" Josie emulated a kitty growling perfectly.

It took most of the next hour for Austin to finish up at his own table. He made sure everyone who wanted a picture with him, or even just to speak with him for a few seconds, had the opportunity to do so. Just before the screening was set to begin, Austin strode up to the front of the bar, a mic in his hand. "It is so great to be here with you guys tonight." The crowed whooped. "*SCI* has the best fans in the world!" The crowd yelled even louder. "Guys, find a seat. Because the mid-season finale starts in …" He glanced at his watch. "One Minute, thirty seconds!"

The crowd grew quiet as a screen rolled down from the ceiling and Austin's famous intro began to play. Austin took his seat next to Casey, as Gladiola, Imogene, and Prudence showed the world a glimpse of the afterlife.

Austin grabbed Casey's hand and swung it back and forth as they made the short trek from the parking garage to the front of his building.

"I think that went well," Casey said.

"It went fantastic," Austin beamed. "I never would have imagined such a great reaction for an episode that wasn't even scary. But the fans loved the farm girl ghosts. I checked the ratings before we left. We hit number one again."

"Of course you did, Control." She smirked at him. "This just proves you don't have to go demon to entertain the viewing audience." The smile shriveled from his face and he shivered. "Are you cold?"

"Yeah, I guess so. This T-shirt's pretty thin." For some reason, bringing up demons dredged up some unpleasant thoughts and made his skin crawl. He yawned. "And I'm pretty tired."

"Me too." The flight, plus the late night party with the fans, did her in. She didn't even feel like taking a shower. As soon as they walked into his loft, they fell into bed.

Early morning sunlight streamed through the tall windows of the loft. Casey sat up, leaning against the headboard. She stared down at her sleeping boyfriend, stretched out on his stomach. With a contented, sleepy hum, he rolled onto his back.

A yearning in her heart grew and expanded, warming her from within. She couldn't remember a time she had wanted someone this much. How had things grown so comfortable with him?

Casey stroked his cheek with the back of her fingertips. Being with Robbie had never been this easy. Their relationship had been dysfunction on a stick, but still, at one time they had been in love. Casey fell for his pretty words and beautiful lies. She couldn't imagine loving him now. A control-freak Spirit Chaser had stormed into her life and banished Robbie from her heart.

Austin walked in the front door of his loft and put his phone and keys down. The weekend had flown by. Saturday night they had a pre-Christmas dinner with his mom and Lyle, then, after Mass this morning, he drove Casey to the airport. A sense of melancholy filled him as he flopped down on the couch. The apartment felt dark and lonely without Casey there. *Cole, you got it bad for this girl.* He certainly did. It was easier to admit that truth than the real reason he was in a funk. There was one thing he knew would cheer him up. His laptop was right where he'd left it on the coffee table. He powered it on and watched the still photos of Enchanted Manor transform into a moving picture show.

The next few days passed slowly. He tried to stick to a routine. In the mornings, he ran. In the afternoons, he went up to *SCI* for a few hours. That was his favorite time of day. He'd call Casey after the shop closed and they'd talk for a couple of hours before he went home.

Austin didn't consider himself to be a real needy person. He didn't have to have people around him all the time and was quite comfortable with solitude, but lately, he didn't like being alone. Especially in his apartment. A rustling noise got his attention. He turned his head to the side. The rustling grew louder. He stood up and walked over to the kitchen. There were scratching sounds coming from inside the wall. He knocked the wall with his fist. The scratching stopped. *Fucking mice. You live in a luxury penthouse and you have a rodent infestation.* He made a mental note to check with building management the next day. He turned to walk away when the scratching noise began again.

Austin tried to ignore it as he stared at his computer screen. Clomp, clomp, clomp, clomp. Goosebumps broke out on his arms. This was crazy. He lived in a single-level unit. So why was he hearing footsteps, stomping up a staircase that didn't exist? His heart sped up and he was acutely aware he didn't want to be here anymore. Austin slammed the laptop case shut, grabbed some clothes, and threw them into a backpack. His mom would love it if he came a day early, and he'd just have to deal with Lyle.

His keys weren't on the entry table like they usually were. He began searching and finally found them on the kitchen table. *What the hell? You're losing it, dude.* He headed to the front door, closing a drawer in the kitchen as he went. His hand was on the doorknob when the sound of wood gliding against wood got his attention. A tingle ran down his spine. Slowly, he turned. The kitchen drawer was pulled all the way out. Austin fumbled with the doorknob and ran for the elevator. On his way down he realized he left his laptop there. *Fuck it.* He didn't go back for it. As he was driving to his mom's, he relaxed. It felt so good to be getting out. His conscious mind didn't register it, but his subconscious was deeply relieved he wouldn't be staying at the loft that night.

25

Casey's eyes lit up as she opened the door to the store. She smiled at a snow-flake covered Austin. Two brightly wrapped red packages lay at his feet. He blew on his hands. "Going to let me in? I'm freezing my ass off out here."

She moved aside. "What are you doing here?"

His eyes moved up and down her form. "Nice flannel. Reminds me of my great Aunt Minnie."

"I wasn't going for sexy; I was going for warm. So answer me, what are you doing here?"

"I spent Christmas Eve with my mom and the new stepdad, and then in the morning we opened gifts.

Sometime around breakfast I got tired of watching the two of them all over each other and realized what a damn shame it was that my fifty-five-year-old mother was getting more action than her twenty-nine-year-old son. I thought to myself, 'I can stay here and watch this guy suck my mom's face, head over to Thai's and have leftovers, or I could drive to Shadow Creek and bug Casey.' Bug Casey won out."

"You drove all the way here?" She peered out the window and saw his black Porsche turning white from the snow.

"Had to. The storm's shut down the airports." Austin picked up a bottle of scented oil and took a whiff. He put it down and looked around. "So this is Shadow Creek's famous health food slash new age store." He grabbed her hand. "Show me where you live."

Casey led him upstairs. "It's not much."

He stepped into her one room space. A striped sofa, floral print chair, and end table with a brass lamp occupied the living area. It had the look of mix-matched garage sale furniture. No television or coffee table in sight. To his right was the bedroom. There was a simple double bed with a black and gray comforter. Red velvet pillows formed a kind of headboard. "Nice," he said and continued his inspection. Directly behind the living area was a harvest gold kitchenette with chipped Formica countertops. He looked around the cramped space. "You don't do much cooking, do you?"

"Mostly I just microwave stuff." She plopped down on the couch. "So, are those for me?" she asked, pointing at the presents.

"Uh, yeah. I know we agreed to open our gifts when we got back to LA, but since I was in the neighborhood, I decided to bring them with me." He handed her the first one. "This one is from my mom."

Casey opened the package. It was filled with all kinds of soaps, lotions, shampoos, loofahs and any other thing she could imagine for showering. She opened a red bottle labeled Raspberry Bubbles. "Umm," Casey said, as she closed her eyes and held it under her nose. "Your mom knows I'm addicted to long, hot showers?"

"I may have mentioned it to her. So what do you think?"

"Nice. Makes me want to try it out on you."

"Promise?" Austin asked with a naughty gleam in his eye. He handed her another package. "And this one is from me. Although, if I had known you were going to greet me in grandma flannel, I would have picked up sexy lingerie instead." She opened it up and found six long skirts in different shades of black, gray, navy, and green. Casey felt the fabric. It was so soft. She stood up and put it up to her waist. "These are perfect." She looked up at him. "Where did you get them?"

"I asked Anna to design them for you."

Casey ran over and planted a kiss on his cheek. "You know, you can be really thoughtful when you want to be."

"I'm not done." He lifted up a key ring with a single silver key on it and pressed it into her hand. "It's to my loft. I want you to come over whenever you want."

Casey bit her lip. "Are you sure about this?" It was only a small, shiny piece of metal, but the significance and seriousness behind the intention made her stomach flutter and her pulse race.

"Positive," he said. This was actually his second choice. If she hadn't been so skittish and so independent, he would have asked her to move in with him.

"My turn." She walked over to the other side of the space and Austin's eyes tracked her movements. When she returned, she handed him a flat, rectangular package. She'd thought long and hard about what to get him, but what did you get the guy that had the means to get anything and everything he wanted? She'd ultimately decided to buy him something he would never get for himself. "Merry Christmas, Austin."

He ripped open the paper. "An e-reader?"

"Yep. With the entire Lux series already uploaded."

"Kat and Daemon?"

Casey nodded. "It's a good thing I did. I don't have a TV. If you're staying here a few days, you're going to need something to do."

Austin bit his lip and narrowed his eyes as he folded her in his arms. "Thanks, Sweet Cheeks. I love it. But, you know, I can think of lots of things to do." He planted a soft kiss on her mouth and was about to delve inside with his tongue when she leaned against the back of the couch.

She stared at her hands. "I have another gift, too, but it's not a package you can open."

"Okay." He sat up, intrigued. "So what is it?"

274

Casey looked up at him through her eyelashes. "Did you bring condoms?"

"Of course. I know how to woo your panties off."

"Throw them away."

"What?"

"I'm on another form of birth control." He looked at her quizzically. "I trust you, Austin."

"Skin on skin?" The side of his mouth kicked up in a grin.

"Uh-huh."

He pulled her to him and pressed his lips into hers. He continued to kiss her as he walked her backward into the bedroom space. When the back of her knees connected with the mattress, he pushed her onto the bed. He crawled over her and began pressing kisses to her forehead, eyelids, and down the side of her cheek. Ocean eyes stared down into her own. "I've missed you, Casey Lawson."

"It's only been a few days."

He pushed a stray lock of hair out of her eyes and repeated, "I've missed you, Case."

The afternoon sun filtered through the window, casting areas of shadow and light in the small bedroom. Casey scooted up next to Austin, laying her cheek against his shoulder. He sat up, pulled her onto his lap, and pressed her to his chest. They stayed this way, him rocking her in his arms for several seconds. She wrapped her arms around his neck and pressed kisses along his collar bone. He squeezed her one last time, then kissed her on the forehead before releasing her.

Casey sifted through the sheets until she found her nightgown and panties. "I'm going to take a shower. Want to join me?" she asked. "If you're good, I'll wash your back with my new loofah."

"What'll you do if I'm bad?" Austin arched an eyebrow.

Casey narrowed her eyes. "Wash your front."

"Very tempting, but I've held you hostage in this bed for most of the day, and I know how dangerous you can be when you're hungry, Sweet Cheeks." He sat up and slapped her bottom. "Go on. I'll make us some dinner." He heard the water running and rubbed his stomach. He hadn't had anything since breakfast that morning. Food was the last thing on his mind when he'd arrived. After pulling on his boxers and t-shirt, he walked into the kitchenette to see what Casey had in the fridge. He was pleasantly surprised to see greens and vegetables. Evidently she'd gone grocery shopping before the winter storm hit. There was even ground turkey. He found a cutting board and started slicing veggies for a salad. While rummaging through the cabinets looking for pasta and sauce, he came across a dozen or so packets of ramen noodles. "What the fuck, Case? You didn't get enough of this shit in college?" he mumbled to himself.

After setting water to boil and putting the meat in a pan, he began pulling out drawers, looking for utensils to cook with. The first drawer he pulled open was full of papers—bills, to be exact—and they were all stamped in large red letters with the words "past due."

He heard the shower cut off. A few minutes later, Casey padded into the kitchen in her long, flannel night gown, fluffy socks, and cardigan. Her hair was wrapped in a towel. "Something smells good."

"Case, what's going on?"

"Huh?"

He picked up the papers. "Are you in some sort of trouble?"

"Not anymore. Thanks to you and *SCI*, I am debt free." She reached for the bills to throw them away, but he pulled back.

"Okay, so what's the deal?"

Casey exhaled. "Nothing. I had some debt after college. No biggie."

"Case, this looks like a little more than college debt. Some of these balances are huge."

Casey bit the inside of her cheek. "Like I said, they're paid off. And what gave you the right to go through my stuff, anyway?"

Austin rubbed his chin. "I wasn't going through your stuff. I was looking for a pasta spoon when I came across it." He leaned against the counter and stared into her eyes. "I'm concerned," he said softly.

Casey bit her lip. "I'm sorry. It's just junk from my past that I'd rather keep in my past, that's all."

"If you don't want to talk about it, I won't make you. But didn't you tell me earlier that you trust me? If you really do, I wish you'd confide in me. I'm not just here for a good time, Case. I'm all in."

Casey exhaled. "You're right." She turned the fire off the stove, took his hand, and led him to the couch. He sat on one end of the couch, and she sat facing him on the other. She brought her knees into her chest and hugged them. It was so quiet she could hear the sound of the second hand tick from the clock on the wall. "Remember at my interview when you thought it was strange that I didn't finish college?"

"Yeah."

"Robbie was the reason."

"Robbie. The guy you were in love with?"

Casey nodded. "He was in deep to some really dangerous creeps. I sold my car to pay them off. I decided to give us one more shot. I had good credit, so I got approval for a bunch of high-limit credit cards. I lived off my student loans and maxed out my cards to pay for him to go to rehab. He got out a month later, but he slipped up and started getting high again. That time I didn't have the money to put him back into a program. I had to babysit him to keep him from getting high. I literally sat on him. It was bad for a few weeks while he detoxed. I couldn't work; I couldn't go to school. We were both prisoners in my small apartment, and the bills were piling up. Then, each day, he got a little better. He'd been clean for over a month. I thought it was safe; I could run down the block to the grocery store and pick something up. I was gone less than an hour, but when I returned, he was wasted. That was the day I finally got it. It took long enough, but I finally realized you can't save someone who doesn't want to be saved. I needed to get as far away as I could. I packed my bag, got on a bus, and took it as far as the little money I had would take me. I ended up in Shadow Creek. Now, I give people one chance. If they fuck up, that's it; I'm done."

He rubbed her arm. "Case, I'm sorry. What he put you through was terrible."

"No, what's terrible is that I was stupid enough to let him take advantage of me."

"Cut yourself some slack. You were in love. You were trying to help him."

"No, Austin. Being in love doesn't give you a pass to act like an idiot. I made some shit decisions. I can get upset at Robbie for using me, but the truth is, I let him. How can I trust anyone else to do right by me when I can't even trust myself?"

"Everyone makes mistakes. That doesn't mean you're an idiot or that you lack good judgment."

"I'm not so sure. Even after I left I wondered for a long time if I'd done the wrong thing. I still loved him, and I felt guilty for leaving him that way. Hell, I don't even know if he's dead or alive."

Austin was quiet for a moment. He lifted her chin so that she was staring into the ocean. "Are you still in love with him?"

"No," Casey answered emphatically. "Definitely not. If there's one thing I did learn, I could never be in love with an addict again."

Austin exhaled and smiled. "You're smarter than you think."

"I don't know about that. It took Tina almost a year to get it through my thick skull. I'm not the one who left; I'm the one who had to get away to save myself. The truth of it was he dumped me for his drugs long before I left him. He's the one who gave up on us."

He pulled her between his legs with her back to his front. "You are entitled to your trust issues. You earned them the hard way." As he wrapped his arms around her, he whispered in her ear. "Case, I'm here. I'm not going anywhere."

Casey gently lifted Austin's arm off her waist and slipped out of bed. He hummed in his sleep but didn't wake. The floor was ice cold, even with her socks on. After taking a long, hot shower, she started the coffee pot and walked to the front window to look at the thermometer. It was eighteen degrees and Austin's car was buried up to the tire wells in snow.

"Woman, where are you?" Austin yelled from bed.

"Getting some coffee."

"Well, hurry up and bring your flannel-wearing ass back to bed."

"I thought you hated my flannel."

"I changed my mind. It keeps me warm." Casey padded back to the bedroom with her coffee cup in hand.

"What time is it?" he asked.

"Eight-thirty."

"Fuck. You are such a bad influence on me. I meant to get up at six and go for a run, but you kept me warm and sleepy, and enticed me to stay naked with you in this bed."

"Yeah, I'm sure that's it. The fact that there's at least a foot of snow on the ground had nothing to do with it. Scoot over." Austin lifted the comforter and she crawled in bed beside him. She buried her cold feet under his warm thighs.

"Shit, Case. Did you put ice cubes in your socks?"

"I can't help it. It's colder than a witch's tit out there." Austin lifted her gown and squeezed her breast.   "What are you doing?"

"Checking the temperature." He squeezed the other one. "Nope. They are definitely warm. Your thermometer's broke." She smacked him in the arm. "Ow," he mock cried out. "You know, we wouldn't be freezing our asses off if you went home to Texas for Christmas instead."

"That's true, but you wouldn't be getting laid, either."

"Good point, Sweet Cheeks."

As long as her gown was up around her shoulder blades, he might as well indulge. He pressed his lips against her naked abdomen. "Umm, you smell like a sugar cookie."

"It's that soap your mom bought."

"Cookies are my weakness. I may never leave this bed." His phone rang and Casey stilled. "We're not going to answer that," he said, continuing to press kisses on her lower abdomen. A moment later, *Tubular Bells* began to play.

"Fuck," Austin muttered.

Casey grabbed her phone off the nightstand and glanced at it. "It's Thai."

Austin leaned over to take it out of her hand. "Damnit, Thai. You and your cock-blocking calls," he muttered under his breath. He put the phone up to his face with his left hand and traced a finger down Casey's face with his right. "Dude, your timing sucks."

"Sorry, Austin." Casey heard Thai yell, "Sorry, Casey." She closed her eyes and felt heat rush to her cheeks. "I hate to interrupt, but I thought you'd want to know. We got the okay for Hillendahl."

"No shit?" Austin sat up straight. He'd been trying to arrange an investigation of the one-hundred-fifty-year-old mansion for years. It was listed in the top ten haunted sites in America. "So, when?" he asked Thai.

"I've set it up for March ninth. We'll have to push back the Bowman Psychiatric Hospital for a week, but I didn't think you would mind." The Bowman hospital had been out of operation for over a decade and wasn't going anywhere.

"Fuck, no, I don't mind." Austin rubbed his hand through his hair. "Holy shit. We're going to investigate Hillendahl." A crooked smile twisted the corner of his lip up. Casey stared up at him. He was twenty-nine years old, but when it came to haunted houses, he was like a ten-year-old kid in a toy store. Thai said some other stuff that Casey couldn't hear. Austin responded with short "yeahs" and "uh-huhs."

"Thanks, man. Later." Austin ended the call, put the phone down, and crawled on top of Casey. His crucifix hung down between them. The morning sunlight glinted off the gold metal.

"This is like a dream come true," he murmured, staring down into her eyes.

"Hillendahl?" Casey asked.

He kissed her long and hard on the lips. "Everything."

26

The bell on the door chimed as Tina bustled in the store. "Brr, it's cold out there. Casey, thanks so much for doing this. It's a good thing we'll be living in different states. Todd's family is cray-cray…." Austin turned to her from behind the counter and Tina gave out a little shriek. "You're Austin Freaking Cole," she mumbled.

He stuck out his hand, "Actually, I'm Austin Gregory Cole, but close enough. You must be Tina. It's a pleasure to finally meet you."

Tina stood there in a catatonic state, and Casey answered for her. "Yes. Austin, meet Tina. I hope you don't mind, but my boyfriend hung out with me here while I worked. But I promise I wasn't a dipshit with the deposits."

They chatted for a few minutes. Tina got a picture and autograph, then Casey and Austin hit the road. With the bad weather, Austin wanted to allow extra time to get to New York for Thai's wedding. Thankfully, the roads were clear and they made it there with no problems. Casey was impressed. For a California boy, he sure knew how to drive on the ice and snow.

In Buddhist tradition, there is no set way to get married. It's up to the bride and groom. Thai and Anna opted for a simple, semi-private, service and a lavish reception for all their friends. The original ghost hunters—Austin, Barrett, and Josie—were the only ones on Thai's side in attendance for the ceremony. Casey smoothed down the formal skirt Anna had designed for her and waited in the ballroom of the hotel with the other crew and Liv for the reception. The bride had put her mad designing skills to work, creating a warm but elegant atmosphere. The tablecloths were a rich burgundy and a single white rose in a crystal vase adorned each table top. The overhead lighting was dim to accentuate the flickering white candles. Casey didn't know if she ever wanted to get married, but if she did, she would definitely ask Anna to help with the planning.

Luis was sitting at a table with his wife and Bob. Gary was chatting with a tall, good-looking blond man Liv identified as Barrett's boyfriend. Casey stood with Liv by the door, watching and waiting. She waved everyone over. "They're here. They're here." The double doors to the hotel ballroom swung open and Thai and Anna walked in. Friends and family ran up and formed a line to congratulate the couple. Austin snuck up behind Casey and encircled her waist with his arm.

She gave him a kiss on the cheek. "How'd it go?"

"Great. Thai's a lucky man, and he knows it."

"So what was it like? Hit me with some details."

"Like a wedding." Casey pursed her lips and Austin winked at her. He walked over to greet Luis and his wife. Casey headed straight over to where Josie and Liv were sitting. She knew Josie would give her the scoop. When it was time for dinner, Austin joined them.

After a delicious, three-course meal, the happy couple stepped on to the dance floor for the first dance. Austin stood behind Casey with his arms wrapped around her and watched. Thai was as graceful at dancing as he was at yoga. As the DJ played a classic first dance, he twirled Anna around and dipped her low. His face couldn't contain the pride and joy he felt. Casey's eyes flitted over to the bride. She couldn't stop smiling, either. They made a striking couple. Anna was breathtaking in the diaphanous white gown she had designed herself, and Thai looked sophisticated and more mature than his twenty-eight years in his black tux.

"They look so happy," Casey observed.

"Yes, they do." The music changed and the atmosphere went from dignified to silly. *Watch Me* by Silento began to play and everyone clapped and laughed as Thai and Anna Whipped and Nae Nae'd in their formal attire. Austin pressed his lips to her temple. He loosened the knot in his red tie. "I'm going to get some air. It's warm in here. Care to join me?"

Casey nodded and took his hand. They hopped in the glass elevator and Austin pressed the button for the roof. He entwined his hand with hers as they ascended into the sky, watching the people in the lobby grow smaller and smaller. When the door opened, they heard a man speaking in a loud voice.

"I knew it was a mistake for you to go back there. You don't give two shits about us, but you'll drop everything for *SCI*."

"That's not true," Barrett protested.

Austin spun Casey around and walked to the other side of the roof to give the men their privacy. He leaned his arms against the railing and looked out on the city. Casey did the same.

"It's beautiful up here," she observed.

"Yeah. I could stare at the city lights all night." He covered her hand with his own, and they stood there, quietly enjoying the view. A smile curled the corner of his lip up.

"What's going on in that head of yours?" Casey asked.

"I was just thinking. Last New Year's I was on top of the world. *SCI* was going great, all my closest friends were also my coworkers. I thought to myself, 'life doesn't get any better than this.'" He leaned back and pushed the toe of his dress shoe against the railing. "Then, less than six months later, everything went to shit.

I lost my best friend and the most talented psychic I'd ever met." He stared straight ahead and cleared his throat. "I never thought I could like you, Casey, let alone love you." Casey's eyes widened as a warm fluttering filled her chest. "I never thought you'd fit in with the team and I was mad at myself for pushing Barrett out the door. But, now, I can see that everything happened the way it was supposed to. Even though I never planned it this way, I got everything I ever wanted. I have my best friend back, and I'm hopelessly in love with the new psychic."

Austin turned toward her and gently rotated her shoulders so that she was facing him. He stared down into her steely blues. Her head was spinning and her hands were trembling. "One day this will end. *SCI* can't go on forever. The show will be cancelled and we'll move on." He took both of her hands in his. "I won't like it; I'm not going to lie. But as long as I have my friends and I have you, Sweet Cheeks, I'll be okay."

"Austin, I...." Casey tripped on her tongue, and her heart hammered in her chest. Despite all her best efforts, she had fallen hard for the Spirit Chaser. *C'mon*, she told herself. *It's just three little words. At some point you're going to have to take a chance. You might get hurt; you probably will. But life without love is no life at all.*

Austin put a finger to her lips. "Don't say it. I didn't tell you I loved you just to get a response from you. I think I know how you feel, but I don't want you to tell me until you're ready. Until it's your idea. But know this: I love you and I want there to be more to our story than just this television series. You're already my present; I hope you'll be my future, too." Before he could finish, she wrapped her arms around his waist and held on like her life depended on it. He pulled her to him, lifting her feet off the ground. She blinked away tears and buried her head in his chest. He lifted her chin with his fingertips and leaned down to kiss her.

The sound of approaching footsteps made them pause. "Hey, Austin, I've been looking for—oh shit, I'm interrupting." Barrett turned to walk away.

"No. Don't leave. Casey and I were just taking a break from the reception. What'd you need?"

"Do you think you could give me a ride home? Derek left. He wasn't feeling well."

Austin watched Barrett. He was twisting the silver ring on his finger. Something was bugging him. But Barrett was a private person and Austin didn't want to pry. "Sure, man."

Another couple exited the elevator and walked over to the other side of the roof. Barrett let them pass, then walked over to the railing where Austin and Casey were standing. "It's hard to believe Thai's a married man."

Austin shook his head. "Not for me. He's wanted this for a long time." Casey didn't know if it was her imagination, but she could swear she felt Austin pull her closer.

"That's not what I mean. It seems like time is flying. Yesterday we were just college kids, ghost hunting on the weekends. Now, shit. It's like, if we blink, it'll be 2025."

"I know what you mean. Casey and I were just discussing how transient this all is. We have to take the time to appreciate each other. Because, one day, we're not going to be here anymore."

There was silence for a beat. Then Casey punched him in the chest. "Geez, Austin, this is a happy occasion. Don't be such a buzzkill."

He looked down at her seriously. "I'm sorry. I'm not trying to be." He grabbed Barrett's hand and pulled him over. He held onto Casey's waist and draped his other arm over Barrett's shoulder. In a low voice, he told them, "You can never know how much you mean to me."

They stood there for a moment, in a close embrace. Austin exhaled and relaxed his grip. Barrett took a step back. "Wow. I didn't know you cared." His lips pulled up into a grin. "I always thought Thai was the special one."

Austin arched his eyebrow. "That was before that woman took him away from me. Believe me, if Thai was out here with us, I'd be hugging his ass, too."

Casey stared up into his eyes. "Everything okay?"

"It's fine, Babe. I should have warned you that I get nostalgic and sentimental this time of year. Auld Lang Syne and all that bullshit."

"Yeah, he does. If you didn't know Austin, you'd think he was sloppy drunk," Barrett said.

The other couple turned to go back inside. "Excuse me," Austin said. "Would you mind taking a picture of us?"

Casey looked up at Austin quizzically. "I want to remember this moment," he whispered in her ear.

"Sure thing." The woman took Austin's phone and put it in front of her face.

Austin pulled Casey and Barrett close again. He pressed his lips against Casey's temple, and the woman snapped the picture.

27

Gina Murphy was sitting in her one-room apartment, drinking vodka on the rocks and looking through her bills. At one time, she had been a Hollywood A-lister, but that had been over ten years ago. Now she was just another aging actress struggling to make ends meet. The sad thing about it was that in her heyday, she had made several million dollars. Unfortunately, a crooked agent took a big chunk of it and the rest went up her nose.

All she'd ever wanted was to be a movie star. Gina was a pretty girl. Her mother put her in acting classes, and she won several local beauty pageants. In high school and junior college, she took drama and was cast as the lead in most of the plays. When she turned twenty, she took off for Hollywood with a dream in her heart and not nearly enough money in her pocket. Less than a month later, she was wondering how she could scrape up enough money to buy a bus ticket home without selling her body.

She was lying on the bed of her weekly rent motel, straddling the line between sleep and consciousness. "I'd do anything to be famous."

Anything? The word came from all around and nowhere. A disembodied female voice giggled.

"Who's there?" Gina sat up in bed.

Out of the shadows, a female form in a flowing white gown materialized. *Your dream come true.* The words came from the woman, but in the darkness she couldn't see any of her features.

"Huh?"

I can make you famous, but I need one, small thing from you. The woman's voice whispered in her ear, and when she heard what the woman wanted, she laughed.

"You're serious? You want my soul?"

Yes.

Gina thought it sounded like a line from one of those old *Twilight Zone* episodes. "Make me famous and you can have it."

Done.

When she woke up, she chalked it up to a wacked out dream. She got dressed and headed out to look for work. There was a diner down the street with a Help Wanted sign. If she got a job there, it would buy her some time to figure out her next career move.

She stepped up to the counter to ask about the position, when a short, balding guy grabbed her by the arm. "You are exactly what I'm looking for. You're perfect." He turned to his buddy. "Isn't she perfect?" He handed her his business card and told her to come down to his studio at two-o'clock.

Gina was skeptical, but what did she have to lose? She took her pepper spray in case the guy turned out to be a total creeper. As it turned out, she didn't need it. He was legit, and helped her get cast in a string of hit movies in the late nineties/early two-thousands. After a few years, she forgot all about the deal she'd made with the mysterious woman. But sometimes, on nights when she was alone, she could swear she heard the woman's creepy laugh.

Gina, a familiar female voice called out. Her head turned to the right, then to the left. She spun around. No one was there. She glanced down at her half-empty glass. Yeah, she'd had a bit to drink, but she wasn't so drunk she should be hallucinating.

I need you to do something for me. The woman whispered in her ear.

A chill raced over Gina's spine as she placed the voice with a memory. She dropped her glass of vodka on the hard tile floor. It shattered and she jumped. With a quivering voice she asked, "Are you here for my soul?"

That depends.

"Depends on what?"

If you cooperate.

Gina shivered. "I am your servant."

Yes, you are.

"What is it you want?" Her voice trembled.

I need to borrow your body.

"Huh?"

I'll give you the details in time.

"What about my soul?" She could see her breath.

What about it?

"Are you here to take my soul?"

The woman cackled. *Not tonight. If you do everything I ask, I will resurrect your career. I'll even give you twenty more years before I come back for what's mine.*

It was stupid to believe her, but what choice did she have? "I will do whatever you ask."

Austin called a meeting of the crew for January fifth. Thai would still be on his honeymoon for another three weeks, but he wanted to get the rest of the crew up to speed before the two-and-a-half month hiatus.

Austin walked into the gym, where the crew was working out. "So glad to see everyone here early. That means we can start now and get out of here. I hope everyone had a wonderful holiday season. I just want to go over a few things before everyone goes their separate ways."

"Luis isn't here. And the meeting doesn't officially start for an hour," Josie said. It still blew Casey's mind that this crew would show up over an hour early for work, just because they wanted to.

"Uh, actually he's going to miss the meeting. Flat tire," Austin said. "Now, I know most of you are going out of town. Be ready to hit the ground running when you get back." Austin grinned and rubbed his hands together. "I have some exciting news that I have been holding in. After much begging and pleading from yours truly, we have finally been granted permission to investigate Hillendahl." Gary and Josie whooped, and Bob and Casey clapped. "Yeah, I feel the same way. We will be the first paranormal team ever granted access to this historical site. Just because it hasn't been investigated before doesn't mean we can go in and pull something out of our ass. The place is a fucking legend and our investigation needs to do it justice. Gary, I want you to check the layout and get back with me regarding the camera locations. JoJo, let me know how that radio frequency communication device is coming along. I'd really like to use it for Hillendahl if it's ready."

"Oh, it'll be ready. I'll make sure of it," Josie exclaimed.

He turned to Casey. "This place is over ten thousand square feet. Be ready for an extended walk through. Let me know if you need to break it up into two nights." He turned his attention back to the group. "We'll definitely need at least two nights for the investigation. Bottom line—we've got to be better than we ever have before. I am prepared to dedicate the whole week to Hillendahl if we need to."

He spoke to Bob next. "Two of the places we're investigating in April have Native American roots. Stop by my office and I'll give you the background info on them. And, Casey, I've lined up some television interviews for most of January."

"And, of course, Luis will return to his day job: exorcising demons," Josie said.

"I don't think so," Austin said, and closed his laptop.

"Huh? Why not?" Gary asked.

Austin shrugged. "Just a hunch." He rose. "Well, that's all I have, guys. We'll meet again for planning on February twentieth."

Austin walked over to his office. He needed his Enchanted Hill fix before he went home. Logically, he knew they were just still photographs. But the more he looked at them, the more alive they became. He was staring intently into the screen when a voice in his head warned him. *She's coming.* He closed out of the page and shut the lid on his computer just as Casey walked in.

"Sorry to interrupt your porn surfing, but I wanted to tell you not to wait for me." She plopped down in the chair in front of his desk.

Austin cocked an eyebrow. "That's not what I was doing."

Casey narrowed her eyes. "Then why'd you slam the lid shut on your computer when I walked in the door? You're hiding something—porn, online girlfriend, My Little Pony fetish—something."

"Or maybe I'm booking a Valentine's getaway for my busy-body girlfriend." He smiled up at her. "And for your information, when a grown-ass man likes My Little Pony, Brony is the preferred term."

"I knew it." Casey smiled at him. "Anyway, Josie and Liv have invited me out for lunch and a movie. One more girl's day out before they take off for their trip. That's okay, right? I mean you haven't made any plans for us?"

"Nothing official. I can always get you naked later. I'll just go home and spend some quality time with Pinkie Pie until you get there."

"You know their names? Okay, now I'm concerned." Casey jumped up and planted a kiss on his cheek. "I won't be out late. Maybe we can get some dinner."

Austin grabbed her ass. "Or maybe we could stay in and have something delivered." His hand slid into the waistband of her skirt.

Casey slapped his hand away. "The door's wide open and the building is full of people."

"So?" His fingers edged over and slipped into the top of her underwear. "Nobody here will care."

She pushed his hand away. "I'll care. Geez, what's wrong with you? Nobody wants to see you with your hands all over my ass. We're at work."

"I need to come in your pussy," Austin blurted out.

"Excuse me?" Casey took a step back.

Austin's cheeks turned red and he covered his mouth with his hand, as if he could take the words back. "I, uh...I don't know why I said that." Austin had a dirty mouth and he did think about sex a lot. He didn't mind cracking a joke about his own anatomy, but he had never in his life spoken to a woman in such blunt terms. He couldn't look her in the eye. "My mom didn't raise me that way." Austin stared down at his hands.

"It's okay," Casey said. Not that she enjoyed hearing it, but the remorse he felt was evident in his face. "Don't feel bad. It's forgotten."

"You're going away for two weeks. That's a long time without seeing you." He ran a trembling hand through his hair. "I'm going to miss you, Case." Actually, he felt sick at the thought. He didn't want her to leave. The idea of being alone for that long worried him.

He looked so pitiful, Casey leaned over and patted his arm. "Well, maybe we could meet up on the weekend. I could fly in or you could fly out."

"Yeah, we could do that," Austin agreed, even though he knew that wasn't going to happen. She waved goodbye as she walked out the door.

As Gary was climbing into his Jeep, his phone beeped. It was a text from Luis.

I'm not going to make it to the meeting. Flat tire.

Gary texted back.

I know. Austin already told us.

I don't understand. How did he know?

You didn't tell him?

No. It just happened. That's why I'm texting you.

Is this a joke? Are you guys playing with me?

I don't understand. What joke?

Gary scratched his head.

Well the meeting's over, anyway. I'll call you later and let you know all about it.

28

Auustinn, her melodic voice echoed. The beautiful brunette opened her robe, giving him an unobstructed view of her perfect body. Her lips pulled up seductively.

"Umm," Austin licked his lips. She had been torturing him for months. Leading him on, then pulling away at the last moment. A straight up cock tease is what she was. He was more than ready to pin her down and hammer into her until she screamed. Wipe that sadistic smile right off her taunting lips. He stalked over to her, grabbed her by the arm, and threw her on the bed. He straddled her, using his legs and the weight of his body to spread her open and keep her from moving. "Is that how you like it?" She squirmed underneath him. He released her, but only so he could grab a handful of her hair and push her down. "Or would you rather suck my dick, you nasty whore?"

"Get off me!" Casey screamed. Austin's back slammed against the headboard. He blinked and looked up. Casey scooted off the bed and wrapped the sheet around herself. Her eyes were wide and she was breathing heavily. "What's wrong with you?"

"Huh?" Austin sat up and rubbed his forehead. "Was I dreaming?"

Her voice trembled. "You were hurting me."

"What?" His eyebrows furrowed in confusion. "Babe." He moved forward and reached out to her. Casey pulled the sheet tighter and backed away from him. A minute ago Casey thought she was going to have to call the cops on Austin for attempted rape. But now, she wasn't so sure. Had she completely misread his intent?

"You were holding me down. I told you last night I don't like the rough stuff."

Austin stared at her and shook his head. *What the fuck?* "Case, I would never hurt you." He patted the mattress. "Come back to bed. Let me hold you."

She shook her head as she backed away. "I'm going to take a shower. We need to get to the airport, anyway." A moment later, Austin heard the sound of running water. He ran his fingers through his hair and picked up his phone. Seven-nineteen. *Shit.* He'd overslept. Last night he'd planned to go for a run before taking Casey to the airport, but that was before their all-night marathon sex session. He smiled as he thought about their evening's activities.

His smile faded as he recalled her reaction this morning when he woke up. She was terrified of him. What the fuck had happened to make her react that way? He crawled out of bed and walked to his closet. As he was pulling on his boxer shorts, a familiar sensation made him pause. There was a rush of blood below his waist and Austin stared down at his twitching cock.

Casey let the warm water flow over her skin. Maybe he had been asleep and didn't know what he was doing. It seemed completely implausible. But the idea that Austin would do something against her will seemed even more unbelievable. She turned the faucet off and stepped out of the shower. After wrapping a towel around her midsection and another around her hair, she walked into the bedroom.

The first thing she noticed was that the bed was empty. The second thing she noticed was the grunting coming from Austin's closet. She opened the door. He was standing with his back to her and his bicep was flexed, pumping up and down rapidly. *Oh shit. He's having an intimate moment with his hand.* She backed out of the closet quietly and crept back into the bathroom. She didn't emerge until she heard him getting dressed.

It was a tense, silent drive to the airport. A million thoughts ran through her mind. Ever since New Year's she'd been working up the courage to tell him she loved him, too. She'd pictured it in her mind. Telling him she loved him before boarding the plane was like something out of one of her romance novels. But, now, after his bizarre behavior, that was the last thing she wanted to do.

Austin drove toward the airport parking lot. "You can drop me off. You don't have to walk me in."

"Nope. I'm going as far as they'll let me." He took her luggage out of the trunk and grabbed her hand as they walked toward the entrance. When they entered the airport, he put her bags down and turned her to face him. He brushed a stray hair out of her face, and cupped her cheek with his palm. "Babe, I don't want you to leave this way. I'm sorry I upset you. I swear to you, I don't remember anything."

Casey gripped the hand he held against her face with both of her own. "It's okay. I may have overreacted."

"Case, there was fear in your eyes. And I put it there."

"I trust you, Austin. You would never intentionally hurt me."

Austin stared into her eyes and swore. "See, I don't like that. I don't ever want to hurt you. Intentionally or not." He leaned in and slowly kissed her. With both hands he pulled her into his chest. "I love you, baby. Hurry home." He kissed her one last time on the forehead and walked her over to the check in. He watched as she went through the security line. She blew him a kiss and headed toward the terminal.

Casey boarded the plane and took out her reader. After staring at the same paragraph for twenty minutes, she put it away. An unease filled her stomach, and she couldn't get Austin off of her mind. It was like he was two different people. She thought back to yesterday. He was aggressive in bed, and rougher than usual. She had to tell him he was hurting her twice. He immediately backed off, but it was weird. Almost like he was trying to cause her pain.

It was early this morning when things really got out of hand. Austin had a dirty mouth and a strange sense of humor, but his language in bed was out of character. He had never called her such nasty names before. She shivered as she remembered him pushing her head to his groin, demanding she go down on him. At that moment, she hadn't felt like his beloved girlfriend. She'd felt less than human. Something to be used and thrown away.

He was right; she had been scared of him. But after it happened, he seemed genuinely confused. No, actually, he claimed he didn't remember.

This morning, at the airport, he'd been the old Austin. The man she wanted to be with. She leaned her head against the window. *What is going on with you, Control? Why do I feel like I'm losing you?* Casey sighed and closed her eyes. *You're letting your imagination get the best of you. He was having a vivid dream. That's all. You're always trying to sabotage your happiness. Austin loves you and you love him. Everything will be fine.*

It took all of about two days for Austin to film the "How Are They Doing Now" episode. All the clients who listened to Barrett's advice were experiencing no paranormal activity or greatly reduced activity. But those who ignored what he said, or procrastinated about getting their houses cleansed, were worse off. Funny the way that worked.

Austin walked in his front door and sat on the couch with his computer. He pulled up the pictures of Enchanted Hill. The more he looked at them, the more real they seemed. In the picture he took of the front of the manor he could now see a woman standing on the front porch, smiling and waving at him. Although she was in the shadows and he couldn't see her features clearly, he knew she was the beautiful woman in his dreams. He sat for hours, staring at the pictures and tracing her silhouette with his finger.

29

Luis met with Brad Thompson for the first time in six months. While he had been filming *SCI*, Brad had been under the care of Father Dempsey. "Let's begin," Luis instructed his lay helpers and opened with a prayer before they began the exorcism. As soon as he began his petition, the demon growled. "Hurry up and get this done so that I can go fuck your mother."

Luis ignored him and continued. "I cast you out in the name of Jesus Christ."

Luis flicked holy water on it and the demon writhed in pain. Lay workers assisted Luis by holding Brad down while Luis continued with the rite of exorcism. Brad's body jerked out of their grasp and he sat up. The demon stared at Luis. In a calm, clear voice it said, "You'll try but you won't succeed."

Luis continued to pray. The demon chuckled. "Such a lovely day to go to the hospital. While you're incapacitated, she'll take over. You'll try to save him, but it will be too late."

"Be quiet, unclean spirit." Luis pressed the cross to his forehead and Brad lay back down. A few minutes later, he came out of the trance state.

One of the lay helpers followed Luis out. It was only his second time to assist, but he was eager to help and his faith was strong.

"Father, what did it mean when it was talking about the hospital and not being able to save him? Was he talking about Brad?"

Luis stopped walking and turned to face him. "Call me Luis."

The man nodded. "Yes, Luis."

He raised his index finger. "Rule number one when dealing with those who are possessed: They're liars. Don't believe a word they say."

Luis came home and had lunch with Maria. Afterward, he thought he'd go lie down for an hour before the kids got home from school. As he walked up the stairs, he felt a draft. At the top step, he paused and looked around. Something dark flicked across the periphery of his vision. He felt heavy eyes resting on him. It grew even colder, and he could see his breath. He mentally prepared himself for battle and began to pray.

"Get away from me, unclean spirit." He heard a disembodied laugh in his left ear and jerked his head to the side. There was a hard shove to his chest. It was so strong it knocked him off his feet. He tumbled down the stairs backwards and landed at the bottom with a loud thud.

Austin was powering up his computer when his phone rang. He let it go to voice mail. What was the point in answering? Gary would just tell him what he already knew: Luis broke his ankle and a few ribs and was in surgery right now. On some level, he recognized it was strange for him to know this information. But mostly he didn't care. All he wanted was to stare at the pictures of Enchanted Hill. And he did so until his eyes grew heavy with sleep.

Austin. The woman came up behind him, placed her hands on his shoulders, and whispered in his ear. *You must give the seer up. I cannot hide from her anymore. She is too sensitive, and you are too con-nected to me.*

"Casey? But why?"

You are mine.

"But I want you both. She's my girlfriend. You only exist in my dreams. I don't see a problem here."

I am more than a dream, and I will not share. If you don't get rid of her, I will.

Austin opened his eyes. He heard a growl and saw a strange creature in the corner curled up on his dresser. It was gray, with wispy tendrils floating around its head. It hopped on his chest and his bed started to shake. He couldn't move; he couldn't speak; and its hands were tightening around his neck.

Austin cried out and sat up in bed. He ran his fingers through his hair as he tried to slow his racing heart. *Damn crazy nightmare.* For just a moment, he could have sworn the bed was moving. He knew he would never be able to go back to sleep.

He got up and walked into the living room. He shielded his eyes from the bright light and glanced at the microwave. Shit, it was ten-thirty. He slammed his hand on the kitchen counter. He'd overslept again. And this was going on day five without a run. *You have a major case of the fuck its. You need to get your lazy ass in gear.*

Austin made a protein drink and sat down on the couch. He thought about going in to *SCI* for a few hours but decided against it. His computer was sitting on the coffee table with the lid open, begging him to power it on. He set it on his lap and leaned back as he scrolled through the pictures of Enchanted Hill. It seemed like only a few minutes, but when he looked up, the sky was dark. He glanced at his phone. It was eight-thirty. *Fuck.* He'd meant to go visit Luis today, but damn if the day hadn't run away from him. And if he was going to go for a run tomorrow, he'd better set his alarm and go to bed right now.

Austin's phone rang and he smiled when he saw it was Casey. "Hey, Babe. Saw you on *The Late Show.* You did great."

"Thanks. But I'm so glad that was my last stop. I miss being home."

"So now LA is home?" He took a sip of water and set the glass on the counter.

"Yeah," Casey said with a smile. "I think it is. How's Luis?"

The drawer holding the kitchen utensils slid open. Austin leaned forward and closed it. "His leg is healing, but now he's got some kind of strange infection. They're going to keep him for a few more days."

"Gosh, I hope they figure out what's going on. The infection thing bothers me."

"He'll be fine," Austin said. *I've seen it.*

Dark shadows darted around him in the periphery of his vision. He looked up and around. The glass of water slid across the counter. *Fuck.* Austin thought, as he stepped away from the kitchen counter.

"Austin? Austin? Did you hear what I said?"

"Hmm? No, I'm sorry, Babe. Bad connection."

"My flight gets in tomorrow night at five-thirty. Are you coming to pick me up?"

"Absolutely." The glass flew off the counter and shattered against the wall. Austin's breathing picked up.

"What was that?" Casey asked.

"I—" he began. Austin wanted to tell her about the strange things going on, and that he was seeing shit, but something prevented him from doing so. *The seer will be angry with you for not having the loft blessed like she told you to.* But that wasn't true and he knew it. He didn't want Casey to know he had been obsessing about Enchanted Hill. "I fucking dropped my water glass on the floor, and now I've got a mess to clean up." He walked away from the kitchen and flopped down on the sofa. "Case, I've missed you. Maybe, when you get back, we could get away for a few days. Just the two of us."

"Or we could just hang out together in LA. I've been on the road for over two weeks, Austin."

"Yeah, that's true. Well, maybe I'll get us a hotel room for a few nights downtown."

"Babe, I'm kind of sick of hotels. What's wrong with your place?"

Everything. "Nothing. I'm going a little stir crazy here with everyone else out of town. If you don't want to go to a hotel, maybe I could come stay with you."

"All right. But you know how tiny and plebeian my apartment is compared to your loft."

"I don't care about that. I just want to see you. Hurry home, Case. I miss you."

Austin was awoken by loud talking and music. He opened his bedroom door and found a shit ton of people in his living room. Metal music jammed from his speakers. It was so loud he was afraid the neighbors would call the cops. The haze of cigarette smoke filled the air. Austin waved his hand and coughed. Ordinarily, it would piss him off to have people getting drunk, high, and smoking in his place, but tonight, it seemed pretty cool.

He dodged and stepped around people dancing and making out. They were in various stages of undress and sobriety. Cigarette butts jutted out of ashtrays and empty bottles of booze littered the coffee table.

"Hey, Austin, it's about time."

Austin turned and looked over to the kitchen where the voice came from. A tall, skinny guy in dark sunglasses was chatting with three chicks that looked like they were dressed in Halloween costumes. One was dressed like a flapper, another looked like one of those old Hollywood stars from the forties, and the third was dressed like Madonna from her *Lucky Star* phase. The guy looked vaguely familiar.

"Do I know you?" Austin asked, as he approached.

"Dude, what have you been smoking?"

Austin's eyebrows furrowed. Then it came to him. He pointed his index finger at him. "You're the lead singer from *Demonsmith*, Sebastian something."

"It's Sebastian Grant. And the band split up. I was about to get cozy with these lovely ladies. Want to join us?" The three women giggled. The flapper batted her eyes at Austin, and the movie star from the forties blew a ring of smoke.

"No, man. I've got a girlfriend. But you guys have fun."

Sebastian put one arm around the flapper and the other around the Madonna look-alike and headed for the bedroom. "Suit yourself."

"Hey," Austin called out. "I thought you died in like 2000. Drug overdose or something."

Sebastian laughed and shook his head. "Actually, it was a suicide." He made a motion of a knife sliding across his neck. "But, as you can see, it was blown way out of proportion. You, of all people, should know better than to believe the tabloids."

"Yeah, you're right." Austin flopped down on the sofa and put his feet on the coffee table. A guy in a white polyester bell-bottom suit and a blond girl with blue eyeshadow in a magenta and green mini-dress were fiddling with a turntable and pulling out an old vinyl record.

"Dude, where'd you get that? I haven't seen one of those since I was a kid. My mom had one."

The guy looked at Austin like he was crazy and turned back to what he was doing. He put the needle on the record and a song Austin didn't recognize began to play. The girl stood up and started dancing.

It sounded like the cheeseball seventies music his mother used to listen to when he was a little kid. But, as he listened to the lyrics, a chill ran down his spine. "What is this song?" he asked the woman.

"Where have you been? It's *Devil Woman*. You know, Cliff Richard."

Austin got a queasy feeling in his stomach and rested his head against the back of the couch. The next thing he knew, he was flat on his back in the dark. It took a moment for him to realize he was on his own bed. He tried to move, but he couldn't. *Must be dreaming,* he told himself. But he knew that wasn't true. The party scene in his loft—that was a dream. This was something different. Shadows darted around him and he felt something crawl onto his chest. He tried not to panic, but the weight on his chest made it hard to breathe.

Relax, Austin. A female voice whispered. He must have fallen back to sleep, because the next thing he knew, he was dreaming again. The beautiful woman with dark hair and eyes was standing next to his bed. "You're not getting away this time." He pulled her down next to him and leaned in to kiss her.

"Umm," Austin groaned as his alarm went off. One eye opened slowly, and he shifted uncomfortably. He looked down to see his hand wrapped around a raging hard-on. Morning wood was one thing, but he couldn't remember ever masturbating in his sleep before. His balls ached, and with his woman out of town, he had to take care of business himself. A few moments later, he sighed his release. He glanced at the clock. It was seven-fifteen. *Son-of-a-bitch.* He'd meant to go for a run before Mass.

He stumbled into the bathroom and turned the shower on. He studied himself in the mirror. Those crazy dreams really wiped him out. Dark circles rimmed his eyes and his California tan had faded a bit. His skin had taken on a gray pallor.

Austin opened the glass door and stuck in his hand to check the temperature. It was warm enough, so he stepped in. As he lathered up, he felt his cock twitch. *Damn, again?* He pressed one hand against the wall of the shower while he pumped his shaft with the other.

It was eight-thirty when Austin stepped out of the bathroom. *Fuck.* If he didn't get his ass in gear, he was going to be late. He dressed in a hurry and ran out the door. He pulled into the parking lot as the bell was ringing. He started walking up the church steps, then paused. He didn't want to go in. Shaking the feeling off, he took a step forward and gagged. The closer he got to the door, the more nauseated he became. He backed away and returned to his car. Perspiration dotted his forehead. *Must be getting sick.* He turned the ignition and headed home.

The farther away from the church he got, the less nauseated he felt. When he walked into the loft, he noticed that several cabinet doors in the kitchen were wide open. *That's weird.* He didn't even remember going into the kitchen before he left. He closed them then headed straight to the bedroom.

Austin exhaled, flopped on the bed, and closed his eyes. He was on the verge of sleep when he felt a pain, not in his chest, but on it. It took a moment for him to realize it was a *burning* pain. Austin jumped out of bed and ripped the chain from his neck. The crucifix made a rattling sound as it hit the hard floor. He looked in the mirror. The skin under which the cross of Christ had lain since his first communion was raised and red. Austin started to shake and slowly sank down on the edge of the bed. He'd tried to ignore the strange goings on in his loft over the last month. Most of the time it was easy to do. He could say he was overly tired and imagining things. But having your skin burned by a holy object was hard to explain away. *This isn't good.* After resting for a moment, he got down on his hands and knees and searched for the crucifix. It was like it had disappeared into thin air. Fatigue overtook him. He collapsed on the bed and fell asleep.

When Austin awoke, he grabbed his phone off the bedside table and wandered into the kitchen. He rubbed his stomach and looked at the clock. It was almost three in the afternoon. *Damn. Sleeping my frickin' life away.* No matter how much he slept, he never felt rested. His strange dreams exhausted him.

He peered into the refrigerator. There was nothing to eat. The last thing he felt like doing was going out, so he reached for his phone. *Shit.* He could have sworn he just put it down on the kitchen counter, but it wasn't there. After searching the kitchen for a few minutes, he walked into the den. There, lying on the coffee table, was his phone. He flipped through his contacts until he found the number for the concierge of his building.

"Mr. Cole. How can I help you?" Jackson answered. The always proper, always polite, fifty-year-old man had worked in Austin's building for a couple of decades.

"Yes. Can you order me something to eat?"

"Certainly. Do you want the usual from Marley's?"

Austin made a face and swallowed the saliva building in the back of his mouth. The thought of baked cod and steamed vegetables made him want to hurl. "No. I want a burger."

"A veggie burger?"

"Beef. And tell them to make it rare."

"Sir?"

Austin was losing his patience. "I want a real hamburger, Jackson. Is that too difficult for you?"

"Certainly, sir. Shall I bring it up to you?"

"Yeah." He ran his hand through his hair. He felt shitty for snapping at the old dude. His tone softened. "That would be great. Thanks."

Austin ended the call and looked at his phone. There were several text messages and missed calls from Casey. "Fuck," Austin muttered as he sat on the couch and pressed her number.

"Austin?"

"Yeah, Case."

"Did you go out after Mass? I've been calling you all morning."

"I didn't go to Mass today."

"What? Why not?"

"I don't feel well," he snapped at her. "What's with the third degree?"

"Sorry. I was just concerned." The line was silent for a moment. Austin rubbed his face. "No, I'm sorry. I shouldn't have yelled."

"Is everything okay? You don't sound yourself."

"I've got a cold or something."

"Oh. Are you taking something for it?"

"I'm fine, Casey. What did you need?" he snapped.

Geez, what crawled up your ass and died? "I was just letting you know I'm heading home. The flight was delayed so you can pick me up around eight."

Austin exhaled. "Shit, Case. I forgot all about it. Can you call JoJo?"

Casey tried to hide her disappointment. "I'll take a cab and swing by your place. Maybe bring you some veggie soup." Austin gagged at the thought. "You okay?"

"I'm not really up for company." He pulled his fingers through his hair. "I just want to rest."

What was this? Last night he sounded desperate to see her, but today he couldn't be bothered? "I didn't think I was company. What's going on, Austin?"

"Nothing. It's like I said. I'm not feeling well." His tone softened. "I'm sorry I'm so grumpy. I'm a whiny bastard when I'm sick. Look, Babe. Don't come by. Trust me, you don't want what I have."

"Okay," Casey said, reluctantly. "I miss you."

"I miss you, too, Case."

He ended the call and reached for his computer. Beside it was a half-full ashtray and an empty bottle of Jack Daniels. *What the fuck?* He put the computer on his lap and opened the cover. Out of the corner of his eye he saw the bottle of Jack start to wobble. It tipped over and fell to the floor, shattering loudly. *Must have shook the table when I picked up the computer. Fuck it.* He'd clean it up later. Right now, he wanted to study the pictures of Enchanted Hill on the computer.

"Hey, Austin," Sebastian yelled over the loud music. Austin walked over to see what was up. There were two people with him, but he couldn't see them well because they were sitting in the dark.

He flicked on the kitchen light, but even with the overhead fixture on, they were still hidden in the shadows. "I want you to meet some friends of mine," Sebastian said. "This is Mason." A guy in a baseball cap looked up and nodded. Where his nose and lips should have been was kind of blurred out. Austin didn't want to shake hands with him, so he stuck his hands in his front pockets and nodded. "And this is Reeve."

"What's up?" Austin said.

Reeve turned to face Austin. "How's your friend, Barrett?"

Austin narrowed his eyes at the stranger in his kitchen. "How do you know Barrett?"

Reeve smiled. "We met him at the Warehouse." He chuckled and Mason joined in. Austin wondered how the guy could laugh without having lips.

"That's not funny. How do you really know him?"

"These are her associates." Sebastian interjected. "They accompany her sometimes. Other times they help her when she needs to be in two places at once." Austin glanced down and noticed that Reeve's lower body looked deformed. His knees were bent forward and his feet were small and oval-shaped. It reminded him of a horse. "Just be ready, man. She's coming sooner than you think." The three of them started laughing. Austin backed out of the kitchen. He gasped and sat straight up in bed. It took him a moment to catch his breath, but when he did, he was immensely relieved to know it wasn't real. *Dude, you need to lay off the red meat and stop eating late at night. Then you wouldn't have these fucked up dreams.* He scratched his forehead and checked the new clock on the bedside table. He'd bought it because lately, he could never keep track of his phone. 3:03. Too early to get up and go for a run. He closed his eyes and fell back to sleep.

Auustinn. She ran her finger over his bare shoulder. He turned to face her, and realized she was standing in front of Enchanted Hill Manor. Two figures, shrouded in shadow, were with her. One had no mouth and the other had hooves for feet. The squeak of rusty hinges drew Austin's attention. Barrett walked out of the front door of the house.

"What are you doing here?" Austin asked.

I asked him to come, she said.

Barrett turned to face Austin, his eyes the color of onyx. "And I couldn't refuse."

30

Austin awoke to pounding on his chest. It wasn't strong enough to injure, but hard enough to hurt. "What the fuck?" He opened his eyes. Small fists were beating on him. "Casey?" He grabbed her wrists to stop her.

She jerked away and jumped off the bed. "Damnit, Austin, I trusted you." Her hair was tousled and she was crying so hard he could barely understand her. The black eyeliner shit was running down her cheeks.

"Baby, what's going on?"

She swiped the hair out of her face. "You tell me, asshole." She crossed her arms in front of her and paced in front of his bed. "Mr. Clean Living. That's bullshit," her voice rose. "So how long have you been using? And don't fucking lie to me." The last part came out a high-pitched scream.

"Case," he said in his most soothing voice. "Using what? What the hell are you talking about?"

"You're fucking high!" She wiped her cheeks with the back of her hand.

Austin's eyebrow shot up. "What? Babe, I would never do drugs. You know that."

"Then what the hell is that?"

Austin's eyes followed where her finger was pointing. A hypodermic needle was protruding out of a vein on the inside part of his elbow. He glanced around the room. On his bedside table there was a container of pills tipped over on its side and an almost empty bottle of Crown Royal. She backed toward the doorway. "I don't get it. You had everything," she said with a sob. All the warning signs were there. Mood swings, strange behavior. Damnit, she should have seen it. She'd been down this road before. *You're an idiot. You let your feelings cloud your judgment once again.*

Fuck, Austin thought. He yanked the needle out of his arm and threw it across the room. He jumped out of bed and caught her arm just as she was about to grab the doorknob. "Case, I know how this looks. But, I swear, you've got the wrong idea."

"Wrong idea?" She wrenched her arm out of his grasp. "'No, you're not going to pull that 'it's all in your head' shit with me. I've got eyes. I can see exactly what's going on." *I can't believe I was going to tell you I love you.* She opened the door and stormed out.

"Case, wait. Fuck!" His eyes darted around the room for some clothes to put on. By the time he'd thrown on some basketball shorts and headed for the elevator, she was long gone. He stood there, scratching the back of his head and staring at the silver elevator doors for a long while. He thought back to the way he'd been living lately. It wasn't surprising that she thought he was messed up.

It'll be okay. She's just pissed right now. When she calms down you can reason with her. Show her you're sober as a judge. Time to get his shit together. No more lying around in bed all day. No more skipping Mass. He needed to get back to running, to eating right, and acting like he gave half a fuck about his life.

It was those damn pictures of Enchanted Hill. He couldn't stop studying them. And now, he could see them moving in real time. Last night, the woman moved out of the shadows and onto the front porch. She was dressed in a long, white gauzy gown. Her hand was raised and she was motioning to someone out of range of the camera to come closer. A part of Austin was frightened, but another part hoped she was waving to him.

As he walked back into the loft, he took a good look around. The place was trashed. Furniture was moved against the wall, as if someone cleared the space to make a dance floor. Empty bottles of booze and full ashtrays lay strewn on every surface. An old 45 rpm lay on the floor. He picked up the record and looked at it. *Devil Woman.* "Hey dude," a familiar voice called out. He glanced over at the TV. Sebastian was smoking a cigarette and staring at him from the other side of the screen.

"Thanks a fucking lot," Austin said. He grabbed a trash bag and started cleaning up.

"What's your problem, man?" He stepped out of the television and plopped down on the couch. It should have freaked Austin out, but with all the other weird shit going on, a guy walking out of his flatscreen seemed almost normal.

"You have a wild party in my place and leave all your fucking paraphernalia lying around so now my girlfriend thinks I'm doing drugs. By the way, how the hell did I end up with a needle in my arm?"

Sebastian smiled and took a long drag on his cigarette.

Austin dropped the trash bag and ran over to the couch. He hauled Sebastian up by the shirt collar. "You fuckin' set me up." Austin could be intimidating, and Sebastian was a scrawny little weasel of a dude. He should have been afraid of Austin, but instead he laughed. After pushing Austin back, he straightened his shirt. He leaned back against the sofa and slowly exhaled his smoke. "Did you a favor, dude. Bitch was getting in the way." With his neck extended, Austin could see a raised scar running across his throat from ear to ear.

"That doesn't make any fucking sense."

"Sure it does." He tapped his temple. "Think about it, Cole. You don't need the redhead. Not when *she's* coming for you." He propped his feet up on the coffee table.

Austin shoved Sebastian's feet off the coffee table. "Leave, man. And don't come back."

Sebastian snatched his sunglasses off and stood up. Austin took a step back. The dude's eyes were solid black. It looked as if someone had poked a needle in his pupils and the dark color had bled out into the whites of his eyes. A chill went up his spine and, for the first time, he felt kind of uneasy around the old rocker.

Sebastian tilted his head and took a step closer to Austin. "You want me gone? Fine, I'll leave. I'm kind of sick of your pussy ass anyway." He stood and stepped up into the television screen. He turned to face Austin. "But *she's* never going to let you go."

It's time, a female voice whispered in Gina's ear. She rolled out of bed and walked to her closet. She tossed her T-shirt aside and slipped on a G-string, and over it, a short, gossamer gown. It ended at the top of her thighs. She grabbed her favorite gold stilettos. As she was slipping them on, she thought about the task her mistress commanded her to do. At least Cole was young and good-looking. She had spent way too many evenings on the casting couch of dirty, fat old men who promised her starring roles in movies and a good time. What they delivered was a "you're not right for the part" and a limp dick. She bet Cole could get it up and keep it up.

Perfect. She-demon's voice echoed against the hard surfaces in the bathroom. Gina turned her head to see where it was coming from. She saw nothing but heard a disembodied female laugh. When she turned to face the mirror, a stranger stared back at her. Her short blond curls and blue eyes were gone. They were replaced by long, dark brown hair and brown eyes. "So you're the Spirit Chaser's dream girl," she said, as she smoothed the long, silky strands. After putting a coat over her revealing attire, Gina took a cab to Austin's loft.

It had taken a good chunk of the day, but Austin had his apartment back in order. He put on his running shoes. As soon as he arrived at *SCI*, he hit the gym hard. He spent a couple hours on the machines, shooting hoops, and stretching out on the mats. On the way home, he stopped at Marley's for soup and salad. As he entered the apartment, he found the bible turned over on the floor with several pages ripped out. The statue of Mary was on the ground and the head was shattered. Austin grabbed a broom and a dust pan and leaned over to sweep it up. Physically, he was feeling better, but obviously the spiritual part of his life was still jacked up. *I'll go to Mass tomorrow. Even if it makes me ill. I'll go to confession and have the Father pray over me. I'll delete every photo of Enchanted Hill Manor and I won't mess with that shit again. Casey was right. That place is no good for anyone.*

First, he had to straighten out things with Casey. He picked up his phone and paced as he dialed Casey's number. No answer. Reluctantly, he switched over to text. Texting was fine for short messages, but the auto correct always changed his "fucks" to "ducks" and "shits" to "shots." If the damn phone was so smart, it ought to know that he never used the word duck.

Case, we need to talk.

Austin rested his elbows on his knees and waited. His phone pinged and he grabbed it off the coffee table.

I hope you get clean. You owe it to yourself and the team. But I can't do this.

I have a lot to say. Pls pick up ur phone and talk to me.

He needed to speak with Casey; to hear her voice. "C'mon, Case," he muttered. Austin held the phone and paced for a few minutes. No response. Just when he thought she wouldn't respond, his phone pinged. He snatched it off the seat cushion. Two words flashed on the screen. *Call me.* He auto dialed her. As soon as he heard the call connect, before she had a chance to say hello, he began speaking.

"I fucked up, but not the way you think. I swear to you, I don't do drugs and I never have. Let me come over and explain."

"This isn't my first rodeo. I don't need you manipulating me and telling me I'm the crazy one."

"Then come over and see for yourself. It wasn't me, Case. A friend threw a wild party at my place and he left all his shit around."

"A friend? Or your dealer?"

"Friend. His name's Sebastian. You don't know him."

"So you let this guy throw a party in your loft, with booze and drugs, when you don't even drink?"

"Well, no. The party was already going when I got there. It wasn't my idea. None of it. It wasn't up to me."

She exhaled audibly. "Let me get this straight: A "friend" you've never mentioned before throws a party in your penthouse loft without your knowledge, trashes the place, and you, Austin Control, don't stop it? It's your place. If it's not up to you, then who the fuck is it up to?"

"Look, he and I are no longer friends. I kicked him out after what happened."

"Even if I was stupid enough to believe that cock-n-bull story, it still doesn't explain the needle in your arm."

"It wasn't my needle. I didn't put it there."

Tears pricked her eyes. "Stop, Austin. Don't."

"Just let me—"

"No. Your story is un-fucking-believable. You need help. And I hope to God you get it. But I'm done with this call and I'm done with you."

"Case, I love you." But she was gone. He wanted to tell her it was that fucking haunted manor messing with him, but she didn't give him the chance. She'd be furious that he'd been lying to her this entire time, but it would still be better than what she was thinking now.

He dialed her back but the call went straight to voice mail. "Shit," he said, as he ran his hands through his hair. *Don't give up. Let her cool down.* But he didn't believe it. The voice in his head reminded him. *She's pissed at you. The seer has no tolerance for addicts.*

She'd be less angry if she'd caught you fucking another woman in her own bed. Finding you with a needle in your arm was the worst kind of betrayal. She'll never forgive you.

His breathing picked up and his stomach was roiling. He'd never had such a strange feeling before. It took a moment for him to realize it was panic mixed with fear. He wrapped his arms around his midsection and leaned over, blinking away tears. *Damnit.* Now he was going to cry like a baby.

He heard a scratching noise and unintelligible whispering. "Who's there?" He sat up and his eyes darted right and left. It wasn't light and bright in the loft anymore, even with the two-story windows. A gradual change had darkened the place. So gradual, it had been virtually imperceptible to Austin. Now he could see dark figures darting around, but when he turned his head they were gone. The shadows appeared to move and expand, irrespective of the time of day or the light of the sun. Austin gazed up at the ceiling. A dark mist hung down from it, filling the loft with its haze. Its negative energy enveloped him and he was left with a void so deep, he felt like he could never crawl out of the hole of his dark thoughts. He shivered and rubbed his hands on his thighs. *Is this what hopeless feels like?*

A shimmer in his peripheral vision caught his attention. He turned. The most beautiful woman he'd ever seen was standing in the entryway. She was wearing a sheer, almost-not-there wrap. Her long, sable-colored hair fell over her breasts and ended just past her waist. Austin saw the outline of a G-string under the iridescent material, and nothing else. The woman pulled her hair back over her shoulders and Austin stared at her hardened nipples for a moment before his eyes moved up to a familiar face.

He swallowed. "You're here. You're not a dream."

The beautiful brunette smiled, revealing perfect white teeth. Austin realized he wanted to feel those teeth biting his skin. "Of course, I'm here. You knew I was coming." He supposed he did. Even before he started dreaming about her, he knew.

Austin rose. He could hear the clack of her gold heels on the hard floor as she approached. She pushed him against the wall, pressing her scarlet lips against his and devouring his mouth. He pulled the sheer wrap over her head and his hands gripped her naked waist. She lifted her leg and rested it on his hip. Damn, he was hungry for her. With one hand he grabbed her tit and the other slid up her thigh. He squeezed her perfectly smooth ass. An ache ran through his groin as the strongest lust he'd ever experienced consumed him. He was like a wild animal. Even if he'd wanted to stop, he wouldn't have had the control. He breathed her in, exploring her neck with his lips and tasting her skin with his tongue. She leaned into him and ground her pelvis into his erection, eliciting a low guttural groan from him. Her fingernails weren't just long; they were sharpened to points. She raked three of them down his back. Even though he couldn't see it, he could feel the blood running down into the elastic of his shorts. His fingers flew up to her neck, running down the center of her spine and circling the crack of her ass. She reached into his shorts and grabbed his dick so hard he gasped. She pumped his cock roughly. "Motherfucker," he muttered as he closed his eyes and let his head fall back against the wall. His lips parted as he exhaled. "So that's how it's going to be?" Cupping her ass in his hands, he carried her to his bed. His mouth attacked hers and she bit his tongue so hard he tasted blood. The coppery taste fueled his desire. Oh, the things he wanted to do to her. He shoved her onto the bed with so much force, the back of her head struck the headboard with a loud *thwack*. Instead of protesting, she smiled. He climbed on top of her, pinning her to the mattress with his hands and legs. With rough, impatient fingers he tore the G-string off her and threw the tattered bits of fabric to the floor.

Fuck, he mentally swore when he realized he'd gotten rid of all his condoms. "We don't need them," she whispered, reading his mind. He looked into her dark eyes and it suddenly seemed ridiculous to worry about protection. She spread her legs and he snarled, curling his lip cruelly as he slammed his erection fully into her with one thrust. She gripped his shoulders and rolled him onto his back. He stared up at her and she grinned at him, the blood from his punctured tongue staining her lips. His eyelids closed as she pulled off, then impaled herself on his cock, sinking all the way down until her ass was resting on his balls.

Leave us, the demoness told Gina. She pulled her physical body back and stepped away. Her evil mistress had wrapped herself around Cole so tightly, parts of her spirit body merged into his skin. *That's some freaky shit,* Gina thought. Now that she was no longer under the spell, her appearance reverted into that of a blond-haired, blue-eyed starlet, who had at least one more box office hit in her. She grabbed her wrap and the coat she'd worn over it, and ran out the door of Austin's apartment.

He opened his eyes. The woman he'd taken to bed had transformed into a discarnate being. She was still intensely beautiful, but she was now united with him in her incorporeal form. He looked down. His body was lying on the bed and he was floating above it with her astral body linked to his. *Holy fuck.* This wasn't flesh to flesh but spirit to spirit. Her touch surrounded him on every level. Nerve endings he didn't know existed came to life, and her energy pulsed through every cell in his body. He couldn't bury himself into her deeply enough. It was pleasure on a scale he could never have imagined. And the pain on the edges of his consciousness only increased his excitement.

Her grip on him tightened, and he gasped as he came harder and longer than he had in his entire life. There was no going back. This experience had forever ruined him for sex in its physical form. Slowly, he drifted down until his spirit collapsed into his physical body. He was weak, almost paralyzed, from the experience. When he caught his breath and got a bit of his strength back, he rolled over onto his side. *Rest,* her voice whispered in his ear. As he drifted into a deep sleep, he focused on the beautiful woman and all the terrible, wonderful things he wanted to do to her and with her. The seer bitch never entered his mind.

31

Austin awoke when the bed started to shake. He tried to get up, but he couldn't move. She was there, sitting on his chest, and he found it hard to breathe. The more he fought it, the worse it became. After a few moments, her form dissipated. The pressure on his chest subsided and he was able to move.

Austin sat up on the side of his bed. Damn, he was tired. Weary. Conflicting thoughts coursed through him. Last night he'd experienced the pinnacle of his sex life. But, this morning, a heavy, dark emotion crept in. He ran his hand through his hair. *This depression stuff sucks.*

He grabbed some boxers out of his dresser and stumbled into the bathroom. He rubbed his face to wake up then flicked on the light. "Fuck!" He jumped back as he stared at his own reflection. An alien, sinister visage flickered across his features, then disappeared. His eyes were the color of onyx. Austin's heart sped up and he squeezed his lids shut tightly. When he gathered the courage to open them, blue-green stared back.

More exhausted than I thought. Fucking imagining things. Austin took a piss and exited the bathroom. He walked into his living room. *Holy shit.* The love seat was now sitting where the couch had been and the couch was jutting out at an angle. The dining room table was shoved against the wall and the chairs were turned with the seats facing out.

Austin walked over to inspect the kitchen. Every single cabinet door was wide open and the drawers slid out. He closed them all and looked down. On the white tile floor he spied a large cockroach. His stomach rumbled. When was the last time he'd eaten? Fuck if he knew. Austin licked his lips. He moved closer and the roach took off, headed for a crack in the wall. With preternatural speed, Austin pounced, and with extraordinary agility grabbed the wriggling bug between two fingers. He tilted his head back and dropped the live insect into his mouth. His teeth tore into it, making crunching sounds as he bit into its body. He swallowed the remains of the roach.

It took a moment for him to process what just happened. *You just ate a motherfucking cockroach. What the hell's wrong with you?* He grabbed a bottled of water out of the fridge and gulped it down. "I need to get the hell out of here," he muttered. *Luis. I'll go visit Luis.* He grabbed his keys and walked over to the living room to get his phone. He'd left it on the coffee table, but now it wasn't there. He started to search for it, but changed his mind. *You don't need it anyway. It's not like she's going to call.* He swallowed down the guilt he felt over what he'd done the night before and entered the elevator.

On the ride down to the lobby he chided himself for not going sooner to visit Luis, who was more of a father to him than his old man ever had been. *You don't want to go see him,* a woman's voice whispered in his ear. By the time he got to his Porsche, he'd changed his mind. He didn't like Luis anyway. Preachy do-gooder. In fact, the whole Roman Catholic religion was kind of wack. Seriously, what kind of pathetic deity would allow himself to be nailed to a cross to save a bunch of sinning sacks of shit who hated him in the first place? Austin shot the bird at the hospital as he turned east toward Hollywood Boulevard.

Casey stepped out of the too-hot shower, wrapped a towel around her midsection, and collapsed on the bed. She bit her lip to keep from crying. She'd done enough of that over the last twelve hours. After leaving Austin's, she'd spent the evening with Ben and Jerry, bawling her eyes out. But she'd discovered that no amount of Cookie Dough ice cream could fill the Austin-shaped void in her chest.

She'd finally settled down, crawled into bed, and pulled out her reader. A few teary hiccoughs were the only remnants of her crying jag. Then, he'd texted her. She shouldn't have engaged. She should have ignored him, but apparently she was into self-torture. Their conversation only confirmed the truth she already knew. Hearing his nonsensical excuses made her sick. *Same kind of shit Robbie used to pull.* Yeah, she was mad at Austin, but she was more pissed at herself. Of all people, she should have known better. *When something seems too good to be true, there's a reason why.*

She didn't leave her apartment that day. In a way, it was a relief that Josie and Liv were out of town. She would have wanted to meet up with them and pour her heart out. They would have listened and expressed sympathy, but it would have put them in a really shitty position—choosing sides. Casey didn't want to be that kind of friend.

She called Tina instead. Her friend could always be counted on for her good ear and shoulder to cry on. She even offered to fly out and stay with Casey a few days. But Casey knew she would have to close the store to do that and told her not to.

Weeks later, she would wonder why she hadn't alerted the others of Austin's drug problem. Even if she didn't have the strength to talk to him about rehab, Thai or Barrett certainly would. But something she wasn't aware of, something she would only later know by name, prevented her from doing so.

At four in the afternoon, Casey finally pulled herself off the bed and got dressed. She walked into the kitchen to get a bottle of water from the fridge and slammed her finger in the door. "Fuck," she muttered as she wiggled her hand back and forth and blew on her finger. Hot tears pricked her eyes, and she slid down the front of the refrigerator until she was sitting on the floor with her knees drawn into her chest. Her finger didn't hurt that bad, but she was bawling her eyes out anyway. Austin's betrayal had reduced her to a crying pathetic heap of heartbreak on her kitchen floor.

"Get out, you sick bastard, and don't come back." Rough hands shoved Austin to the ground, and his palms scraped against the concrete. He looked up and turned to see colorful neon signs surrounding the hulking man who had thrown him on his ass. The bouncer's thick, muscled biceps were crossed in front of him and he had a "you don't want to fuck with me" look on his face. A group of women in thongs and bustiers was standing behind him, staring at Austin with disgust. Someone snapped a photograph.

Austin blinked and put his hand in front of his face to shield it from the bright light of the camera's flash. The last thing he remembered was getting in his car that afternoon and heading for the hospital to see Luis. So how did he end up at a strip club on Hollywood Boulevard?

He was losing time more and more often. At first, he thought he was sleeping later than he realized. But now, there were several hours a day that he had no recollection of. He pulled himself up and stumbled down the block. His eyes drifted over the street. *Think, man. Where'd you leave your car?* It was almost two in the morning, and only the hard-core partiers were still out and about. After wandering around for twenty minutes, he spotted the Porsche parked in front of a bakery. There was a ticket on the windshield from long overdue meter fees. He crumpled it up and hit his key fob. The lights blinked on and the alarm beeped. As Austin was reaching for the door handle, the car disappeared. *What the even fuck?* He blinked, in case his eyes were deceiving him. He put his hands on his head and spun around. He paced back and forth in front of the bakery. What did he do now? Call the cops? It's not like it was stolen. The son-of-a-bitch just plain vanished. After muttering a string of curse words, Austin started the long walk back to his loft. He arrived just before sunrise, collapsing on his bed where he slept for most of the day.

Bright sunlight spilled through the bedroom window. Austin's eyes flew open and he awoke gasping for air. He stared at the clock. It was eight in the morning of the *following* day. Fuck. Had he been in bed for twenty-four hours? Most of it was a blur, but there were snatches of disquieting memories—being held down while she forced him to service her. Pleasure mingled with pain. Her insatiable need was wearing his ass out.

Each night she came to him and each night they had sex on the astral plane. Actually, it was more like very rough fucking, and she was becoming more violent. Austin looked down. There were scratches up and down his chest. It looked as if someone had taken a sharp, three pronged cooking utensil and scraped his flesh with it.

Out-of-body sex wasn't as great as he'd first thought it was. He couldn't even say he enjoyed it anymore. Instead of fulfilled, he felt drained. Melancholic. Thoughts of harming himself crept into his mind with increasing frequency. In fact, if he had to admit it, he was a little afraid of her and hoped she wouldn't be back. *Well, that's not going to happen. You've seen what she wants. The only way it's going to stop is if she grows tired of you.*

And what would happen if she did grow tired of him? Nothing good, he was sure. Slowly, he rolled over on his side and sat up. He was sore all over, but now, he noticed his back was stinging like a son-of-a-bitch. Moving like a ninety-year-old man, he slipped on a pair of not-so-clean boxers he found lying on the floor and slowly ambled to the bathroom. He flicked on the light and turned his back toward the mirror to see what kind of damage she had inflicted to his backside.

His face contorted in disgust. A large tattoo of the beautiful woman was etched in his skin. She was dressed in a gauzy, dark gray gown. Long, black wings extended over each one of his shoulder blades. Her index finger was curled toward her body in a beckoning motion, and even in ink form, her eyes bore right through him. Austin blinked. He remembered none of it.

Shit. He didn't want a tattoo and he sure as hell didn't want *her* face inked on his back. *Casey,* he thought, as he stepped into the shower and turned on the water. He let the cold water douse the heat from his inflamed skin. *What have I done? What the fuck have I done?*

Barrett pulled into the driveway of the luxury townhome he shared with Derek. They had returned from their ski trip in Colorado a day earlier than they originally planned. He and Derek were fighting anyway, so what was the point of staying? He checked his messages. Gary had called him last week to let him know about Luis's fall, but he was surprised when he heard Casey's message. Apparently, Luis was still in the hospital suffering from an infection. He would have to call her later and find out which hospital he was in.

Barrett rubbed his stomach and popped a Tums. Over the past few days, he hadn't felt well. Not real sick, just a subtle, constant nausea and burning in his belly. And he'd been having his dreams again. He hadn't experienced vivid dreams since the exorcism, but now, almost every single night, an old, dreary mansion appeared to him while he slept. The gray stone edifice reached three stories into the sky and black ravens circled round its pointy spires and rock chimney. It was like a black and white horror movie from the nineteen-thirties.

Barrett decided his stomach was too upset for breakfast. He crossed to a small building Derek had built for him in the backyard. He pulled out his key and opened the door to his art studio. He hadn't had the urge to draw since the warehouse, but now, he needed to get the picture out of his head and onto paper. Taking a charcoal in hand, he began to sketch the house from his dreams. Within moments, he was lost in the drawing. He didn't stop to eat or drink. Hours passed. The sun headed down in the west and, when the final gasps of daylight gave way to darkness, he put the charcoal down. Barrett took a step back to appraise his work. He shivered and broke out in a cold sweat. The picture reeked of evil. And *she* was calling to him. He ran to the sink to throw up.

32

o. Feed. I need you strong. A violent shaking of his bed woke Austin up. He tried to wiggle his fingers. They moved back and forth for the first time in almost fourteen hours. He bolted out of bed. For whatever reason, he was now free.

On his bedside table, he spotted his phone. "You decide to come back now?" he asked, as he reached out to grab it. When he lifted it, he realized he was holding a Beretta 9mm pistol instead. He studied the gun. It was beautiful and sleek; the weight of it felt so right in his hand. He pressed the cold, dark metal against his cheek and closed his eyes. If it felt this good against his cheek, he could just imagine how wonderful it would taste in his mouth. He slid the barrel between his lips to test the theory when it apported into thin air. He exhaled. "Okay. Now you're just fucking with me."

He walked into the bathroom. Lifting an arm, he inhaled through his nose and nearly choked on the smell of sweat mixed with sex on his skin. There was something else there, too. It was a cloyingly sweet smell, like overripe fruit well on its way to going rotten. *Her scent,* he thought. As he waited for the water to heat up, he leaned over the vanity and looked in the mirror. The haggard man staring back at him looked nothing like Austin Cole, star of the silver screen. Dark circles rimmed his eyes and he was paler than he could ever remember. He'd always been lean and muscular, but now his ribs jutted out in an unattractive way. His stomach rumbled and he realized he couldn't remember the last time he'd eaten, either. It might have been the cockroach appetizer.

He stepped into the shower and let the hot water run down his head and face. He lathered up from head to toe and washed his hair twice. After drying off, he smelled his skin. Although the sweat and sex odor was gone, the cloying fruity smell remained. But he could not feel her presence. Should he try to leave? Austin quickly dressed in a pair of jean shorts, a semi-clean T-shirt and flip flops. He stepped out of the bedroom and tripped on the edge of the coffee table. "Son-of-a-bitch," he muttered as he walked off the stubbed toe. Something had decided to redecorate again. The love seat was pushed against the wall and the recliner was lying on its side.

Austin shoved the coffee table out of the way and ran to the front door. He exhaled in relief as it turned easily in his hand. She was actually going to let him leave. He didn't bother with a hat or sunglasses to avoid the paparazzi. No one would recognize him as the Spirit Chaser. He looked more like the homeless meth addict living under the bridge. As he rode the elevator down, he formulated a plan. If he could just get in touch with Casey and explain what was going on, she could get him some help.

He approached the concierge desk and Jackson's eyes widened at Austin's appearance. He smoothed his features. "Mr. Cole, is there something I can do for you?"

"Um, I was wondering if I could use your phone." Austin struggled to sound as normal as possible. He cleared his throat. "The line in my loft isn't working and I've misplaced my cell."

"Certainly, Mr. Cole. Right over here," he said agreeably. He was speaking in low, gentle tones and completely ignoring the fact that Austin smelled like overripe cantaloupe and looked like hammered dog shit. It reminded Austin of the way the family treated his grandmother, who had dementia. They pretended she was completely sane, agreeing with whatever she said, even when she told them about the train tracks running through her house and how the television was sending her messages from Jesus.

Austin turned away from the doorman and picked up the receiver. He started shaking. Fear and panic spurred his heart rate higher as he realized he didn't know Casey's number off the top of his head.

Jackson was staring at him, fearing he was going to lose his shit any second. "Is there a problem, Mr. Cole?"

Austin took a faltering breath and ran his trembling hand through his still damp hair. "Uh, yeah. I don't know my girlfriend's number."

The doorman gently pulled the receiver out of his hand and placed a call to directory assistance. "What's her name?" Austin told him and he got the operator to patch him through. He returned the receiver to Austin's hand.

On the third ring, Casey picked up. "Hello?"

"Casey, thank Go … thank Go …" Forming the word was an impossible feat. He gave up and said, "I'm glad it's you."

"Austin?" she asked. This was the first she'd heard from him in a week.

"Yeah. Case, I need your help. Something is wrong with me." He touched his forehead with his fingers. "Something's in my brain. I can't think straight."

No shit. That happens when you're fucking high. Casey blew out her breath. "Where are you? Do you even know?"

"Uh. The lobby of my building, I think."

"Stay there. I'm calling Thai. He'll get you some help."

"I can't wait for Thai. He's too far away."

"Thai lives in your building."

"He's not here. He's still in Denver."

"No, he's not. He was flying back in yesterday, remember?"

Austin ignored her. "Please, Casey, I'm running out of time." He swallowed. "I need *you.*"

"What you need is to get clean. And it's not just so you don't flush your career down the bowl. I thought you were a smart guy. Why would you put that poison in your body?"

Austin pulled on his bottom lip. He tried to explain about the woman from Enchanted Hill invading his brain and his body, but the words came out garbled, slurred. Even he could tell he was incoherent.

"Enough, Austin. You are messed up, and I don't have the patience to talk to you in this condition."

"Listen," he screeched. "You're not understanding me."

"Yeah, well you're not making much sense."

He could have called Barrett; he definitely would have believed Austin. But along with his newfound psychic abilities came hidden knowledge. The demoness wanted another shot at Barrett in the worst way. There was no way he'd risk his friend's life again. "Case, please." Austin ran his hands through his hair. "She's after me. She's coming to get me."

"Listen. No one's coming to get you. The drugs are making you paranoid."

"No, you listen. I'm scared," he said sharply. A sob escaped from his throat and he swiped at his cheeks as a few tears spilled down. "Please, Casey. Make them stop. Make her stop. When I'm with you, I don't hear the voices."

Casey was prepared for lies, broken promises, and excuses. But a frightened Austin, desperate and crying, was never something she'd considered. Tears welled up in her own eyes. *Stay strong. There's nothing you can do to help him.* "I'll call Thai," she said wearily. "Go back up to your loft and wait for him there."

"Please, let me come over. I ... I ... don't want to be alone."

"Austin, listen to me," she spoke firmly. "Don't get in your car. You are in no condition to drive."

"I ... I ... don't even know where the Porsche is. I'll walk."

Fuck. Casey thought. Losing a ninety-thousand-dollar car meant he was pretty far gone. But not giving a shit that it was missing was the very definition of rock-bottom. "No, Austin." Her voice cracked, and she wiped away a tear with the back of her hand. "That's not a good idea. I'm sorry." She took in a breath. Her throat ached from straining to hold back the tears. "I'm sorry you're fucked up and my heart is broken. But I can't do this. Not again." She ended the call.

Austin stared at the phone for a moment before hanging it up. He glanced up at the ceiling. No way in hell was he going back up there. His hand twitched against the side of his leg. She would be back soon. This would be his last chance to stop all the evil shit she was putting into motion.

Jackson eyed Austin warily. "Mr. Cole, is there something I can do for you? Someone else I can call?"

Austin looked up, confused for a moment. "No, no thanks." He stumbled out of the building and headed down the street. A small, white dog ran up to him, barking and nipping at his ankles. He looked down at it and was filled with rage. Thoughts of snapping the little turd's neck ran through his mind.

The owner pulled hard on the leash, but the dog wouldn't budge. It planted its paws and growled low in its throat. "I'm so sorry. Honey never acts this way. I don't know what's gotten into her." She looked up into Austin's face and her eyes widened in horror. His eyes flashed from blue-green to black and his features blurred. She snatched the dog off the ground and backed away. Then, she ran from him as fast as she could. Austin turned and continued down the street.

Rays of early morning sunlight filtered into the bedroom as Barrett awoke from a restless sleep. It was the kind of dream-filled sleep that was so detailed and vivid, his muscles ached from acting it out. He sat up and stretched his neck, hearing it pop. Damn, it felt like he'd drank half a bottle of bourbon.

He stumbled out of bed and into the kitchen. He powered on the coffee machine and as the water was heating, bits of dream memories played in his mind. Barrett grimaced as the taste of bile rose in his throat. He rubbed his upper abdomen to ease the burning in his stomach. This was bad. Very bad. There was a block; a barrier erected in his mind, preventing him from knowing the why and the how. But this is what he did know: She-demon was back and that dreary mansion he had drawn figured prominently into her plans.

Four hours and several missed calls later, Casey finally got in touch with Thai "I need you to go check on Austin. He sounds completely fucked up." Casey explained how she found him in his apartment the week before with booze and prescription drugs laying around and that she had ended it with him.

"What? That can't be right."

"I swear to you, it's true."

"All right," Thai said with hesitation. Nothing about that scenario sounded possible. "As soon as I get back to LA, I will. I'm still in Denver. My flight got delayed."

"Oh." She was quiet for a moment. "Well, when's the last time you actually spoke to him?"

"Last week."

"Last week!"

"Casey, I've been on my honeymoon. Austin wasn't on the forefront of my mind. I did try to call him a few days ago, but he didn't pick up and his voice mail was full."

Casey exhaled and pushed the bangs out of her eyes. "So explain how he knew your flight was delayed?"

"I have no idea." To Thai, none of it made sense. Austin on drugs? Not something he could even imagine. He was starting to wonder if Casey was all there. "Try not to worry. I'll check on him as soon as I get in this afternoon."

"What'll it be?" a harried waitress asked. She hadn't made eye contact with Austin and that was probably a good thing.

Austin didn't remember how he got to the diner or being seated at a booth, but he was here now, so he might as well eat. *Damnit.* He'd left his wallet at the loft. Just as he was about to tell her never mind, he felt something hard materialize under his right butt cheek. He checked his back pocket. His wallet was there and full of cash. "Steak and eggs with hash browns. Actually, make it a double order and make the steaks rare. And a large Coke." His phone appeared next to his right hand. He picked it up and scrolled through pictures of Enchanted Hill.

"He's not here, Casey." Thai was standing in the lobby of his building, looking around. The man behind the desk told Thai that Austin had seemed "out of it," refused his help, and wandered out into the street. That was the last he'd seen of him.

"I'll try his cell again in a few minutes. Try not to worry. I'm sure he's fine." Thai said it to calm Casey down, but he had his doubts. "I'm going upstairs to unpack. If I still haven't heard from him in an hour, I'll head up to *SCI*. Maybe his phone's jacked up."

Casey chewed her bottom lip. She should have gone to him when he asked. What if he hurt himself? "Okay. Call me as soon as you hear from him."

Austin peered up into the sky. It was already afternoon. *Damn, where had the time gone?* It seemed like it should still be morning. But he was losing hours and he couldn't remember where he'd been. He headed down the road, setting his sights on the Catholic Church a few blocks down. Relief swelled in his chest. If he could just make it inside, he knew everything would be okay.

The closer he got, the farther away it seemed. It was like the building was moving away from him. *Only a few more steps, Cole. Then, you'll be free.* Dark shadows appeared in front of him, tricking his eyes and taking his attention away from the front doors. An unseen force gripped his legs; it took all his strength to press forward. The wind picked up and pushed him back. Austin heard a cawing sound overhead. He turned his attention to the sky. The California sun had disappeared behind dark clouds and a flock of ravens circled above his head.

A few people stared at him as he shooed away invisible birds and trudged along as if fifty-pound weights were attached to his legs. Austin reached out a shaking hand and tried to pull on the door handle. As soon as his fingers touched the metal door handle, an intense pain shot through his arm. He jumped back and blew on his fingers. His fingertips were a bright angry red. *C'mon Cole. Mind over matter.* He grabbed on to the curved iron and despite the burning, pulled as hard as he could. Droplets of sweat broke out on his forehead. He was grunting from the pain and exertion, and yet the door wouldn't budge. Austin looked down at his hand. It was covered in blisters.

"You want to go in?" a man standing near the steps asked.

Austin nodded his head vigorously.

The man opened the door and Austin forced his unwilling body forward. As he tried to cross the threshold, he was met by an invisible wall, as hard and unwieldy as concrete slab. He could see the large crucifix hanging in the front of the church and hot tears pricked his eyes as he gazed at the image of Christ's sacrifice. "So beautiful," he gasped. And completely unattainable. He shoved his shoulders into the wall, but it wouldn't give an inch. Over and over he tried, but the only thing it got him was a bruised shoulder to go along with his blistered fingers.

Despair welled up inside his chest as he realized she would never allow it. He turned and walked away from the church. "Wait," the man who opened the door called out. "Sir, are you okay?" Austin didn't answer. It was growing dark and she was summoning him. Powerful invisible energy pulled at him, and like a dog on a leash, led him away from the church and toward his loft.

As he exited the elevator of his building, his front door opened. Hunched over, he stumbled into his living room. *You are well and truly fucked,* he thought to himself. The door slammed behind him.

33

Honeymoon's over, Thai thought. What the fuck had he come home to? Thai related to his wife the hysterical conversation he had with Casey. "Austin doing drugs—that's not possible," he told her.

"Go upstairs and check on him. I'll unpack," Anna told him.

"No. I want to call first." He hit connect. This time the call went through.

Thai's ringtone sounded. Austin's eyes flicked to the couch where his phone appeared. Before he could think, she commandeered his hand and picked it up. She latched on to his vocal cords and answered.

"Hello?"

"Austin, you okay?"

"Yes, I am fine. What do you want?" *I'm in trouble.*

"Casey's worried about you. She's been blowing up my phone all day."

"Why?"

"She says you're acting weird."

"I'm not acting strange." He laughed and after a few seconds stopped. Then he laughed again for an uncomfortably long time.

What the fuck? Thai thought. Finally, Austin stopped laughing and spoke. "I'm no longer her concern, anyway. We broke up. Actually, she's the one who broke up with me."

"Yeah, well, that doesn't mean she stopped caring about you."

"You can tell her I am well, if it makes you feel better."

"Why don't you tell her yourself?"

"I don't think that's a good idea. While you were out of town, we got into an argument. She caught me in bed, fucking an escort I had sent to my place. She started screaming and crying and throwing my belongings around." He laughed again, and it was odd. "She can be one crazy bitch. I suppose it is better I found that out now, before things actually got serious."

Last I knew, things were already serious. And since when do you pay for sex? Thai's eyebrows furrowed. "Austin, what goes on between you and Casey is your business. But I don't think you need to talk shit about her just because you're no longer together."

"She's a stupid, interfering cunt and I will talk about her however I like."

Damn, Thai thought. *He really is a cold bastard.* "You know, if that's your attitude, I think it would be better if I spoke to Casey myself." Thai chewed his bottom lip. "Hey, mind if I come up? I think she'll feel better if she knows I've actually seen you. She's convinced you're on drugs."

"That's absurd." In all his life, Thai had never heard Austin use the word absurd. "Maybe some other time. I've got company, if you know what I mean."

"Yeah, whatever." Thai hung up the phone. He made himself a cup of tea and checked his emails. Procrastination wasn't in his nature, but for some reason, he couldn't get up the nerve to go see Austin or call Casey back.

Austin closed his eyes and tried to concentrate. *C'mon, what are the words? I know the words.* Finally he spat out. "Evil from us deliver." He leaned back against the couch and rubbed his forehead. This was not good. He'd either transformed into Yoda, or he was reciting the Our Father backward.

His eyes drifted skyward. *I can't say Your name, but You know who You are. I need Your help.* Something grabbed him by the throat and threw him against the wall. Great, so he couldn't even *think* about calling on the help of that deity he used to worship. He opened his eyes and watched as a black cat darted in front of him.

Austin. Her beautiful, cruel form materialized in front of him. This was the first time she had appeared to him in a waking state. All the breath left his lungs.

Be cool, he told himself. *There aren't many people on Earth better equipped to handle this situation than you.* "Whatever you are, you aren't welcome here. This is my house. I want you gone."

The sound of disembodied female laughter surrounded him. *It's a little too late for that.* He spun around, looking for the voice's origin. He tensed and held his arms in front of his body. "What do you want from me?" he cried out. Austin's eyes widened as the dark entity approached. Red slash marks appeared on his arms and he could feel the burn from them on his torso. He looked down to see his shirt was ripped. He slowly backed into the kitchen, his eyes darting back and forth as he did so. "This ends now." More female laughter. This time it split into a disharmonious chorus. Austin grabbed a knife out of the block on the counter and held it out in front of him. "Don't come near me." The hand holding the knife trembled and slowly turned inward until the blade was facing Austin. It went up to his neck and Austin's heart began to pound. Damn. She was going to force him to slit his own throat.

Without warning, his hand moved down and he stabbed himself in the leg. Austin dropped the knife and gripped his thigh. Blood trickled down his leg and dripped on the floor. When he looked up, her dark presence was surrounding him. He inhaled sharply and her spirit rushed into his open mouth and through his nose. Austin let loose a tortured scream. He was slipping away. The spark of life that made him Austin was being overshadowed by the entity. With a forceful pull she ripped him from his world and thrust him into her own.

Casey wrung her hands as she paced in her apartment. She needed to get out for a bit, get her mind off Austin. *I'll go see Luis.*

She walked to the corner grocery store to get some flowers and, in the check-out line, her eyes drifted over to the tabloids. On the front cover of one was a picture of an almost unrecognizable Austin Cole. His face was scratched up and he had one arm around a woman in a thong and bustier and the other hand was holding a drink. The caption read: *Austin Cole Dumps Psychic Girlfriend to Chase Women and Spirits of a Different Kind.* Another magazine showed him passed out on the ground in front of a strip club. It read: *Spirit Chaser on Downward Spiral.* Casey tore her eyes away and tried to concentrate on Luis.

She entered the hospital room to find a gaunt, but smiling, Luis lying in a hospital bed hooked up to an IV. His wife, Marie, was sitting next to him. "Casey," he said with a smile. She leaned over and gave him a hug.

"Sorry I didn't come sooner. How are you feeling?"

Luis waved her concerns away. "I'm feeling better."

"Then eat something, Luis," Marie scolded. "You are too thin."

Luis shook his head and rubbed his abdomen. "I can't. My stomach is unsettled." He glanced over at Casey. "I've had some complications. That's why I'm still in here."

"Yes, I know. Austin told me you got an infection."

Luis blinked. "How did he know?"

Casey's eyebrows drew together. "What do you mean?"

"I didn't think he knew. I haven't seen him."

"I don't understand. He hasn't been here?" Casey asked. Luis shook his head.

"Maybe Gary told him," Marie suggested. Neither Luis nor Casey supported her assertion.

"How *is* Austin? I've been trying to call him, but I can't through. It's like his phone is turned off."

"I don't know. We broke up." That was all she got out before *Tubular Bells* began to play. "Excuse me, Luis. I've got to take this."

"Thai?"

"I just got off the phone with Austin."

"How is he?" Casey tried to keep an even tone to her voice.

Acting like a total asshole. "He seemed sober. But I agree with you. He's acting strange." Thai paused, not sure how to phrase his next question. "Can I ask you something?"

"Yeah sure."

"Was there anyone with him in the apartment when you found him with the drugs?"

"No. He was alone. Why do you ask?"

He just lied to me. Why would he tell me he was fucking around on Casey when he wasn't? "I just wondered if he was getting high with someone else."

At that moment, Casey's other line beeped in. She saw it was Barrett. "Thai, let me call you back." She ended the call with Thai and answered Barrett. "Yeah."

"Casey," Barrett blurted into the phone. "I've seen it. We have to hurry."

"Seen what? What are you talking about?"

"Austin's in trouble. That unholy bitch has got her claws in him."

34

Barrett instructed Casey to get over to Austin's building as quickly as she could. *C'mon. Hurry up.* Casey mentally told the cab driver. Traffic was a ridiculous piece of shit. It was bumper to bumper all the way from the hospital to Austin's building. She exited the cab at Marley's and ran the rest of the way.

When she arrived, Barrett and Thai were standing outside of Austin's loft. The door was ripped off its hinges. Casey peeked into the space. The couch was upended. All the cabinet doors in the kitchen were wide open and broken plates and glasses were strewn across the loft. The stuffing was ripped out of cushions and the television was lying screen down on the floor.

"What the hell happened?" Casey pointed at the space. "Where's Austin?"

Thai pressed his lips together. "Beats the fuck out of me."

Barrett was twisting the ring on his finger, lost in his thoughts. They all turned when the elevator dinged and Gary and Bob stepped out. "What the hell?" Gary said as he pointed at the door off its hinges.

Thai shook his head. "I came up here when Barrett called me. Austin's missing and his place is trashed." Bob walked through the front door and into the apartment.

"I want to show you guys something." Barrett pulled a folded paper out of his jacket pocket. When he opened it up, Casey could see it was about the size of a large picture frame. "Recognize this?"

Casey's hand flew to her mouth. She closed her eyes. "Enchanted Hill Manor."

"I drew this yesterday. The night before, I dreamt I was in Austin's head and I was thinking about this house. Isn't this the place you two visited while you were in Texas?"

Casey nodded. Cold tingles raced up her spine. Bob poked his head out into the hallway. "Come inside, everyone. You need to see this."

They entered, stepping over Austin's personal belongings and broken furniture. Bob turned and pointed. "Look at this." Along the wall extending from the kitchen to the front door were two long red streaks. Her eyes dropped to the ground. Drops of blood dotted the hardwood floors. "See here." Bob pointed at what looked like two bloody hand prints gripping the inside of the door frame. "Whatever happened, he didn't go willingly."

Casey rubbed her arms as fear welled up in the pit of her stomach. Austin was missing and his blood was all over the floor. Her eyes were drawn to the ceiling. She had been so concerned about Austin that she failed to notice the place itself. The paranormal funk was back and it had brought its friends. A depressing gloom filled the entire space. It made Casey want to crawl into a corner and cry. *What if he's...*

Barrett rubbed his forehead. "Stop it, Casey. Don't think like that. I would know if she'd killed him. And you would, too."

Thai spied Austin's phone on the coffee table. "Austin never goes anywhere without this." He reached over to grab it and it disappeared. "What the fuck?"

The room went silent. Perspiration dotted Barrett's upper lip. He closed his eyes. "You okay?" Casey asked.

"Just a little nauseated. I need to get out of here." Barrett ran out of the apartment and the others followed. He sat on the floor against the wall and rested his head on his knees. The elevator door opened and they all looked up.

Luis slowly stepped out. He was unsteady on his feet and Casey ran over to help him. "What are you doing here?"

He took a handkerchief out of his pocket and dabbed his forehead. "I had to come." He peered in the front door but went no further. "So the demon has taken him?"

"We think so," Casey said.

Gary nodded. "It makes sense now."

Thai's eyebrows furrowed. "What do you mean?"

"Austin's new ability to see the future."

"What are you talking about?" Thai asked.

"He knew before it happened that Luis would have a flat tire and miss the meeting. He even said Luis wouldn't spend the off season doing exorcisms like he usually does. A few days later, Luis falls down the stairs."

"I didn't fall. I was pushed by an invisible entity," Luis said. All heads turned toward him.

"Why didn't you tell us?" Casey demanded.

"I was planning to tell you at the hospital. Then Barrett called."

"Shit." Casey put her hand to her forehead. "I should have known. The personality changes. The sleeping all the time." *Masturbating in a closet.* "That's not Austin."

Thai pushed off the wall and faced Casey and Barrett. "No shit that's not Austin. Some psychics you two are. He gets abducted by an evil entity right under your noses."

Barrett raised his head. "C'mon, dude. Don't be a dick. I can't see the future anymore and she-demon was blocking me. Think about it. Most of us were out of town when things started to get weird. Do you honestly not believe that was by design?"

Thai crossed his arms and tipped his head toward Casey. "What about you? What's your excuse?"

"I already told you. I thought he was on drugs." *No. She made you think he was on drugs.*

"Damnit, Casey. This is Austin we're talking about. He doesn't do drugs."

"Thai, leave her alone," Barrett said. "It's not her fault. Satan is called the deceiver for a reason."

Luis held up his hand. "This isn't accomplishing anything." He inclined his head to the loft. "The evil is affecting our tempers. Let's go to the office and figure this out."

"What about the apartment? We can't just leave it like this. One of the staff is bound to find it and call the cops," Thai pointed out.

"Then let them," Luis said. "Austin's penthouse has a private elevator. If we're lucky, no one will venture up here for a day or two and that will buy us some time. I'm not trying to interfere with the law, but if we report this to the police, they will detain us for questioning. They're not going to accept that this was a supernatural incident, and we don't have the time to waste. Getting Austin away from the demon is all that matters."

As soon as they arrived at *SCI*, Gary called Josie in Louisiana, gave her a quick rundown, and video conferenced her in via Skype.

"First things first. We need to locate him. Does anyone have any ideas about where she could have taken him?" Luis asked.

"Here," Barrett said, unfolding his drawing. "Enchanted Hill Manor. Casey knows where it is. She's been there."

Thai glared at her. "Don't look at me that way. I told him it was evil as hell and to leave it alone."

Thai pressed his lips together. "I can get us on a flight out of here in a couple of hours."

"Good. The sooner the better," Luis said.

"Liv and I can meet you out there. If we leave now, we can be there a few hours after you arrive," Josie said.

"Let's get moving. Pack a bag and get to the airport." Thai said, standing up. Casey grabbed her purse and her sweater and everyone began to scurry around.

"I'll head over to the airport now and buy tickets," Barrett said. "I can grab a change of clothes at the gift shop."

"The hell you will," a booming male voice cut through the frenetic activity. In an instant the background noise went to zero. "You're not flying out there. You're not going anywhere near that place," Derek said. His hands were on his hips and his gaze was dead serious.

Barrett stood up to face him. "This is a private meeting."

"Don't change the subject. How in the fuck do you think this is a good idea? You just got it out of your body and now you want to invite it back in?"

"It's not your decision. Austin needs us, and I'm going."

"Just like that." Derek crossed his arms. "You'd go anywhere and do anything to save him after he nearly got you killed." He pointed at Barrett's chest. "You really need to check your priorities."

Barrett opened his mouth to respond, but Luis put his hand on his shoulder. "Derek is right. You can't go. It will come after you. It would love nothing more than to crawl inside your head again."

Barrett shrugged out of Luis's grasp. "I can't sit around here doing nothing while my best friend is suffering." He leaned over with his palms flat on the table. "I understand what he's going through. None of the rest of you do." He averted his eyes from Derek's penetrating gaze.

"Yes, that's true," Luis agreed. "We could never understand what it's like. And when we get him back, he's going to need you more than any of us to help him through his recovery."

"Let's go," Thai jumped up. Everyone else bustled out of the room. Derek stared at Barrett, the irritation and disappointment evident in his glacial expression. Finally, he turned and left. Barrett raked his fingers through his hair and collapsed into a chair. Now he was all alone.

35

As soon as they deplaned, Thai and Gary walked over to the rental car desk. Casey was tired of sitting. She paced back and forth, worrying the pocket of her cardigan. Bob stood, sipping on a cup of coffee and staring out the window. Casey stared down at the boot cast on Luis's leg. "Why don't you sit down? You look kind of gray." He had to feel awful—getting out of the hospital and then hopping a plane.

"No. The nurse was kind enough to give me a shot to prevent blood clots, but if I don't keep moving, I'll develop one anyway."

Casey narrowed her eyes. "They didn't release you, did they?"

Luis smiled weakly. "No. I left against medical advice. Doctors ... they worry too much." Casey paced and chewed her fingernail. "Would you feel better talking about it?" he asked her.

She turned and looked out the window. After a long sigh, she spoke. "Thai's right. This is all my fault. He was trying to tell me he was in trouble, and I wouldn't listen."

"Casey, it's not your fault. Demonic possession is rare. I'm telling you this and I'm an exorcist. Whenever I am contacted regarding a possible possession, I insist the individual go through a thorough medical and mental evaluation first. I also ask for a drug screen and look for any evidence—past or present—of drug abuse. We are taught to suspect other things first because demonic possession is so rare. The demon lied to you. It showed you what it wanted you to see."

Casey shoved her hands into the pockets of her sweater and continued to pace. "I just want him to be okay. He's got to be okay."

Luis squeezed her shoulder. "Trust in God, daughter. And pray. Prayer is the most important weapon we have."

"Casey, Luis, let's go." Thai waved them over.

Gary drove, Thai rode shotgun, and Casey sat in the backseat between Bob and Luis. As soon as they got in the Suburban, Luis pulled out his rosary and kissed it. With the lights from the parking lot, Casey could see his lips moving.

Bible memory verses from her youth surfaced in her mind. *This kind can only be driven out by prayer. Pray without ceasing. The prayer of the righteous availeth much.*

Casey pulled out her phone and dialed her parents' phone number. "Mom? Is Dad there? I really need to talk to him." She tapped her hand against her thigh as she waited for her mom to put her dad on the line.

A moment later she heard, "Sweetheart, what's going on?"

"Daddy, it's Austin. He needs your help."

Casey dry-swallowed three Excedrin as the Suburban pulled up to Enchanted Hill. The dead sensed her presence and flocked to her like a moth to the flame. They were banging on the windows of the car door before it even stopped. Casey closed her eyes and tried to ignore them.

Gary cut the ignition and Luis nodded his head at Thai and Casey. "Maybe you two should stay here while we check things out."

Thai said, "Hell, no," at the same time Casey said, "Not happening."

"C'mon, we're wasting time," Thai muttered as he unlocked the door and kicked it open with his foot. Casey scooted over to get out of the car, but Luis put his hand over hers.

"I know you've seen evil before, daughter, but this is different. This is affecting someone you love."

"And that's why I have to go with you."

"No. That's why you should stay back until we know how he is. He was still fighting it back in LA, but if the demon was able to drag him half-way across the country, there's no telling what we'll find. He won't look like the Austin we know and he will say the vilest things you can imagine."

"I understand, Luis. Demons are vulgar. I get it."

"No, I don't think you do. It will know your thoughts, Casey. It will use your love of Austin against you. It will lie to you. Demons don't fight fair. You must guard your heart and mind against its attacks."

"What that thing says doesn't matter to me. Getting Austin back is all that does." She looked at the other four. "We walk in together. Austin's rules."

The four men entered through the gate and started up the steps. Casey followed as quickly as she could. Wading through all the dead surrounding her was impeding her progress. She sandwiched herself between Thai and Gary. Thai looked at the rest of the group, unsure of how to proceed. Casey took his hand. "Ready?" she asked as she reached for Gary's. They all clasped hands and nodded in the affirmative.

Luis kissed his Crucifix. Thai put his hand on the doorknob and with more courage than he actually possessed said, "Let's do this." The door opened silently. The first thing Casey noticed was the temperature drop. She rubbed her upper arms, and when she glanced up at Luis, she could see the steam from his breath. The foyer was dark, but up ahead there was a soft orange glow. *Candlelight,* Casey thought. Shadow figures and dark spectres darted in and out of her periphery. The group tiptoed quietly down the hall to the main living area. Casey was sure the demon knew they were here before they even pulled into the drive. But still, entering in a stealth manner seemed like the prudent thing to do.

Casey's breath caught as she entered the main room. Floating a foot off the ground and slowly spinning in a circle was a naked Austin. He was covered in bruises and scratch marks. His hair was greasy and matted, and his neat facial stubble had grown into a scraggly beard. He looked too thin; she could count his ribs from across the room. But that wasn't the only change. As he slowly turned with his back toward her she saw a tattoo of a beautiful woman with long, dark hair. She had thick, leathery-appearing black wings that extended across each of Austin's shoulder blades. Casey's hand went to her throat.

The stench of old blood, urine and feces was suffocating. Thai covered his nose and coughed. At the sound, the Austin thing awoke from its semi-catatonic state. It opened its eyes and Casey whimpered. Her skin erupted in goose bumps and all the air escaped from her lungs. Thai clenched his fists and took a step back. Austin's beautiful blue-green ocean eyes were gone, replaced by pools of black. Shark eyes. They were staring at pure evil. The hatred that shown in its eyes was clearer than any message it could declare with its lips. It smirked and inhaled deeply. Three distinct voices spoke at once. "Casey, I can smell your wet pussy from here."

"Let us speak to Austin," Luis interjected.

"He's indisposed." It laughed and continued to slowly spin. With Austin's hand, it gripped the shaft of his cock and rubbed up and down until he was fully erect. Casey averted her eyes. It began speaking in Italian. Although she didn't understand, she knew Luis did. He stared straight ahead and his features never wavered, but a flash of emotion in his eyes belied his calm state.

"God, we ask you to look with mercy on your servant—" Luis began to pray.

"I am tired of you, Father. Go away." Luis continued his entreaty while the entity focused his dark eyes on Casey. "Where's Barrett? I was hoping he would be joining us. I've missed him. I've missed being inside his head." It pointed to his temple. It spoke again, this time with a male British accent. "Imagine this, Casey: You, me, and Barrett in a threesome. Brilliant! Whilst I fuck you, you give him a nosh." Casey's breathing hitched and hot tears stung her eyes. "What's the matter, my little whore? Why so shy? Usually you splay your legs wide open for me." It cackled and other voices joined in.

Casey turned and ran. Thai was right behind her as she sailed through the front door. On the north side of the old mansion was a stone courtyard. She stopped there, with her arms wrapped around her midsection. She breathed in slowly. *Be strong. Don't let it get to you.*

A moment later, she felt a hand on her shoulder. She turned to face Luis. "It is not Austin saying those vile things, dear daughter. Try to remember that."

Casey nodded. "I know," she said in a trembling voice, "But I still don't want to go back in there." Although the demon that possessed Austin was definitely the main attraction, Casey sensed other dark entities scattered throughout the house. It was safer to remain in the courtyard.

"I told you, it knows how to get to you. You must keep calm no matter what it says. In fact, do not listen to it. All it does is lie." He patted her shoulder then glanced over at Gary. "Help me get my things?" Gary nodded and followed the priest to the Suburban.

Casey walked over to the table and chairs in the courtyard. The ghosts milling around grabbed at her sleeves, pulled her hair, and clung to her skirt. When she turned away they crowded in closer and reached out with their incorporeal hands. She sat down and hunched her shoulders. "Go away. I'm not here for you. I'm here for him." Casey swatted at the air. They pressed closer. She covered her head with her arms.

Bob knelt down next to her. "Tell them to follow me."

Casey looked over at him. "Huh?" Her thoughts were with Austin, not out here with the others.

"You are the strongest psychic signal. That's why they won't leave you alone. If you tell them to follow me, I'll help them cross."

"Thank you," she whispered to him. Casey picked up her head and announced. "Go with Bob. He will help you." She watched as the dead lined up behind him. They followed him like he was the Pied Piper over to a corner of the courtyard.

Gary walked out of the stone gate and smacked into an unmovable barrier. He pushed against the air but couldn't move forward. "What the hell?"

Luis placed his palms against the flat invisible surface. "It seems as if it doesn't want us to leave."

Thai ran over to see. First he placed his hands up against the invisible wall. Then he shoved hard against it with his shoulder. "Shit." He moved down farther and ran into the barrier again. He repeated the process all around the perimeter of the mansion. "We're trapped. It won't budge."

Casey looked over at the corner of the courtyard where Bob was ushering the ghosts through. "The dead don't seem to be having any trouble moving across."

Thai turned his head to see. Light gray auras floated up and out of the manor's grounds. "So only the living are stuck," he noted.

Luis tipped his head to the side. "What about objects?" He bent down and picked up a rock. Everyone watched as he flung it over the stone courtyard fence. It sailed through the barrier easily and landed with a soft thud on the overgrown grass.

"What does this mean?" Gary asked.

"We can't get out. But hopefully, our things can get in." Luis answered.

"So what do we do now?" Thai asked.

"We wait for Josie. When she gets here, she can toss us our things," Luis said.

$$\mathcal{Q}$$

Gary and Bob found a stack of tree limbs on the side of the house. Thai helped the guys break them up and with Bob's lighter, they were able to start a fire. They were gathered around it when Josie and Liv pulled up. Josie dashed out of the car and everyone yelled at her to stay back. "There's some kind of invisible shield around the place. If you come in, you won't be able to get out," Gary said.

Josie blinked. "What in the hell?"

Gary tossed Josie the keys to the Suburban. She took out their luggage and one at a time, heaved the bags over the fence. "How's Austin? Have you seen him?"

Gary shook his head. "That creature in there is more animal than human. He's levitating; speaking in different voices."

"Worse than Barrett?"

"Way worse. And the smell? Like rotten meat that's been rolled in cow shit. I hope to God Luis can help him." Liv threw them some bottled waters she kept in a cooler in the car.

"We need to figure a way to break down this barrier, then we can get Austin and ourselves the fuck out of here," Thai said. "Any ideas?"

"The demon created the barrier." Luis said. "The only way to break it down is to weaken its hold on Austin. And the best way to do that is through exorcism." He turned to face Josie. "We'll need supplies. Food. Water. We're not going to be able to move him away from here like we did with Barrett." He looked over at the crew. "We're going to be here for a while."

"A while?" Thai smacked the table with his hand. "Define 'a while.'"

Luis patted his arm and gazed at him with understanding eyes. "I don't know. But I think we need to prepare for an extended stay." He turned back to Josie. "And get some blankets, coats, gloves, sleeping bags, and thermal underwear for Austin. We don't want him to succumb to hypothermia."

"Bob says that old stone fireplace is in decent shape. He's knocking a bird's nest out of the flue now. If he can get it functional, we can heat the main room for Austin," Gary said.

"That will help," Luis told him.

"I'll call Marcus and Steve from the tech team. They can drive the tech trailer and the lounge here," Josie said. "At least with the lounge on site, we can prepare hot meals for you guys."

"That's good. We'll need the help. But please, ask them to keep quiet about this. The last thing we need is the paparazzi here."

"Will do. I'll get the cameras set up as soon as they arrive. I'll call Barrett and let him know. He can analyze the video from *SCI* headquarters." She reached into her pocket for her phone.

Casey's eyes widened in shock. She pointed toward the front door. "You're going to film this for the show?"

Josie shook her head. "Film it yes, but not for the show. Sometimes we catch stuff on camera we can't see with our eyes. Maybe Barrett can see a way around this force field."

"She's right," Luis agreed. "This demon has been one step ahead of us this whole time. Maybe a little *SCI* high tech can level the playing field."

Thai shoved his arms through the sleeves of his coat. "Whatever we do, we need to hurry up. It's already February. Filming for the show starts up again in March."

Luis walked over. "First things first. We loosen her hold on him and we all get out of here. But Thai, even if we manage to get him away in a few days, it's going to take time to cast the demon out."

"Why? She left Barrett after the first exorcism."

"That was different. The demon didn't inhabit Barrett for very long. But with Austin, it's been slowly invading his mind and body for months. It isn't going to let go easily." Luis stared him in the eyes and spoke in a low voice. "He's not going to be ready to film in a few weeks."

Thai thrust his hands into his pockets. "If that's what you think, you don't know Austin. There's no way he's missing Hillendahl."

"I pray you are right, my son." He glanced over at Bob. "I won't ask the two of you to violate your beliefs by reading responsively during the exorcism. And it would do more harm than good for you two to state things you don't believe. But if you wouldn't mind holding Austin down and keeping him from hurting himself while the rest of us pray and chant, it would be greatly appreciated."

"Of course, we will," Bob said. "We'll do whatever we can to help." Thai didn't speak, but grunted a half-hearted assent.

"Good, let's go." Luis headed for the front door wearing his purple stole and crucifix and clutching the Ritual in one hand and his Aspergillum of holy water in the other. Gary stood beside him and Bob and Thai lined up behind him. He turned to Casey. "That goes for you, too. It's not just about labeling yourself Christian or believing in God in your own way. You have to have a strong faith and believe in the power of the prayers you speak. It would be better for Gary and me to pray the rite alone than for someone weak in the faith to try to help."

"I believe," Casey stared into his eyes. "Christ is the one man I've never doubted."

Luis chewed the inside of his cheek as he considered her words. He straightened and placed his hand on her head. "Casey Lawson, do you repent of your sins and ask God for forgiveness."

"Yes."

"Will you strive to lead a God-pleasing life?"

"I will."

"Do you renounce the devil and all his works and all his ways?"

"I do."

Luis made the sign of the cross. "I am no longer a called servant so I cannot offer you absolution. But know that Christ forgives you. And pray. Never stop praying."

He patted her shoulder and waved everyone over to the front door. "Do not listen to the demon. It lies. Do not engage the demon. Don't ask it anything. Ignore it completely. Casey and Gary concentrate on the prayers and responses. Thai and Bob, don't be distracted by his bizarre behavior; just hold him down. Remember, we aren't the ones who will rescue Austin. It is God who will cast the diabolic out." He exhaled. "It's time." The group followed the priest back into the house.

Luis put on his readers, kissed his purple stole, and opened the text. The Austin thing was no longer floating in the air. It was pacing back and forth. Casey didn't recognize this creature in front of her. Its black orbs looked with such intense hatred upon the former priest that Casey feared for his safety.

Luis began with a lengthy litany to the saints, readings, and prayers. Austin growled and steam came out of his mouth and nostrils. He grabbed his penis and directed a stream of piss toward them. They moved out of the way, and it laughed.

Luis motioned for Bob and Thai to come closer. It growled and spit at Luis. Bob grabbed one of his arms and Thai the other to hold him in place. He made the sign of the cross over Austin. He placed the stole over Austin's neck and his right hand on Austin's head.

"See the cross of the Lord; be gone, you hostile power!" Austin roared like a lion. Luis blessed him and sprinkled him with holy water. "I cast you out, unclean spirit, along with every satanic power of the enemy, every spectre of hell, and all your fell companions in the name of our Lord, Jesus Christ." He made the sign of the cross. The Austin thing pushed Bob and Thai, but they held him down. "Lord, heed my prayer."

"And let my cry be heard by you," Gary and Casey answered.

Austin leaned over and vomited a pile of screws at their feet. Gary glanced down, remembering another container of screws spilling out of a container on a vacant warehouse floor. Austin writhed out of Bob and Thai's grasp. His body began floating up, supine, and five feet off the ground. Luis made the sign of the cross and spoke in Latin. A chorus of voices erupted from Austin's throat. "Your Latin will not work. God will not hear the prayers of an ex-priest."

"How long will this go on?" Casey whispered to Gary.

"Until he comes out of his trance state," Gary answered.

Luis recited the Hail Mary and the Our Father. The creature groaned in pain as Luis flicked holy water on him. Its hands clawed at Austin's face and it wailed in three octaves. Finally, as the first bits of orangey light crested the horizon, she let out a pain-filled shriek. Austin's body fell to the ground.

35

Gary covered him with a blanket. Casey ran to his side and cradled his head in her lap. His eyes flicked open for a moment then shut. "Let him rest. As soon as he awakes, he'll need water." The priest rubbed his forehead and swayed on his feet.

"Easy," Gary said, supporting Luis.

"Outside, please, Gary." He glanced up at the ceiling. "I need to put a little distance between myself and this house." He leaned against the larger, stronger man. Thai crossed his arms and pressed his lips together as he stared down at his broken, fucked-up friend. He shook his head and exhaled, then followed Gary and Luis out.

Austin began to snore. When Bob and Gary returned, they lifted him off the floor, placed him on a cot next to the fireplace, and placed a warm blanket over him. Bob walked over to the fireplace and added some wood. Gary took out padded wrist cuffs with straps.

"What's that?"

"Restraints," Gary said as he attached them to Austin's wrists and ankles. "Part of Luis's exorcism kit. He says they're necessary."

Casey stared down at her hands. "I suppose they are." Austin didn't even stir while they put them on.

Bob turned to her. "He'll probably sleep for a while. Why don't you get some rest, too? We'll stay with him." Gary unpacked his own sleeping bag and settled in on the floor beside Austin. Bob took the other side.

"No," she said simply. She gathered her skirt underneath her and sat next to Austin, lightly stroking his head. She shivered as she caught glimpses of two shadow figures darting in and out of the room.

Bob glanced over to where the shadow beings faded into the wall. He knelt down beside her. "You know, we could take turns. You'll feel better if you step away for a bit. I know with your sight, this can't be easy."

Casey continued to stroke Austin's cheek. "Thank you, Bob. I appreciate the gesture, but I want to be here when he wakes up." She turned to face him. "You have the sight, too. It's probably just as terrible for you."

Bob shook his head. "I've got my spirit guides. I can still see, but they protect me from the worst of it."

"I guess so." Casey thought his spirit guides must be the Incredible Hulk and Iron Man if they could protect him from this evil.

Austin's head rolled back and forth on the cot. Casey sat on her heels.

"I am your servant. I belong to you," he muttered. "I will do whatever you ask."

Her eyebrows furrowed and she looked over to Bob. "Is he conversing with the demon?"

"It sure sounds like it." A disembodied female laugh echoed through the room. Casey jumped and Bob put his hand on her shoulder. "She's trying to scare you. Don't let her."

After a few hours, Austin began to stir. "Water," Casey commanded and Bob handed her a bottle.

He was too tired to open his eyes, but when Casey pressed the water bottle to his lips, he took a sip. "Careful. Don't drink too much. We don't want you puking it up."

"Case, is it really you?" He strained to open his eyelids. Bob stood and alerted the others.

"Yeah, it's me," Casey smiled. A flicker of hope warmed her soul. For the first time since she arrived, she heard Austin speaking in his own voice and staring at her with those gorgeous ocean eyes. They were weary and bloodshot, but they were the most beautiful sight she'd ever beheld. She put the bottle of water to his dry, lacerated lips and he took another sip. Thai and Gary ran in the front door.

Her eyes stared into his and she pressed his hand to her cheek. "I love you, Austin. So much."

He turned his head away. "Don't say that."

"Austin," she said sharply. "I love you. And I'm going to show you every day how much I mean it." A sad smile tugged at his lips. "This is not the response from you I was hoping for. I thought you'd be happy."

He sighed. "The selfish part of me is happy, but it would be so much easier if you didn't." He wrapped his finger around a lock of her hair. He was too ashamed to look her in the face. "You don't know the awful things I've done."

"Shh. It wasn't you." She leaned over to kiss his face. A tear rolled down her cheek. "Austin, I'm sorry. I'm so sorry I didn't listen or believe you."

"No, Case. This is not your fault. I fucked up so bad," his voice was a raspy whisper. He shivered and Casey bundled the blanket tightly around him. "You told me to stay away from Enchanted Hill and I didn't listen."

"But if I hadn't been so stupid and stubborn, we could have stopped this from happening." She lifted his head and gave him another sip of protein water.

"No, Case. I won't let you take the blame. She was gunning for me. I don't think you could have stopped it," he said through chattering teeth.

Thai crossed his arms and looked at both of them with disgust. "Allow me to settle this. You're both fucking assholes." Austin cocked an eyebrow at Casey. She shrugged. Thai turned and walked out the door. He nearly ran into Gary, who was carrying a steaming bowl in his hands.

"Austin, Liv made your favorite. Vegetable soup."

"Liv's here?"

"Yeah. She and Josie both."

Vegetable soup sounded terrible to Austin, but he didn't want to be rude. Casey lifted his head and fed him a couple of spoonfuls. He managed to swallow it down, but shook his head when she tried to give him another.

"Please, Austin. You need to—" Before she could say "eat," Austin began gagging. He leaned over the cot away from Casey and vomited. Watery soup came up, along with shards of bloody glass."

Bob brought Casey a damp rag and she wiped his mouth. Luis limped in. "What's going on?" he asked as Bob and Gary cleaned the floor. Austin frowned and wouldn't look Luis in the eye.

"It's okay," Luis told him. "I know the demon is hostile toward me. I just came to see how you were."

"Have you ever seen this?" Gary pointed to the glass mixed with blood on the floor.

"Yes," he answered calmly. "It happens."

Casey blinked incredulously. "If we don't get him to hold down his food, he'll starve." Her words came out more pointed than she wanted, but she was frustrated by the calm demeanor of the priest. Austin's lip curled downward and he growled. Everyone looked to see if she had returned.

"We'll discuss it later, daughter." Luis told her. He blotted the perspiration on his face with his handkerchief and limped out, heavily favoring his leg.

Austin took another sip of water and closed his eyes. Sleep was creeping up on him. Fuck, he couldn't keep his eyes open for more than a few minutes. Or maybe she just wanted to keep him in a dream state where she was in full control. His eyes closed involuntarily, and a moment later he was out.

Bob glanced over at Casey. "Why don't you try to get some rest, too? I'll stay with him."

"Are you sure?"

"Positive. Don't worry. I'll let you know when he wakes up."

Casey nodded, glanced back at Austin one last time, and stepped out into the courtyard. Bob was right. Even putting a few feet of distance from that house made a huge difference.

"Luis," she called, running to catch up with him. "What are we going to do? He needs to eat."

"Yes. I know that." The priest rubbed his brow. "I'm going to speak with Liz now about creating a menu he can tolerate."

Casey looked around the courtyard. While she had been with Austin, the guys had been busy unpacking the supplies Liv and Josie had brought back. A few tents were set up on the pavers. Thai pointed to a red one. "That one's yours. I suggest you get some rest. We'll repeat this whole thing once she-demon comes back."

Casey crawled into her tent and collapsed onto her sleeping bag. She tried to relax. It had been almost twenty-four hours since she'd slept. Every time she closed her eyes and tried to rest, her third eye shook her awake, warning her of the innumerable evil entities and dangers that surrounded the manor. She lay there, staring up at the red plastic material of her tent for hours.

"Casey, are you up?" she heard Josie yell. She crawled out of her tent. It was overcast, but she could see the noon-day sun poking out from behind the cloud cover. Josie waved her over from the other side of the fence.

She pulled her hair up into a ponytail. "What's going on? Is Austin awake?"

"Not yet. There's someone here to see you."

Casey gave Josie a questioning glance. "Come see," Josie told her.

She walked over to where Josie was pointing. Her father was standing by the gate with his hands folded and head bowed. The dead watched him curiously, but kept their distance. His lips were moving silently. She waited until he finished his whispered conversation with God and opened his eyes. "Daddy, what are you doing here?"

"What you asked me to do. Praying for Austin." His gaze flickered over the ghosts, then returned to Casey.

"But I didn't mean for you to come all the way out here."

"I had to come. Sweetheart, your mother and I are so worried for you."

"I'm fine." Casey crossed her arms. A scream and the crash like the sound of shattered pottery erupted from the house. "You've lost," three distinct voices proclaimed at the same time.

"Casey," he said.

"Later, Dad. She's back. I gotta go."

She followed Bob and Thai into the manor. Luis was already standing there with his head bowed in prayer. A cool wind swept through the room. Luis pressed his hand down on the pages of the Ritual to keep them from turning. That was when Casey noticed the entity. She glided over to Austin from a dark corner. His eyes rolled to the back of his head and his head flopped onto the cot. She-demon smiled.

Two of her evil sidekicks joined her, one at her right and one at her left. Casey recognized them as the two shadow figures she had seen in the house earlier. The one on the left had the lower body of a goat and the one on the other side had a blank spot where its mouth should have been.

Luis looked up from his text, but did not stop his reading. Despite the effort of Thai and Bob to hold him down, Austin's body began to rise, with only the restraints tethering him to the cot. A moment later, the cot lifted off the ground as well. He opened his mouth, and Casey watched in horror as her mist-like form poured itself into him. Austin's head turned toward her. Shark eyes. The demon's spirit form adhered itself to his body and wrapped her leg over his hip. She caressed his face and licked his lips with her long forked tongue. She pointed at Casey and whispered in his ear.

Casey was scared, but she was upset, too. "Whatever you want to say, say it to me," She yelled. Luis looked up from his reading and shook his head at her.

Demoness cackled and made long scratch marks on his skin with her sharp, black fingernails. No one but Casey and Bob could see what she was doing, but they could see the results as long lacerations appeared on Austin's chest and abdomen. The bloody scratch marks formed the words "He's mine, now."

Casey began to shake. "Stay away from him, you bitch!"

A cold, disembodied hand shoved Casey back and she landed on her butt five feet away. It cackled. Austin's voice joined with hers. "Corpulent cunt. You're only good for fellatio, and you're not even very good for that."

"Casey, go. Get out of here," Luis told her.

She wiped her eyes. "No, I'm fine."

"Go, Casey," Luis commanded. Demoness took this moment of distraction to knock the text out of Luis's hand. He reached down to pick it up and she slammed him into the wall. Austin opened his mouth and globs of something resembling black gelatin poured out. As soon as they hit the floor, they dissolved with a hiss and a puff of steam. Luis righted himself and spoke to Gary. "Get her out of here."

Gary hauled Casey up to her feet and marched her outside. She tried to shove him aside and edge around him, but he held her firm. He bent over to look her in the eye. "Take a minute. You're upset, and it's not helping." Gary gave her a warning glare before heading back into the mansion.

Casey vacillated, wondering if she should go against Luis and head back in. Josie walked up then. "Don't even think about it, Casey." She handed her a cup of coffee in a thermal mug.

"What are you doing? You realize you just trapped yourself inside the gate."

"I know. Liv and I talked about it. We both agree my place is with you guys. Marcus and Steve can handle the tech end."

"They're here?"

"Yeah. They arrived while you guys were inside. The tech trailer is up and running. Barrett can now see what's going on here. Liv is still on the other side to go on supply runs and meal preparation and junk."

"That's a lot of work—taking care of our crew. Are you sure she's okay with it?"

"Are you kidding? Liv is Ms. Organization. She lives for this shit."

Movement behind the gate attracted Casey's attention. Liv was waving them over. Casey trudged over to the courtyard and Josie followed. "Barrett's on the phone. He wants to talk to you." Casey held out her hands and Liv underhand tossed the phone to her. She caught it and hoped the demon brigade in the house wouldn't wipe out the battery before she had a chance to speak with him. "Hello, Barrett?"

"How are you feeling?" he asked.

"Like someone hit me in the forehead with a sledgehammer."

"I can just imagine." Barrett stared down at the wastebasket he had placed next to the desk. He couldn't watch the footage of Enchanted Hill without it upsetting his stomach and he was over a thousand miles away. "Have you been able to speak to Austin?"

"Once."

"How was he?"

"He seemed surprised to see us. I guess he thought we wouldn't come for him."

"That would never happen."

"No. But she's got him so wrapped up in her lies, he doesn't know what side is up."

"Casey, stay strong."

"I'm trying, but it's hard. She abuses him and he still tells her 'I am your servant.' It's sick. It sucks being witness to her and those creepy shadow figures tearing his skin and torturing him." Casey shook her head and shuddered.

"Then don't watch."

"Huh?"

"Close your third eye."

Casey wasn't sure she heard him correctly. "You can't be serious. I'll be blind and helpless."

Barrett twisted his silver ring. "Trust me. You'll feel much better."

There was silence from Casey's end for a moment. Finally she said, "That seems dangerous."

Barrett knew what he was asking. He also knew that if the situation were reversed and Casey was telling him to block his sixth sense, he'd tell her no fucking way. "Is it more dangerous than going insane? You can't be getting any sleep as it is. You don't need to see all the grisly details to help Austin."

Casey exhaled. "Okay. I'll do it."

"Good," Barrett said, relieved. "I know it's scary, but I think it's the best thing for you." He believed it, too. So why did it seem like a lie coming off his lips? "I'll be your eyes. I'll warn you."

"Yeah. Okay."

"Put Josie on the line. I need to tell her about some stuff I noticed on the static camera. And take care of yourself." She handed Josie the phone and walked over to the edge of the courtyard. She grasped the old stone gate with both hands and closed her eyes.

Visualizing her pineal gland, she focused all her concentration as she willed it to shut down. Her third eye realized what she was doing and tried to force itself open. She felt a sharp stabbing pain in the base of her brain and a screech like nails on a chalkboard as her third eye begged her to stop. Then, silence. Casey looked around. It was eerily quiet. For the first time since she'd arrived, she couldn't see the dead milling around the yard.

36

Luis walked slowly out of the mansion. Perspiration dotted his upper lip. Casey took one arm and Josie the other to help him over to the table.

"You're done?" Casey asked. Josie handed him a bottled water.

Luis removed his glasses and rubbed his eyes. "For tonight. She's left him. He's asleep."

Casey turned and headed toward the house. Luis put his arms out to stop her.

"Let me go. I need to see him."

"We need to talk first. I realize that you can see more than the rest of us and that has to be upsetting. But you must not engage the demon."

"She was scratching him; hurting him. So, what? I'm just supposed to let her abuse him?" Casey shook her head.

"Calling it names won't help. If you can't get hold of your emotions, I cannot allow you back in there. Remember, before the fall it was an angel of God. In the order of creation, you are not above it. It is not our place to speak ill to them. Let the Lord rebuke them. You cannot overcome evil with hate. You can only overcome evil with love."

Casey nodded. She knew he was right, but it wasn't something she felt like hearing. "I've got to go to Austin." She hurried into the mansion and knelt by his cot. Bob was stoking the fire, but the room was still cold. Thai was turned away from them, staring out the window. She kissed Austin's forehead and he stirred.

"Case?"

"Yeah, baby. It's me. I'm here."

Josie brought in a basin with warm water and soap. "Welcome back."

"Hey, JoJo. I've missed your blue hair." Josie grinned up at him and placed the bowl on the floor while Casey uncovered him. Casey wrung out the excess water from the soapy sponge and proceeded to clean his bloody, lacerated, and filthy body. Josie put shampoo on a wet washcloth and scrubbed his dirty hair and beard. A grin spread across his face. "Thai, check this out. I've got two hot chicks giving me a sponge bath."

Thai turned from the window and looked at him with disgust. "Nice." He muttered between clenched lips. His gaze returned to the courtyard.

"Don't get used to this type of treatment," Josie told Austin. "It's not in my job description and you definitely don't pay me enough to wash your ass." Casey covered all his sores in antibiotic ointment then undid his restraints and got him dressed.

With Josie's help, she pulled a clean, long-sleeved shirt over his head and slipped on some pajama bottoms and warm woolen socks. Bob brought over a blanket he had been warming by the fire and they bundled him up.

Gary walked in carrying a fast-food bag and a Coke. "Eat up, Austin."

Austin's stomach rumbled. He hadn't realized how hungry he was until he smelled the burger and greasy fries. Casey opened the wrapper and handed it to him. He shoved it into his mouth, devouring half the double cheese burger in two large bites.

Austin stared up at Casey and his fingers gently caressed her arm. "You look different without all that black shit around your eyes."

"Making myself up hasn't been high on my priority list."

"You're beautiful."

"Shut up and eat." He took a large sip of Coke and grabbed some fries.

Thai was leaning against the wall with his arms crossed. Austin turned his head to look at him. "Have you been filming this?"

Thai glared at him. "What kind of question is that?"

"It would be great for the ratings. This could be one of our most popular episodes. Enchanted Hill Manor: The Possession of Austin Cole."

"Get fucked," Thai replied, and his gaze returned to the window.

Austin chuckled without mirth. "I already am."

Thai stomped off and slammed the door on his way out. Casey watched him leave then turned to Austin. "He's a little on edge. You probably shouldn't joke about it."

"It's better than crying."

Casey squeezed his hand. "Actually, we are sending footage to *SCI* for Barrett to analyze. He's helping us find a way around the force field she's erected so we can get you out and all go home." Austin knew all about the force field. It was part of her plan. He was relieved to hear Barrett was far away. At least she hadn't succeeded in bringing him here, too.

Austin burped loudly. Then farted. "Sorry about that."

"It's okay. You can't help it."

"I'm tired," he said.

"Just rest." Casey tucked the blanket tight around him and kissed his forehead before returning to the courtyard. She spied Thai standing close to the fence where the oak tree stood. His back was facing the manor as he gazed out into the early morning fog that always seemed to surround the place. By his demeanor, Casey knew she should leave him alone.

The following afternoon, Casey awoke to the sound of tools banging and opened her eyes. She crawled out of the tent to see what was going on. Gary was constructing a rectangular wooden structure at the side of the house. Her eyes drifted to the other side of the gate. Steve and her dad were unrolling a garden hose on the other side of the gate.

"What's going on?" Casey yawned.

Gary didn't look up from his work but did answer her question. "I don't know about you, but I'm starting to smell as bad as Austin. If we can get this thing to work, we'll have a shower by the end of the day."

"Anything I can do to help?"

"Yeah, take that shower curtain Liv bought and put it on the pole. I'll hang it as soon as I'm done nailing the enclosure together."

Later that day, Casey entered the very basic shower with a water hose for a faucet and coated every millimeter of skin with soap. She washed her hair three times. How she missed personal hygiene! Now she felt almost human.

On Sunday morning, Luis performed Mass in the front room of the house. Gary and Casey sat on either side of Austin's cot, listening to the divine service. Luis had already decided there would be no formal exorcism tonight. Everyone, including Austin, needed a day of rest. And Luis needed to get his strength back. His leg had been bothering him, and now he was running a low-grade fever. Everyone thought, but no one dared to say, that his infection had returned.

The demon remained quiet during most of the service, but when Luis lifted the host and said, "This is my body," she growled in four part harmony, and Austin bucked and thrashed against the restraints.

After the service, Casey walked over to the courtyard table. "Something smells good."

"Liv's making a roast," Gary told her. "She thinks we all need a good, home-cooked meal."

Bob approached. "Is anything wrong?" Casey jumped up.

"Relax. Austin's sound asleep. I figure I can join the land of the living for an hour or two." Bob had appointed himself Austin's personal caretaker.

"Bob, if you need a break, one of us can spell you."

Gary brought him a coffee and he took a sip. "I'm good. I know the spirits would bother the rest of you."

"So why don't they bother you?" Casey knew if she tried to stay in the house with Austin, she'd never get any rest. But Bob had told her he'd had no problems sleeping on the floor in the main room while the others slept in their tents outside.

"It's a difference of belief systems. I mean no disrespect to Luis or your father, but I don't agree with them about the spirit realm. I have had many impassioned discussions with Luis about this, and it usually ends up with me telling him not to worry about my soul, and him telling me he's praying for me. Neither one of us is swayed. Catholics and Christians anger the spirits. The goal of those religions is to get rid of them. My people try to live in harmony with nature and the spirit world."

"Even the bad spirits?"

"Spirits are like people. Some are nice; others aren't. That doesn't mean you can't get along with them." He nodded to the mansion. "The ones in there are hostile to Austin because he is Catholic and because he antagonizes them on his ghost hunts. They downright hate Luis, but they leave me alone. If there was a danger, my spirit guides would alert me."

Liv whistled. "Come and get it."

The meat was fork-tender and well-seasoned. The rolls were the frozen kind you put in the oven, but to Casey they tasted like heaven. For dessert they had warm apple crisp a la mode. It would have been a pleasant afternoon cook-out with friends, if they forgot about the fact that a few feet away their possessed friend was chained to a cot, imprisoned in a house created in the bowels of hell.

After dinner they gathered by the gate, the crew on one side and Liv, Marcus, Steve and her dad on the other. Bob licked his fork. "This sure is good. Too bad Austin is missing it."

"Don't worry," Liv said. "I'm making him a to-go plate for when he wakes up. I substituted the vegetables with pork rinds and chili-cheese fries." She shook her head. "Serving Austin this junk food crap seems so wrong."

Austin awoke when he heard the sounds of laughter outside. Bob had moved his cot close to the window and cleaned the grime off so he could actually see onto the courtyard. Josie was standing next to the fence, laughing and joking with Liv. The others were gathered around a fire pit. *They're all here,* he thought to himself. *They came here for me.*

She-demon's spirit form wrapped around him and clung to him like wet fabric. *No. They're here because of you. If I release them, they'll flee and not give you a second thought.*

"No," he whispered. "That's not true. They're my friends."

She pointed her discarnate finger to the fence. Austin stared to where she was pointing. Josie was standing on one side of the fence with her palm pressed against the force field. Liv pressed her hand to the force field on the other side. *You've separated them. They'll blame you for this. And Thai? When's the last time he came to see you?*

37

At twilight, Casey rose to check on Austin. Gary and Bob unfastened his restraints and let him walk around for a few minutes. She watched him as he took a few steps. When he got too close to the foyer, sharp pains rolled through his stomach and head. She-demon wasn't going to let him outside. Ball and chains, invisible to the others, kept him house-bound. He was unsteady on his feet, and the short walk around the room exhausted him. When he sat back down on the cot, Casey could see dots of perspiration on his upper lip. It was hard to believe this was the same man who used to be able to run five miles, barely breaking a sweat.

Casey brought him his plate and he was able to feed himself. "How are you feeling?" She sat down next to him and rubbed his back.

"Tired. Ashamed. Alone." He stared straight ahead. His former life seemed like an unreal dream. Rising early, running most every morning, working ten and twelve-hour days. Now, he slept most of the time. And when he wasn't asleep, he was often in a trance state while she operated his body and mind. What was the point of getting off the cot? It's not like he could go anywhere. "I don't really feel like talking." He lay back down and extended his arms and feet so that Gary could attach the restraints.

She kissed his forehead. "It's okay. You don't have to talk. I'll just stay here with you." She took his hand but he pushed her away.

"Casey, go. Please."

"You just said you were lonely. I'm here to cheer you up."

He stared at her for a moment. "I wish you could." Austin closed his eyes. In a few minutes she could hear him snoring.

Casey held his hand and studied the mansion. On the right side of the main room was a grand staircase. At one time it must have been beautiful, but now, the banister was rotting, and Casey wondered how sturdy it was.

Bob stoked the fire, then sat down next to them.

In a low voice, so she wouldn't wake Austin, she asked, "Does he seem any better to you?"

"In some ways," Gary said. "Today he was able to piss in a bucket instead of on himself. And he's able to stay out of his demonic trance state for a few hours each day now, minus the time he's asleep. But come tonight, she'll be back. And he'll be slithering around the room like a snake." Bob said nothing but nodded his head in agreement.

A few hours later, Bob shooed Casey out the door so she could get some rest. She headed over to the courtyard where the others were gathered in a circle around the fire. Josie sucked her pierced lip into her mouth. She stared up at Luis. "I was wondering. Is Austin the worst case of possession you've ever seen?"

Luis put down his water. "One of them, yes. This demon is very strong."

"You said one of them. What happened to the other ones?" Josie asked.

"I was thinking of a woman in her forties. I'm still working with her and probably will for many years to come."

"How long have you been working with her?" Thai asked.

"About fifteen years." Casey's eyes grew wide.

"You mean he's going to be like that for at least fifteen years!" Josie gasped.

Luis chuckled. "No, I don't think so. The woman I'm referring to has shown remarkable improvement. She comes in once a month and I perform part of the Ritual. She doesn't curse anymore, but she does clear her throat and drool when I pray over her. She lives a mostly normal life. She's married with kids and holds down a full-time nursing job. Most people would never know she's possessed."

"How long did it take her to get to that point?" Casey asked.

"About five years." Casey gasped. That seemed incredible to Casey. "You mustn't think of exorcism as a one-time fix," Luis continued. "For most, it's like ongoing outpatient therapy. The poor lady was cursed by a relative early in life. Her parents were unchurched and she was never baptized. She lived with the demon for a long time before she sought help. Possessions from curses are some of the most difficult to break."

"Then how come it only took Barrett one exorcism and he was cured?" Thai asked.

"Barrett's case was a rarity. Most possessions happen gradually over time." Luis snapped his finger. "Barrett's possession happened just like that. It didn't take long to liberate him because the demon wasn't entrenched. But even so, he still suffered from the effects of the possession long after."

"So how long do you think she's been in Austin?" Thai asked.

"It's impossible to say. But it obviously hasn't been years."

"Any idea how long it will take to free him?" Gary asked.

Luis shrugged. "Every possession is different. I'm still exorcising Brad, and he was possessed sometime last spring. When we started, he was in the trance state almost every day, but now the demon only manifests when he is prayed over. He undergoes the Ritual once a week and he is steadily improving. His parents are currently home schooling him, but hopefully, next year, he will be able to function in society."

"Well, what does that mean for Austin?" Thai asked. "When will he be able to get back to work?"

Luis rubbed the bridge of his nose and exhaled. He had tried to avoid this conversation with Thai, but Thai kept pressing the issue. "I don't think ghost hunting is a viable career path for someone who's under demonic influence."

Thai frowned. "He's the Spirit Chaser. That's not something you can walk away from."

Luis spoke gently. "I'm not concerned about Austin getting back to work; I'm concerned about Austin's spiritual and mental health."

Thai stood up and walked away. It was quiet for a moment as everyone watched him go. Gary turned to Casey's dad. "Reverend Lawson, have you seen many possessions?"

Casey's dad shook his head. "Contrary to popular belief, Bible College does not teach a pastor how to cast out a demon, or even how to handle snakes." Everyone chuckled at that, and Casey glanced up at her dad. "I've seen one case of a young girl who might have been possessed. I was at a conference and attending a church in another town. A woman came to the front of the church with her daughter, who was muttering profanities and writhing around. The minister and the elders of the church laid hands on her and prayed. She seemed to calm down." Reverend Lawson took a sip of his coffee. "I still don't know for sure if it was real or she was faking it. That's what I've always believed—that it's someone trying to get attention. Trouble is, I've never been taught the signs of true demon possession like Father Ramirez." He nodded toward Luis. "I pray that if I ever were in that situation, the Holy Spirit would guide me."

Luis nodded. "You certainly don't want to perform the Ritual on those who aren't possessed. If they are mentally ill, that could do more harm than good. But a prayer of blessing never hurt anyone. And if the demon is hiding, it could drive it out and then you would know for sure."

"I don't understand why the churches either ignore exorcism completely or act like it's a dirty little secret," Gary said.

Luis sighed. "Possession is rare. But rare isn't the same as nonexistent. Exorcists are in short supply, and it is difficult and time-consuming to train them. Most of the ones I know are aging and completely overworked. We are supposed to fast and pray before we exorcise the sick. But most of us see several sick souls a day. We can't go without food all the time. We'd starve."

"Is that why you only eat once a day?" Casey asked.

"Yes. But I do eat a big meal. Even so, it takes a toll." Casey thought about it. Over the past four weeks, Luis had suffered a broken leg, hospitalization, surgery, infection—all at the hands of a demon. He was currently running a fever and there was a rattle in his chest that wasn't there a few days ago. He was frailer now than she had ever seen him. And still, he performed the Ritual most nights on Austin.

"So why is it so rare? Is it misdiagnosed?" Gary asked.

"I don't think so. While possession is certainly the most visible sign of his power, Satan employs other, more subtle means to separate us from God. One of the worst tricks he ever perpetrated on mankind was convincing us he doesn't exist."

38

Casey stepped out of the shower Gary had constructed. It wasn't very warm, and the water pressure was for shit, but at least she was clean. She slipped into a new blouse and skirt and pulled her wet hair up with a big clip.

Casey dropped her dirties in the trash bag by the gate. When it was full, Liv would take everyone's soiled clothes to the laundromat in town. Between the spitting, vomiting, and cleaning up Austin's bodily fluids, the laundry bag filled up quickly. Austin's clothes could not be salvaged. If the evil bitch didn't rip them off of his body, they were so filthy, throwing them out was the only option. Tired of running to the store, Liv bought him sweats, underwear, and shirts in bulk. That would keep him in clothes for a little while.

These were her days: Clean Austin up and shove a bacon and egg sandwich down his throat. Pray he keeps it down. Take a shower, eat breakfast, and sleep for a few hours. Wake up in the afternoon and feed Austin. Talk with him until Demon-bitch returned. Perform the rite of exorcism most of the night. Then repeat. It was a strange routine, but one she had become accustomed to over the last week and a half.

"Look who's up," Bob called out. Casey and the others turned to the house. Austin was standing at the open front door, fully dressed, waving at them. He tried to put his foot out the door, but winced as a hot pain shot through his leg. He pulled back and stood inside the foyer. Casey ran over.

"Bob, you should have called me. I could have gotten him dressed."

"I didn't have to. He dressed himself."

"She let you up?"

"Sort of," Austin shrugged. "I still can't leave her house, though."

"But this is an improvement," Bob observed. "Yesterday you couldn't even get close to the front door."

"That's a good sign, isn't it?" Casey asked.

Luis nodded. "The evil hold on Austin is weakening."

As a rule, Luis didn't interact with the demon. He prayed over the sick person and cast out the spirit in the name of Christ. The Rite allowed for two exceptions to this rule: asking the evil spirit its name and when it would leave. Of course, there was no guarantee he would get a truthful response, or any response at all.

The demon had broken free of its restraints again. Currently it was floating above the cot. It glided up to Luis and spit at him.

Luis wiped his face with his handkerchief. "I command you, unclean spirit, whoever you are, along with all your minions now attacking this servant of God, by the mysteries of the incarnation, passion, resurrection, and ascension of our Lord Jesus Christ, by the descent of the Holy Spirit, by the coming of our Lord for judgment, that you tell me by some sign your name, and the day and hour of your departure." She laughed. "I command you, moreover, to obey me to the letter." He laid his hand on Austin's head and he bellowed and swore.

"You must answer. By the authority of the Lord, Jesus Christ."

"You can call me Lillith," the Austin thing growled.

"The day and hour of your departure." Luis did not remove his hand from Austin's head.

"NO! Fuck you and all the saints."

"The day and hour of your departure," Luis said calmly.

It growled and its head rolled around. "Twelve." It grunted.

"Twelve what?"

"Cocksucker."

"Twelve what?"

"February."

"When?"

"Before the sun rises, we will be gone."

Josie handed Casey a cup of coffee and Luis a bottled water. "Fantastic news. Barrett Skyped Liv. The area of distortion on the north side is getting larger and thinning out. I can almost push my hand all the way through. A few more exorcisms and we can talk about getting out of here."

"It can't be soon enough. Luis can't keep this up. He's sick and should probably be in the hospital. And Austin. At least now he's keeping down the red meat. But he's cold all the time. We can't keep him in clothes or warm blankets, because she's always ripping them off." Casey dabbed at her eyes as her voice broke. "How long can a person survive this way?"

Josie put her arms around Casey and held her. "Austin is strong, Casey. Stronger than you think."

Casey turned when she heard Thai's voice. "This is good. February twelfth is only a few days away," It was the first time Casey could remember Thai with a smile on his face since they'd arrived over a week before.

Luis turned to him. "If it was telling the truth and if it meant the current year, then yes, it is a good thing. We can't rely on anything it says."

Casey stayed inside with Austin for the rest of the day. She spoke about all the stuff they would do as soon as he was free of the evil one's influence. She was careful to avoid the subject of *SCI*. He nodded, content to let her ramble on. Mostly, he was just glad of her company. He entwined his fingers in hers and smiled up at her.

When he started twitching and clearing his throat, it was her cue to leave. She-demon was close, and Austin didn't like Casey around when he was trying to fight her. She walked out of the house and into the courtyard. Her father was sitting on the steps of the lounge, drinking coffee with Marcus and Steve. She spotted Thai at the edge of the courtyard, stretching out on his yoga mat. She waited for him to finish his poses, then walked over to him.

"Gary tells me you won't be joining us tonight."

"Nope. Josie's volunteered to take my spot from now on." Thai said. He wouldn't look her in the eye. "It's not helping anyway."

Casey thought it was, but decided not to argue the point. "What's going on with you? Why are you so angry with everyone?"

Thai sighed. "I don't know."

"Better question. Why are you so angry with *him?*"

"I can't stand to be around him. It's too …." He exhaled and looked away.

"I try to remember the old Austin. I'm doing it for him, not for the thing he becomes at night. You should come and see him in the afternoons. He has moments when he seems like his old self."

Thai shook his head. "No can do. Not when he's spouting that crazy shit. Not when he's jacking off. Not when he smells like sewer water and he's covered in scratches and pus-filled sores. I hate this. He's my best friend, and I fucking hate how I feel about him." Thai shook his head. "Demon bitch is fucking up everything!"

"It will get better." Casey rubbed his upper arm.

"Will it? He's Austin Cole. He's supposed to be fearless; not frightening." He turned his gaze toward the manor. "And what she's turned him into is scaring the shit out of me."

"It's time," Bob announced, stepping outside. He glanced over his shoulder into the manor. Hisses, snarls and scratching could be heard emanating from inside.

Josie and Casey looked on as Gary helped Luis up. "Geez, he looks bad," Casey observed.

"Yeah," Josie agreed. "Luis asked Liv to get some first-aid supplies at the store. According to Gary, his leg's infected again." Casey exhaled. It was too much to worry about. If she didn't release Austin soon, Luis would get sicker. Or worse.

The front room was freezing. Casey rubbed her arms to keep warm. Luis began with prayer. He skipped the Litany of Saints and went straight to the Psalms. Luis swayed on his feet and Casey wondered how long he would be able to perform the Ritual tonight.

Josie swatted the air. Then she began to wriggle and scratch. Luis didn't look up from the book.

Bob leaned over and whispered, "What's wrong?"

"Ants! They're crawling all over me." Casey and the others couldn't see the supernatural insects now attacking their pixie tech guru. Austin leaned back on the cot and giggled in a school girl's voice. A moment later, Josie ran out into the courtyard. Bob tried to hold down Austin by himself but quickly gave up. The demon untied his straps and Austin's body floated up like a helium balloon.

Gary began to cough. Then he started to gag. He ran for the foyer and Casey could hear him vomiting. *Great,* she thought. *Thai's a no-show, and we already have two men down.* A minute later Gary returned, looking a little green. She glanced up from her reading to see Austin's mouth, controlled by Demoness, pulled up in a smirk. *You're responsible for this. You can't stop the exorcism, but you can make us all ill.*

Casey brushed the hair out of her eyes. Luis's voice sounded far off, and the room began to spin. Her vision grayed out. The next thing she knew, she was sitting on the steps by the front door, leaning against Thai.

She tried to sit up and he helped her. "What happened?"

"You passed out."

Casey pushed off the step. "I've got to get back in there. Josie's gone and Luis is weak enough as it is."

Thai pulled her back down. "Relax. Josie went back in after Liv tossed her some Calamine lotion and Benadryl. Your dad's filling in. He told me not to let you back in there."

"My father? He came through the gate?'

Thai handed her a bottle of water. "Yes. Luis wasn't feeling well, so your dad kind of took over. Obviously, he can't perform the exorcism, but he's reading bible passages and praying over Austin. He was serious about you not going back in. Don't make me tie you down."

Emotion welled up in her. Her feelings for her father were complicated; this act of kindness from him undid her. Her throat tightened up and tears gathered at the corner of her eyes. She wiped them away as Gary opened the front door and helped Luis over to the courtyard.

"Are you all right?" she asked Luis.

"I'm fine. The demon is growing desperate. It is trying to attack us physically to stop us from continuing." Even though it was cold and windy, he took a handkerchief out of his pocket and blotted perspiration off his forehead. "I'm going to lie down."

"I'll get you some Advil and Gatorade," Gary told him.

Luis called out to Casey. "Austin's back now, if you want to go to him."

Casey jumped up and ran through the door. Her father was sweeping the floor and Bob was following behind him with a mop. It looked like tonight Austin had regurgitated broken glass again. She stepped around the pile and approached her father. "You don't have to do that, Dad." She tried to take the broom from him.

"No. I'll sweep. You go be with Austin." His eyes drifted down to the floor as he continued his task.

Casey paused. "Dad?"

"Yes, sweetheart?"

"Thank you." She wrapped her arms around his waist.

He dropped the broom and pulled her into his chest. "Casey, I love you. Never doubt that."

"I know. I'm sorry I ... well, thank you. And I love you, too." She swiped at her eyes and walked over to Austin's cot.

Josie was removing Austin's vomit-stained shirt and was starting to clean him up when Casey approached. "I'll do that."

Josie rose up from where she was kneeling. Her face was covered in white polka-dots from the calamine lotion. "I want to go check on Luis." She patted Austin's shoulder and strode off.

Casey wrung out a washcloth and wiped down his face. "How are you feeling?"

"Not bad for someone who vomits non-food items on a regular basis." He pulled himself up as far as the restraints would allow and stared into her eyes. "What about you? You weren't here when I woke up. Did I say something?" He bit his lower lip and stared at the floor. "Do something to hurt you?"

She squeezed his hand. "Nothing like that."

"Then what?"

"It's kind of embarrassing."

"Case, you're talking to a guy who goes into a trance and chokes his monkey in front of his best friends. Nothing you say could be that bad."

She scrunched her face up. "I sort of fainted."

Austin's lips tightened into a thin line. "I did that to you. You're exhausted. Luis is ill. Thai's pissed at me. Josie, Liv, Gary, Bob, even your dad—they're all stuck in this hell hole. I'm ruining everyone's life."

"I think you're being just a tad melodramatic." She kissed his forehead. "We love you, Austin. We're a team. When one of us falls down, the rest of us are here to pick him up."

Austin's eyes focused on something on the other side of the room. Casey wasn't sure he heard anything she said to him. "Thai hates me." His voice was small and pitiful.

She ran her fingers through his hair. "You're wrong about Thai. He doesn't hate you. He hates seeing what she's done to you."

"Isn't that the same thing?"

"No. It's not." Austin nodded, but his eyes were dull and vacant. "Are you hungry? Do you want me to get you something?"

"Food can wait."

"You sure?"

He shook his head and swallowed. His chin was trembling slightly. She stared into ocean eyes teeming with fear. "Just stay with me, Case. I need you to stay." She scooted onto his cot and loosened the restraints so that he could lean into her chest. She wrapped her arms around him tightly and rocked him back and forth.

39

The following afternoon, Austin appeared at the front door again. Bob stood beside him and helped when he slowly stepped outside, squinting into the sunlight. "Austin," Casey jumped up and ran over. Gary and Josie stood up and stared at the front door. Thai sat at the table alone. Casey stared at this changed man in front of her. There were scratch marks and bruises on his face and arms in various stages of healing, but he was clean, dressed, and clarity shone in his eyes. He was back in control. If his beard had been trimmed and his eyes weren't so weary, he would have looked like his old self.

"You want to sit on the front porch?" Bob asked.

Austin shook his head no. He pointed to the courtyard table. "I want to sit at the table with the other guys." Bob held one arm and Casey took the other.

His jaw tightened, and with that Austin-Cole-determined-glint in his eye, he pressed forward and trudged down the steps. The heavy, supernatural shackles binding him to the manor made for a slow and difficult trek. It took about ten minutes to make it the thirty feet from the front of the house to the courtyard. Austin stopped about a foot from the table. "This is as far as I can go." Bob moved the bench closer to Austin and he collapsed onto it. "It's great to see you, man." Gary said. Josie nodded and smiled up at him. He patted her blue hair. Thai said nothing but made no move to leave.

Austin rubbed his palms on his pants legs. "What's wrong?" Casey asked.

"Being this far from her ... from the house, is uncomfortable," he said through clenched teeth.

"We can move the bench closer."

"No, I want to be here with you guys." He squeezed her hand to let her know he was okay. "Where's Luis?"

"He's still asleep," Josie answered.

The wind blew cold against his thin T-shirt, and he shivered. "Here. I'll get your coat," Casey said.

Austin shook his head. "I want to feel the sun on my skin."

"But it's freezing out here," she said.

"It's warmer out here than in there."

Liv, Marcus, and Steve approached their side of the fence. "Look who decided to grace us with his presence."

Austin smiled. "Liv. Man, it's good to see you." His eyes moved around the table and settled on Thai. "To see all of you." He turned his head back toward Liv. "Thanks for accommodating my strange dietary needs. I owe you big time."

"Yes, you do," she chided. "And I expect an Austin Cole bear hug as payment in full as soon as you get out of there."

"Anything for you, sweetheart."

"I was just starting lunch. Any special requests?"

Austin shrugged. "What's everyone else having?"

"Turkey chili."

"That sounds good to me." Liv's eyes lit up and Casey stared up at him.

Liv smiled broadly. "You got it. It's simmering on the stove right now. You get the first bowl as soon as it's ready."

Reverend Lawson approached the group and everyone grew silent. "How are you feeling, Austin?"

Austin cleared his throat and stared at the ground. "Good, sir." It reminded Casey of when she was little and got called into his study for doing something wrong. *Shame. He feels shame around my father.* Even though she knew her dad wasn't trying to make him feel bad, she still felt sorry for Austin.

"I'm glad to hear it." He clapped his hand on Austin's shoulder and kissed the top of Casey's head. "Liv, if you have some coffee ready, I'd like to bring a cup to Luis."

"Sure thing."

"How's he feeling?" Bob asked.

"He's better. No fever this morning." Liv passed the coffee over to Reverend Lawson. "Well, I'm going to head back over to the tent." Casey knew her father's routine. He was going back to pray and study the bible, as he had every morning of his life.

After Reverend Lawson departed, Austin glanced over at Thai. "How's it going?"

Casey held her breath and braced for something smart ass and shitty to erupt from Thai's mouth. He crossed his arms and his eyes flicked up over Austin. "You're looking better, so I guess things are improving."

"Yeah." He stared at his hands awkwardly. With Thai, he'd never had to struggle with words. Their friendship had always been more intuitive than that. Finally, he lifted his fist up. "We cool?"

Thai stared at it for a moment, then brought his own fist up and bumped it against Austin's. "Yeah."

Austin smirked. "You think you can handle being lead investigator on the Hillendahl investigation? After all the hard work and groveling I put into it, I'd hate to see you fuck it up."

Thai's eyes darted over to Casey. Neither one said anything. "Relax guys. I get it," Austin said. "I know my days as the Spirit Chaser are over." This was Never-Give-Up-Never-Quit-Austin Control. His quiet acceptance of the situation was worse than if he'd thrown a shit fit. Casey softly swallowed her heartache.

Thai shook his head and grinned. "Are you fucking kidding me? The fans are going to wonder why you were ever in charge in the first place. The ratings are going to skyrocket with me at the helm. We'll probably have to change the name of the show to *TNI*, Thai Nguyen Investigations."

"Is that so?" Austin raised an eyebrow at him.

"You gonna run the show all by yourself, then?" Casey asked.

"Okay, Thai Nguyen and *Company*, Investigations. Better?"

Austin glanced around the courtyard. Steve and Marcus were staring at the fence and poking their hands at the invisible barrier. Luis was up now and he walked over to him with just a slight limp.

"Austin, my son. It is so good to see you up and about." He put his hands on Austin's shoulders and kissed the top of his head.

Austin stared down at his hands. "How are you feeling, Luis?" Casey could see the sadness and guilt on Austin's face.

"Much better. No fever, and my leg isn't hurting. Thanks be to God. It is a good day."

When dinner was served, Austin scraped the bowl clean.

"You're not going to hurl, are you?" Casey asked.

"Don't worry, if I need to get sick, I'll aim away from your shoes, Case." He rubbed his stomach. "What's for dessert?"

"Liv's made some of her famous oatmeal cookies, or you can have you some berries with whipped cream," Josie said.

"I'll take both," he said. Josie brought over a bowl of berries and a couple of cookies. He closed his eyes and hummed with satisfaction as he took his first spoonful. Casey took a napkin and wiped a bit of whipped cream from the corner of his mouth. They sat quietly, listening to the wind rustle through the trees. In this still, soft moment, they were granted a respite from the crazy evil that defined this place. Finally, Austin pushed the bowl away. He straightened up, wrapping his arm around Casey's waist as he pressed his lips to her temple. She closed her eyes, savoring his warm touch. This was the strong, yet tender man she'd fallen in love with.

Josie observed their body language. "Hey," she said to Gary, Thai, and Bob. "Get off your lazy asses and help with the clean-up. Liv may have to cook and clean for you right now, but we are not your mothers." She winked at Casey as the guys stood up and picked up their trash. The table emptied, giving Casey and Austin some alone time.

Casey snuggled into Austin's chest. "I've missed you," she said, staring up into the ocean.

"I've missed you too, Sweet Cheeks. More than you could ever know." He traced circles with his finger on her arm. This simple gesture soothed him. Night would come too soon, but at least he could forget about her hold on him for a few hours.

Austin stared up at a sky that was somewhat overcast, but infinitely lighter than anything inside the house. He breathed in deeply and imagined he was far away. *If I could be free, I'd run out of the gate and keep on running. I'd run until my lungs burned and my sides cramped up. And I'd still keep running. I'd get so far away from this place, she'd never get her hooks in me again.*

None of them should be here. They should be at *SCI* planning for the next investigation. Thai at his side, his loyal ghost-hunting partner. Barrett with the tech crew and Casey doing her walk throughs in her signature Casey way. He stared down at his woman who'd wrapped her arms around him and was sitting so close to him, she was halfway on his lap. She was hanging on to him so tight, like she was drowning and he was her life preserver. *If only,* he thought. *I can't save anyone. I can't save myself.* He tucked her head under his chin and exhaled.

"So you think Lyle's a good guy? Good for my mom?"

Casey stared up at him. "That's pretty random. Where did that come from?"

Austin shrugged. "I was just thinking about Mom. I haven't seen her since this whole thing began."

"I told you, Austin. Lyle's great. When you get out of here, maybe you should try to get to know him."

"Probably," Austin said in a far off voice. "Does she know … about me?"

Casey nodded. "Yeah. Luis told her the night we came. Since then, Barrett's been checking in with her every few days."

"That's good. I know Luis broke it to her gently. And Barrett's like a second son to her. He won't hurt her unnecessarily. He has a soothing way about him." He stared into Casey's eyes seriously. "My mom can never know about what went on here. It's too upsetting. And she's been through enough."

"Austin, I would never tell her. The tabloids will make up whatever suits their purposes. When you get out of here, you tell her as much or as little as you want."

Austin relaxed, and Casey leaned into his shoulder. "I know you wouldn't, Case. I'm just saying in general. My mom's had a rough life. The last thing she needs to hear about is the various ways her adult son has humiliated himself." He gazed down into her steely blues. "Come here." She lifted her face and he took her cheeks in his hands. Gently, he guided her toward him and with trembling lips, pressed his mouth against hers.

This kiss was different. Casey felt it in his gaze and in his actions. There was a hunger to his kiss, but not from passion. He put one hand around her back and pressed her against him. Pulling her into him, he held on tight. Just when she thought he would crush her in his arms, he broke away.

"I hate to interrupt," Josie yelled at them from across the courtyard. "But Barrett's on the line and he really wants to talk to you." Austin looked up. The tech crew had turned a monitor to face the mansion. Barrett was staring at all of them from *SCI* headquarters.

"Austin, wow man, did you forget how to shave? You look like shit," he joked. Then he saw the seriousness in Austin's face. His smile faded and his brow furrowed in concern.

Austin's chin trembled and his eyes welled up. "You okay?" Casey asked, as she rubbed his arm.

He nodded. "It's just. I wasn't expecting to see you, Barrett." He rested his arms on the table and clenched his fists to get control. "I miss you so much."

"I've missed you, too, my friend." Barrett said sincerely. "No need to get all choked up about it. When you get back to LA, I'm going to be around so much, you'll get sick of seeing my ass."

"I hope so," Austin said.

"We're going to get through this. Together. We're *SCI*. That's what we do," Barrett told him. Casey put her hand over Austin's. Then Thai put his hand over Casey's. Josie ran over and did the same. Gary and Luis approached the table. In a matter of moments, the whole crew joined their hands with Austin's.

The crew, plus Casey's father, all gathered around the courtyard table as Luis outlined the plan for that evening. "We'll proceed with the exorcism as always, but before dawn, we're going to start moving Austin away from the house. Tell them what you discovered today, Josie."

"As you know, we've been in close communication with Barrett. He told me earlier today that he could see fluctuations in the density of the barrier."

"In English, please," Casey said. "Some of us don't speak tech."

"It means the whole force field is unstable. There are now a few areas of distortion. She's lost control over it. Marcus and I were conducting an experiment to see if we could cross the barrier. He was able to pass through it and go back over to the other side and so could I."

"That means as soon as Austin is able to cross, we'll all be able to leave," Luis said.

"So, do you think the demon was telling the truth about leaving Austin? Tomorrow morning is when she said she'd take off," Gary asked.

"Not necessarily," Luis shook his head. "But it doesn't matter. Look how much stronger Austin is. The demon only has the power God allows it to have. If it leaves at four-thirty tomorrow morning, great. If it doesn't, there's no need to get discouraged. We'll probably still be able to get across the barrier after tonight's exorcism."

Everyone whooped. Austin's lip kicked up in a half-smile. "Now, prepare yourselves. Tonight the demon will likely do everything in its power to stop us. Remember, Satan is strong, but God is stronger. We must keep our focus and pray very hard for Austin's liberation." Luis rose. "I'm going to prepare now." He squeezed Austin's shoulder and headed for his tent.

The afternoon was drifting away. The rays of sunlight were descending into night. Austin stared off into the sunset and shivered. "Are you cold?" Casey asked.

Austin closed his eyes and cleared his throat. "No. She's coming back." His head twitched to the side. "Bob, help me back inside. Gary, you'd better come, too. She's strong tonight." He rose and walked toward the mansion. Casey jumped up and followed.

Austin turned to her and cleared his throat. "Don't come in. Not yet." He twitched and closed his eyes. "Wait until they have me strapped down. I don't want to hurt you." He reached out and caressed her cheek. She nodded and remained where she was as Austin made his difficult trek back to the manor. He was continuously grunting and clearing his throat now. When he got to the front steps, he turned and his eyes surveyed the courtyard.

"Austin," Casey cried out. "Hang on. This will all be over soon."

He smiled bleakly at her before turning to go into the house.

Thai joined Casey on the front steps. "You're going in, too?" she asked.

He smiled at her. "Hell, yeah. I want to be there when we pull Austin out. This shit ends tonight."

Casey took his hand and they walked in together.

40

Something about the whole Skype with Austin bugged Barrett, but he couldn't put his finger on what it was. He was ruminating on the encounter as he drove back to his townhome. It would be a while before he found out if they had succeeded in getting Austin away from her, so he might as well go home and get some rest.

As soon as he closed his eyes, he was plagued by a terrible nightmare. The crew was back in the warehouse and she-demon was whispering her evil predictions in his ear. All the fear and negative emotion from that day broke the dream barrier and consumed him. A scream erupted from his throat as he jolted awake. He was breathing heavily and was drenched in sweat. *Damn. Where did that come from?* It had been almost a year since he thought about the warehouse.

Barrett rubbed his face and glanced at the clock. It was one o'clock, and Derek still wasn't home. There was no way he was going back to sleep, so he decided to head back up to *SCI* and wait for news of Austin there. His thoughts returned to the video chat with Austin that afternoon. He was used to being blocked by Demon Bitch. If she wasn't outright possessing his body, she was fucking with his mind. But this was different. He couldn't read Austin's mind. Austin was keeping something from him, and he didn't know why. He could see the actual padlock in his mind. It was still gnawing at him as he pulled into the parking lot.

Instead of going to the conference room, Barrett headed for the tech lab. He thumbed through files of the various episodes until he came across *L&D Warehouse*. He had never seen this episode—had sworn he never would—but he was missing a piece of the puzzle and he needed to know what it was.

Barrett pulled up the episode and rewound it to the part just before devil woman invaded him. He forced himself to watch the clip several times, but nothing seemed amiss. Finally, he let the video continue to play. The next clip was of the other side of the warehouse. Austin and Thai were searching for anything that could have made the deafening noise that greeted them when they first entered that wretched place. A black being, wispy like smoke, appeared at Austin's side. A frozen finger trailed down Barrett's spine. Austin, unaware, turned right into the creature. Barrett watched as the evil entity entered his best friend's body, taking his breath and settling in his chest when Austin inhaled. Barrett couldn't believe his eyes. He replayed the video three times to make sure.

Oh shit! Thai was right! A sick feeling pooled in his stomach, and he felt all the blood drain out of his head. This was it. He knew what she planned to do. His hand shook as he reached for his phone. "She wasn't after me. I wasn't the target; I was the fucking diversion."

He dialed Liv's cell phone and paced as he waited for her to pick up.

Austin's body fought against the restraints. When Luis began to recite the Canticle of Mary, an unholy trio of voices issued from Austin's mouth. "Shut up! Close your fucking mouth! Do not bring her into this!"

After the canticle, Luis began the exorcism. He put his hand on Austin's head and sprinkled holy water on his face. "I command you in the name of God most Holy, and his Holy precious Son, and by the power of the Holy Spirit, to depart from this child of God, unclean spirit."

"Never. I'll never leave."

"Our Father," Luis began.

Austin began thrashing and swearing. Bob, Thai and Josie tightened their grip. At least he wasn't levitating. Gary, Casey, and Reverend Lawson joined in the prayer. "Who art in heaven. Hallowed be Thy name."

He threw-up violently and they all held their noses and waited to see what would come up. Oddly enough, it was just his lunch. Bob removed Austin's soiled shirt and Josie grabbed the basin with the washcloth.

"Forgive us our trespasses," Austin's eyes opened—ocean blue. Casey stared at him as she and the others continued to recite the words. "Deliver us from evil. Amen."

"Amen," Austin gasped out weakly. Everyone turned to face him.

"Did he just say amen?" Gary asked.

"Yes," Luis said with a wan smile. He waited for Gary and Josie to finish cleaning Austin up, then instructed Gary to refasten the restraints. When Austin was again strapped down he asked, "Do you repent of your sins?"

"I ... do," he managed.

Luis pulled out the consecrated host and placed it on Austin's tongue. "This is My body, shed for you for the remission of sins. Do this in remembrance of Me." Austin grunted and made a face. The demon wanted him to spit it out, but with some holy water, he was able to choke it down. Luis pulled off his readers and closed his prayer book. "I think we'll take a break." He placed his hand on Austin's shoulder. "Get some rest, my son."

The quiet was disrupted by the sound of shattering glass. A rock flew through the window. Josie and Thai ran outside. A moment later, Thai yelled. "Casey, Luis, come out here. It's Barrett and it's important."

Casey ran outside, and her father went with her. "Stay with Austin," Luis instructed Gary and Bob. Then he joined the others in the courtyard.

Her evil laugh reverberated in Austin's ear. *Poor stupid sheep. Trying to stop me. They'll never succeed.*

"Shut up. Just do what you came here to do."

Bob and Gary glanced back at Austin. He was having one of his conversations with the demoness in his head. Nothing new. At least now he was starting to fight back. They faced the window to see what was happening in the courtyard. While their backs were turned, she swiftly and silently relocated Austin to the third floor balcony.

During the exorcism, the she-demon had closed the distortion in the field around the house, and now Liv couldn't cross. She shouted at them. "Sorry about the rock, but we're locked out again and we needed to get your attention. Barrett's on the phone. He says it's crucial he speak with you and Thai." She threw the phone over the stone fence and Casey caught it. She held it up and Thai leaned in so he could hear, too.

"What's going on—" Casey began.

"There's no time. Austin's in grave danger."

"I just left him. Relax, Barrett. He's okay."

"No, Casey, listen to me. He's not okay. The demon is not weakening; Austin is."

"That can't be right," Thai told him. "He said amen after the Lord's Prayer and took communion."

"Listen. I've been reviewing the raw footage from the warehouse. Thai was right. The shadow figure stole his breath."

"So? What does that have to do—"

"Don't you see?" Barrett cut Casey off. "She killed him that night at the warehouse. He just hasn't died yet."

Casey's eyes widened as realization dawned. She dropped the phone and took off toward the mansion, with Thai, her father, and Luis right on her heels. As she ran through the door, her stomach twisted in fear. "Where is he?" she cried out. Gary and Bob turned. When they saw the vacant cot with the restraints intact, they appeared just as shocked as she was. She pulled her hair back from her face. *Where could he be?* Desperate to find him, she opened her third eye.

An explosion of supernatural sound and sight overwhelmed her senses. The atmosphere was thick with negativity. Inhuman wailing and shadow figures darted through her vision. The hooved shadow figure and the one with no mouth cackled at her. She ignored them. Her third eye was leading her up to the third floor. She began climbing the ramshackle stairs. Every few steps, her feet would sink into a rotten wood plank. Dead were lying on the staircase grabbing at her and moaning a doleful dirge as she climbed. *The damned,* Casey thought. Their spirit forms were dark gray and they wore tales of their torture and suffering on their faces.

When she finally ascended to the third-floor landing, she spied Austin, wearing only his underwear, staring out of a window that had to be at least five feet tall. "Austin?" she called out meekly, not sure whom she was addressing. He turned to her and relief flooded through her. *Thank God,* she thought. *Ocean eyes.* She stared at his bruised and broken body. "Baby, what are you doing?"

He put his hands over his ears and shifted from one foot to the other. "The voices. I can't listen to them anymore." He began pacing back and forth in front of the window.

"No, baby," Casey said, as she slowly approached. She put her hands out in front of her, like she was talking to a skittish foal. Gary and Thai caught up to her and were now standing right behind her. "Don't listen to her. She lies."

He stopped pacing and stared at Casey. His features were contorted in anguish. "I can't stop it. She's making me. She's too strong."

"We're going to get you out of here," Thai said.

Austin shook his head back and forth. "No. no. You can't. She won't let you take me away."

"It's not up to her," Casey declared.

Austin's shoulders drooped and he took in several breaths before speaking again. "I'm so tired. I can't." His voice hitched, and a single tear rolled down his cheek. "I can't fight her anymore." He rubbed his hands together as he rocked back and forth.

"Austin, you don't have to fight her alone. We're here to help." Casey walked toward him, extending her hand. "Please, step away from the window."

"I can't do that, Case. Trust me. This is the best thing for everyone." He turned away from her and stared out the window again. "I've destroyed everything."

"That's not true." She pushed her fear and upset down in her belly and spoke to him softly, like he was a child. "I love you, Austin. We all do. All you have to do is turn around, take my hand, and we can walk out of here. All of us. Together. Easy peasy." Casey looked up at the ceiling and put her hand out, palm up. "Can't you feel it? The air is lighter; her power is waning."

Austin reached out his hand and took a couple of tentative steps toward her. Their fingertips touched. *Gotcha.* Casey thought. But then something changed. Something inside of Austin broke, and he pulled his hand back. "You guys, you can get out of here now."

His eyes brimmed with tears. *One will be hurt and the other one killed.* "This is the only way." He placed a palm to his forehead. His eyes turned dark and he growled as she took over his body. Then he turned away from Casey and sprinted toward the third-floor window. It was like a slow motion horror film, and Casey was helpless to stop it. The last thing she saw was the tattoo of the woman on his back as he dove head-first through the glass.

41

"NO!" Casey screamed, running after him. The loud shattering set her teeth on edge. Casey shielded her face from flying shards of glass. She winced as she heard the heavy thud of a body hitting the hard ground.

Casey stood stock still. It took about two heartbeats for her brain to register what her eyes were telling her. The sound of her own blood pounded in her ears. She turned one hundred and eighty degrees and dashed down the stairs. The old staircase was crumbling beneath her feet, but she didn't slow down. She was flying past Gary and Luis, still frozen in place. A loud crash like thunder exploded around the house. They all jumped and Casey froze in her tracks. She met the eyes of the others. They all felt it. The dark emotions and malevolent atmosphere lifted. She was letting them go. But not without exacting a price.

"Casey, don't go out there." Her dad grabbed her arm, but she wrested it out of his grasp. Casey ran as fast as she could through the first floor parlor and out the double front doors. Once outside, she picked up speed, ran at an all-out sprint to the North side of the old house.

There, on the courtyard stone, lay Austin's unmoving body. His arms were splayed and one of his legs below the knee lay turned to the side. The shards of glass, discolored by his blood, surrounded his body and created a macabre stained glass. By the misshapen contour of his head, there was no doubt of the way he landed. Blood dripped from a gash in his forehead, turning his hair a reddish-brown, and part of his brain peeked through a crack in his skull. Her hand flew to her mouth, and she mumbled soft prayers to God. Praying her eyes were deceiving her. Praying that she was wrong in her belief that nothing could be done.

In the east, the first hint of sun lightened the sky. *Before the sun rises, we will be gone.* Casey's vision blurred. The wind whipped her long hair into her face. Annoyed, she swatted it away. A tortured sob broke from her throat as she knelt down beside him. She rocked back and forth on her heels, and her hands shook as she gently touched his bloody and broken face. His unseeing eyes were closed and his chest was no longer rising and falling. *No more ocean eyes,* she thought to herself. "Oh, Austin. Please God, no," she cried out, over and over, as she pressed kisses all over his face. Her tears fell on his cheeks, mixing with his own blood, turning it a watery pink.

She was vaguely aware of the sound of a siren in the distance, increasing in volume and pitch. Two sets of strong arms pulled her up and away, as someone in a uniform began chest compressions on Austin's still form. She looked to see who had grabbed her. It was Gary and Luis. They placed her next to Thai. He was hunched over, hands on his knees. When he straightened, all she could see was grief and pain etched on his face. His jaw trembled. He crossed his arms over his midsection, pacing back and forth. "Fuck," she heard him gasp, his voice choked with tears.

Gary stood quietly, calmly, watching the paramedics do what paramedics do—try to resurrect the dead. Luis's eyes were closed, but she could see his lips moving in silent prayer.

"This isn't happening. This isn't real. That's not Austin," she mumbled. She could lie to herself. She could pretend that the fractured body of the man lying five feet from her was someone else. Not the man she loved more than her own life. She could do whatever it took to deceive herself and keep from ripping apart from the inside out. Casey sank to the ground, her legs no longer able to hold her.

One of the ambulance crew shook her head. It was over. The two other men loaded Austin's body onto a gurney. Casey watched as the woman gently draped the sheet over him. Her kind, sympathetic eyes met Casey's for a moment, in a silent, sincere "I'm sorry." Gary and Luis turned and made their way to the *SCI* trailer. Casey's gaze followed their retreating forms when the doors to the ambulance slammed shut. Her head snapped back in time to see it take Austin's body away.

With a slow and shaky breath, she pulled herself off the ground. Thai was still standing there, staring at the ground Austin's body had formerly occupied. If there was a visual representation of agony, it would have to be the expression on Thai's face. Casey wanted to say something to him, but she had no words, and even if she had, she was too numb and in no condition to comfort anyone. With her sleeve, she wiped the tears and the snot off her face. Like a zombie, Casey stumbled back over to the trailer.

Josie flew down the steps as soon as she saw Casey approach. She pulled her into a fierce hug. The two women held each other, rocking back and forth. Josie's eyes were glistening as she told Casey, "I'm sorry. I'm so sorry." Her voice hitched. "Oh, God, this hurts so bad!"

"I know," she whispered softly as she gripped Josie's forearms. "I know."

"You're freezing," she told Casey. Josie led her out of the gate and into the lounge. Someone, Liv maybe, sat her down, put a blanket around her and shoved a cup of coffee in her hand. She looked at it and thought, *As if I could drink anything ever again.* The silence was broken by the sound of *Tubular Bells.* She closed her eyes as laughter mixed with anguish caught in her throat.

She swiped the screen and saw that it was Barrett. He had left several messages, voice mails and texts. While Austin had been speaking his final words, Barrett had been blowing up her phone.

"Hello?"

"Is it true? Please tell me what I'm seeing isn't real."

"It's real," she said. Then her throat closed up and tears strangled her words. She felt like she had swallowed all the broken glass from the third floor window. "Austin's dead." The words came out a whisper.

"Oh, God, oh, God," he said.

Luis grabbed the phone out of her hand and spoke softly to Barrett. So softly, she couldn't hear what he said.

Marcus and Steve were picking up the tents and sleeping bags to load into the truck when the first set of headlights turned onto dirt road that winded its way to Enchanted Hill. "That didn't take long," Gary remarked. Reporters and cameraman jumped out of vans and cars. They converged on the manor, flashing microphones and video cameras. A woman who seemed to be in charge approached the crew. "We've received reports that the body of Austin Cole was recovered from this location."

No one said anything. Gary stared at the ground. When it became obvious that they weren't going to leave until someone spoke to them, Luis approached. *He's not limping anymore.* The random thought appeared in Casey's mind. *Now that she's gone, he's better.* Luis allowed the reporter to thrust a mic in his face. "Tonight, we have lost a dear friend. I have lost a son. It is true. Austin Cole has passed away."

While the reporters were distracted with Luis's interview, Casey's father led her down the path to his car. Her father held her in his arms and whispered soft words in her ear. They must have been comforting, because she felt calmer after he spoke, but she couldn't recall one thing he said.

They drove in silence. The only sound was the soft music from the Christian radio station her father listened to. Old hymns and popular Christian Contemporary wafted through the speakers, just barely noticeable in the background hum of the road.

Her mother ran out on the front porch as soon as they pulled up. Tears were shining in her eyes and she folded Casey in her arms. She murmured, "I'm sorry" and, "I know how much you loved him" over and over.

Casey mumbled something akin to thank you and slowly pulled away. There was only one thing on her mind and she remained focused on it. That one thought propelled her weary body up the stairs when all she wanted was to collapse on the floor in a heap and cry her eyes out. She flung the door open to her old bedroom. She closed it behind her and leaned against it. "Austin," she whispered. Silence.

"You told me you would say goodbye. You told me you would never leave your friends wondering about you. I'm here. I'm waiting for you to appear."

She stood there quietly for several minutes. The only sound was the beat of her heart, thudding in her hollow chest. "Please," she finally begged. "I need to know you're okay." She swiped at tears forming on the inner corners of her eyes. No response. Not even a chill in the air or a tingle down her spine. Casey's extra-sensitive radar for the dead failed to detect any trace of the newly deceased Austin Cole. "Where are you, Baby? Why won't you talk to me?" Casey crumpled to the floor and wrapped her arms around her chest.

It was dark outside when her door swung open. She had been lying in her bed, watching the moon ascend from the ground to high in the sky as the minutes slowly ticked by. "Mom? What are you doing up?"

Mrs. Lawson, in her pink nightgown and flannel robe, sat down on Casey's bed. She stroked Casey's hair and kissed her forehead.

"Checking on you." She lifted the comforter and climbed in next to her daughter, and pulled Casey into her chest. "I can't imagine what you're going through." Casey blinked in the dark. In a low voice, her mother said, "You don't have to talk. Just listen. I know how much you loved him. My heart breaks for you." A lump formed in Casey's throat. "I'm praying for you, sweetie. I'm praying hard." She tucked Casey's head into her shoulder. Hours later, Casey was still wide awake. The moon was descending, moving closer to the horizon, when Casey heard her mother stir. "Mom?"

"I'm here, sweetie. It looks like neither one of us is going to get any sleep tonight. You want to join me downstairs for a cup of coffee?" Casey nodded, even though her mother couldn't see the gesture in the dark.

The numbers on the microwave clock read 5:40. Her mom started the coffee pot, and as soon as it was ready, poured Casey a cup with lots of cream and sugar. Casey took the mug and headed for the den. She passed by her father's study. The light shown from under the door. *It looks like no one got any rest tonight.*

She plopped down on the couch in the dark and thought of Austin as she took a sip of coffee. A moment later, her mother flicked on a lamp. "Mind if I turn on the news?"

Casey shook her head and returned to thinking of her boy-friend. Her dead boyfriend. She barely heard the drone of the newscaster in the background. Her mom slipped on her readers and picked up her needlepoint. No matter the circumstance, Sarah Lawson could be counted on to keep the house running and her routine going. The quiet strength her mother possessed was reassuring in the midst of all of her emotional turmoil. *You're gone, but the earth keeps spinning. The sun will rise in less than an hour, even though you're no longer here to see it.*

The news station covered a local story on a school shooting in Dallas before turning to national headlines. It took a moment for Casey to register what the newscaster was saying.

"For the last month or so, rumors of strange behavior and possible drug abuse have been swirling around the Spirit Chaser. After he and girlfriend Casey Lawson called it quits, he was thrown out of a Hollywood strip club for allegedly trying to assault the women."

"I'm so sorry, Casey," her mother said as she grabbed for the remote. Casey put up her hand, motioning for her mother to be quiet and not turn the channel at the same time.

"Paramedics recovered his body outside an old mansion ten miles north of San Antonio. It is unclear why he was there, but early reports identify suicide as the cause of death."

"So tragic," the anchorman said. "He fought everyone else's demons but he couldn't fight his own."

The female co-anchor nodded. "Austin Cole, dead at twenty-nine. Now let's check in with Bill for the weather." Casey sat numbly watching the yellow, blue, and green from the Doppler radar for a few minutes. Finally, she turned from the television and ambled over to her father's study. She knocked, but instead of waiting for a response, walked on in. He was sitting at his desk with his bible open.

"Sweetheart." He took off his readers and started to rise.

"Don't get up, Dad. I just wanted to ask you something." Casey fingered the hole in the pocket of her cardigan. "I don't want you tell me what I want to hear. I want you to tell me the truth." She leaned against the back of the door. "Is Austin damned?"

Her dad pressed her lips together. "I'm not God. I can't make that determination."

"Please don't do this to me, Dad." Casey took a calming breath. "I'm asking you, as someone who has studied the bible his whole life, what is your best guess about what happens to a believer's soul who commits suicide while under the influence of a demon?"

Reverend Lawson stared into his daughter's eyes. He sat forward and steepled his fingers on his desk. "Sweetheart. You shouldn't be thinking about this right now. You have just endured a terrible shock. Give yourself some time."

"Time won't help me. Knowledge will. Are you going to answer me, or do I have to call Seth and ask him?"

Reverend Lawson sighed. Seth would answer her, but he would not speak the truth in love. He motioned for her to take a seat. "That is a complex question that I will have to answer in two parts. Are you sure you want to hear it?"

"Yes," Casey said definitively.

"Let's start with this: you say he was a believer."

"Yes. He was a baptized and devout Catholic."

"My first inclination is to doubt that. Demons cannot dwell in the same space occupied by the Holy Spirit."

Casey gripped the arms of the chair so hard her knuckles turned white. With rocks in her throat she spoke. "You said there were two parts to your answer. What's the second part?"

"The suicide. Many Christians believe that suicide is an unforgivable sin. I don't agree with that. There are many reasons a person might take his own life, including mental illness. I can't accept that a loving God would condemn one of his own who is suffering and can see no other way out. According to my reading of the bible, dying in unbelief is the only unforgiveable sin."

"So where does that leave Austin?"

"In the hands of a merciful God. We leave room for God's grace."

Casey blinked away tears and ran from the room.

Casey took the first flight available to LA. Her coworkers were already back, having left the morning he died. Casey was greeted at the doors of *SCI* by hundreds of Austin's fans. Flowers, candles, and teddy bears, along with signs declaring love for Austin, were strewn all over the front of the building. The crowds moved aside to let Casey through. They squeezed her hand, hugged her and murmured condolences to her. Before entering she turned and said, "Thank you all."

A somber mood hung over the offices of *SCI*. Everyone was moving in slow motion. Casey gave a small wave to Gary. He nodded his head but didn't even glance her way. She ran past Austin's office, not wanting to see it dark and empty. She bypassed her own as well and headed to the tech area. Casey entered and flopped down in the chair in front of Josie's desk. "You're back," Josie remarked. It seemed to take great effort to pick her head up. Her eyes were red and puffy and she looked like she hadn't slept in two days.

Josie studied Casey's face and must have made a similar assessment of her appearance. "There's going to be a private service at St. John's chapel tomorrow morning for friends and family of Austin. Luis is officiating. Tomorrow afternoon, the network is going to televise a public memorial for the fans. Molly Lyons, that reporter who always did interviews with him, is going to host it. They will play some clips from his time on Spirit and give the fans a forum to grieve. We've kind of nominated Luis to be the spokesman for *SCI*. He's going to make it perfectly clear to the entire viewing audience that Austin was not on drugs. On Thursday, we're heading to Alabama for the interment.

Casey didn't give a rat's ass what the public believed about Austin. She knew the truth. "Why Alabama?"

"His mom wants him to be buried next to his sister."

Casey's hand flew to her mouth. Mired in her own misery, she had forgotten the pain and grief his mother must be feeling. What could be worse than outliving both your children? "How's she doing?" Casey asked when she trusted herself to speak.

Tears shimmered in Josie's eyes and her voice hitched. "Austin was her baby." She shrugged and grabbed a tissue. The silence in the room completed her sentence. Really, what else was there to say?

Josie blew her nose. "Barrett was looking for you."

"Yeah, I need to speak to him, too."

She stepped out of Josie's office and walked over to where the tech crew hung out. The room was dark. Barrett was alone, staring at a blank television screen. Casey picked up the remote and flicked it off.

"Have you seen him?" she asked.

Barrett twisted the silver ring on his finger. "No," he said simply. "You?" She shook her head.

"Where could he be?"

Barret shrugged. Casey started pacing. "He said he would come back. He promised he would come back."

"I thought so, too," Barrett stared off into the distance.

"What does it mean that he hasn't?"

After a moment's silence, Barrett spoke. "I think you already know."

Barrett and Casey sat next to each other on an uncomfortable, upholstered sofa, waiting for the burial service to begin. The scents of various floral arrangements competed with one another, overwhelming the space. The tranquil funereal music piped into the room didn't improve the atmosphere. If anything, it put Casey more on edge. Barrett closed his eyes. He looked nauseated.

She hated that Austin was dead, but she could survive it. Losing him wrecked her, but she would eventually heal. That he hadn't returned to say goodbye bothered her, but she could live with it if he was in a better place. What kept her up at night, twisting in the depths of despair, was the thought that he was doomed to hell for all eternity. She thought of those wretched beings on the staircase of Enchanted Hill. She couldn't imagine Austin in that state. His earthly suffering was horrible, but the idea that his suffering had increased with no end in sight—that sent her completely over the edge.

Luis was rushing around, preparing for the service, but he stopped suddenly when he saw the devastation in Barrett's and

Casey's faces. He motioned for them to follow him into an unused office to speak with them. "I know this is incredibly hard. We all loved Austin. But we will see him again."

"Will we?" Barrett asked.

Luis blinked. "Of course. What's going on here?"

"What happened to Austin's soul?" Casey demanded, her voice quivering. "Is he damned?"

Luis cupped her cheek and smiled gently. "No, dear child. A demon can only possess your body, not your soul."

"But he committed suicide," Barrett said.

Luis held up his index finger. "No. The demon drove him to take his own life. If even I can see the difference, God can, too." Luis squeezed their hands and looked from one to the other. "Austin was a child of God and God does not forsake His children."

Casey bit her lip, anger welling up inside her. "But He did forsake Austin. The exorcism didn't work. He didn't hear our prayers. It would have been so easy for God to heal Austin, but instead He just handed him over to She-demon."

"No, dear daughter. He healed Austin perfectly. He brought him home."

Breathe. Casey reminded herself. She stared at the grave next to the mound of dirt where Austin would be buried. Audra Christina Cole. August 19, 1984 – October 15, 1998. Beloved Daughter and Sister.

"Ashes to ashes, dust to dust." Luis shut his book and stepped away from the casket. Leaning on Lyle, Austin's mother approached and placed a single white rose on top. Casey looked away and tried to swallow the lump in her throat. Through her blurred vision, she saw Anna holding Thai up. With the heel of his hand, he wiped tears from his eyes. Together they walked out the cemetery gates.

Breathe. Josie and Liv approached the casket. Liv pressed two fingers to her lips and touched the lid of the casket. Josie's hand shook as she placed a rose next to the one alongside the one from his mother.

Breathe. Bob stood and followed Josie and Liv out. Gary approached the casket. He put his hand to his mouth and cleared his throat. He stared at the casket for a moment longer then locked his gaze on Casey. With his eyes, he communicated how sorry he was and how much he missed Austin. How much they all would miss Austin. He shook his head and walked away.

Breathe. Barrett inched closer to Casey. He took her hand then pulled her in for a hug. They were the only two mourners left in the cemetery.

Breathe. Slowly the funeral director began lowering Austin's casket.

Breathe. Barrett choked out a sob. He held onto Casey tighter.

Breathe. Together they held each other up. Austin's casket descended into the ground and out of their view.

42

Casey's doorbell rang. She pulled herself off the sofa and opened the door. Barrett was leaning against the door frame, holding a half empty bottle of Maker's Mark.

She pulled him inside and took the bottle out of his hand. "I'm sorry to bother you." He tried to focus through his blood shot eyes. "But I didn't have anywhere else to go." He glanced around the space. Unfocused eyes finally latched on Casey. "I need to be with someone who understands. Someone who loves Austin, too."

Casey was surprised he wasn't slurring. "How'd you get here?" she asked as she helped him to the couch. He flopped down haphazardly.

"I called a friend." *Thank God you didn't drive.* He reached for the bottle, but Casey held it out of his reach.

"You've had enough." She stood up and walked to the kitchen.

"Just trying to feel better."

"This won't help. Drowning your sorrows may work temporarily. But later you won't just be sad, you'll be sad and puking your guts out, feeling like shit." She twisted the top off and began pouring it down the sink. Halfway through she stopped, took a glass out of the cabinet, and poured herself two fingers. After throwing it back she dumped the rest of the bottle down the drain.

Casey returned to the living room and sat beside him on the couch. "What's all this about nowhere else to go?"

"Derek broke up with me after the funeral."

"Geez, Barrett, that's awful. And shitty. Couldn't he have waited a little bit?" *Talk about kicking someone when they're down.*

"No. Actually, he's a pretty decent guy. He knew I didn't have the same feelings for him that he had for me, and yet, he was still there when I needed him. Honestly, he put up with a lot. When he broke it off he told me, 'Battling Austin when he was alive was one thing, but I'm not going to compete against a dead man's memory. Not a fair fight.' He's in Europe now. He gave me a month to find a new place, but I want to get out of there ASAP."

She patted his arm. "Well, Barrett. What's mine is yours. You're welcome to stay here and crash on my couch for as long as you need to." She pulled him into a hug. They stayed up late, telling funny Austin stories until they both collapsed from exhaustion.

The following week, Casey and Barrett met Josie and Thai at the Austin's attorney's office. Casey sat down across from Barrett and stared at the desolate team. Dark purplish circles rimmed Barrett's eyes. Josie looked worn and bone tired. Thai was still in shock. They were all empty husks, lost and disconsolate without their fearless leader. Casey felt all those things and more. Underneath the despair was a shit ton of guilt. 'If onlys' surrounded her, invading her every thought. If only she had believed him. If only she hadn't jumped to conclusions.

The attorney cracked the door. "Everything's set up. If you'll follow me." He led them to a room with a television screen and four chairs in front of it. Josie and Casey sat in the middle with Thai on Josie's left and Barrett on Casey's right. After they were seated, the attorney began. "Mr. Cole updated and recorded a new will shortly before his death. He asked that you four be in attendance for the video reading of it."

He turned down the lights. Without speaking a word, the four friends took each other's hands.

A haggard Austin appeared. The time and date were printed on the bottom right of the screen. January sixteenth. Casey's heart jerked. This was four days after she called it quits. His ocean eyes were filled with sadness, and something else. It took a moment for her to realize what it was. The stubborn, hard-headed man looked defeated. A voice on the recording said, "State your name, please."

Austin nodded. "I am Austin Gregory Cole and these are my last wishes." He pulled at his bottom lip. "You guys are sitting here watching this, so you know how it all played out." He pointed to his temple. "I've gotten pretty good at this precog thing. And Barrett, I agree with you. It sucks to know the future, especially when all you see is bad shit headed your way." He took a breath and continued.

"To JoJo. You've been a mother to a group of overgrown, rowdy boys for a long time. You kept us in line and you gave your heart and soul to *SCI*. There is no better technology specialist in the field of ghost hunting than you. Period. You astound and impress me every day I work with you. I don't know how to thank you enough. But I do know you love my ride." He held up his keys. "The Porsche is yours." Josie wiped tears from her eyes and Thai patted her back.

"To Thai….Where do I begin, man?" He blinked and cleared his throat. "If I am the head of *SCI* you are definitely the backbone. You love this organization as much as I do, and that's saying something. You are the most loyal, trustworthy friend I've ever had. I'm leaving you *SCI*. It's all yours, man. I hope you will continue the show as long as the network is willing to air it. But, of course, dead men don't control anything. You do what you want." Thai closed his eyes. He swiped at the tears rolling down his cheeks. Josie pulled him into her shoulder.

"To Barrett. My friend. My brother." He was silent for a moment and he stared down at the ground. He shook his head and his gaze returned to the camera. "I don't believe in fate, but I also don't believe what happened at the warehouse could have been avoided. Over the years I have relied on you so much. My reckless behavior and dangerous actions placed an unfair burden on you. I know that now. So many times, you saved my ass, even to your own peril. I didn't know how much I loved you until I lost you. I thank God you came back for the last few moments of my life." He cleared his throat. "To you, I leave my loft. Its creep factor is high right now, but I'm sure you and Luis can fix it. It sure beats sleeping on Casey's couch."

Barrett cleared his throat. "Damn, this is hard to watch." His voice came out a trembling whisper. Casey entwined her hand in his.

"To Casey." Austin paused and looked up, trying to get control of his emotions. He sniffed and rubbed his nose, then looked right into the camera. "I know you're done with me." She stared into ocean eyes, shimmering with unfallen tears. "But that doesn't matter." He inhaled and his voice cracked. "Because I'm not done with you." The screen blurred as Casey's eyes filled up. His words broke what was left of her mangled heart. He couldn't see her now, just as she couldn't see him then. But the connection was always there. "Case, it's hard to think about you. When I think of you, I have so much regret. I think of the future we could have had. I think about all the things I wanted for us and I realize how I fucked us both over." He straightened his back, pulling himself together. "To Casey, I leave my whole heart and the remainder—" But Casey didn't stay to hear the rest. She ran through the doors of the office and leaned against the wall, sobbing. She didn't try to contain it and knew she couldn't even if she wanted to. Her insides felt hollow and ached with the absence of him. She slid down the wall and pulled her knees into her chest. After a few minutes of ugly, snot-filled crying she glanced up. The others were standing around her, staring at her with concern in their eyes.

Barrett knelt beside her. "Are you going to make it?" he asked softly.

Josie handed her a tissue. She wiped her eyes and cry hic-coughed. It took her a moment to speak, and when she did her voice was barely a whisper. "Do I have a choice?"

Thai and Barrett grabbed her arms and pulled her to her feet. "I know you didn't stick around to hear, but with the exception of a trust fund for his mother, Austin left you the remainder of his estate. A little over fifteen million dollars," Thai told her.

"What? Why would he do that?"

"Something about not wanting you to worry about bill collectors and ramen noodles," Barrett told her."

"I .don't. want. his. money." She was sobbing so hard, her voice was jerking. "I. want. him." She wiped her nose with the tissue Josie handed her.

"It could be worse." Josie wrapped an arm around her friend's shoulder. "At least he didn't leave you a car that no longer exists on this plane." Then she pulled Casey into her arms for a big hug. Thai went to go speak to the lawyer and Barrett stepped away to give the women a moment. Josie held on to her tightly for several seconds. She brushed the hair out of Casey's eyes, and told her everything was going to be okay.

Thai walked up and cleared his throat. "You guys are free to go. The lawyer's going to bring your paperwork over to *SCI* tomorrow. I have more forms to sign with the transfer of *SCI* from Austin to me, so I'm going to do that now. Barrett, could you give Josie a ride back?"

"Sure," Barrett said. Casey climbed into the passenger seat of Barrett's Lexus and Josie hopped into the back.

"Where to?" Barrett asked.

"Just drop me off at *SCI*. I can get Liv to pick me up from there. They rode in silence, but, as they pulled into the parking lot, they heard Josie scream, "Holy shit!" Casey glanced up, her gaze following Josie's pointed finger. There, in Austin's spot, was his shiny black Porsche with his vanity plate SP1R1T.

Josie jumped out of the Lexus and ran over. Barrett parked and they walked over and joined her.

"Well, now you don't have to call Liv to come get you."

Josie approached it and gingerly placed her hand on the hood. "Do you think it's safe to drive? I mean, who knows where it's been."

Barrett shook his head. "I don't think Austin would have left it to you if it wasn't safe."

"What if it doesn't start?" Josie pulled her lip piercing into her mouth.

"Well, there's only one way to find out," Barrett told her.

Josie jumped up and down excitedly. "I'll run inside and get his keys out of the office." Moments later, she was outside revving the engine. "Who wants to go for a ride?"

"I'm in," Barrett said as he opened the passenger door.

"What about it, Casey?"

"No, thanks. You two go ahead." She waved at them as they pulled out of the parking lot. It wouldn't be the same riding in that car if Austin wasn't the one shifting gears.

43

Casey exhaled and closed her eyes. She rang the bell and waited for Barrett to answer. The door swung open. "Welcome to the new and improved Austin's Loft," he said with a grin. Casey glanced around as she entered. The air was so light. Lighter than she ever remembered. The décor was simple, masculine. Barrett had replaced all the furniture. Most of it had been torn up, and the remainder was tainted by evil. The new sofas were black leather, and a square, dark wood coffee table sat in between them. The artwork was simple and modern. Two matching geometric designs in red and blue in the living room. Austin's abstract painting of the outline of a naked woman was unharmed, so Barrett kept it. A simple wooden cross hung on the wall across from the front door. She glanced back at the entry automatically, halfway expecting to see Austin's bloody handprints.

"So, what do you think?"

"I think this place has never felt so right. You and Luis did an excellent job of cleansing it."

"It was a project," Barrett looked around, with his hands on his hips. "But I think it was worth it." He motioned for her to have a seat. "Would you like something to drink?"

"Maybe later." She rubbed her fingers on the arm of the sofa. It felt odd to be here again. "You know, I like your design choice, but it doesn't look very Barrett." To Casey, it looked more like something Austin would have selected.

"No, it doesn't. But my tastes are changing. I'll probably redecorate one day, but for now, this is what I want." He sat on the arm of the sofa with his arms crossed and a smile on his face.

"Well, whatever you're doing, it's working. You look fantastic."

"It helps that I've stopped drinking."

"Stopped drinking or cut back?"

"Stopped for good."

"What's this?" she asked, as she brushed her fingers over his chin. He had let his beard grow out a little. Bad boy stubble. "Are you channeling him?"

"Nah," Barrett looked down for a moment, then his gaze returned to hers. "The loft, the beard—it makes me feel closer to him."

"You seem … happy," she said, a tinge of envy in her voice.

"I'm not sure that's the word I'd use, but I've made peace with what happened." He squeezed her hand and stared into her eyes. "I can see you haven't."

Casey shrugged. She was afraid to speak because her throat was tightening and her eyes were filling. Barrett pulled her into his chest as the sobs overtook her. "Shh," he whispered as she wet the front of his shirt with her tears. He rocked her slowly, smoothing her hair and rubbing her back. She tried to calm herself by thinking of something, anything, other than Austin. It was silent in the loft except for the thump of Barrett's heart. She concentrated on that, counting the beats. When she reached seventy-two, he finally spoke.

"Did you call the therapist I recommended?"

She shook her head and wiped a stray tear from her eye.

"Casey," Barrett scolded, as he handed her a tissue. "Why not?"

"I don't know." She shrugged. "He'd probably just give me drugs. I don't want to get hooked on antidepressants or have to take them for the rest of my life just to function. And I don't see the point in talking about it, either." *Even if I could.* "There's no way it could make me feel any better."

"That's what I used to think, too. When I look back on all the years I spent feeling like shit when I could have been getting help, I could kick myself." He bent over and stared into her eyes. "Look, I wouldn't worry too much about the drugs. Unless you have some underlying chemical imbalance, you probably won't have to take them for that long. But if you're that concerned, tell him up front that drugs are a deal breaker for you. He can suggest alternatives." Casey pulled on her bottom lip.

"C'mon. At least give it a shot. If you can do something to make things better for yourself, why wouldn't you?"

Casey sniffled but smiled up at him. "That sounds like something Austin would say."

"Yes, and if Austin were here, he'd be pissed at you for not going."

If Austin were here, I wouldn't need it. "I know."

"So you'll go?"

"I'm moving back to Shadow Creek in a few days. I'll find a grief counselor once I get there."

"Promise?"

"I promise," Casey said. "Trust me, my friend Tina won't let me blow it off." Casey exhaled. "Did I mention that I love what you did with the loft?"

"Yeah, but you can tell me again." He smiled. "Making it right for Austin's memory was good for my soul." He got up, "Speaking of, I have some things for you."

He walked over to the entry table and returned with a package. "You know how you told me you can only think of Austin the way he was at the end of his life?"

Casey bit her lip. "That's still true."

"Well, maybe this will help." She opened it up. It was a framed photograph of them on the roof from New Year's. Barrett had photo-shopped himself out of it and enlarged and centered the picture.

Austin's arm was wrapped around Casey's shoulder and he was kissing her temple.

Casey placed her finger on his image. "Happy times."

Barrett turned to face her and took her hands in his. "Whenever you're feeling down, whenever you can't see past the images of him when she was in control, I want you to look at this picture and remember how happy you were and how much he loved you."

Casey squeezed his hand. "Thank you."

"I also found his crucifix. I know he'd want you to have it." He uncurled her fingers and dropped the gold necklace into her palm. Casey stared at the image of Jesus nailed to the cross. How many times had she stared at this very image dangling from Austin's neck?

Her smile turned to anguish and her hands shook. "Barrett, where is he?" she whispered hoarsely.

"Obviously, he's crossed."

"But this is Austin. He always said he'd come back. He'd at least check in with us before he left for his eternal rest." Her voice rose with emotion and she put her hands out. "What if he hasn't come back because he's in the other place?"

Barrett knelt in front of her and placed his hands on her knees. "I'll admit I'm new to this Christianity thing. But Luis is right. Austin was a believer. From my understanding, that's a ticket straight to heaven."

"Then why didn't he tell us good-bye?"

Barrett chewed his bottom lip, remembering that last day at Enchanted Hill. "I think he did. But we just didn't listen."

Liv and Josie gave Casey a ride to the airport. Josie hugged her tightly and told Casey she would call her every day until she returned. Casey nodded but she wasn't sure she'd ever come back to LA. Casey was sitting in the terminal, waiting for her plane to board, when *Tubular Bells* began to play. *Shit, I really need to change that ringtone.* She glanced down at the name on the display.

"Hey, Thai. What's up?"

"Barrett said you were flying out today."

"Yeah."

"He also said you weren't sure if you were coming back to *SCI*."

Casey pushed her bangs back. "I don't know." She knew Austin would want her to return, but that didn't make the decision any easier.

"Well, don't write us off yet. You've got time. We don't start filming until September. And even then, Barrett's offered to do the walk throughs on the first episodes if you're not ready to return that soon."

"I thought he wanted to stay behind the scenes."

Thai cleared his throat. "That was before. With Austin. He knows I'm not about to risk the crew with a house from hell just to boost the ratings. That, and we're short an investigator." He was silent for a moment, not stating the obvious reason for their need of another member for the investigation team. "Just promise me you won't shut the door on *SCI*."

"I won't. I'll let you know."

"Okay. Tell Tina I said hi."

"I will. Talk to you later."

Tina folded Casey in her arms the minute she exited the terminal. She yammered all the way home from the airport, filling her in on the Shadow Creek gossip. Casey was thankful for the distraction. She stared out the window while her friend spoke, watching the scenery turn from concrete gray to lush green as they headed out of the city and into rural farmlands.

Tina cleared her throat. "Barrett called me." Casey turned to stare at her friend. "He's worried sick about you, and who can blame him? I've seen zombies more animated than you. Don't take this the wrong way, honey. But you're a mess. I've made you an appointment with a therapist in the city on Tuesday. I hope you won't give me any trouble about going."

Casey shook her head. "No, I won't. I think it's past time to do something about this." She exhaled. "I want to feel good again."

Tina helped her unload her stuff and carry it into the store. "Your apartment's ready and waiting for you. Not that I understand why you want to stay here when you could afford the ritziest place in town."

Casey frowned at her. "Anyway, go put your stuff up, then come back downstairs. I'm taking you to my place. Lifetime's playing a Terrible Mothers marathon tonight." Casey grabbed her luggage and headed up the stairs. She unpacked her bags then sat on the edge of the bed. It was good to be back. Like coming home. She closed her eyes and let the safety and security of Shadow Creek envelop her.

Casey planted herself in front Tina's big screen with a beer. She promised to tell Tina all about what happened to Austin in time, but she wasn't ready to go there yet. Tina patted her hand and said she would be there to listen whenever she was.

Early Easter at sunrise, Casey dragged herself to Mass. She wasn't sure if she did it for herself or for Austin's memory. It was difficult to sit through the joyful service of the risen Christ, knowing that all earthly happiness for her was forever gone. *It's a pitiful existence when all you have to look forward to is your own death,* she thought.

That afternoon, she leaned against the old oak tree next to Tina's store, drinking a beer and fiddling with the bottle cap. She looked up at the sky. It was clear blue and full of fluffy white clouds. The sun shone a little too brightly. Shadow Creek had awoken from its winter slumber, green and full of life. All around her, the world was a thriving, cheery place, and that seemed so wrong.

I think Barrett's right; you're in heaven now. And it's not just my own wishful thinking. It's the only thing that makes sense. You may have been the one possessed by evil; you may have been the one who committed suicide, but I'm the one in hell. Every single day. And you aren't here with me, so you must be in heaven.

Casey took a sip and pointed the neck of her beer bottle up to the sky. "I miss you and envy you in equal parts."

Casey crawled into her bed that night and glanced up at the picture Barrett had given her, as she did every night. A sad smile tugged at her lips. She picked up her e-reader, determined to finish *Opposition*. *At least some people get a happy ending*, she thought as she read. Her eyelids grew heavy and shut involuntarily.

Casey? Are you asleep? His voice. *Just another fucked up dream.* Casey sighed but didn't open her eyes. She was determined to stay in this dream state where Austin existed as long as possible. "Come lay next to me," she mumbled. She felt the covers shift and the air around her grew cold. She shivered as goose bumps pebbled her arms. For a dream, this was as real as it got. One eye popped opened. She bolted upright and her heart sped up. "Austin, is it really you?" Her voice was quivering. She turned and saw his form sitting next to her on the bed. He was as she remembered, dressed in basketball shorts, an *SCI* T-shirt, and running shoes. But now his skin was semi-translucent, a luminous blue, and his ever-present crucifix was but a ghostly glimmer dangling from his neck. "Shit, where have you been?"

Arctic eyes stared back at her, and blinked. His head tilted to the side, but he didn't answer her question. She wanted to see those beautiful orbs looking at her like he used to. Like she was the most precious thing in the world to him. But something was off, out of focus. *I've been here before*, he mumbled. He stood up and walked over to the wall that separated the bedroom from the living area. He stared at it for a moment, then stepped around and walked through the doorway. A few moments later, he walked back through the doorway and over to the bed. Casey blinked. Walking through walls was ghost 101. So why go out of his way to use the doorway?

It was then that Casey noticed the two other ghosts in the room, Gran and Prudence. They motioned her over. "What's going on? What's wrong with him?" she whispered.

Prudence showed her an image of Humpty Dumpty falling off the wall. When Casey looked to the ground it wasn't Humpty Dumpty she saw, but shattered glass and Austin's broken skull. Casey turned her head to see what Austin was doing. He was sitting on her bed, preoccupied with her reader. After finally finding the on switch, he stared at the images on her virtual bookshelf. *Opal. Daemon and Kat.* He frowned. *How do I know Daemon and Kat?*

Gran looked over Casey's shoulder to make sure Austin wasn't paying attention. *Prudence found him wandering around the streets of LA. He was confused and frightened. He didn't know where he was. He kept mumbling "Spirit Chaser" over and over. Those first few days, he didn't even know his own name.*

Casey's lip trembled as she imagined the nightmare he'd been through. Gran's voice broke into her thoughts. *Prudence took him to a vacant apartment she was staying in. She didn't know how to locate you, but she found me. He wanted to go home, but we didn't think it was a good idea. We had no idea who was living in his place now, and that would have thrown him for a loop. When some of his memories started to return and he asked for you, we knew it was time to bring him here.*

"So, he doesn't know?"

No, Gran said. *And I don't think it's my place to tell him. It will be better if he hears it from you.*

Casey turned toward Austin, but before she could approach him, Gran materialized right in front of her. *Be gentle, Casey. You've had time to adjust to the idea. He hasn't. You don't have to tell him everything tonight.*

Cold fingers passed over Casey's arm. Prudence smiled sadly at her. Casey squeezed her ghostly hand. "Thank you for taking care of him." She walked over to the bed and sat down next to her dead, brain-damaged boyfriend. "Austin," she said softly. He looked up from the reader with questions in his eyes. "What do you remember?"

He scrolled through the pages of Opal. *I remember that you like cheeseburgers and you like to read. I remember lots of things.*

"Like what?" she asked gently.

I remember I like to run. I know we used to look for ghosts in haunted houses. He laughed. *You and Thai were scared sometimes. Barrett came, too, but not all the time. There were others, but I can't think of their names.* His brow furrowed in concentration. *I know we had this big building with a gym, but when I looked for it, I couldn't find it. We worked there, I think. It was our job. I want to go back there. I miss that. Will you take me?*

"I miss it, too." She paused and took the reader out of his hand. "Austin, this is important. What is the last thing you remember? Do you remember the big old house on the hill?"

Austin bit his bottom lip, and his brows furrowed as he concentrated. *I don't remember an old house. I remember sitting in my loft, and I was alone. I remember you were upset with me. I did something really bad and you were mad at me.* He rubbed his hands on his thighs and rocked back and forth on the bed.

A lump formed in her throat. "Do you remember what that was?"

No. I just know it was really bad. You told me not to do it, but I did it anyway. His hands went up to his hair and he ran his fingers through it. *I remember being scared.* He shook his head and slammed his incorporeal hands against the mattress. *I don't want to think about that anymore. It makes me sad.*

"Shh," Casey put her warm hand over his cold one. "You don't have to."

He pinched his bottom lip between his thumb and index finger. *Are you still mad at me?*

"No," Casey said, her eyes brimming with tears. "I'm not still mad at you. I love you very much."

A smile illumined his ghostly features. He stared down at his hands, then up into her eyes. *I haven't told you the best part.* He clapped his hands together. *You'll never guess what I can do.*

"What?"

I can see ghosts now. Just like you, I can see ghosts.

Casey gave him a sad little smile. "I know, baby, I know."

Dear Reader,

    If you have come with me this far, you may want to punch me in the face. I wanted to let you know, I do have a plan for the intrepid Spirit Chaser. When your livelihood is chasing ghosts, death is not the end of the story. The entire *SCI* team will return in *Melancholy Ghost*, coming 2017.

Blessings,

Kat

BIBLIOGRAPHY

Rite of Exorcism. 2013 ed. Lexington, Kentucky: The Credo Institute, 2015.37.

Armentrout, Jennifer L. (2012) *Opal. A Lux Novel* Fort Collins: Entangled Publishing.

Verses have been paraphrased from the King James and New International Versions of the Bible.

The author acknowledges the use of wordmarks Starbucks, In-N-Out, Guinness, O'Douls, Walmart, Bud, Coke, My Little Pony, Chuck Taylors, Hello Kitty, Maker's Mark, Crown Royal, Jack Daniels, and Heineken.

Other books by this author under the name K.M. Montemayor:

The Circle

The Circle Broken

The Circle Complete

Connect with me on FB. K.M. Montemayor.

Or visit my Website: www.kuriositykilledthecat.com

Printed in Great Britain
by Amazon